# Aunt Bunny's Will

by Kathleen Willett

Chapter 1

There was nothing quite like travelling down a dusty road in Kansas. Except maybe gargling with sand.

Mitch checked twice to make sure the window was rolled up all the way by opening it just a crack and then closing it again. By doing so, she let in even more dust. Reb didn't seem to notice. She was raised on this stuff. Can people develop an immunity to grit?

"You're awfully quiet," Reb stated the obvious as she drove the van. She was getting to be quite the expert at this, even with her disability. In a car accident that now seemed lifetimes ago, Rebecca Fairbanks, Governor of Colorado and U.S. Senate hopeful had been paralyzed from the waist down. An injury that could've driven a stake through the heart of many relationships had only drawn Rebecca and Mitch closer together. They considered themselves a committed lesbian couple.

Not that they had had a ceremony like their good friends, Trish and Robbie. Reb just had a thing about weddings, as how her first one hadn't worked out. Jeff was nice enough, he just hadn't been female enough once Reb had discovered her true nature. Their divorce was graceful, but then, when Mitch and Reb began to explore their mutual attraction, it was as if they had gotten trapped in some sort of macabre carnival house ride. Reb was the only thing that had made it all worthwhile. When the ride started, Reb was the newly-elected Governor of Colorado. Now, she was a U. S. Senator from the same. Which was really kind of stunning since conservative politics was well known for its anti-gay bias. The first official act of thugs, when the news leaked out that Mitch and Reb had consummated their love, was an attempted torching of the Governor's Mansion. That was barely old news when a zealot shot Mitch in the elbow. In a more recent unrelated incident, Mitch had endured another gunshot wound to the shoulder as well. Needless to say, her left arm had seen better days.

"Hey you," Reb prodded again. "Are you asleep or meditating?"
"I'm just quiet. Death has that effect on me."

"It was my relative who died."

"It's still death."

The phone call had come a day ago. Reb's Aunt Bunella had passed away. Rather than be at the mercy of airlines and rental cars, Mitch and Reb opted to drive from Washington D.C. to Kansas. It sounded like such a good idea at the time. Now, Mitch wasn't so sure. She sneezed twice.

"Are you getting sick, Sweetie?"

Reb had become such a nurturing soul over the past year. When they had first met, a kind description of Governor Fairbanks would've been "aloof." Mitch had seen through the tough act pretty quickly and from there, they had gotten to intimate terms in a respectable amount of time. Then, due to true love and nothing but, they found themselves in a relationship.

"It's the dust."

"What dust?"

Mitch couldn't believe this.

"The dust all around us," Mitch waved her hands in the air like an erratic symphony conductor.

"Gee, and it isn't even dust season yet."

"Dust season?" Mitch echoed. "It has its own season?"

"Oh, yeah. It gets a lot worse around here. This is mild."

Mitch sneezed again. Maybe it was a cold after all?

"How many more miles before we get to, where was it we're going?" Mitch asked. It still sounded better than "Are we there, yet?"

"Utopia."

"Utopia, yeah, right. How much farther?"

"Thirty more miles."

"Thirty more light years is more like it," Mitch half grumbled.

"After a thousand miles, what's another thirty?"

It had been a long stretch, no doubt about it. Good thing the burial wasn't subject to any religious time restrictions. Two very long days on the road was making Mitch cranky. In theory, that was an okay sort of mood for funeral going.

"Why don't you try and squeeze in a nap before we get there?" Reb suggested thoughtfully.

"What? And miss all this lovely scenery?"

If sarcasm had truly been able to drip, it would've cut the dust.

2

"Now, don't tell me I've gone and hooked up with a scenery snob?" Reb teased gently. As usual.

"Living in Colorado will do that to you," Mitch half-explained, half-defended as they drove over land as flat as Mitch's singing voice.

Balancing out Mitch's cantankerous mood was Reb's peaceful attitude. It had to be the fact that they were nearing the homestead, and even in the face of death, the close proximity must be bringing back good memories.

"Did you have a happy childhood?" Mitch asked suddenly. It had only taken over a year to inquire, so the rush now seemed ludicrous.

"It was happy enough," Reb nodded.

"Even with Aunt BeBe for a sister?" Mitch asked knowingly. Mitch's first ever encounter with the formidable Aunt BeBe occurred when Reb was in the hospital after her accident. Trish had asked Mitch to go with her on a trip to the U.S. Holocaust Museum in Washington D.C., a trip Trish needed support to get through. When the news hit about Reb's accident, Mitch flew back to Denver and right to the hospital. In the waiting room, she encountered Aunt BeBe, whom she knew absolutely nothing about. More accurately, she encountered Aunt BeBe's strong hand as Mitch found herself on the receiving end of a right cross to her mouth. And only because she wasn't expecting it did she find herself on the floor. And pressing charges. And then later dropping charges when she found out that it was her sister-in-law, so to speak. There were no loose teeth involved, so Mitch's forgiving nature let bygones be bygones. Besides, you couldn't very well jail such a pillar of the community, even if the community was hundreds of miles away. In Utopia, Kansas.

"I guess when you're reared to believe that you're among the chosen few, your childhood couldn't be anything but happy," Reb answered as she turned down still another dusty road.

"The chosen few?"

"Right."

"By that, you wouldn't be referring to 'lesbian' or 'gay' or anything even resembling that, I take it?"

Reb laughed a throaty chuckle. The kind that made Mitch want to snuggle up close and listen to. Over and over.

3

"Oh, no," Reb went into sermon mode. "About the farthest thing away from being amongst the chosen round these parts is to be gay. Or lesbian. Or, frankly, now that I think about it, anything other than missionary-position straight."

"How long are we staying again?" Mitch asked with only a tiny bit of panic creeping into her voice.

"Well, the funeral shouldn't take too long, but then there's the legal work. You know, the estate."

Nobody had bothered to mention to Mitch that Aunt Bunella was rich until it came up in conversation with Jeff. The catch was that anyone who had wanted to inherit the money or estate had to be married. When Reb left Jeff for Mitch, she knowingly kissed off a fortune. Third world countries had less GNP than Aunt Bunella. All of which, straight Aunt BeBe of the Right Cross was next in line to inherit.

"But, you're not going to get anything, right?" Mitch was still looking for an express route home.

"Right."

"So, why stick around?"

"I want to be supportive to BeBe."

Mitch nodded. This was truly Reb-like. Were the reverse true, would Aunt BeBe be so helpful? Mitch thought not and kept this in mind as she asked still another question.

"Does BeBe have a husband?"

"Of course. You didn't think she'd be caught without one with Aunt Bunny so advanced in years."

"What's his name?"

"Henry Knight."

"Okay, so it's Aunt BeBe and Uncle Henry and Aunt Bunny. Is there anything else I need to know?"

"You sound nervous."

"I just don't want to embarrass you in front of your family."

"You never embarrass me."

"I'm not through trying!"

Reb shook her head and then pointed to a spot on the near horizon.

"Is that Utopia?"

"Oh, no, that's the farm complex. Utopia's about ten miles further down the road."

4

"God, it looks huge!"

"It sort of is."

"I feel just like Ali McGraw in Love Story."

"Thanks for the warning."

Reb drove to the front door of the sprawling house in the midst of a sprawling ranch. The word 'mansion' didn't exactly come to mind as Mitch slipped down out of the passenger side of their van and stretched her legs. How did Reb ever get by without this simple pleasure? Mitch made a mental note to help her stretch later tonight. They were sort of behind schedule on that stuff. Stretching, that is.

Reb was out and wheeling around as Mitch pulled a suitcase out of the van. The land was flat enough to make it easy for Reb to maneuver her wheelchair. It was as if Kansas had been made with paraplegics in mind. By the time they got to the front door, it was flung open by Aunt BeBe with the same force that she delivered a punch. Ka-Wham!

"Where have the two of you been!" she asked more like a school principal confronting tardy students than a loving relative. What a surprise.

"In Washington D.C., a thousand miles away," Reb answered in a tone that suggested that she didn't care much to be interrogated the moment of arrival.

"Well, get inside before anymore dust blows in."

"My sentiments exactly," Mitch agreed as she crossed the threshold, only hoping that she wasn't considered a part of the dust BeBe was referring to. Then, as she bent over to place the luggage on the floor, BeBe fairly shrieked in her ear,

"HENRY!!!" Perhaps he was in the north four thousand? The tingle in Mitch's ear drum stayed with her for a good ten minutes.

"Where is that man?" she asked everyone irritably, like it was their fault her husband wasn't within screaming distance.

"Maybe he's in the barn?" Reb offered an explanation to avoid another outbreak of the shrieks.

"He'd best better be gettin himself down here. He needs to meet Mary's flight!"

"I could've done that," Mitch was already looking for ways to escape.

"You have driven too much as it is!" BeBe was actually understanding. "Somebody go find him. I'm cooking dinner!" Reb gave Mitch one of those head bobs that communicated volumes. Like, for instance, follow me and I'll show you where the barn is. They carried their suitcases to the ground floor bedroom that Reb had grown up in, and quickly unpacked the hanging clothes. Took about fifteen seconds.

"See that big, red building out there?" Reb pointed out the window.

"The one that looks like a barn?"

"That's where Henry hides out from BeBe. She won't go to the barn unless it's absolutely necessary.

"She prefers the farmhouse?"

"Always has. Could you do us all a big favor and see if Henry's in there?"

"Anything for you, my darling," Mitch kissed Reb with a flourish, like she was going off to slay a dragon or something. "And then, hurry back to my rescue."

"Depends on what you need rescuing from?" Mitch said over her shoulder as she exited the room. Mitch picked her way through the pathway to the barn. It wasn't exactly an obstacle course, but the walkway was uneven and could make even the most sober preacher appear to be drunk. If Reb wanted to visit the barn anytime soon, she would need an escort. Mitch opened the barn door carefully, hoping that there weren't any cows planning to stampede to freedom once they saw the light of day.

Inside was cool and quiet, a nice break from the outside. "Who would want to escape from here?" Mitch wondered to herself as she tiptoed around like a specter. Horses were scarfing down hay like it grew on trees. And considering where the intake eventually ended up, things didn't smell too bad. For a barn, that is. In her scouting around, Mitch didn't see anything resembling an Uncle Henry. She was about to leave when she heard voices. Maybe they were the ones in her head? She strained to hear more and located the sounds somewhere above her head. In every good barn, there was a hayloft. The ladder looked like true

Americana and it was all Mitch could do not to get a sliver as she quietly ascended.

When she reached the top, and could look around, she indeed found Uncle Henry. She also found someone of the female persuasion and the word that jumped to the front of Mitch's vocabulary was, "Boink!" Before she could duck out of sight, the woman noticed her. Loudly.
"HENRY!"
"Oh, I know, my precious. I need you, too!"
"NO! HENRY! LOOK!"
"I'm lookin, I'M LOOKIN!"
"Not at me! At HER!"

Mitch could sense that for a frightening split second, Henry thought he'd been made by BeBe, so Mitch tried to waylay his trepidation.
"It's only me," Mitch pulled herself one more step up the ladder. It was warm up here. The farther you came up the ladder, the hotter it got. Imagine, all that heat...
"Who in the hell are you!" he scrambled to cover himself. A hankie would've been sufficient.
"I'm a shirttail relative," Mitch remarked, having articles of clothing or lack thereof on the mind. "I live with Rebecca."
"Oh, yeah, you're the queer," Uncle Henry the Fornicator nodded thoughtfully.
"Right," Mitch took the remark in stride. She'd been called worse by people who had all their clothes on.
"And you are?" Mitch asked the woman who was amply proportioned and by now had covered herself with her blue cotton sun dress.
"I'm the church organist," she said, as if that explained everything.
About three off color remarks floated through Mitch's brain and she struggled to hold back a burbling giggle.
"Of course, you are," Mitch managed to say before Uncle Henry butted in.
"What are you doing here?"
"BeBe wondered if you were going to meet Mary's flight?"

7

"It's not time yet!"

Boy, was he irritated. Who wouldn't be when interrupted on the verge of getting some?

"I'm just the messenger. The real yelling is going on back at the house." Mitch said as she started to descend.

"Nice meeting you," the organist stammered a polite goodbye.

"Pleasure was all mine," Mitch smiled back and then went down the ladder. A horse snorted in her general direction.

"I couldn't agree more," Mitch nodded.

Back at the house, things were strained. It was to be expected. After all, there had been a death in the family.

"Did you find Henry?" BeBe launched in faster than a torpedo.

"Yes."

"And?" she asked like it was all a conspiracy.

"I'm sure he'll be down," Mitch was all serious and straight-faced, at least as much as she could be, "in a minute."

"I don't know what's gotten into that man!"

"We all mourn in mysterious ways."

"Well, he's been in mournin for two years, if that's the case!" she huffed.

Mitch only nodded. Two years, huh? By the time Mitch got a chance to use the bathroom and freshen up from the marathon road trip, Henry was present and accounted for and taking orders like any good soldier in marriage.

"Stop at the store on the way there, so you don't bother Mary with the shopping. That's why you needed to get an early start or did you forget! Again!"

"The store," he said dutifully.

"And," BeBe continued on like some run-on sentence, "Don't get that pricey bacon like you did the last time. You can afford that when you become a pig farmer!"

"Bacon," he nodded.

Mitch wondered why they would need to buy bacon if they were pig farmers one day, but wisely kept her mouth shut.

"And eggs! At least five dozen. Maybe six!"

"Six dozen!" his eyes widened.

Mitch had seen this particular expression already at least once today.

"Well, I'm not going to cook for a dozen people a day with no eggs!"

Mitch started to count on her fingers. Who exactly were these dozen people? BeBe, Henry, Reb, Mitch, Mary. That was five so far.

"Who else is going to be here?" Mitch finally got brave enough to ask a question.

"People will be in and out and nobody ever came into this house what didn't leave with something in their stomach!" BeBe explained curtly.

Mitch refrained from making a remark about her observations to date. There was a shopping list to consider.

"And about fifty pounds of potatoes…"

It went on. And on. Mitch hadn't seen fifty pounds of potatoes since her days at the Lucky U and wondered how Henry was going to transport all this and Mary, too.

"You want me to go with you, Henry?" Mitch offered real neighborly.

"No!" he answered quickly. Maybe he was meeting you-know-who at the store? Or maybe he just wasn't the kind who liked a tag-a-long. Or maybe he just didn't want to be seen with a queer. Whatever the case, Reb looked relieved that Mitch was staying behind. This was going to be a long week. Whatever peacefulness Mitch had sensed in the drive here was long gone and forgotten.

Henry took off after appearing to memorize the list. BeBe went back to the stove to cook. If ever there was a classic farm kitchen, this was it. It was built back in the days when people took baths in the kitchen, so it was plenty roomy. Along the way, it had been modernized to include state-of-the-art appliances. Maybe they couldn't afford good bacon for company, but it looked like Aunt BeBe got her way with the appliance budget. You could cook a dinner here for a dozen people every day with one hand tied behind your back. Which is how Mitch felt in the kitchen since she had been shot. Still, if she tried real hard, she could peel a potato with the best of them.

Well, maybe not the best. She offered. BeBe refused, "Company don't cook!"

Mitch tossed a glance to Reb, who shrugged and then offered to help.

"Knife's in the drawer. Taters in the bin. Just like always."

And so, the line was drawn. Mitch wasn't family enough to help, but that didn't stop her from pulling up a coffee cup and settling in for a chat.

"What was it like to grow up around these parts?"

"Dusty," was BeBe's answer.

Reb had to smile. "She's right about that."

"Not at all like the dirty thirties when Bunny, *God rest her soul*, was growing up."

"Dirty thirties?" Mitch asked. It sounded like the title of a porn film.

"Kansas was a dustbowl in the 1930s. Topsoil blew away. You couldn't grow beans nor soybeans nor much else."

"Don't mention soybeans," Reb intoned with exasperation.

When Reb had first arrived in Washington D.C. to begin her term as Senator, the first thing she got embroiled in was a soybean scandal. Between Rebecca, her daughter, Mary, and Mitch's old girlfriend and Mary's new girlfriend Lisa, things had gotten very complex. For a while, everyone thought that Lisa had been in cahoots with the bad guys, so for a few weeks, Mary and Lisa had split up. Mitch and Lisa had split up long before that, which made things interesting, to say the least, whenever Lisa and Rebecca ended up in the same part of town. Actually, for two women who had slept with Mitch, they got along. Mostly, for the sake of Mary. It would be good to see her again. Since Trish and Robbie's wedding, Mary and Lisa had been renting (wink wink) Mitch's old house in Denver. What little cash they sent Mitch's way, she turned around and funneled to Jane. Jane, otherwise known as Antoinette Scarpeli, was a hooker who Mitch picked up in a bar. Well, it didn't exactly happen quite that way. She had met Jane in a bar. After a brief exchange of unpleasantries, due solely to the fact that Mitch had been turned down for a minimum wage job, Mitch ended up too drunk to find her way out of the bathtub at home. That was where the nice cab driver had deposited her as per Reb's instructions.

When Mitch managed to sober up, regret propelled her to seek Jane out to apologize. They became friends and subsequent business partners, which in no way is meant to imply that Mitch got into the prostitution business. She actually wanted to make money! As soon as matters were settled, they were planning to open a restaurant. Jane was going to do the cooking, and could that woman cook!

"Can't you peel potatoes any faster than that!" BeBe chided Rebecca. The remark pulled Mitch back to the present.
"Let me help," Mitch went to the counter and commenced to peeling before BeBe could raise a fuss. If she spoke to Reb like that once more, they might very well have flying spuds. Reb had a temper. Mitch had seen it once. Or twice. Or maybe three times? So she kind of knew what it looked like. And it, like every other feature of Reb was still absolutely stunningly gorgeous. She was beautiful when she laughed. She was beautiful when she cried. She was beautiful when she was awake. She was beautiful when she was asleep. It just wasn't fair. Then again, what is?

Mitch hated to admit it at first, but it was this stunning beauty that had first caught her eye. If this was the only attraction, things might not have lasted very long. But it wasn't the only attraction. For two women who were supposed to be polar opposites, they found too much in common to fight it for very long. And now, here they were, peeling potatoes under the scrutiny of Aunt BeBe.
"You need to clean this one up," she firmly placed a reject in front of Mitch. "You missed an eye!"
When BeBe said it that way, she made it sound like Mitch had broken the eleventh commandment. One of those "eye for an eye" dictates. Mitch examined the potato for the interloper.
"I don't see it?"
BeBe took the potato and pointed to a swear-to-God microscopic blemish before excising it with the flash of a paring knife.

11

"Nobody's ever had to eat mashed potatoes with eyes in them in this house since I've been in charge and by goodness, they're not going to begin tonight!"

The visualization of eyes in mashed potatoes made Mitch ask, "What else are we having?"

Hopefully, BeBe would be more prone to be conversational about cooking than anything else. Like politics. Or religion. Or sex?

"Roast beef, mashed potatoes WITHOUT the eyes, green beans, gravy, apple pie!"

"Those are all of my favorites! How did you know to make them for my first night here?"

"I didn't," BeBe made it clear.

"If you keep cooking like that, I might stay longer than a week," Mitch was warming up to how to best approach BeBe. Took her long enough.

"You can stay as long as you want, as long as you learn the right way to peel a potato!"

By the time they helped BeBe set the table, Henry was back with Mary and groceries. Reb monopolized Mary's attention for quite a while, understandably. They had things to catch up on. Dinner was lovely. Nothing less from a master. Mitch helped clean the kitchen and learned the correct was to polish a copper bottom pan. She might be allowed in the kitchen of her new restaurant if she kept up this apprenticeship.


Begging off any late night activities, Mitch and Reb turned in early. They were snuggled up close for about five minutes before Mitch wanted to talk theory.

"If you were having an affair, would you tell me?"

Reb looked straight at Mitch. "Are you having an affair?"

"No, of course not."

"You could tell me if you were."

"I'm not. It's a hypothetical question."

"Who would you have an affair with, if you ever did?"

"Well, I've ruled out Abraham Lincoln…"

"That doesn't count."

"Why not?"

"He was gay."

"He was?"

"There were letters."

"Like, love letters?"

"That's the rumor."

"Uh huh," Mitch got really quiet, hoping the subject she brought up would now go quietly away.

"Who else would you rule out?"

"It's your turn," Mitch countered.

"Okay, I'd never have an affair with Bob Dole."

"I'm glad to hear you say that. Since we're in Kansas. So close. The temptation would no doubt have been so strong."

Reb laughed. "I knew you'd be relieved! Now, if you're not having an affair and I'm not having an affair, who exactly is having an affair?"

"Henry."

"Henry!" Reb came up on one elbow.

"Shhh," Mitch warned, fearing the walls had ears. Or air ducts at the least.

"You've only been here a few hours. How did you find out so soon?"

"You're the one who sent me out to the barn."

"Oh please! Don't tell me-"

"It isn't one of the animals if that's what you're wondering."

"It wasn't, but that's a relief to know. So, who is it?"

"The organist. At the church."

How Reb knew that Mitch had struggled so very hard not to make a pun in front of Henry was anyone's guess.

"You behaved yourself, didn't you?"

"I don't think it's my behavior that needs to be called into question here."

"You're right. I'm sorry."

They were both quiet for a moment, almost long enough for Mitch to drift off to sleep. Reb's voice stemmed the tide.

"I guess I'm not surprised," she said with a certain resignation in her voice.

"Why?" Mitch carried her end of the conversation. Barely.

"Living with my sister can't be all that easy."

"Hmmmm," Mitch was noncommittal.

"I think I'd tell you."

13

"Tell me what?" Mitch yawned.

"About an affair. I'm pretty sure I'd tell you because I think you would already know about it anyway."

"You think?"

"You're pretty smart."

"If this unabashed flattery is leading somewhere, I'm way too tired to do anything about it."

"You just get some sleep. Tomorrow's going to be a busy day."

"Yes, Ma'am."

Mitch followed orders well. Her snoring might very well have kept up the entire household, (save Reb, who was used to it), judging by everyone's mood the next morning. Mitch breezed into the kitchen at an hour when she thought she would be the first one up. But no! BeBe was standing guard over a pot of oatmeal at the stove and a stranger to Mitch was seated at the table.

"Good morning," Mitch greeted the duo.

"Mornin," BeBe answered without turning around. Apparently, oatmeal had to be watched every minute.

The girl seated at the table remained silent. Maybe someone had read her her rights?

"I'm Mitch Tanner," Mitch held out her hand.

"That's my daughter, Miranda," BeBe explained.

Mitch held back a laugh. At this rate, she was going to require hernia surgery.

"Nice to meet you, Miranda."

"She's late for work," BeBe explained. Again.

The girl shoved in two more spoonfuls of oatmeal and then stood to leave.

"Kiss your mumsy!"

The girl obeyed and then left the kitchen without so much as a glance back. She was old enough to drive, but apparently not polite enough to be civil.

"She's a lovely young lady," Mitch remarked to BeBe's back and then noticed the unmistakable stiffening. Mitch now pretty much understood what the instructions to Miranda had been.

"Steer clear of the queer!"

14

Mitch helped herself to a cup of coffee and sat down at the table. Reb wheeled in soon after, brightening the entire room with the smile she cast Mitch's way. As always, Mitch's heart thumped. Almost clear out of her chest.

"It's a lovely morning!" she greeted everyone.

"Now that you're here," Mitch paid a compliment. The remark was punctuated by the bang of bowls of oatmeal thrust in front of them by BeBe. Romantic nonsense wasn't tolerated at the breakfast table. So said the scowl on her face.

"Thank you," Mitch said.

This was certainly a far cry from the bacon and eggs that she had expected based on Henry's shopping list.

"I told BeBe how much you like oatmeal," Reb explained.

"And so, you made this for me!" Mitch smiled her best company smile at BeBe.

"I made it for everybody," she deflected the remark with her flat reply.

"If you have any oatmeal left, I can make some cookies," Mitch offered.

"If you want cookies, I'll make them!"

"It sounded more like a warning than an offer.

"I wouldn't mind, really."

"I don't want the kitchen to be a mess. I have too many people coming over tonight for the meeting."

"The meeting?" Mitch asked.

"The meeting before the funeral tomorrow of course!"

Reb had a look on her face that said, "I'll explain it to you after breakfast. Eat your oatmeal!"

"And if anyone needs their black clothes washed and ironed, they'd better get them to me right now."

"Mine are fine," Reb assured quickly.

"And what about yours?" BeBe confronted Mitch.

"I brought a blue pant suit. It should be okay, since I hung it up yesterday."

"That WON'T do!" BeBe nearly shrilled the words. Everything Aunt BeBe said sounded like she was hollering to the farm hands, of whom there were none.

"What won't do?" Mitch asked back quietly.

"Blue isn't black!"

Mitch had taken enough art classes to know *that* already.

"Right," Mitch agreed.

"You're not wearing blue to the funeral!"

"Why not?"

"It just isn't done!  Nobody from this household is going to this funeral in anything but black!"

Mitch really didn't feel like arguing, no matter how much goading BeBe was prepared to do.  Instead, she just looked at Reb for guidance.

"How about I take you shopping in Utopia after breakfast?" Reb smiled.

Who could refuse such an offer, especially with the element of escape crafted into it?

"I can't think of anything I'd like better," Mitch smiled back.

"Hmpf" was BeBe's comment.

One nice thing about oatmeal; you could eat it up quickly and be off.  Just like Miranda had done.  Mitch took a moment to thank BeBe before heading out with Reb.

"What about Mary?" Mitch asked.

"She's sleeping in."

Reb gathered her purse and wheeled outside.  Mitch never thought she would be so happy to be back in a car so soon after their cross country trek, but it beat sitting around in the hostile environs of BeBe's kitchen.

"You have some explaining to do," Mitch intoned playfully as they were safely in the van and five miles down the road.

"I do?" Reb asked, as if surprised.

"Yeah.  Why didn't you tell me that BeBe had a daughter?"

"Well, I did, a long time ago."

"I guess I thought that she was moved out of the house?"

"Nope."

"She didn't say a word and gave me rather wide berth."

"She's that way with everybody."

"Does she have a job?"

"She works in the library."

"Great place if you don't like to talk to people much."

"I suppose so."

"Now, tell me about the meeting before the funeral."

"It's a family tradition. Tonight is the viewing of Aunt Bunny and then everyone gathers at the house for coffee and cake and stuff like that."

"That's a wonderful tradition, except for the viewing part."

"You don't like looking at dead people?"

"It's not on my top ten list. Can I stay home and fix the coffee or something?"

"It's okay with me, although BeBe might judge you harshly."

"I'm sort of getting used to it."

"I'm sorry about that."

"It's not your fault."

They grew quiet for a mile or two."

"Would it be better for you if I went?" Mitch asked.

"I always feel better when you're at my side, but not if it means that you would be uncomfortable."

"Let me think about it."

"Whatever."

"I hope they have something black in my size in Utopia."

"I'm sure they will. And as long as we're shopping for something in black, let's not forget to go through the lingerie department."

"Oh, yes?"

"Aunt BeBe's not the only one who has a thing for black."

Mitch didn't say anything, but she sure wondered for there was a nice motel somewhere between here and Utopia. Just in case the barn was reserved. Due to their early departure, or escape, the stores weren't open when they pulled in to the town. They had over an hour to kill.

"Are you hungry?" Reb asked.

"I could eat something. The oatmeal was a nice appetizer."

Reb pulled into the one and only one handicapped parking spot in front of a quintessential diner. Mitch could smell the fried food before they even got to the door. Folks coming out were kind enough to hold the doors open for them, and with no real fuss, Mitch and Reb were seated at a table next to a window. Everything on the menu sounded absolutely sinful. Pancakes, sausage, eggs, chicken fried steak, biscuits and gravy and blueberry pie in season were the first items Mitch scanned on the menu. She wondered if she could order one of each without

17

sending the management into a tizzy. Heck they had a whole hour. When the waitress brought coffee and two cups, she asked, "Whatcha gonna have?"

"I want one of everything," Mitch said as easily as if she were ordering a side of toast.

"One of everything?" the waitress clarified.

"It all sounds so good."

"You know how many eggs comes with one of everything?"

"No."

"Well, a whole lot, I can guarantee!"

Reb was listening to this without comment until now. "Probably a good two dozen, maybe more?" she estimated.

"Okay," Mitch thought that sounded like almost enough.

The girl looked from one to the other as if she was on hidden camera.

"Is this one a them blooper shows on TV? Am I on TV right now?" she asked as she wiped imaginary lipstick from her teeth.

"No," Mitch assured her.

As the waitress checked over her shoulder for a TV crew, she asked, "Are you paying by check?"

Mitch understood the concern. She had her share of bounced checks at the Lucky U.

"I have cash," Mitch pulled a money clip out of her pocket and showed a bundle of hundreds."

"How would you like those eggs?"

"Three over medium and the rest scrambled."

"Okay. Now, you'll also have about a dozen pancakes, if you get all the stacks."

"Okay."

"And if you want, we can get the steak and biscuits and gravy all on the same plate.

"Good idea."

"And what are you going to have?" she asked Reb.

"A bowl of Wheaties."

"'Kay. One bowl of Wheaties and one of everything comin right up."

"Oh, and if my order gets in the way of anybody else's, go ahead and serve them first."

"'Kay."

18

Reb studied Mitch for a moment. "You're a character, you know that, don't you!"

"I couldn't make a decision."

"What are you going to do with dozens of scrambled eggs?"

"Get a really high cholesterol reading?"

"We're burying my Aunt Bunny tomorrow. I don't want you to be next."

"I promise to reform once we leave this place."

Reb sensed they were getting to the heart of the matter.

"This particular diner or the entire state?"

"It's hard to love this side of your family. Particularly when they don't love back."

"I wish you could've met Aunt Bunny," Reb said as the first plates were brought out.

"You here for the funeral?" Jessie, their waitress, asked as she set food in front of them. She had found her nametag in the interlude. Reb looked up. "Yes, we are."

"It sure is too bad about Ms. Bunny. She was a sweet old lady. Too bad she had to up and die."

Reb nodded.

"You related?"

"She was my aunt."

"Oh yeah, like you said, Aunt Bunny! Well, here's the first of your order. There's plenty more cookin!"

"Thanks."

Mitch started in on the steak. It was as tender as the biscuits and combined with the cream gravy made it hard to keep the moaning down to a simper.

"You're whimpering," Reb reported with an arched eyebrow.

"I can't help it. There's only one thing better than this."

"And I bet you're not referring to Aunt BeBe's oatmeal."

"You know full well what I'm referring to and if you don't tone down your charm, I'm going to check us into a motel after breakfast."

"Eat your pancakes!"

Mitch did her best to eat a respectable amount of everything she had ordered, but had to surrender about halfway through the feast. Jessie didn't mind and happily boxed up the rest for transport. As tempting as it was to explore that motel option,

Mitch knew that there was shopping to do. It would be easy with Rebecca. She had a flair for selecting clothes for Mitch. If they could only do this without causing a stir in the little town, it would be an accomplishment. By noon, Mitch was outfitted in funeral duds and Reb had a box or two of drop-dead sexy underthings. Aunt BeBe would've thought it scandalous, which was probably why Henry spent his time in the barn. They were back at the ranch central in good time. They changed and were ready for the viewing well within the strict timetable of Aunt BeBe. At four-thirty, a mortuary limousine pulled up to the house. Mary, Reb and Mitch sat in the back. BeBe, Henry and Miranda sat in the front. Due to some unspoken rule, nobody talked. Every time it looked like Mitch was going to say something, Reb squeezed her hand tightly. The ride would've been torture had Reb not eventually acquiesced and allowed Mitch to put her arm around her shoulders. She pulled her close and comforted her. BeBe could eat sand.

It took little effort to extract Reb from the limousine and into her wheelchair. She was getting so strong that she required hardly any assistance. And although Mitch had joked earlier in the day about needing a crane herself to lift her out of the chair at the diner, she had regained some poise after much digesting. The group made their way slowly to the mortuary chapel. It was small and already filled with old friends and acquaintances of Aunt Bunny, the operative word being "old." The front row had been set aside for the family and BeBe marched to it like a soldier on a battlefield. If she was trying to command attention, it wasn't working. All eyes were on the Senator and her sidekick, Old Bent Arm.

Since they really didn't know anyone but the immediate family, there was no need to stop and chit chat with the other mourners. Mitch only recognized the organist, even with her clothes on. She was actually a stately woman, and it struck Mitch that at least Henry had the sense to fool around with women his own age rather than chase after some twenty-year old in a miniskirt. He got brownie points for that in Mitch's tally. Reb stayed in her wheelchair through the quick prayer service and subsequent process as people passed by Bunny's open casket. As people came over to speak to her, their soothing words all sounded the same, more or less, to Mitch. For the most part, no one was particularly distraught. Bunny had lived a long, rich fulfilling life. Her time was up and she went gracefully. All the milling about gave Mitch a chance to catch up with Mary.

"How is Lisa?"

"She's fine. She couldn't come. She had to work."

"I understand. How's your class going?"

Mary had decided to take the courses necessary to work in the daycare industry. Her work at the abuse shelter had helped her make this career choice. She couldn't take the stress of the shelter any longer, but wanted to continue to work with children.

"It's great."

"How long can you stay?"

"I fly out tomorrow, right after the funeral."

"Too bad you can't stay longer."

"They're getting to you already?" Mary watched carefully for an answer.

"I'm learning how to peel potatoes the right way. Feels like KP duty."

"Ah yes, the old 'they'll be no eyes in my mashed potatoes' speech."

"You've heard it?"

"Just about every Christmas."

"How did you endure it?"

"Distance, my dear friend. Distance. When things get too overwhelming, go hide out in the barn."

"I'll keep that in mind," Mitch nodded sagely.

BeBe came over to them and directed them to go back to the car for the ride home. It was essential to arrive before the crush of guests showed up at the house. The ride home was as silent as the ride there. Even Reb was subdued. There was nothing like looking at a deceased relative to bring home the reality and finality of death. Both Mitch and Reb had lost their parents before they met, so it wasn't like this was their first death. It was just their first death as a couple. And as far as Mitch was concerned, every experience was a learning experience. They held hands. That was enough for now.

There was still a parking spot left in front of the house by the time they arrived. It seemed as though everyone had jumped in their cars and zoomed straight to the farmhouse. As Mitch mingled about, the motivation was crystal clear. Aunt BeBe had put out a spread. What had started out as coffee and cake developed into a buffet supper for fifty people. No wonder she needed all those potatoes and eggs!

"Looks like about what you had for breakfast," Reb remarked with just a hint of humor.

"Not enough eggs," Mitch joked back.

Although Reb had brightened up a bit, she still looked drawn and pale. Hopefully, everyone would know when to go home so they could go to bed. As she talked with the guests, Mitch noticed that Henry and the organist stayed a safe distance away from everyone. Or maybe it was the other way around? Mitch knew what it was like to be the odd man out, so she went over for a visit with the organist.

"Hi, I'm Mitch."

"Yes, I remember."

"And I don't think I caught your name?"

"I'm Harriet Baker."

"Well, it's certainly nice to meet you. You play very nice music."

"Thank you."

"Have you lived here all your life?"

"I was born in Nebraska."

"So, when did you move here?"

"After I was married. My husband and I lived here."

"Do you have children?"

"No, we were never blessed with children."

"I see."

"I'm a widow now."

"I'm sorry."

"So am I."

Mitch waited a moment to see if there would be further conversation. There didn't seem to be much more to say. Once you've seen someone naked, it just didn't feel right talking about things like nothing ever happened. Reb came to the rescue.

22

"Could you help me find something for a headache?"

"Of course. Please, excuse me, Ms. Baker."

Mitch wheeled Reb down the hallway and into their guest bedroom.

"So, how bad is your headache, Sweetie?"

"It's just that pain when you hold it all in."

Mitch nodded. She knew exactly what that felt like.

"Why don't we stretch out on the bed together and talk about it?"

"What about all those guests?"

"They'll just have to find their own beds."

Mitch handed Reb two tablets and a glass of water. When she downed the medication, Reb allowed Mitch to help her change into her pajamas and arrange her in the bed. A pillow here, a pillow there. Mitch was then beside her after performing a quick change herself.

"My Aunt Bunny was a good woman."

"She seems to have a lot of friends."

"Most of the people are here for the food."

"I'm shocked."

"No, you're not!"

"No, I'm not," Mitch admitted.

"She looked good. It's amazing what those morticians can do."

"Do me a favor?" Mitch asked.

"Keep in mind that I have a headache."

"It's not that kind of favor!"

"Okay. What then?"

"When I die, don't do this to me."

"Do what?"

"Don't fill me full of formaldehyde and put me on display."

"Put it in writing."

"That's not a bad idea."

"It's the only way your wishes will truly be followed."

"Even if I ask to be stored in an upright freezer?"

"You may want to check state statutes on that one."

"First thing as soon as we get home."

"You'd go back tomorrow if you had the chance, wouldn't you?"

"Heck no! I'm having the time of my life."

"Well, you're certainly having the *meals* of your life."

Mitch chuckled. "Yes, indeed. You never told me your sister could cook like that."

"She's had a lot of practice over the years."

"Well, she certainly knows her way around the kitchen."

They were quiet for another long minute or two. Reb's color was slowly returning.

"How's your headache?"

"Better."

"Will it bother you to not inherit any of this?"

"No."

Mitch thought that was an awfully short answer to such a complex question so she tried another avenue.

"If you could have changed one thing about your childhood, what would it be?"

"What is this, twenty questions?"

"Only two so far," Mitch countered.

"Three," Reb argued. "You asked me how my headache was."

"Well, excuse me for being worried about your health," Mitch said, though not unkindly. She recognized a stall when she saw one.

"What would you have changed?"

"The wallpaper."

"Anything else?" Mitch wouldn't let go. Whenever Reb was this evasive, it was usually worth the effort to do a bit more excavating.

"I wish that the attitudes would have been different."

"What attitudes?"

Reb checked to see if Mitch was really interested in hearing this. "You're that curious?"

"Yes."

"Okay. I wish I had been raised in a more tolerant atmosphere. By the time I figured out how intolerant I was, I was almost a lost cause."

"Keep going."

"You want the ugly details?"

"I'm stuck in Kansas for five more days. A long story will break the monotony."

"My father ridiculed Blacks and gays. I know I should say African Americans instead of Blacks, but when I was growing

24

up, it took a lot of guts to use the word Black. Especially when everyone else around you was being disrespectful. You can only imagine what they called gay people."

"I've heard the word, "Queer.""

"That's an upgrade, believe me."

"So, what did your mother do when she heard all this?"

"She was too busy denigrating Jews and people of religions other than hers. Everyone was going to hell but her."

"Ah, yes. Celery and tomato juice."

"What and what?" Reb was dumbfounded.

"It's an old joke. A guy is in heaven three days, all he gets to eat is celery and tomato juice, so he asks God why the lousy food and God replies, 'You know how hard it is to cook for two!'"

Reb chuckled politely. "My mother loved celery."

"She loved celery and hated Jews. Why do you suppose she was like that?"

"I know why she was like that. I know why my dad was like that as well. They put other people down so that they could feel superior. Some people are just like that. It's a pass-fail mentality."

"I feel sorry for people like that," Mitch said. "I can't imagine going through life trying to judge everybody else and find illusions of fault just so I could feel morally or physically superior. I'd think you'd end up distancing yourself from everyone and feeling very lonely."

"Unless you find a way to break the cycle. For some reason, Aunt Bunny wasn't like that at all."

"Was she your mom's or dad's sister?"

"My mom's."

"And what about your grandparents?"

"I didn't know them any other way except pillars of the community. If they harbored prejudice, I didn't know about it."

"So, it was just the two girls?"

"Oh, yes! And was *that* a bone of contention! Leaving a homestead farm to two girls!"

"Well, it survived."

"Henry and BeBe have stuck with it, I'll grant them that."

"And so their reward is to inherit the place."

"And my reward," Reb tugged at Mitch's sleeve, "is you."

"I'll try to live up to the billing," Mitch said and then kissed Reb goodnight.

Mitch wasn't quite used to farm noises and slept well past the rooster's alert. She reached over, but Reb was gone. The clock read eight. The funeral was at ten. It was so tempting to want to fall back asleep for five minutes. Or five days. She fended off the sleepiness and dragged herself out of bed. A ten minute shower woke her up thoroughly and then she dressed for the funeral before making an appearance in the kitchen. The atmosphere was subdued. Subdued in the normal way when a funeral was on the agenda. Reb was rested and refreshed, a welcome sight to Mitch. She gave her a peck on the cheek, only slightly nauseating BeBe, Henry and Miranda. Maybe this was what had given Reb her headache last night. All this undisguised disapproval could create volumes of stress.

"Morning, everyone."

They muttered replies and then scattered to get ready for the trip into town.

"You probably shouldn't kiss me when they are watching," Reb stated quietly.

"If we were straight, it wouldn't matter."

"If we were straight, we wouldn't be kissing at all, probably."

"And think how terrible that would be," Mitch smiled and then kissed her again. This time with feeling.

"Still, we should honor their feelings. It is their house, after all."

"And I think they should grow up a little. All three of them."

"I'm taking Mary to the airport after the interment. You want to go with?"

"No. I think I'll stick around here. You two can have some time alone together."

"She seems really happy."

"I think things are working out well."

"I still owe you that thousand dollars."

When the bribery scandal had hit its apex, Reb was convinced that Lisa was guilty. So convinced, in fact, that she bet Mitch a thousand dollars. The IOU was still outstanding.

"I'll take it in trade," Mitch leaned close and playfully kissed Reb. Again.

26

"Do funerals always have this effect on you?"

"I celebrate life."

The sound of approaching footsteps made them move farther apart, but it was only Mary, who was used to these displays of affection.

"Hi, you two."

"Hi, back."

"So, how are you liking Kansas so far, Mitch?"

"Do you have room in your suitcase to smuggle me out?"

"Had enough of the Bible Belt already, I see."

"You know, I've heard a lot about the Bible in my lifetime, but never once has anyone ever quoted from it, 'And Jesus was rude.'"

"What's that mean?"

"If Jesus never found occasion to be rude, I don't understand why so many of his so-called followers do."

"I think they just run out of things to say," Reb offered for the defense.

"A simple 'Good morning' would suffice."

"Give them time. They'll warm up."

The only warming up that happened during the morning was the weather. For a land-locked state, it was a sticky heat, and wearing black didn't help. As they entered the church for the funeral, Mitch noticed a knot of protestors milling around with signs and Bibles. They were wearing blue and white and yellow and about every other color except black. By the time Mitch and Reb were seated, it had dawned on her who the protestors were. It was that same group who carried anti-gay placards at the funerals of HIV related deaths. The same group who appeared at Trish and Robbie's wedding. But that didn't make sense. This was neither the wedding of a gay couple nor the funeral of an AIDS patient. Aunt Bunny had died of natural causes.

It wasn't until Mitch noticed that BeBe kept glaring in her direction that the horrible truth dawned. It was Mitch and Reb's presence at the funeral that had sparked the demonstration. As far as BeBe was concerned, it was their fault that this awful desecration had happened and there would be hell to pay. It

27

wouldn't be Mitch's life were there not hell to pay once in a while. She consoled Reb as best she could during the proceedings without making it appear to be a public display of affection. After the final song and dismissal, she mingled out of range of Aunt BeBe as they followed people out of the church. It was a short drive to the cemetery and the protestors were there as well. When the graveside prayers were over, Mitch stirred up her courage and approached the protestors. There was a brief, one-sided exchange, and then Mitch rejoined Reb by the car.
"What did you say to them?" Reb was concerned.
"I invited them back to the house for a bite."
"You did *what*?" Reb was thunderstruck
"It seemed the polite thing to do. They must be hungry. They've stood a long vigil."
"My sister is going to ream you out."
"I don't see why? I'm only doing the Christian thing."

Once again, a feast was ready when they got back to the farmhouse. Fried chicken, potato salad, and a pie in every flavor. Eventually, the protest group assembled outside the house. And Mitch hadn't even given them directions. Guess everyone knew where Aunt Bunny had lived. Mitch fixed up several plates of food and carried them out two by two to the group. At first, they refused to acknowledge her, and then, one of them sneered at her, "It's probably poisoned."

Mitch understood their suspicions. People who hated that much always expected the worst in others. Undaunted, Mitch produced a fork and ate a bite, sometimes two, of everything she had dished up. When she went back in the house to get them something to drink, they waited until she had given them a pitcher of tea before they dumped the plates of food on the ground and threw the tea in the general direction of Mitch's feet. Then, they dispersed, leaving the mess behind for her to clean up. Before she could even bend down to pick up the empty pitcher, Harriet, the church organist, was at her elbow.
"You go into the house. I'll clean up."
"No, I'll help. I caused the mess, in a round-about way."
"I'll have more than enough help."

As Mitch turned, she saw almost everyone coming forward to help. They had things picked up and hosed down faster than Mitch could believe.

"You sure showed them up," Mary came down the walk and gave her a hug.

"That wasn't the plan, but as long as no one got hurt, I guess all's well that ends well."

"How Shakespearean!" Reb said. She looked at Mitch with one of those combination expressions which Mitch couldn't quite decipher.

"I'm taking Mary to the airport. We'll talk later."

After they left, two women fussed over Mitch, guiding her to a comfy chair and bringing her a plate of food. She accepted the hospitality graciously and chatted with them as she ate. They treated her like some sort of folk hero, which served only to nettle Aunt BeBe even more.

"There are children starving and they throw food on the ground," the first woman huffed.

"Terrible waste of BeBe's wonderful food," Mitch agreed. Loudly.

"Please don't think that everyone is like those troublemakers," woman number two announced.

"I don't think that at all. Everyone here has been so nice to us," Mitch assured them both.

By the time Reb returned from the airport, Mitch and her two new best friends, Millie and Carol, had traded recipes, gossip, and weather predictions. It was all Reb could do to extract her from her fan club.

"I need your help with a personal matter." was the magic phrase. They went to their room and closed the door.

"A personal matter?" Mitch didn't know if this was good-personal or bad-personal. She was about to find out.

"I just wanted to tell you that if you ever pull a stunt like that again, I want fair warning!"

"Why?"

"So I can have a trophy engraved."

"What would the inscription be?"

"To the biggest damn fool who I ever fell in love with."

"Is that grammatically correct?" Mitch was being studious for the first time in a long time.

"Like, I give a damn."

"A big part of you is still really angry at me, am I right?"

"Why do you court danger?"

"Taking food to hungry people isn't dangerous. Except if you don't take enough, I guess?"

"You don't think these people are dangerous?"

"Not any more than Senators protecting their stolen art work," Mitch shrugged. "And even you got in on that deal."

It was true. Not so very long ago, when Mitch and Reb confronted the now deceased Senator Schnell with the truth of his crimes, he tried to shoot Mitch in the head. Thanks to the bullet of a deadly accurate police officer, Mitch's shoulder took the worst of it.

"Why don't you change your clothes? Then, join me out in the living room," Reb instructed.

Mitch finally noticed why she should change after Reb had wheeled out. Her black slacks had been splattered by the tea. Maybe she had been just a touch more affected by the incident than she realized? She had nothing else black to wear, so she changed into navy blue and rejoined the crowd. It had thinned considerably since the mini lecture. Most folks didn't stay around as long at a funeral as they did at weddings. Those who remained were either picking up the food or cleaning the kitchen. BeBe was commandeering the troops like a drill sergeant. From what Mitch could see, these people didn't need much in the way of orders. This crew had polished plenty a kitchen in their day. Then, as quickly as they had assembled, they vanished, leaving the bereaved family with no further distractions.

"The lawyer will be here at nine-o'clock sharp tomorrow morning. He charges by the hour! Be on time!" BeBe warned everyone before closing herself up in her sewing room. Miranda had long since vanished in her car and Mitch would've only needed one guess as to Henry's whereabouts. Not that he was engaged in any certain behavior as much as just needing a few quiet hours to himself. Which left Mitch and Reb to their own devices.

"If I change into something more comfortable," Reb ventured, "would you take me to the movies or something?"

"Wonderful idea!" Mitch agreed. Anything to get out of the house. They dressed in light clothes and took off after leaving a note that they wouldn't be home until late. It was a squeeze, but they made the matinee at the movie theater. Mitch bought two popcorns, two drinks, and four boxes of bite-size Butterfinger candy and then had the self-deprecating sense of humor to ask Reb what she was having. They laughed like fools. Grief was a funny thing. After the movie, they stopped in at the diner for a cup of tea and a roll of heartburn medicine.

"Heard the two of you are famous," Jessie said as she brought tea bags, hot water and Tums.

"What did we do?" Mitch asked. A silent "this time" was floating between Reb and Mitch.

"You stood up to the 'Citizens United for Morality" group."

"That's not exactly what happened and how did you hear about it anyway?" Mitch was curious.

"Oh, it's all over town. See, here comes Ned now."

"Ned?" Mitch looked at Reb who now had a deer-in-the-headlights look about her.

"Guy who owns he newspaper. Probably wants an interview." Jessie went to another table before Reb said, "Can we give the appearance that we were just leaving?"

"Why?"

Reb didn't get to explain further. From the doorway, she heard a booming voice, "Senator Becky!"

Mitch mouthed the words in Reb's direction with a somewhat bemused expression on her face. Reb would've kicked her under the table had she been able. At the same time, she flashed a gorgeous smile in Ned's direction. He came over and sat right down at the table like he'd been asked.

"Hello, Ned. How are you after all these years?"

"Not nearly as well aged as you," he delivered it as the compliment he intended it to be. It still sounded a bit cheesy to Mitch.

"And look where you ended up!" he exclaimed.

Mitch scanned the room. It was still the diner as far as she could tell.

"A Senator!" he beamed.

"Are you so surprised?" she asked in a teasing way that old friends understand.

"Yes! I mean NO! Our little Becky a Senator. One of a hundred."

"Thank you, Ned. I'd like you to meet Mitch Tanner."

"Oh, you're the one who was attacked! Can you tell me about it firsthand?" he asked as he skillfully pulled out a small tablet and pen.

Mitch wasn't quite in quote mood yet, and instead asked a question herself.

"How do you two know each other?"

"We grew up together!" Ned nearly wriggled with the news. Remember Mrs. Evan's English class?" he quizzed Reb.

"Like it was yesterday," Reb nodded.

"She was Juliet in the school play," Ned the snitch informed Mitch. Meanwhile, Reb looked like she was about to jump off the balcony.

"Who was Romeo?" Mitch followed up like she was the reporter. Ned blushed like a ten-year-old schoolboy.

"I was," he admitted.

"How *sweet*," Mitch directed the remark toward Reb.

"Hollywood never called back," she remarked dryly.

"I can't imagine."

"Now," Ned was back to business. "About that attack?"

"There was no attack," Mitch started off with the truth.

"I heard there was! Something about things getting thrown at you?"

"Some food was spilled. Nothing more," Mitch refused to embellish, even though it would've been easy enough to do so.

"I heard a pitcher was thrown."

"A pitcher was dropped. Folks cleaned up the mess in a few minutes. No harm was done."

"The only casualty was a piece of fried chicken," Reb backed up Mitch's version of things.

"Well, not much front page about that," Ned sighed dejectedly.

"Sorry," Mitch apologized.

"But I can still do a nice write-up about our Senator!"

"That might not be such a good idea, Ned," Reb warned.

32

"Why not?"

"I'm a Senator from Colorado, not Kansas. Your Senators might be put out if you do a story about me."

"You're right, of course. Well, I guess that's it. Except…"

"Except what?"

"It is true about Bun's will?"

Reb furrowed her brow. "What do you mean?"

"I thought you could tell me," he remarked evasively.

"We're talking to the lawyer tomorrow. That's all I know."

"Things are quiet on the home front, then?"

"More than you can imagine," Mitch said.

"It's been a long day, Ned," Reb patted Romeo's hand.

"I understand. Call me before you leave town. Promise?"

"Promise."

He buzzed out of the diner like he was on deadline. Mitch watched Reb carefully.

"Romeo and Juliet?"

"It was a school play."

"Pretty racy stuff for a small town."

"Mrs. Evan was a visionary. Besides, we couldn't very well do Inherit the Wind."

"Mrs. Evan was a visionary who wanted to keep her job?"

"Exactly."

"What do you suppose he meant about the will?"

"I figured he wanted my opinion on being cut off without a penny."

"Then why didn't he just ask that?"

"You expect me to understand the mind of a reporter?"

"I just thought it was an overly-broad approach."

"Not everyone is as direct as you!" Reb arched an eyebrow.

"He got right down to business with the food incident."

"You want to go across the street and ask him?" Reb was tiring quickly of the topic.

"No. I can wait until tomorrow. Your family must be something else."

"Why?"

"How many lawyers do you know who make house calls?"

"It's just always been that way. Besides, I'm sure he charges for travel time."

After Mitch got her popcorn heartburn under control, she talked Reb into a steak dinner. It wasn't very often that they indulged in a heavy-duty meat meal, but when in Kansas, it seemed so fitting. They had managed to find a restaurant that had candlelight. Not exactly twelve-inch tapers, but the flickering from the glass jar was still just as romantic. Keeping the sparks to a minimum was difficult.

"I love every day I spend with you," Mitch gazed into Reb's eyes.

"Death makes you appreciate life."

"And love."

"And the people around you."

"Tell me how to better appreciate your family."

"I don't know what to tell you. It's hard to reach out to people who don't much want to be reached."

"I did it with you."

"So, if you know the secret, why are you asking me?"

"Well, I wanted to sleep with you," Mitch tried to wriggle around the topic.

"And you don't want to sleep with my sister."

"That's right!"

"What is it that you do want?"

"I want to get out of Kansas with no recurring nightmares."

"Why don't you just continue to be your relaxed, charming self?"

"Did I mention that I love every moment I spend with you?"

"Did I mention I want to sleep with you?"

"Did I mention that that can be arranged?"

Chapter 2

That damn rooster! Mitch opened up first one eye and then the
other. Reb was up and gone. Where did that woman get all her
energy? They had been awake until well past midnight. It just
wasn't fair for Reb to be that talented when she was no longer
capable of sexual function herself. Of course, she insisted that
Mitch was still the greatest lover since Casanova, but it couldn't
possibly be the same. Mitch dragged herself out of bed and
checked her eyes for bags. She might look presentable by
lunchtime. A knock at the door broke into her reverie.
"Come in."
Reb appeared. Damn, she looked great. What a show off.
"The lawyer's going to be here any minute."
"Yeah, I guess so."
"Are you ready?"
"Why do I need to be ready?" Mitch asked. She had never
expected to be in on the meeting. She wasn't a legal part of the
family.
"You're supposed to be there."
"I am?"
"That's what BeBe said the lawyer said."
"That doesn't make sense."
"You'll have to take that up with BeBe."
Mitch dressed casually but quickly and then made an appearance
in front of the coffee pot. BeBe was looking daggers her
direction so she didn't ask about the lawyer's directive. Going
with the flow seemed to be the better part of discretion. The
family lawyer, a sweet gentleman by all accounts, arrived five
minutes early and cordially greeted all interested parties. BeBe
herded them into the formal dining room so that they could sit
and shuffle paperwork.

"If it's convenient with the family, I will dispense with the
reading of the entire will and just discuss the items I feel you are
most interested in."
Everyone nodded. Especially Aunt BeBe. She just wanted to
hear it was all hers and get it over with.

"The will, for the most part, leaves everything to Ms. Rebecca Fairbanks and her life partner."

If the world stopped on its axis, it wouldn't have made a bigger impact on the people seated around the dining room table.

"That can't be!" Aunt BeBe sputtered. "That's not right!"

"I have the will right here if you wish to see it."

"The will leaves the money and estate to the person who is married!" Aunt BeBe explained the obvious mistake to the lawyer.

"Aunt Bunella had seventeen wills the last time we checked," the lawyer intoned. "The will you're referring to was number nine, I believe."

"Aunt Bunny had seventeen wills?" Reb asked.

"Yes."

"And the 'you did not need to be married to inherit' will was the ninth one she had written?"

"That's correct."

"And there were eight prior and eight after."

"Correct."

Mitch was trying so hard to keep a straight face. Reb would have been proud of her effort had she only seen it.

"Why did she write so many wills?" Reb asked.

"Your Aunt Bunella was an eccentric, even among eccentrics. She amused herself by rewriting the condition of inheritance clause."

"Can you give me an example?"

"Most certainly. Will number three stated that people could only inherit if they lived in a state beginning with the letter C."

Aunt BeBe gasped. She would've been aced out with this deal as well.

"Will number seven excluded everyone who ate pork."

"Why?"

"She had a pet pig at the time," the lawyer answered.

Too bad Aunt Bunny was dead. She sounded like a real hoot.

"So, when it's all said and done, in her final will," the lawyer explained, "Ms. Rebecca Fairbanks and Ms. Mitch Tanner inherit the entire estate."

BeBe was nearly panic stricken. "Isn't there any inheritance for those of us who stayed and worked the land and took care of Aunt Bunny!" she asked in a shrill voice choked with rage.

"There is one gift that Bunny wanted to bequeath to Henry."

"To Henry!" BeBe was turning a dangerous shade of beet red.

"He is the new owner of the barn."

The dangerous red color in Aunt BeBe's face now started to drain out, but not nearly at the rate of Henry's. Between the two of them, there might be hospital bills to pay.

"This can't be. This just can not be," she muttered as her hands shook. "I stayed married to the likes of *him* all these years and all I get is a barn! Aunt Bunny told me to my face that I needed to be married to inherit!"

"Perhaps you misheard her. Or maybe she misspoke. Either way, the will is clearly written. If there are no other questions, I do have another appointment," the lawyer stood to leave. Henry saw him out, due to the fact that BeBe was no longer capable of perambulation. She looked squarely at Reb. Her ability to speak had not been adulterated.

"I'll fight this," she hissed. "I'll contest this will! The old woman was batty and I'll have no trouble proving it. You'll be left without one penny!"

Apparently, the venting of the spleen made it once again possible for BeBe to move. She stood up so quickly that her chair tipped over and she stormed out without setting it upright again. Now, it was Reb's turn to be shaken and wan. Mitch sat steadily and held Reb's hand.

"This isn't what I expected at all."

"Seems like everyone has had a bit of a shock."

"I can't let this happen. I never wanted to ace BeBe and Henry out of their rightful inheritance. I'll just sign everything over to them."

"You ought to think about that for a long minute," Mitch voiced her one true opinion.

"You want this farm?" Reb looked skeptical. "The woman who's counting the hours until she gets to leave?"

"I'm just saying that you should consider all the options. Like, for instance, Mary."

"What about Mary?"

"This is her birthright as well.  If anyone needs a bit of a helping hand right now, it's Mary and Lisa."

"You think they want to move out here and become lesbian farmers."

"I just think that we all need to catch our breath and do some serious thinking."

"I think we're expected to pack our things and vacate the premises."

"Is there a good hotel in town that's handicapped equipped?"

"Sounds like we're about to find out."

"Let's go start the packing."

"Okay."

It took about twenty minutes to secure everything in their modest luggage.  A quiet knock on the door made them look at each other with dread.  One more confrontation they didn't need.  It was Henry.  He hadn't done any of the yelling earlier.  Maybe he thought he was due some.

"I hate to see you leave like this," he explained in a voice that sounded full of regret.  Maybe the presence of Mitch and Reb had been like a cold drink on a hot day.  A refreshing change from the usual.

"I think it's best," Reb said calmly.

"Oh, I agree," he nodded.  "I just hate to see it."

"Thank you, Henry."

He was waiting for something.  It wasn't clear what.  Maybe an opening?

"You should come visit us soon, Henry."

"Oh, Washington's too big a place for me.  Too many important people."

"You would enjoy it," Reb assured him, "and Miranda could see all the sights."

"And BeBe could eat out every day and not have to cook for a month," Mitch tacked on.

"You leaving town today?"

"No, we're going to check into a hotel for a night or two."

"Meet me tomorrow at the bank."

"Why?"

He heard footsteps and needed to escape.

"Just meet me there 'bout noon. Oh and one more thing, I don't want the barn."

Then, he was gone. And so were the footsteps. Reb led the way through the house, seeking out BeBe to say a proper goodbye. She was in the kitchen and stood a stony silence as Reb told her of their plan, except the part about the meeting with Henry at the bank of course. Then, they left. Quietly.

A hotel in the middle of the Main Street was a pleasant surprise. It had made every effort to not only conform to the ADA, but with a certain amount of panache. The senator and her cohort were ensconced in a suite before lunchtime. By now, Reb was a bit ragged around the edges. No one could blame her. She had gone two or three rounds with the undisputed champ of Utopia and was about to be declared the winner.

"How about room service?" Mitch suggested.

"I'm not hungry, but you go ahead."

"Sure," Mitch proceeded to order for two. Just in case.

"I'm going to clean up a little and then rest."

"Holler if you need help," Mitch remarked without her usual twinkle. It was just a hunch, but Mitch felt that Reb wasn't in a twinkly mood. Having a major falling out with the family could have that effect. By the time lunch arrived, a scrumptious array of deep fried veggies, steak covered in mushroom gravy and cherry pie, Reb was out of the shower and comfortably arranged in bed. Mitch sat next to her while she cut up the steak.

"Want a bite?" Mitch asked.

"Whatever happened to our sensible diet?"

"I forgot to pack it."

"I think I'll pass," Reb moved restlessly. Mitch could sense her sadness and set the food aside.

"You want to talk about it?"

"No."

"You want me to hold you while you cry?"

"I'm not crying."

"Not yet, but the minute the adrenaline wears off, you will be."

"You're right," Reb said as she reached out to gather Mitch close to her. As good cries go, this was a real humdinger. Between the death, funeral and family fireworks, Reb had a lot of stress to cry out. Mitch just held steady and encouraged her to get it all out.

Soon, two things were true. The food was cold and Reb was hungry. Some days, timing was everything.
"You want me to send it back to be warmed?"
"No. Just give me the pie to start with."
Mitch surrendered the dessert and popped cold pieces of crusted zucchini and mushrooms into her mouth.
"Anything good on TV?"
"Let's check it out."

A movie about spies and counter spies gave them something entertaining to doze through. By dinner, Reb was almost back to her usual self. Fearing that if she took Mitch to the diner, they would have two of everything on the dinner menu to sample, she suggested a restaurant that specialized in low-fat entrees. Nothing like a charbroiled piece of skinless chicken breast to satisfy taste buds that craved guilt-free eating. That, with a salad, baked potato (No butter! No sour cream!) and steamed broccoli brought contentment to Reb. As Mitch was wondering whether or not she could cram down some non-fat frozen yogurt, surprise, surprise, Ned showed up at the door of the restaurant. Perhaps it was the subdued atmosphere of the dining room, but he refrained, thankfully, from hollering out Rebecca's name. Instead, he sidled over to the table and asked if he could join them.
"Please, have a seat."
"Can I buy you dinner?"
"We're just finishing up," Reb shook her head.
"I'll pick up your check."
"You don't need to do that, really," Reb shook her head again.
"It would be my pleasure! Besides, after the reading of the will who knows when we'll see each other again?"
"Why would you say that?" Reb was putting on mental ice skates and going full speed toward thin ice.
"Well, rumor has it that you were getting cut out of the will. I guess I figured that you'd pack up and move on pretty quickly."

"I just can't stay long, Ned. I have work back in Washington."

"So, you *were* disinherited?"

"Not yet," Reb answered carefully. After all, it would soon be a matter of public record when the court battle broke out.

"So, the rumors aren't true?"

"How many rumors turn out to be true?"

"You're right, of course," Ned nodded his balding head. "I mean, remember all those rumors that floated around after we were in *the play*?"

"I never heard any rumors," Reb said forthrightly.

"Oh," he sounded deflated.

The conversation trailed off. By now, Mitch had lost her appetite for dessert and went ahead and paid the check over the half-hearted protestations of Romeo. They extracted themselves gracefully and returned to the hotel room to rest. Since they had slept in the afternoon, their resting consisted of chatting and holding hands. All things considered, they were good company for each other and the relaxed atmosphere soon led to sound sleep. So sound, in fact, that they had to hustle to make their appointment with Henry the next morning.

"How do you know which bank to go to?" Mitch asked as Reb drove.

"Bunny only ever banked at one place."

"Why?" Mitch wondered out loud, mostly just to keep a conversation going.

"I suppose because she was on the board of directors."

"That would be a good reason," Mitch mused, wondering to herself just how much money a person would need to have to be on a Kansas bank's board of directors. They parked in a handicapped parking spot and entered the bank. It was quiet for the lunch hour and Henry was right there to greet them. He didn't seem quite so nervous now that he needn't worry about being intercepted by BeBe.

"I made a promise to Bunny before she died," he said by way of hello.

"Okay," Reb figured he was a man who would keep his promises. Except, maybe, his wedding vows? But, then again, Reb hadn't done so well in that area either. Except that she had had the decency to give it a rest before launching into another

41

relationship. Not eons, mind you. But she hadn't dallied in a hay loft.

"BeBe doesn't know." Henry explained the obvious.

"I figured as much."

"We need to go to the safety deposit box area."

Which was all the way across the room. Henry signed a log book and the clerk studied it like it was Al Capone's autograph. He produced a key and was led back to an area while Reb and Mitch stayed behind in the waiting area. Mitch pondered reading the latest issue of Fortune, but time didn't allow. Henry was back out in thirty seconds. He handed a thick, sealed envelope to Reb.

"What's this?"

"I don't know. She just wanted you to have it."

Reb didn't want to open it in front of the all-seeing, all-nosy eyes of the bank personnel and cameras so she put the parcel in her lap and rolled out to the van. She thanked Henry when they were outside. It was painfully obvious that Henry would've given a square mile of farm land to know what was in the envelope, but had been a man of honor. Besides, it seemed that he no longer had a square mile of farmland. He had a barn. It was probably all he ever wanted. He headed back in silence.

From what Mitch could tell, there could be several things in the envelope. A stash of handy cash would be nice to pay a lawyer to fight Aunt BeBe? Even if it were in hundreds, it wouldn't be enough at today's prices. Perhaps it was a stack of bills to be paid? Maybe Aunt Bunny was a stickler for that. Reb didn't seem to be worried about it one way or another and tossed the bundle in the back seat.

"You want some lunch?" she asked.

"You buying?" Mitch asked back.

"Sure, as long as you don't order two of everything!"

"I promise to behave myself."

"Oh, don't promise that!" Reb winked as they drove to the diner. Jessie saw them coming and had a table ready and waiting.

"Want some coffee or is it tea time yet?" she asked as she handed them menus.

"I think I'll stick with water," Reb said.

"You know what?" Mitch started out with a look in her eye. Reb almost seemed to cringe. "I've been craving a root beer float for days."

"Good choice. One scoop or two?"

"Make it three. I'm in a vanilla mood."

"Comin right up."

Mitch didn't notice the look until she took stock of Reb's face. "It was either that or a chocolate milkshake."

"You've been on quite the rampage, calorie-wise, lately."

"I've lost ten pounds since the shooting. Consider it part of the healing process."

"You're going to heal yourself right into a triple bypass."

"I've got the blood pressure of a teenager. Don't bug me about what I eat!"

Mitch rarely snapped. Usually, when there were words of discord between them, they emanated from Reb. As did flying dishes. She was the one with the temper.

"I'm sorry. I didn't mean to nag."

"It's okay."

"It's Kansas, isn't it?"

"No, it's the way things are turning out."

"Tell me what's bothering you," Reb had that soft look in her eyes. It melted Mitch every time.

"I'm scared."

"Of what?"

"Honestly?"

"Uh huh."

"I'm worried that one day, we'll turn into BeBe and Henry."

"Are you going to have a sex change operation?" Reb asked.

"Not without a fight," Mitch answered.

"You're terrified that I'm going to become my sister. All nagging and directives and dead on the inside, right?"

"When do people lose their ability to enjoy life and the people around them?"

"Some people never have that ability to begin with," Reb explained.

"Is that what happened with BeBe?"

"She's pretty much always been that way. I guess she believes that only stiff-necked sanctimonious people can go to heaven."

"Well, you know what I think about that," Mitch remarked like she and Reb had already had this conversation.

"Remind me."

"I think that if heaven is going to be filled with people like your sister, then I'd just as soon be in hell."

"I'll be right beside you," Reb smiled.

Mitch's root beer arrived. Reb held up a finger. "Could we have one more of those?" she indicated the drink.

"Sure thing!"

With just a hint of a flourish, Mitch handed the treat to Reb.

"You start on this one. I'll catch up."

"Are you sure?"

"Delayed gratification is always better."

"Yeah, but like, how would you know?"

Other than the liquid appetizers, they ate a sensible meal and then headed back to the hotel. All that talk about gratification had given them inspiration. It really hadn't been all that much talk, granted. But, then again, they didn't need much lately. Mitch snuggled up to Reb just to snuggle. If it bothered Reb that their sex life was awfully one-sided anymore, she never breathed a word.

After brief consultation with a therapist after Reb's accident, Mitch had worked hard to hone her pleasure-giving skills. Finding new places to touch and different ways of letting Reb know she was still the most sensual woman on the planet was all part of Mitch's learning curve. All the practice was beginning to pay off. Reb was glowing.

"How do you make me feel so fulfilled?" Reb kissed her lazily.

"Creative genius," Mitch smiled back.

"You've been reading up on this, haven't you?"

"Chapter three was fun."

They giggled in unison.

"Speaking of reading, why don't you check out whatever's in that envelope that we got today?"

"Why do you think it's reading material? It could be cash."

"Well, that's fun reading too. One-hundred. One-hundred. One-hundred."

"Okay, okay. Get the envelope. I've made you wait long enough."

Mitch had a look about her like it was Christmas Eve and she had wheedled permission to open just one gift. She ripped open the seal and looked inside. It seemed pretty boring overall, just a bunch of letters, hand-addressed to Bunella. Mitch pulled them out and handed them to Reb. It was an interesting assortment of letters and cards that appeared by postmark to span several years. One fact was evident. They were all from the same person, a Ms. Evie Newton.

"Who is Evie Newton?" Mitch asked.

"I have no idea," Reb answered as she began to read one of the letters. The handwriting was beautiful. Something you'd expect from a penmanship teacher. Reb wasn't reading aloud, so Mitch had to wait patiently for updates. It didn't take too long.

"Oh, my dear God in heaven," Reb breathed it like a prayer.

"What?" Mitch looked worried.

"I don't believe it."

"What?" Mitch was coming out of her skin with worry.

"Ms. Newton is, was, my Aunt Bunny's lover."

"Oh," Mitch nodded. That wasn't such bad news. Except if Ms. Newton hadn't heard about Aunt Bunny.

"What's the latest postmark?"

"Why do you want to know that?"

"Just curious."

"The most recent date appears to be four weeks ago."

Mitch looked at the postmark. It was from Idaho.

"Did Aunt Bunny take a lot of vacations to Idaho?"

"Not that I know of. BeBe would have better information, but asking her is out of the question. I mean, even if we were still speaking, I wouldn't get BeBe to volunteer information without first having to explain why I was asking."

"Henry might."

"Maybe."

"Or maybe Ms. Newton is our best source. I bet that no one has told her about Bunny's death."

"And you think that this was Aunt Bunny's way of arranging for that?"

"Maybe she knew that you were the right person for the job."

"I should track her phone number down."

"I think you should do it in person."

"Go all the way to Idaho?"

"We've gotten this far. What's another thousand miles?"

"I do have the Senate to think about."

"Oh, fuck the Senate!" Mitch snapped for the second time in twenty-four hours. "This is your Aunt Bunny's lover. Imagine if you and I had to keep our relationship a secret and one of us died. Wouldn't you want someone to deliver the news with a modicum of compassion?"

Mitch stood up and started to get dressed.

"Where are you going?"

"In search of something to clog my arteries!"

"Try a chocolate milkshake. And bring me back one. I'll be here reading through these letters."

"Fine," Mitch left quietly, as opposed to stomping and slamming doors. She wandered around the main street for a while. It helped to calm her nerves. Why she kept snapping at Reb was anyone's guess. There had to be a bottom to get to around these feelings. She located an old fashioned soda fountain and ordered two milkshakes to go. As she waited, she noticed that people were giggling and looking over and then avoiding her glance. Didn't take long to get recognized in a small town. No wonder Bunny and Ms. Newton kept it to correspondence.

"That's four and a quarter," the clerk intoned. Mitch handed over a ten and told her to keep the change.

"Wanna bag for those?"

"Sure, thanks."

The bag was a true blessing. Otherwise, Mitch's hand would have gone numb from cold by the time she got back to the hotel room. Reb was still there reading the letters.

"Hi," she said without looking up.

"Hi, back."

Reb placed the letters aside and patted the bed. "Come here." Mitch obeyed. As usual.

"Here's your milkshake."

"Thanks," Reb said as she took a long draw. "Oh, now that's good! I had forgotten what it was like to have an old-fashioned milkshake."

Mitch sipped hers. It tasted like any old milkshake, but she didn't argue.

"Cuddle up to me. I want to tell you something," Reb requested. Mitch complied. Reb usually wasn't this direct, so it must be important.

"Okay. I'm cuddled. What's on your mind?"

"I can count on this hand," Reb wiggled the fingers on her left hand, "the number of times you have snapped at me in our entire history together."

Mitch thought back through time. They has such a rich history together. Even at the beginning, when newly-elected Governor Fairbanks considered Mitch to be an adversary, Mitch had never done much snapping. She had dared Rebecca to face facts on several occasions, but for the most part, if there was snapping to be had, Reb was the snapper.

"Okay. Five times," Mitch nodded.

"But what worries me is that two of them happened today."

Mitch nodded. Again. "I guess so."

Reb made eye contact. "Would you talk to me? Tell me what's on your mind?"

Mitch held on for a moment, trying to gather her thoughts. They refused to be corralled, like so many sheep, and wandered aimlessly. So she just let them roam free.

"I hate to be giggled at just because I'm gay."

"When did that happen?"

"Just now. When I went to get the milkshakes."

"So, it didn't happen before?"

"No. It's just on my mind."

"Okay," Reb said, trying her best to not have a nagging detail like timing derail their dialogue. She followed up with a neutral, "What else?"

"I don't like it when families fight."

"It makes you edgy?"

"It makes me feel like a kid again. In all the worst ways."

"Did your family fight a lot?"

"Define 'a lot.'"

"Once a week."

"Once a week! Jesus, my family set a record if they fought once a year. Once a week? Is that how often your family fought?"

47

"We had our share."

"And now you can't even speak to each other."

"It's a strain. Now more than ever."

Mitch became silent for a while. Reb prodded, "Tell me what else?"

"I guess I just don't like it here. I didn't know at first if I was going to like living in Washington, but it's a whole lot better than being here."

"It doesn't seem all that bad."

"That's because you're looking at it through the rose-colored glasses of nostalgia."

"I am?"

"All your fond memories are clouding your vision."

"Tell me what you see."

"Okay, well, first off, this isn't the best milkshake on the planet."

"Okay."

"And I don't like being observed like some vermin under a microscope. People gawk at us like they'd never seen a gay couple!"

"Okay."

"And I don't like being called a 'queer' by a man who is diddling the town organist in a hayloft."

"Is that about it?"

"No. There's one more thing. I really detest the fact that not only does your sister treat us like dirt, but she's also managed to poison the mind and heart of her only daughter as well. I almost checked to see if I had horns growing out of my head and a pointy tail coming out of my-"

"I get the picture!" Reb cut her short.

When Mitch realized that she was talking a lot louder than she had intended, she lapsed into silence.

"People in a small town can be like that."

"That's just a convenient excuse for treating people like they aren't even human."

"For what it's worth, I think you're handling it very well."

"No you don't. You've already pointed out how many times I've snapped today."

"That's only because it's so monumental when you do so."

48

Mitch chuckled. For the first time in a long time.

"How do you know when to grill me, Detective Fairbanks?"

"When you talk like a fish!"

"Glub, glub."

"We'll leave tomorrow. How's that?"

"Sure. Fine," Mitch shrugged, figuring it was time to go home. "To Idaho."

"Idaho?" Mitch raised up on one elbow. "But what about the Senate?"

"Oh, fuck the Senate. I have simply got to meet this friend of my Aunt Bunny."

"You mean, lover."

"Lover," Reb concurred.

"You read through all the letters?"

"About half."

"And?"

"Maybe we could leave today?"

"Today?" Mitch sat clear up now. "You're kidding, right?"

"Okay. Early tomorrow morning."

"Those must've been some letters!"

"I don't want to talk about them right now."

"Do you know what you're going to do about the farm?"

"I figure that the family lawyer will contact me soon enough. BeBe will be getting her own lawyer very soon, and then the fireworks will begin."

"If we're going to hit the road bright and early, we'd better get some sleep."

"It doesn't have to be that early," Reb compromised as she ran a knowing hand up and down Mitch's back.

"Oh really?" Mitch responded by moving closer to Reb.

"Five thirty, maybe?" Reb teased.

Mitch teased back, but not with words.

Chapter 3

Mitch heard the stirring before she could believe that it was already morning. Reb was up. Ever since the accident that had left her paralyzed, Reb had become an even earlier riser. It was due to two separate causes. The first was that she simply needed a bit of a head start in order to accomplish all of her morning chores. Secondly, and probably more important, she was in better overall physical condition and required less sleep. Mitch had remained a lazy slug and was even more so after last night's lovemaking. Reb always could wear her out and yesterday was no exception.

"You gonna stay in bed all day?" Reb greeted the morning.

"If you come back in here with me."

"Idaho isn't getting any closer."

"Neither are you, apparently."

"After last night, how could you and I *get* much closer?"

"Is that an esoteric question?" Mitch rubbed the sleep from her eyes.

"You need a cup of coffee?"

"I need a kiss."

"You want a kiss, you come over here and get it."

Mitch got up slowly and then took her turn in the bathroom. Since they were going to spend another long day on the road, she spent leisurely time showering and washing her hair. After all, you never knew when you'd have access to hot water and plenty of it. Lately, Mitch had begun to let her hair grow. To say that she appeared a bit on the butch side when she and Reb had first started going together would have been an understatement. But, hey, a whole lot of straight women wore their hair short. Right? Mitch did it for convenience as much as anything. However, life had conspired against her of late, and she just hadn't had time to get a haircut. She brushed her squeaky clean mane straight back and emerged clean, if not decent.

"Oh, my," was Reb's only comment.

"I think I'll take that kiss now."

"Sure. Just tell me where you want it," Reb was tempting fate.

"You did actually want to leave the hotel today, right?" Mitch bantered back good-naturedly.

50

"Well, yes," Reb used her best mock crestfallen expression. They shared a simple kiss. The kind that people celebrating their twenty-fifth wedding anniversary would've shared. Mitch could've lingered, but she didn't. She dressed quickly, only too willing to shake the dust of this town off of her shoes. Biblically and literally speaking. They grabbed a bag of breakfast from a national food chain outlet and nursed their heartburn through Colorado. It was tempting to drop in and visit Mary and Lisa, but then they would feel obligated to explain why they were heading still further west instead of backtracking due east. Explaining was something Reb wasn't ready to do. Not until she was able to talk things over with Bunny's lady friend.

They stayed overnight at the last handicapped equipped motel room in Rock Springs, Wyoming and then wheeled into Pocatello by midday. Mitch looked around for a good diner. She was acquiring a taste for small-town food. Yum. Yum. "There's a place. Let's try that." Reb was pointing to something called Eight Potatoes.
"Gee, I wonder what's on the menu there," Mitch tried not to drip too much sarcasm.
"Hopefully, whatever it is isn't all slathered with butter, sour cream and chives."
Mitch didn't nod. She was hoping for the opposite. Maybe praying would be a more accurate description.

The hostess showed them to a corner table and inquired as to their drink orders. Mitch wondered what kind of wine went best with spuds before ordering a beer. Reb ordered a whiskey sour.
"Who's driving?" Reb asked when the hostess had gone.
"I am. I figured that a potato would more than soak up one beer."
"Particularly with butter, I suppose?"
"Good idea!" Mitch acted real surprised.
"You are so bad!"
"That's not what you said last night," Mitch reminded.
Further critique was stayed by the arrival of the waitress. Mitch ordered a steak and fries. Reb wanted a salad and baked potato.

"How did this place get its name," Reb asked as she handed over the menu.

"You know the old rhyme. 'One potato, two potato…'"

"Ah, I see," Reb nodded.

"I wonder how many times she has to answer that question every day?" Mitch wondered.

"I'm sure the locals know."

"Are we going to visit Bunny's pen pal this evening?"

"I thought I'd call her as soon as we've finished here."

"Let's get a room, first."

"Have I worn you clear out?"

"Yes, and thank you very much."

For an early dinner, it was lovely. The potatoes lived up to their reputation and Mitch's steak was prime.

"You having dessert?" Mitch asked Reb.

"Gosh, no. I'm full. Aren't you?"

Mitch thought it over. She could've squeezed in a slice of cheesecake or pie, but on second thought, there was no use getting uncomfortable.

"Stuffed," she reassured.

Reb paid the bill with a fifty, and had plenty of change to leave a generous tip. The rest she folded and placed in her breast pocket. A large motel right in the middle of town had all three amenities Mitch and Reb could ever want: Handicap access, cable TV and king-size beds. They were in motel heaven. From the room, Reb researched the person they came to visit. She was listed in the phone book. Reb took a couple of deep breaths and then placed the call. A friendly voice picked up.

"Hello?"

"Hello, Ms. Newton. My name is Rebecca Fairbanks."

"Why, hello, Senator."

"You know me?"

"Yes."

"May I come by and see you?"

"Of course. Do you need my address?"

"No, I have it. I'll be there in about ten minutes, then?"

"I'll make some coffee."

"Thank you."

"Bye, now."

Reb replaced the phone on its cradle and looked at Mitch. "She already knows, doesn't she." Mitch could tell just by the look on Reb's face.

They were on Ms. Newton's front porch before they had time to wallow in the dread that had been building up over the course of a day. She was waiting for them at the door.

"Please, come in."

For the most part, Mitch and Reb had good luck with the steps leading up to the porch, and the last little bump up to the doorway was no challenge. Ms. Newton had cleared a path by rearranging the furniture.

"I'm Rebecca," Reb held out her hand.

"Yes, Senator. I recognized you. Welcome to my home."

"And this is Mitch Tanner."

"You're the one who steps in front of bullets. Bunny's told me all about you!" she said with gusto and then, in an instant, her lower lip began to tremble.

"I know why you're here. It's Bunny. She's dead."

"Yes, I'm afraid so."

"And buried."

"Yes. I didn't find out about the letters until after the funeral."

"And that's how we planned it. Won't you have some coffee? And I have some apple pie."

Mitch's expression brightened.

"I'll take that as a yes!" Ms. Newton smiled that wonderfully crinkly smile of many senior citizens. She took off and kept busy in her small kitchen for a few moments.

"I knew I skipped dessert at the restaurant for a good reason," Mitch smiled at Reb.

"You always do have good luck where these things are concerned."

"I have good luck in many facets of my life," she assured back. Their hostess returned with a tray. She was steady as a rock for her age.

"You can call me Evie," Ms. Newton said as she handed out coffee cups. It smelled glorious. The slices of pie had scoops of vanilla ice cream nestled beside them. So much for sticking to a diet. Mitch ate as Reb talked.

"Henry gave me the letters two days ago."

"Bunny said she would let me know about her death. She had it arranged. That was our plan."

"You two kept in touch?"

"We wrote a lot of letters."

"When did you first meet?"

"Oh, years ago!"

"Really?"

"I used to live in Kansas myself. Years ago," she explained wistfully.

"And you knew Aunt Bunny back then?"

"We had what you youngsters call an 'affair.'"

"I see," Reb had figured that much out on her own.

"But you knew that already."

"I had an inkling."

"You're clever. Just like your Aunt Bunny."

Mitch didn't say it, but that's not all they had in common.

"How long were you, uh, friends with my Aunt?"

"Not nearly long enough. Three lifetimes nor thirty would've been enough."

"But, then, why are you here?" Reb asked, somewhat confused.

"Life brought me here," Evie answered as if explaining to a child.

"I still don't understand."

"You must remember the times. It was years ago. Nowadays, people are more tolerant of folks like us. But, back then, it was brutal. I couldn't put Bunny in a position where she would lose everything. Her farm, her money, her standing in the community."

"So, you split up?" Mitch chimed in. Keeping quiet wasn't her long suit.

"That's one way of putting it. We were never really, well, together, in the sense you mean."

"You didn't have a relationship?" Reb was doing her best to cut through the nomenclature.

"Oh, of course we did! We just were careful about outward appearances. We never dated, is what I'm trying to say."

"And then, you moved away?"

"I came to live here. BeBe and Henry had taken to spying on us day and night. We never had a moment to ourselves. They even had peepholes drilled into the walls! Can you believe them?"

"The bedroom walls?" Reb asked suddenly.

"Those, too. They even spy on Miranda so, well, you know."

"Have a boyfriend over?" Mitch took a guess.

"That too, but mostly because of, oh, what do they call it nowadays…"

"We understand, now!" Reb interrupted quickly.

"They watch for that!" Mitch asked both Reb and Evie, mostly to check for consensus.

"Of course!" Evie nodded wisely.

"I guess it's cheaper than renting a porn movie," Mitch said with obvious distaste. Between being monitored at home and working in a library, that poor young girl must be ready to explode. No wonder she acted the way she did. Mitch remembered the bout of bugging that she and Reb had endured not so very long ago. It tends to create an unbearable amount of tension.

"And, so, I had family out here," Evie carried on with the story, "And we figured it was best if I lived here and Bunny lived there. But, we never stopped loving each other. Ever."

"That was obvious from the letters you wrote."

"Did you read them all?"

"No. Just one or two. Until I got the drift. I brought them to you," Reb handed over the envelope.

"I can't thank you enough," she trembled again.

Feeling so all of a sudden inadequate, Reb asked, "Is there anything else I can do for you?"

"Keep an eye on Miranda. Watch over her. Just not the way BeBe does."

"Anything else?"

"You inherited the farm, right?"

Everybody was apparently in on this secret but Reb and BeBe.

"That's right, but I'm sure there will be a court battle."

"Don't back down. BeBe has been stashing cash away for years! They won't go broke even if they never earn another dollar the rest of their lives."

Mitch heard the double negatives but understood the gist. Apparently, if BeBe had recently acquired a taste for Swiss chocolate, it might not be a random occurrence.

"Is there anything that you would like from the farmhouse, if it hasn't been gutted in the meantime?"

"That's a big 'if.' I'd like Bunny's bed, if it isn't too much trouble."

Reb only nodded. They finished up their pie and coffee and headed back to the motel. It was a little early for bedtime, but that didn't stop them. It never had before. Idaho hadn't changed that. Rather than engage in passion, they chose to chit chat instead.

"What would you want if I died?" Reb asked after they were settled.

"What do you mean?"

"Evie wants Bunny's bed. What would you want?"

The question utterly stymied Mitch. She had never even given it a thought. She stalled for time.

"What would you want?" she turned the question back on Reb.

"I'd want your paintings."

"My paintings," Mitch was astonished. "Those crappy things?"

"Your paintings are beautiful!" Reb assured her.

Mitch only giggled.

A while back, when she had needed some time and space, she took off for sights unseen and ended up in Santa Fe, New Mexico. The art capitol of the Southwest. She was three sessions into painting a nude man named Tim when Reb walked in on them. Tim liked Reb. It was obvious. Mitch managed to capture the essence on canvas and then unofficially titled the masterpiece, "Boy Woodpecker."

"So, you like paintings of wildlife?" Mitch quizzed.

"Better than that Rosenthal that's going up for bid soon."

"Ah, yes, the Rosenthal."

Chapter 4

Trish had died and gone to heaven. There was no other way to explain it, she thought to herself as she stretched out in bed. Robbie was up already and in the kitchen cooking breakfast. God, what a woman!"

Trish had met Robbie through Robbie's parents, Max and Rose Goldstein, while doing research on the Holocaust. Their acquaintance had soon bloomed into full-blown love. Not that anything had happened quickly. Robbie had been a stickler in that department, chastely waiting until their wedding night to bestow her passions unto Trish. Trish was still recovering after a month of bestowances. Robbie appeared at the bedroom doorway, spatula in hand.
"You want breakfast in bed?" she asked in her shy yet appealing way.
"I want you in bed."
"You've already had me in bed!" Robbie waggled her spatula.
"Breakfast will be such a step down," Trish waggled back, except she didn't have a spatula.
"Oatmeal in two minutes."
Trish sat up and pulled on a T-shirt. Just in case she dribbled. Robbie brought in oatmeal and coffee for two. They relaxed and talked as they ate.
"What are we going to do today?" Robbie asked her usual question.
"As soon as breakfast is over, I'm going to wrestle you back into this bed and make mad, passionate love to you."
"And then what?" Robbie asked in a pretend-mundane way.
 They both chuckled. Ah, the life of newlyweds. When Trish had considered Robbie's chaste behavior, it hadn't been just about their relationship. Robbie had never been on intimate terms with anyone else, a fact Trish attributed to Robbie's shyness. Robbie was harder on herself and put the blame on her weight. She would never be mistaken for a super-model, even in a funhouse mirror. It hadn't mattered to Trish, who frankly had had enough relationships with reedy women to know that it wasn't what you looked like that counted in the loving

department. Robbie had exceeded in each and every criteria of lovemaking. Like we said, Trish was still catching her breath.
"This is great oatmeal," Trish complimented the cook.
"It's just oats and water," Robbie tried to explain away the magic.
"That's just like saying that all there is to love is hugs and kisses," Trish set her bowl down and started to nuzzle Robbie's shoulders. It had only taken about three days into the honeymoon to find this particular spot. Robbie moaned softly. Oats and water were never this mushy.

Completely sated, Robbie again asked, "What's on the rest of the schedule?"
"I don't know. You have any ideas?"
"My parents wondered if we could come for dinner."
"Absolutely!" was Trish's enthusiastic reply. Going to the Goldstein's was always a treat. In a world where the situations involving in-laws were for the most part adversarial, Trish had managed to beat the odds. She loved Max and Rose as if they were her own parents and in return they hadn't damned her to hell eternal for what others would incorrectly term "recruiting" their daughter. They had even paid for the wedding. Which had nothing whatsoever to do with the blinding diamond that Trish had sprung for. It now rested firmly in a platinum ring on Robbie's finger. In her old age, she would need help raising her left hand were she to grow frail.
"They will be happy to see us."
"I love your parents," Trish proclaimed the truth to Robbie.
"And, I yours."
"You got the short stick in the draw," Trish muttered as she crawled out of bed.
"Not with you in my life."

They dressed casually and then went out on another of their famous shopping sprees. Up until the time they had met, Robbie had lived on a nurse's salary, which wasn't exactly cause for complaint in her book. In fact, nothing much was cause for complaint in Robbie's book, except for an encounter with a mugger soon after Trish and Robbie had started going together.

It turned out that the mugger was after some paperwork giving ownership of a painting to Trish. Not just any painting, mind you, but a Rosenthal. Trish had, unbeknownst to all concerned, been interviewing Albert Rosenthal about his experiences in the Holocaust. As a gay man, he had a unique perspective. He also had painted a masterpiece titled "Paradise on Earth" and subsequently had it stolen by a Nazi. The painting's worth had risen by leaps and bounds since its disappearance and, thanks to Mitch, Trish managed to retrieve the painting as Mitch was creating a diversion. Said diversion included getting shot in the shoulder at point blank range. Which was better than getting shot in the head at point blank range. It was then and there that Trish vowed to take part of the proceeds from the Rosenthal auction and reimburse Mitch for all of her medical bills. Mitch had requested a tonsillectomy in jest, just to run up the bill.

With another part of the proceeds, Robbie and Trish were inheriting the medical maintenance bills of Albert's nephew, Connors. Connors Rosenthal was the only child of Albert's sister, and apparently during birth there had been a glitch. A serious glitch. A glitch that had deprived Connors of oxygen for a critical period of time. He was, by all accounts, what some call a vegetable, residing in a care facility. Needless to say, it wasn't cheap. Other minor Rosenthal's had been sold over the years to cover the costs to date, but the bills were coming due.
"What do you think about this pair of jeans?" Robbie asked the meditating Trish.
"You are beautiful."
"What about the jeans?"
"They make you look even more beautiful."
"I could be wearing nothing and you'd say that!"
"And your point?" Trish smiled.
"I shouldn't spend too much money."
"Why not?"
"Because the auction has been delayed for another month."
"That's a good sign. Bidders are trying to raise more money."
"You think it will sell at value?"
The thumbnail value was 65 million dollars last time they checked.

"I have no idea," Trish said like it was a bother to even be discussing it in the middle of a shopping trip.

"How can you be so blasé about so much money?"

"Because it's *only* money. My real treasure is standing in front of me in the most flattering pair of jeans I have ever seen." Robbie turned a shade of crimson that the sunset would've been envious of.

"You stop that. We are due at my folk's for dinner in an hour."

"We should buy them something. I hate to go empty-handed." They stopped by the florists and liquor store. Wine and roses were always welcome in the Goldstein home. Robbie's finger hadn't even gotten within ringing distance of the doorbell when the door swung open. It was Max.

"Rose! It's the kids! Come in! Come in! What's this?" Max indicated the gifts as he herded them into the house.

"Hello, Max," Trish gave him her usual quick hug. Max and Rose Goldstein were both Holocaust survivors. Max's story was well known. He had talked about it to high school groups and people like Trish who were researching the subject. Rose's story was a secret. Only one other person in the room knew the real story. It just happened to be Trish. When Rose and Trish looked at each other, it was with the understanding that they should carry the story to their respective graves. Today's exchange of looks seemed to carry a greater sense of urgency.

"Hello, girls!" Rose hugged Robbie first and then Trish. Trish loved the coddling and warm family atmosphere. Her own parents had adopted her, and kept her Jewish heritage a secret from her. When she informed them that she was marrying Robbie, they asked who the groom was. Robbie's parents, for all their old-fashioned ways, accepted Trish into the family with a ceremony covered by all the major networks. They blamed the coverage on Robbie's choice of matron of honor, Senator Fairbanks. Reb had stood up with Robbie as Mitch was Trish's best man. The right-wind press had a field day. Mitch and Rose seemed to be having a contest to see who could cry the most. It was judged a draw.

"What smells so wonderful?" Trish started right in with compliments.

"Must be my after shave," Max quipped.

"Oh, hush!" Rose took center stage. "She's referring to my cooking."

"Can I help?" Robbie offered as Max opened the wine and steered Trish to her favorite chair.

"Of course, Dear."

Mother and daughter disappeared into the kitchen while Max and Trish passed the time of day. Neither Max nor Rose had ever inquired into the sex life of Trish and Robbie, somehow knowing that they were too happy to be having any difficulties. Today was no exception. The conversation was strictly about weather, sports and the impending art auction. Although Robbie had never been instructed to seek out a rich husband, the fact that she accidentally had must have given Max a sense of relief. He was downright chipper. The fact that Trish had enabled Robbie to move closer to home helped raise Trish's good-provider stock even more. By the time dinner was served, Trish had downed two glasses of very expensive wine and was feeling no pain. Rose's chicken and dumplings helped soak up the alcohol and then to avoid a repeat performance with after-dinner aperitifs, Trish coerced Robbie into sitting with Max while she helped Rose with the dishes. Rose usually refused Trish's offers of K P duty. Tonight, she was uncharacteristically happy to enroll her in the program. Rose waited until they were about halfway through their chores before she gripped Trish's arm. The grasp was so tight that Trish feared for an instant that Rose was falling and Trish was her stabilizing force.

"Are you okay?" Trish asked as she looked carefully at Rose. The expression she saw was fear.

"I need to tell someone," Rose hissed in a whisper.

"About what?" Trish worked to keep her voice down as well.

"About this," Rose fished a piece of paper out of her apron pocket. Her hands were shaking. Trish took the paper. It was folded like a letter. She opened it and saw letters cut and pasted like a ransom note. It read, "W H E E   N O   H O O   U   R"

"This looks like nonsense. Maybe some neighborhood kid left it for you to find?"

"They know who I am and where I live!" Rose explained quickly.

"How did it get here?"

"It was mailed."

"You kept the envelope?"

"Of course. The postmark was Cleveland."

"Cleveland? Do you know anybody in Cleveland?"

"No, but they must know me. They found me!" Rose was beginning to get agitated and shaky.

"Who? You speak like you know who this is."

"I don't know. Not exactly. But I know who they are!"

The story was interrupted by footsteps. Rose gave a look of warning and then beamed a smile at Robbie.

"You two are taking your sweet time doing the dishes," Robbie smiled. "You want my help? Dad fell asleep in the chair and I can't hear the television for his snoring."

"I thought I heard a buzz saw," Rose giggled like a schoolgirl. Trish noted for the record Rose's ability to change from fear to silliness in an instant. They finished up the chores together and visited over tea until it was time to go. Trish gave Rose a look that conveyed her willingness to continue their conversation. Sooner rather than later. She was quiet for a suspicious length of time during the drive home.

"Are you okay?" Robbie inquired after they got back to Trish's condo. Well, make that "their" condo now. For better or for worse, they were joined in paperwork as well as bodies and souls.

"Yeah. Why?"

"You are so quiet."

"I'm a quiet person."

"You and my mom find a lot to talk about."

"She does the talking and I do the listening."

"I know how that goes. Sometimes." Robbie let it go at that. Thankfully. Trish wasn't one bit comfortable keeping secrets from Robbie that concerned her mother. It had started long before tonight. Trish had harbored the sinking feeling that one day, Robbie would discover that Trish knew more about Rose's Holocaust experiences than anyone else. Seems like someone was intent on pushing the envelope. Quite literally. But from Cleveland?

Chapter 5

"You're back early!" Lisa had gathered Mary in her arms when she picked her up at the airport.

"I couldn't get out of there fast enough," Mary answered.

"Was it Kansas?" Lisa asked. She was always up for a bit of delving.

"It was the family," Mary cleared up the confusion readily.

"Your Aunt BeBe? The one with the famous right cross?"

"More like the old rugged cross. They don't call it the Bible Belt for nothing."

"So, it was Kansas, too? In a way?"

"I guess so."

"Wouldn't you hate to be gay there?"

"I never hate being gay. It's just more of a struggle some places than others."

"You make it worth any amount of struggle."

Mary held Lisa's eyes as she changed the subject. "We've had a few struggles of our own. I haven't been as patient, or as trusting as I could have been."

"You had good reason for having doubts. We were taken in by professional crooks."

"That doesn't excuse my knee-jerk reaction. I'll never doubt you again."

"I'll never give you reason. Now, will you stop beating yourself up?"

The remark slipped out before Lisa could think about what she was saying. Mary's first and former lover had had a mean streak. She was out of their lives now, getting therapy and working on a medical degree. She was out east, they were in Colorado. All was right with the world. A world, for them, that now included a whole lot of hard, honest work. While Lisa was tending bar at night, Mary was going to school. She had decided to work toward a child-care license. During her stint at the Women's Shelter, she had grown accustomed to being around youngsters, and had missed the experience. That was all she missed. In the meantime, she took a job as a receptionist at a school. Lisa, meanwhile, took the bulk of the housekeeping chores under her jurisdiction. The house was squeaky clean, and their meals were fabulous, even if they didn't have many together. Sunday was their big day and they particularly enjoyed lounging around in bed. For obvious reasons.

"Do you *ever* miss it?" Mary asked after they had made love for the second time that morning.

"Uh, what?" Lisa asked warily. She didn't think she had missed anything so far.

"The money."

"Oh, the *money*!" Lisa was relieved, to say the least.

"What did you *think* I was talking about?"

"The money," Lisa lied.

"Oh, no you weren't!" Mary pulled her close and kissed her like she was ready for a third go around just any time.

"No, I wasn't. I confess!" Lisa squirmed under the tickling fingers.

"So, do you?"

"It certainly was fun while it lasted," Lisa admitted honestly. "But I wouldn't trade it for what I have now."

"And what do you have, now?" Mary egged her on, needing to hear reassurances of this Sunday morning.

"I have a job and a nice house and a clunker of a car and the most beautiful, loving, giving woman in the whole entire world by my side. That's what I call real wealth."

"Speaking of understanding landlords, have we heard from them lately?"

"I haven't."

"Me, neither. Maybe I'll call them."

"Do it tomorrow."

"Why tomorrow?"

"Because I have the rest of today booked solid for you," Lisa smiled. "And I promise you'll be exhausted."

"Promises, promises!" Mary wiggled her eyebrows.

Chapter 6

The trip back to Washington was exhausting in more ways than one for Mitch and Reb. Adding up all the miles made their journey home even more tiring. Added to that were all the diesel fumes along the way. By the time they pulled into the driveway of their Georgetown house, they didn't care to take any more extended driving sojourns for the rest of the week. Maybe longer.

For the first time in a long time, Reb's body was sore. At least, the parts that she could feel. The rest she had Mitch check over very carefully for any sign of possible pressure sores. This was a task that Mitch was only too happy to do any old day of the week, whether or not it led to anything sexual. Just the experience of running her hands over Reb's body was a comfort and pleasure.
"I really need to get back on a therapy regimen," Reb said as Mitch stayed happily busy with the task at hand.
"We should both get a little more on the active side," Mitch agreed.
"How are you going to do that while running a restaurant?"
"You ever wait tables?" was Mitch's total reply.
Reb acknowledged her point, and then followed up, "Have you and Jane made any plans?"
Jane, the hooker who Mitch discovered was also quite the cooker, had stopped turning tricks for a living and was staying busy working out new recipes. Mitch was paying her rent and had been scouting around for a restaurant to buy before the timely death of Aunt Bunny.
"I think I'm going to need some professional advice," Mitch admitted.
The place she had her eye on buying, a deteriorating spot called Wagner's, was finally up for sale. Apparently, the current owner had finally realized that this was the best option all around.
"Like a restaurant consultant?" Reb asked.
"I was thinking more along the lines of therapy," Mitch quipped.
"You think it's a crazy idea?"
"Let's just say that I lay awake some nights wondering about it."

65

"But now, you're responsible for Jane."

"And I always fulfill my responsibilities. Besides, if I didn't have this to keep me occupied, I'd just be causing trouble for you."

"And without even trying," Reb smiled sweetly.

"Right," Mitch was agreeable.

"Make me a promise?"

"Sure. What?"

"Next time you're wide awake some night worrying, wake me up."

"Why?"

"Because I've never seen you worried. About anything."

"I hide it well."

Chapter 7

As anxious as Trish was to follow up on her conversation with
Rose, it was hard to tear herself away from Robbie. They were
typical newlyweds in every sense. Although they enjoyed
making love, they were inseparable in other aspects as well.
They dined together, watched movies together, shopped together,
sat quietly together. Time spent apart would come all too soon,
as with all typical marriages. If Trish was to talk to Rose again
soon, they would need to invite them over for dinner. Trish
suggested as much and Robbie subsequently dove into her recipe
box for the perfect menu.

"What we had last night was good," Trish thought it best to
begin with a nice word.

"Toaster waffles and syrup?"

"I thought it was great," Trish assured honestly.

"I don't think we can get away with waffles and syrup for my
parents."

"They're not wafflers?"

"You've met them!" Robbie intoned.

"Well, what did we have the night before?"

"Chinese takeout."

"Oh, yeah! That was okay, too," Trish praised faintly. It wasn't
Robbie's cooking, so it was best to hedge.

"We could take them out?" Robbie offered the idea. Trish had to
think fast. Any conversation with Rose in private would be
relegated to the ladies room in a restaurant setting and even then,
Robbie would probably tag along.

"Oh, I'm sure that you can cook ten times better than any
restaurant," Trish steered back toward the recipe box.

"You have that much faith in my culinary skills?"

"If they're anything like the rest of your skills, dinner should be
superb!"

Robbie studied Trish for a moment, wondering perhaps if there
was more to this dinner party than met the untrained eye. Trish
pulled an innocent moue. She was impenetrable at best.

"Okay, well, pork roast is out of the question." Robbie noted.

"Do your parents keep a kosher kitchen?" Trish asked suddenly.

"Not strictly. But they do keep alive some traditions."

"So, it isn't just Max's strict diet that prohibits pork?"

"I never had a pork chop until I moved to Arizona."

"Wow! I was raised on them."

"We could do a beef roast."

"That's probably not on Max's diet, either."

"What do you suggest?"

"How about an old fashioned turkey dinner! We could watch the amount of butter we cook with and skim all the fat. That with a green vegetable or two and it would fit into everyone's food plan."

"That would be a lot of work," Robbie warned.

"I'll help," Trish was enthusiastic. "Call your folks. Set the date."

Robbie did just that. Now, they had two days to pull it all together. Anyone who has ever cooked a turkey dinner knows that the turkey is the easy part. Except if the two chefs involved couldn't agree on a size.

"I think we should get a thirty pound turkey," Trish stated like she knew what she was talking about.

"Thirty pounds!" Robbie echoed incredulously. "Geez Louise, you'd need a pan the size of a bathtub to cook it!"

"You would?" Trish was genuinely surprised.

"And by the time we stuffed it, it would take hours and hours to get it cooked through."

"Okay, so what size would you suggest?"

"Twelve pounds is nice."

"That's not enough turkey for four people," Trish maintained.

"We're inviting my parents. Not a couple of bodybuilders."

"I want a lot of leftovers so we don't have to cook for a couple of days."

"Whatever would we do with ourselves if we didn't need to cook for a couple of days?"

"You just leave that to me."

"Okay. How about a twenty pounder?"

"Make it twenty-two and I'll do all the dishes."

"You've got yourself a deal. When do we go shopping?"

"How about now?"

They were in the truck and off to the store without further discussion. It was quite a chore to find a premium turkey in the off season. Between Thanksgiving and Christmas, shoppers were knee deep in turkeys. Now that it was summer, only the brave of heart would roast something for hours in an already hot kitchen. Turkeys were few and far between so they ended up buying two twelve pound birds. The only cranberries were in a can and pumpkin pies were in the freezer case. But the potatoes were reliable and fat-free gravy straight out of a packet was always stocked on the shelf.

"Getting an early start on Thanksgiving?" the clerk inquired as she ran the items through the scanner.

"We're having the folks for dinner."

"You two sisters?"

"No, we're married," Trish announced matter-of-factly.

"Oh," the woman said and then lapsed into utter silence. Dead people talked more, according to some psychics.

After they were bagged up and heading toward the truck, Robbie asked a good question.

"Are you going to tell everyone that we're a couple?"

"Does it bother you?"

"I know that I'm still sorting it all out."

"You tell me to stop, I'll stop. But there's one thing that you should know."

"Just one?"

"Maybe two. First, I'm so proud to have you as my significant other that I'd tell anyone who'd listen."

"I noticed."

"And although I'm not on a one-woman mission to change the world, I'm not inclined to remain silent about my life on the off chance that it might make someone else a teensy weensy bit uncomfortable hearing about it. I mean, I'm really sorry if people need therapy or something to get over their homophobia, but I'm not keeping quiet like I have something to be embarrassed about. Which I don't."

All through the soliloquy, Robbie was putting groceries in the truck and nodding thoughtfully. A store employee approached her to gather the buggy.

"We're married," Robbie said to him.

"How wonderful for you," he remarked in monotone like he'd heard it all before.

69

"You about done with that cart?"

"Sure. Here."

He lumbered off to catch other carts before they dented more expensive cars.

"See!" Trish said. "That wasn't so bad, was it?"

"I guess if I ever need a conversation stopper, I'll know what to say."

"Oh hey, I can come up with better stuff than that!"

"I bet you can."

They headed home and spent a companionable afternoon doing the prep cooking for a lavish turkey dinner. Robbie could chop celery and onions faster than any food processor and before long, they were simmering in a modicum of butter. When this was done, it would be gently tossed in with the proper amount of bread crumbs and left overnight. In the meantime, Trish unwrapped the turkeys and cleaned them thoroughly. Although many people boiled the giblets, Robbie didn't include them in any part of the recipe.

The following morning, she omitted any eggs in her stuffing recipe. Enough fat would cook out of the turkey to make up for those. They flipped a coin to decide if they would make the stuffing dry or moist. Dry won out so Robbie used scant milk until the mixture barely held together. By nine a.m., the birds were nestled in a huge roasting pan and cooking away. Trish and Robbie came up with the brilliant idea of going back to bed and engaging in a little nestling of their own.

Robbie certainly had a special touch in everything she did. Her expertise in the kitchen was clear and her growing knowledge of sexual pleasuring in the bedroom was nothing short of phenomenal. Trish was a happy recipient in both matters.

"You are something else," she murmured in Robbie's ear as she lay resting. "You make me look like an amateur."

"You're too hard on yourself," Robbie answered as she stroked Trish's hair.

"I'm so lucky to have you."

"I know."

They chuckled and then went back to work. There were dishes to wash and potatoes to peel. Max and Rose arrived a little after noon and they sat around chatting amiably about the hot weather, baseball, and yard work. No one in America on that particular day had a more typical conversation. Until, that is, Rose cornered Trish in the kitchen.

"I got another note," Rose whispered.

"Did you bring it?"

"Here," she jammed the paper in Trish's hand. It crinkled loudly as Trish spread it out to study it. If it were dusted for fingerprints, Trish would be suspect number one. Rose would be second in line.

"The next time you get one of these, put it in a plastic bag."

"Why?"

"So we can have the police check it for fingerprints."

"We can't do that!" Rose was terrified.

"Why not?"

"No one must ever know."

Trish scanned the note. It read, "WE KNOW WEAR YU LIV."

"They still need spelling lessons," Trish observed.

"They know where I live. I'm sure of it!" Rose was petrified to the point that she was beginning to panic.

"They knew that with the first letter. The question is, who are they?"

"They are from the past."

"Long past?" Trish quoted Scrooge.

"My past! My days in the war!"

Trish developed a crinkled brow over this concept.

"If that's true, then why have they waited all these years to contact you?"

"They didn't know where I was until…"

"Until what?"

"Until the wedding."

Trish thought back. She remembered that there was a lot of media at the event. So Rose's theory was that someone had seen the press footage and picked her out of a blur of activity.

"You think someone recognized you?"

"Do you have a better explanation for these letters all the way from Ohio?"

71

Trish had to admit, "No."

"They'll kill me if they can catch me."

"Then, why warn you?" Trish inquired patiently.

"Because," Rose answered with an agitated voice, "that's half the fun for them! Scaring old ladies half to death was their favorite sport."

"What do you think we should do?" Trish figured Rose had worked out the beginnings of a plan.

"I think we should move."

"How long have you lived here?"

"Forty-four years."

"You won't be able to get Max to move. If it hadn't happened in forty-four years, no amount of cajoling nor dynamite is going to blast him loose."

"And I can't tell him the real reason."

"It would make it easier," Trish reasoned.

"I can't. I just can't."

"Okay," Trish calmed her down. "Let me work on a plan."

"Hurry."

"In the meantime, what if I arranged for some sort of undercover protection?"

"A body guard?" Rose's eyes got as round as saucers.

"I'll try and find a good-looking guy for you."

In spite of the seriousness of the situation, Rose blushed. Like mother, like daughter. Speaking of whom, Robbie appeared in the doorway.

"You two need any help?"

"Thought you'd never ask," Trish teased and then handed her dishtowel to Robbie.

"What's Max doing?"

"You get one guess!"

"One is probably all I need."

"He even fell asleep before dessert. I'm making coffee. How many takers?"

Everyone nodded so Trish made a full pot. By the time Robbie and Rose whipped the kitchen into shape, the coffee was poured and the pie divided. The clatter of forks must've roused Max. He asked for, and received a sliver of pie. He was such a good role model for how to keep your arteries squeaky clean. After

72

many polite phrases, Rose and Max left. Rose's parting glance to Trish spoke her concern better than words ever could've. Trish retreated to her study to think things through. What was she going to do about this mess? Rose could use an extra police patrol. How daring would it be to call her old friend, Detective Forrest, at police headquarters to request an occasional drive by? He had pulled his gun on Mitch. Maybe that would be a bargaining chip. She would call him. In a few minutes. As soon as she came up with a plausible story. At least, a little more believable than a grudge match dating back to WWII. Which brought Trish back to the second prong of the problem, how real could this be? Were there really secret societies who kept tabs on war heroes? It made sense after Trish realized that there were people who had spent a lifetime hunting down Nazi war criminals. It followed that someone of the Nazi persuasion could be tracking down people they considered to be criminals. Everyone who was involved in the sabotage of the crematorium was hanged. Except one. Trish had thought about it so long that Robbie came in to check.

"You coming to bed?"

"In a minute."

"You sure?"

Trish realized that not only was she being reticent, but also a touch recalcitrant. She hated it. And if she felt this strongly, Robbie had to be sensing a problem. She stood up and stretched. It had been a long day with an uneasy ending. She took Robbie's arm and together, they went to bed.

It wasn't until the following morning that Trish came to the conclusion that she would need to confide in someone, if only to relieve the tension. She mulled over the prospects. Mitch was too far away. Reb was out of the question. That left Mary and Lisa. Of the two, Trish got along better with Mary. No surprise there. Trish had never really forgiven Lisa for breaking Mitch's heart. It was foolish to feel that way because Mitch had grown past it. She now was beginning to understand lifelong grudges. When Robbie headed to the gym for her new self-improvement project, Trish stayed home like a lazy slug and called Detective

Forrest. He was out. Strike one. Next, she called Mary's house. Lisa answered. Strike two.

"Hello?"

"Hi, it's Trish. Is Mary there?"

"She's at work."

"I see. Will she be home tonight?"

"No. She has class."

This was beginning to feel like strike three territory.

"Can I have her work phone number?"

"Why?"

"I want to call her."

"They don't like her getting a bunch of personal phone calls at work."

"I'll keep it brief."

Lisa was quiet for a moment and then rattled off a number. Good thing Trish had a pencil ready. She remembered to thank Lisa, and then hurriedly hung up. She then quickly dialed the school and Mary picked up on the first ring. What an efficient gal she was.

"It's Trish."

"Hi! How are you? It's so good to hear from you. How's Robbie?"

Gee, so much for not getting to have personal phone calls at work.

"I'm fine. Robbie's fine."

"Are you sure?" Mary pierced through the façade. God, she was good.

"Would you...Could we..."

"You want to get together?"

"That would be wonderful. What time is good for you?"

"Probably after class tonight. We could go for a drink."

"Somewhere downtown. How about the Brownstone? Is that close to your campus?"

"Sometimes too close!" Mary laughed. "I have to go. See you there about eight?"

"Eight. Great. See you."

Trish hung up much more reluctantly this time. All she needed to do now was to come up with a plausible excuse to be away for the evening. Maybe she could kill two birds with the one proverbial stone by spending a stretch of time at the library. Researching fringe groups could take hours. Hours that Robbie would accept without question. Trish left her a note and took off before she had to explain it all in person. By the time Trish got to the library, found a parking lot that had one space, looked up the reference books she was interested in and found a table in a secluded part of the second floor, it was nearly one o'clock. Not really knowing where to begin searching, she ended up with an eclectic selection of books. She had found several shelves of information about the Holocaust concentration camps on prior visits, but now she leaned more toward books about espionage. One book in particular detailed the work of women in the OSS. If there were American women spying on Germans during WWII, maybe one of them had kept notes or knew of whoever was trying to intimidate Rose. Trish thought back to the notes Rose had received. There was really no inherent threat. They only detailed the fact that they knew who Rose was and where she lived. It could still be just a prank of a neighborhood kid. Except for the pesky Cleveland postmark. Now, even Trish's mind was beginning to swim in the mystery.

One of the books Trish picked off the shelf was an expose of various hate groups. It was the stuff of which nightmares were made. There were very few areas in America that were not stained by these types of organizations. Apparently, some of these groups were very organized. Others were looser. Still, they all had hate as a motivating factor, with that venom being directed toward the usual targets: African Americans, Jewish Americans, Hispanics and Gays.

Trish usually avoided reading epistles of hate directed toward gay and lesbian people, because it gave her a nearly intolerable feeling of frustration. She felt it grossly unfair for people to judge her without knowing her. It was arrogance in the extreme as far as she was concerned. However, as she scoured the materials for Anti-Semitic groups, it was inevitable that she would find horrible slurs and blatant lies against her people as well. Why did people make up lies anyway? She assumed it was all tied into money somehow. People who could drum up such fear could also manipulate the wallets of their fearful flock to the tune of millions. Too bad the greenbacks were covered in blood.

Trish rubbed her eyes from the fatigue more mental than physical. She reverted back to the books about women in the war. Maybe something would jump out at her. It probably wouldn't have qualified as a jump, but Trish more or less stumbled upon an idea. Perhaps the authors of these various books would have an insight. She busied herself by writing down book titles, authors and publishers. A well-crafted letter might pique someone's interest. All this transcribing took about half an hour, by which time Trish realized she was getting hungry. She folded her studies tent and went looking for a spot that served either a late lunch or an early dinner. Her plan was to eat light in case Mary wanted to share a meal after class. Ah, but as with all other best laid plans, this went out the window when Trish sat down to order at one of the best Mexican food restaurants in the city. She started with a frosty beer and some snappy salsa and chips as her order of one enchilada, one tamale and one taco was being assembled. It arrived smothered in melted cheese with a side of guacamole. If Mary wanted dinner, Trish would order a salad. After cleaning her plate and drinking another beer to quench the fire rumbling in her taste buds, she drove to the Brownstone Hotel. She had barely ordered another beer in the stunningly elegant lounge when Mary appeared.
"You're early!" Trish said.
"Getting a head start?" Mary smiled easily.
"More than you know," she was a tad sheepish as she flagged down the crisply tuxedoed waiter.
"Did I keep you waiting?"
"Not at all. I didn't expect you for another hour."
"We had a test tonight. I got done early."
"Doesn't surprise me one bit."
When the waiter came over, Mary ordered a beer. He had a look on his face like he had suddenly inherited the white trash section of the bar. As far as Trish was concerned, he could stick it. When he whirled away, Trish turned her attention back to Mary.
"I thought you were a wine drinker?"

"I thought you were?"

"I went to Dos Enchiladas for lunch. They should've called it Dos Beers."

Mary laughed. It was a charming sound.

"How is Lisa?" Trish asked, mostly just to get the pleasantries out of the way.

"She's great," Mary effused.

Trish just sort of, "Uh huhhed." And then said, "And school is great, obviously."

"You said it."

"And work is?"

"Busy and noisy and rewarding."

As they drank their beers, Trish glanced around. Maybe it was just all those books about spies, but Trish could've sworn the man two tables over had taken an interest in their conversation.

"Uh huh," Trish answered distractedly.

"What's wrong?"

"Shhhh."

"What?" Mary was puzzled.

"We can't talk here," Trish wanted to be extra careful.

"We can't? I thought we were doing pretty well."

"Come on," Trish put a twenty on the table and led Mary out of the lounge.

"Where are we going?"

"Upstairs."


Trish walked over to the hotel registration desk and requested a room. The clerk, a man who had a face like a goldfish, gave her the bad news.

"We are booked solid."

Trish thought she picked up on a silent, "except."

"You must have one room available?" Trish had that moneybags expression on her face.

"The Honeymoon Suite is available. Apparently, someone got stood up at the altar," he burbled out of puffy lips.

"We'll take it."

"One Honeymoon Suite for two…ladies?"

"We only need it for an hour or so."

"We rent by the night at the Brownstone. *Not* by the hour!"

"Of course," Trish nodded. Seems some people only have one thing on their minds, but the true explanation wasn't going to be one bit better, so Trish just shut her mouth and pulled cash out of her pocketbook.

"I'll need a credit card imprint."

"I'm paying with cash."

"I still need a credit card."

Trish didn't hesitate. It would look suspicious. She handed over a platinum hued card. Her credit limit was astronomical. Next time Robbie was in the mood for a surprise, they could spend the entire week here.

The Honeymoon Suite was on the fifth floor. They went up in the elevator, sans luggage, to the floor and found the room with no trouble. All the excesses of the twenty-first century were represented within the confines of this room. Mary just sort of gawked.

"I thought they were kidding about the heart-shaped bed," Mary voiced her first impression.

"At least it's heart-shaped," Trish muttered as she closed and bolted the door.

"I wonder where they get the sheets to fit it?"

"You want something from room service?" Trish asked, mostly to stall.

"I'm sure Lisa will have something cooked up for me when I get home," Mary sat in a red plush chair.

"I'm sure she will," Trish agreed.

"You really don't like Lisa, do you?"

"If you love her, that's good enough for me. You do, don't you?"

"I absolutely adore her. Even when she was bad, I still loved her."

Trish just nodded. Her eyes were everywhere in the room but on Mary.

"Trish?"

"Yes?"

"I don't mean to put too fine a point on it, but what are we doing up here in the Honeymoon Suite? I've been pretty patient."

"You have, and I really appreciate it. I need to talk to someone."

"Okay. About what?"

"And I can't talk to Robbie about this. You seemed to be the next best choice."

Mary nodded. She understood more than most the way people need to tell their own stories.

"Why can't you tell Robbie?" Mary prompted.

"I promised Rose I wouldn't tell."

"Her mother?"

"Right. You met her at the wedding."

"She's a delight."

"Yes, she is. But she has a problem. You see," Trish settled into the story, "everyone knows that Max and Rose are both survivors of the Holocaust."

"Okay."

"And everyone with two ears has heard Max's story."

"Right."

"But, hardly anyone knows Rose's story."

"Obviously you do."

"I do."

"And Robbie doesn't?" Mary guessed correctly.

"Robbie doesn't and Max doesn't."

"But she told you?"

"I guess I sort of bullied it out of her one day."

"I doubt that. It would be my guess that she just finally needed to talk about it."

"That's not exactly the case. You see, Rose is a hero."

"Really? Then why can't Robbie and Max know?"

"Because being a hero in the Holocaust wasn't always as easy as it looked. She worked in a munitions factory as slave labor. There, she got involved in a plot to sabotage a crematorium."

"Now, that is a true act of bravery!"

"And everyone involved was caught and killed. Except Rose."

"How did she escape detection?"

"She didn't. She just escaped being hanged."

"How?"

Trish paused. This was the difficult part of the story.

"I think I understand," Mary said quietly.

Trish nodded.

"And then, when she discovered she was pregnant the father aborted the child out of fear."

"Oh, my God.  That must've been so frightening."

"It was.  And to make matters worse, it made it very hard for her to have a child when she and Max were trying to start a family."

"That makes sense."

They were both silent for a moment, as if in grieving.

"But why did we need to rent the Honeymoon Suite to talk about it?" Mary wanted to know.

"Because that isn't the whole story."

"There's more?"

"You know that there are people who have spent their entire lives ferreting out Nazis?"

"It's a vocation for some."

"Then it stands to reason that it would be the case also for the other side."

"I don't quite follow?"

"What if there were people whose only goal in life was to find and punish Jewish heroes of the Holocaust?"

"Is there such a person?"

"Ever since the wedding, Rose has been getting weird letters."

"Threatening letters?"

"Maybe veiled."

"Why did this happen after the wedding?  Why not before?"

"The wedding pictures were telecast coast to coast.  Remember?  Rose thinks someone spotted her on a news program."

"After all these years?"

"Spooky, isn't it?"

"And so, she asked for your help."

"Right.  And I'm really not sure where to begin."

"Are the letters local?"

"No.  They are postmarked Cleveland."

"How many letters are we talking about?"

"Two so far."

"Both from Cleveland?"

"Both from Cleveland."

"Sounds like that's the place to begin."

"Cleveland's an awfully big place.  I don't think it would do much good to go there on the strength of a postmark."

"What about fingerprints on the letters?"

"Between me and Rose and a dozen postal employees, I'm sure we've obliterated most of the useful ones so far."

"Do you have any other ideas?"

"I've been reading up on espionage circa World War II. I had hoped to find someone or some group that had insight."

"Like counterespionage?"

"I really don't have much of an idea what I'm doing, frankly. All this talk about spies has started to make me paranoid. I imagined that guy in the bar was trying to overhear our conversation."

"What guy?"

"The guy who was at the next table."

"Oh, him. I figured he was just trying to hit on us."

"I suppose you're right. I just forget all about that possibility from time to time."

"Well, if anyone had any doubts, renting out the Honeymoon Suite certainly removed them," Mary smiled sweetly. Lisa was so lucky.

Trish grinned back. "We'd better get going."

"Will you promise to keep in touch about all this?"

"Absolutely. But let's keep this between us for now."

"Of course. I understand. Tell me one more thing."

"Sure."

"What's the latest news on the art auction?"

"All the buzz is good. The experts feel that the painting will easily fetch the price that Robbie quoted at the beginning."

"Sixty-five million?"

"Staggering, isn't it."

"Maybe that's why guys are hitting on you in bars!"

"If that's the case, I'm joining a cloister."

They parted ways in the parking lot after dropping the room key at the front desk and settling the bill. It was a lot for a thirty-five minute visit.

Robbie was cleaning the kitchen when Trish got home. From the wonderful aroma, she had been making pie. Or something?

"What's that marvelous smell?" Trish thought it wise to say something nice since she had disappeared most of the day.

"Well, hello! Did the library finally close?"

"Actually, it did so a couple of hours ago. I've been drinking beer."

"Have you had dinner?"

"I had a late lunch."

"So, you're ready for dessert, I hope."

"What did you bake?"

"Who mentioned anything about baking?" Robbie winked.

"Gee, remind me to stay out all hours of the night more often," Trish pulled her closer.

"You're not so late," Robbie noted generously, "but you're reeking of garlic."

"I had lunch at Dos Enchiladas."

"Remind me to take you there again soon. It must be good."

"I stuffed myself. I'll go gargle with mouthwash."

Trish wandered into the bathroom and ended up taking a long, hot soak in the bathtub. It helped to cleanse her of the smells of being downtown as well as the garlic that seemed to seep out of her pores. She washed her hair and then emerged from her baptism. Maybe she felt the need to be washed of her sin of not telling the complete truth. It would take more than one bath to accomplish that, but in the meantime, she felt more relaxed. Robbie was waiting in bed, propped up on her pillows. She was more lovely than any vision.

"Did I tell you today how beautiful you are?"

"I think you mentioned it," Robbie smiled shyly. This alone melted Trish's heart.

"You're beautiful," Trish made sure to say it, just in case.

"And so are you," Robbie held her close. Trish couldn't think of anything else to say. Her day's activities were pretty much unrepeatable.

"Are you okay?" Robbie asked like she knew something.

"Sure. Why?"

"You just seem distracted. Like something is bothering you."

"I'm fine. I just get all bookish when I spend time at the library."

"You would spend the rest of your life doing research if you could, wouldn't you?"

Trish thought this concept over. "I guess I never had much time for idle reading when I was working. Now that I'm a lady of leisure, I enjoy reading about history."

"You could be a professor someday."

"Only if I donated a ton of money to a university. Maybe not even then. They do have their standards, you know."

"You would make a very lovely professor," Robbie kissed her hand.

"I'd rather remain just your lovely lover. After all, I've not even gotten a good start at studying you."

"Now, that's research I can appreciate!"

You're home early," Lisa said as Mary walked in the door of Mitch's ranch house in the dusty suburbs of Denver. When Mitch had first won her fortune in the lottery, she went house shopping. The first house she bought was way too big so she donated it to a down-on-their-luck family. Her next choice was this very modest house surrounded by dirt. Lots and lots of dirt. For a while, it was something the Kettle's would've considered a downgrade. The driveway made the dustbowl days look like a monsoon season, and the floor sagged like a ten-year-old bra. But it was likewise comfortable. Early in Mitch and Reb's courtship, they were forced to reside here for a while when the Governor's Mansion was being cleaned up after a fire. Someone had decided to bring fire if not brimstone to the forefront of the Governor's conscience in a big way. So, Mitch, Rebecca and about fifty of their closest Federal agents set up camp in the boggy, soggy ranch house. Mitch had nicknamed it such not because it was a sprawling mansion worthy of an oil-rich Texas brood, but rather because everything was on the same level, which happened to come in very handy when Reb ended up in a wheelchair. Now, Mitch and Reb were in Washington D.C. and Lisa was waiting for an explanation.

"What are you doing here at all?" Mary asked back, equally surprised.

"I live here," Lisa was just a bit on the snappish side.

"I thought you'd be at work?"

"I traded with Minnie."

"Does that mean you'll have to work the whole weekend?" Mary sounded truly disappointed at this development.

"Yup!"

"Why did you do that? You hate working weekends."

"I had to be here when you got home to find out what Trish wanted."

"Is that all? Trish only wanted to talk."

"About what?"

"I can't tell you."

"Don't tell me you're going to keep secrets from me?"

"I won't keep *my* secrets from you. Just other people's."

"I don't see the difference."

"If someone at work told you something, like maybe they were pregnant or something, and asked you to keep it a secret, you would, wouldn't you?"

"I guess so."

"Good! Any other questions?"

"Just one."

"Okay."

"How long has Trish been pregnant?"

Mary rolled her eyes. "Trish isn't pregnant! I was just using that as an example."

"Well, did she specifically tell you that she wasn't pregnant?"

"No."

"And if she had said specifically that she was and asked you to keep it a secret, then you wouldn't tell me, right?"

"Right," Mary agreed, hoping that she was correctly following the logic after such a long day.

"So, she could very well be pregnant."

Mary had to think about this a second more to fully answer Lisa's question.

"If Trish is pregnant, she didn't tell me about it. But she didn't look one bit pregnant from where I was standing."

"You can be three months pregnant before it shows, no matter where you're standing," Lisa remained unconvinced.

"Besides, why would she tell me something like that and not tell Robbie?"

"She's keeping her pregnancy a secret from Robbie!"

84

Mary had to put forth a great deal of effort to avoid outright groaning and gnashing of teeth.

"Is there going to be dinner around here soon, or do I need to order a pizza?"

"Trish didn't feed you?"

"She wasn't hungry."

"Morning sickness at night. I've heard about that."

"You have? From where?" Mary played along as she opened the phone book to find the nearest pizza place.

"From my mother. She had morning sickness all hours of the day with me. What are you doing?"

"Looking for dinner."

"Check the oven first, unless you're taking me out somewhere nice."

"Not on my salary. Sorry."

"How about my treat?" Lisa closed the phone book gently.

"I thought you said something's in the oven?" Mary reminded, hoping that it wouldn't begin anew talk of pregnancy.

"It's just a tuna casserole. I can heat that up for lunch tomorrow. I'll buy you a steak. I just got paid."

Mary looked into Lisa's eyes for so long that she began to fidget. It had finally, not soon enough, dawned on Mary that Lisa was full blown jealous over the meeting with Trish and was doing anything to cover it up.

"What are you looking at me like that for?" she finally asked.

"Come here," Mary pulled her closer and held her face in her hands.

"What?"

"I love you," Mary said.

"I love you, too."

"I love you a lot."

"I love you more."

"Do not."

"Uh huh."

"You'd buy me a steak?"

"I'd buy you a steak and cut it up for you and feed it to you one damn bite at a time."

"Is there a restaurant in town that doesn't frown on that sort of thing?"

"Probably not."

"You could feed me that tuna casserole one damn bite at a time," Mary suggested a workable alternative as she slowly lost interest in going out to eat. Lisa moved closer.

"You'd prefer my tuna casserole to a steak?" Lisa whispered it like a prayer. Mary answered her prayer with a kiss. Lisa made a mental note to pray more often.

Chapter 8

The war of the paperwork had begun. No sooner had Rebecca
gotten back in the groove of her Senate duties than she received
official notice that Aunt BeBe was contesting the will in court.
And although it would've taken a stack of law books to
understand the situation, it all boiled down to whether or not
Aunt Bunny was mentally competent when she wrote the final
will. This much Reb conveyed to Mitch across the kitchen table
during a fabulous dinner.

Ah, the kitchen table in the fabulous kitchen of their fabulous
Georgetown house. Mitch was so happy here once she got used
to it that it gave her the excuse she needed to eschew the
functions of the other Senate wives. Not so long ago, Reb had
smashed to smithereens every good dish in the house. After the
cathartic experience, Mitch had sent Mary and Trish out
shopping and they found a lovely set of melmac. You could
drop this stuff twenty stories with nary a scratch. Besides, it
matched the wallpaper. Sort of.
"Well," Mitch had to ask, "Was Aunt Bunny mentally
competent?"
"Why would you even ask such a thing?" Reb countered back, a
little edgier than usual. Maybe it was a good time to cover the
melmac with her body, just in case. Actually, Mitch was very
understanding of Reb's moods by now. Running your little piece
of the free world could make anyone edgy. For a perfectionist
like Reb, it could be downright nerve wracking.
"Maybe because I never met Aunt Bunny?" Mitch offered the
comment as an olive branch. The good senator from Colorado
took note.
"I'm sorry. Does your head still hurt where I bit it off?"
"If I said yes, would you kiss it and make it feel better?"
"Oh, hush!"
Mitch couldn't help but smile. When she first fell in love with
Rebecca, she thought that that was as deeply as anyone could,
fall in love, that is. It was heaven on earth to be wrong about
that.

"What are you grinning about?" Reb followed up in the split second of silence.

"I'm thinking how lucky I am to have you in my life."

"Most days, we don't get a lot of time together," Reb said, "and I shouldn't waste it by snapping at you."

"Was it a tough day at work?"

"Just long."

"Are you sitting too long?" Mitch constantly worried about things like that.

"What are you going to do about it?" Reb made the usually gruff question sound so sensual that Mitch nearly dropped her fork. In fact, she was speechless for a moment.

"Well?" Reb cocked an eyebrow.

"How about a nice, long, hot shower after dinner. Maybe that would help ease some of the tension?"

"It might ease tension or then again, it might build tension."

"Either way works for me," Mitch nodded.

"That's what I like about you," Reb winked as she wheeled by to get a head start. "You're always willing to compromise."

"And be compromised!"

Later, in bed, after Mitch had been *thoroughly* compromised, she went back to the subject that had set off Reb earlier.

"Do you think BeBe has a case?"

"I don't know. I'm not that kind of lawyer."

"But you still know a lot more than the average person."

"Well, you just can't go into court and say that someone is mentally incompetent."

"You have to have proof?"

"You need documentation. It would be a case of having dates and times and incidences written down. Otherwise, it's just opinion."

"But isn't there even more opinion in it than that?"

"What do you mean?"

Mitch thought carefully about what she was trying to say.

"Suppose one day I wear one blue sock and one red sock. You write it down, but it doesn't prove I'm incompetent. Maybe I was just in the mood to wear two different colors of socks on that day."

"Are you going to start doing that?" Reb had to know.

"Will it make me look even sexier?" Mitch had pure hopefulness in her voice.

"It will drive me over the edge," Reb giggled.

"I didn't know you had a sock fetish."

"I didn't know I had a lot of things until I met you!"

"So, back to the court case. Do you think BeBe has actually written down things to present in court?"

"She probably has a ream of paper covered in notes."

"What are you going to do?"

"I'm going to get a good lawyer and pray."


The praying part was easy. God didn't require retainer fees up front. The lawyer was another matter, but Reb managed to find one that was local to Kansas and willing to stand up for the integrity of the eccentric elderly. Besides, the money involved wasn't half bad, either.

"Can I ask just one more question?" Mitch said as the conference call was over and she and Reb had a quiet moment.

"Sure."

"What are you going to do when you win the case?"

"Don't you mean 'if.'"

"I said 'when.' I mean 'when.'"

"I haven't thought much about it."

"Why not?"

"Because I never considered the possibility of owning the farm before and I'm not about to get my hopes up now."

"So, you would want to live there?" Mitch asked with just a hint of skepticism in her voice.

"Don't I strike you as an old farmhand?"

"Oh, yeah, sure," Mitch agreed much too blandly, like she had often pictured Reb with a straw hat and a pitchfork.

"It's just…"

"Just what?" Reb asked.

"How can you be a Senator from Colorado and reside in Kansas?"

"Well, I suppose I'd keep my Colorado residence intact. For now. But it is something to think about."

"There aren't enough Democrats in Kansas to vote you back to the Senate."

"If I own a farm, I won't have time to be a Senator."

"Gee, I suppose not," Mitch nodded.

"You hate this idea, don't you?"

"I'll go anywhere you go. Don't worry about me. I can learn to milk a cow. Eventually."

"That alone would be worth winning the case."

"You can hardly wait to get me in the barn."

"It's been my secret ambition for years."

Mitch only smiled. Serenely.

Chapter 9

An entire week passed with no more notes from Cleveland.
Trish was relieved.  So much so that she was now planning that
romantic weekend that seemed like such a good idea at the time
of her meeting with Mary.  She called the Brownstone and
reserved the Honeymoon Suite for Friday night.  Now, all she
had to do was to come up with a plausible story to lure Robbie
out of the house.  Dinner out was the logical choice.
"But we always stay in on Friday nights," Robbie reminded
Trish when she suggested the outing.
"I thought it would be a nice change."
"But we pop popcorn and snuggle up in front of the TV."
"We can go to a movie, too," Trish was wondering what sort of
rentals they had at the hotel.
"It sounds like an old-fashioned date."
"Too corny?"
"I think it's a lovely idea.  Let me go and change.  I'll be right
back."
Robbie managed to transform herself from lovely to gorgeous in
eight minutes.  She came out wearing a black sequined top and
matching black slacks.  It was a good thing that they were
heading to the Brownstone or Trish would've been tempted to
call the whole thing off and snuggle up right then and there.

Soon after the excitement of the wedding had died down, they
had purchased a sensible small car.  It was easier to find a
parking place if you didn't need space for a truck.  Trish drove
and before Robbie knew it, they were in the parking lot of the
hotel.
"Is this where we're going to have dinner?" she exclaimed.
"Actually, I've reserved a room for the night.  The Honeymoon
Suite."
"You didn't!" Robbie was flabbergasted and bubbly all at the
same time.
"You deserve some real romance," Trish intoned.
They walked in past the valet parking and taxi cab stand and
right up to the front desk.  As luck would have it, old Fish Face

was the clerk. As Trish gave her name, he looked from her to Robbie and said, "Back again so soon?"

"Excuse me?" Trish said, hoping against hope that her tone of voice would stem this inquiry.

"I said 'back so soon'!" he repeated loudly enough to engage Robbie fully in the conversation.

"What is he talking about?" Robbie said quietly.

"You bring all your girlfriends here?" he pressed on with a slight sneer. Trish felt a sudden rush of anger. A hundred, no, make it a thousand, bucks says that if they were a straight couple, this conversation wouldn't be happening. If Trish were a man, there would be no mention of any other visits.

"What does he mean, Trish?" Robbie was turning redder by the minute, besotted with flames of embarrassment and anger.

"Last week's date was a lot prettier and a whole lot thinner, too." With that, Robbie was gone, headed to the front door.

"I hope your hotel can afford a lawsuit," Trish said angrily.

"You can't be sued for telling the truth."

Fish Face had a point. Trish picked up her credit card and stormed back outside. Robbie must've gone to the car. When Trish checked, she saw no sign of her. She walked back to the cab stand and found out from the doorman that she had taken a cab. Even in her state of mind, she was still nice enough to leave Trish the car.

"Did you hear what address she gave the driver?"

"No, Ma'am."

It didn't help to ask which way the taxi went. They were at an intersection of one-way streets. Trish went back to the car and drove home. There was no sign of Robbie, which meant that there was only one other logical place to look. Trish picked up the phone and dialed the Goldstein residence. Instead of saying, "Hello," Max answered succinctly, "What is going on?" Obviously, they had caller ID.

"There's been a misunderstanding."

"Must be a real humdinger."

"Is she pretty upset?"

"She's in talking to her mother."

"I'm coming over," Trish hung up before she could be talked out of it. By the time she pulled up to the house, Max was ready with a full pot of coffee. They sat at the table with a cup apiece. "Does Robbie know I'm here?"

"I told them a few minutes ago that you were on the way."

"You think this is a bad idea?"

"I think it's good to talk things out."

Realizing that it was going to be extremely difficult to explain to Robbie why she had met with Mary while still keeping Rose's secret, Trish said, "Maybe I'd better go."

"No. Don't go. Not yet, anyway."

Trish couldn't tell if Max had hope or he was just afraid to be left alone with two emotionally distraught women. He was outnumbered by estrogen big time.

"I'm gonna tell them you got here. This can't go on like this." Max disappeared down the hall. Trish followed the sound of his footsteps, listening for any clue. A door opened. There were muffled voices. Two sets of footsteps came back down the hallway. It was Max and Rose. Rose sat down at the table and when she finally made eye contact with Trish, the look riveted her to the chair.

"Robbie needs a few minutes."

"It isn't what you think," Trish stated.

"I don't know what it is at all," Rose explained. "I only know it's serious."

Trish glanced up at Max, who was fidgeting. She asked him, "Do you have something for a headache?"

"Of course. I'll go and get it." he welcomed the escape.

It gave Trish the thirty or so seconds she needed to explain to Rose why it happened that Trish and Mary ended up in the Honeymoon Suite and what had happened an hour ago.

"Why did you tell someone else?" Rose asked quietly.

"Because I needed to confide in someone and get some good advice."

"And did you?"

"She is a very smart woman. Maybe she'll think of something before I do."

"This is all my fault," Rose admitted as Max finally found the way back to the room. He must have taken a long cut.

93

"What's all your fault? How could that be?" Max asked as he handed the two pain reliever tablets to Trish.

"It just is. Max, you sit down here. I'll go and get Roberta."

"Rose?" Trish asked and then met her glance.

"It's time. It's been too long as it is."

Rose walked down the hallway. Max looked confused.

"What is she talking about?" he asked.

Trish couldn't speak. She offered the tablets to him and when he refused, she washed them down with one good swallow of coffee. In a moment, Rose was back with Robbie in tow. She had been crying and now Trish felt the sting of tears as well. Since Robbie had not yet heard the whole story, she sat with her hands in her lap and wouldn't look up.

"Max and Roberta, I have something to tell you."

"You do?" Robbie sounded surprised.

"Trish isn't seeing another woman."

"How did you know about that?" Robbie asked, looking from her mother to Trish and back again. Robbie hadn't been very specific with her mother about the details.

"Because she told me," Rose answered simply.

"I see," Robbie said and then continued, "So, why would she be taking a hotel room with another woman?"

"It wasn't just any woman," Trish said, "It was Mary Fairbanks."

"You're having an affair with Mary?" Robbie was still in shock and not processing information well. Meanwhile, Max was all ears.

"I'm not having an affair with Mary," Trish assured everyone listening.

"Then why take her to the Honeymoon Suite at the Brownstone?"

"It was the only room left."

"The only room left?" Robbie was trying really hard to connect the dots.

"Mary and I were talking in the bar and I thought we were being overheard."

"Overheard? By whom? Why would anyone be listening to you and Mary?" Robbie asked each question without waiting for answers.

"It was just a feeling I had," Trish answered as best she could.

94

"Must have been some feeling. The Honeymoon Suite isn't cheap."

"You're telling me," Trish agreed. She had already paid for it twice and had yet to sleep there.

"So, what were you and Mary talking about that made you worry about being overheard?"

Trish looked down rather than at Rose. If Rose wanted to jump right in, now was as good a time as any.

"They were talking about me," Rose answered.

"You?" Max asked now. "What about you?"

Rose reached over and grasped Max's hand. "It's a long story."

"I'm listening."

A story forty-plus-years old took a scant ten minutes to tell. The sabotage, the rape, the forced abortion. Rose ticked them off in a monotone voice. Max and Robbie absorbed the revelations with thunderstruck concern.

"You couldn't have told us this years ago?" Max held on to Rose's hand like he was afraid she'd drift off.

"I didn't want to worry anyone."

"But you told Trish?" Robbie reminded gently.

"I needed help," Rose elaborated.

"What kind of help?" Max asked point blank.

"Help with this," Rose pulled the crank letters out of her apron pocket and handed one each to Max and Robbie. They read them and exchanged puzzled glances.

"Rose believes that these are threats. I tend to agree with her," Trish expounded, mostly to fill the void.

"Why would these be threatening?" Robbie asked Trish.

"Why would anyone in Cleveland be sending Rose letters like this?" Trish asked back.

"Maybe it's just a joke?"

"Maybe it is. But I still think we should be careful."

"Let's move," Max interjected suddenly.

"You move if you want to. I'm staying right here. No Nazi is going to chase me out of my home!"

"That's my Rose. You're right. You're always right," Max beamed.

"I'm sorry I kept this from you all these years. I was wrong about that," Rose held Max's hand as she started to cry.

"I understand.  I was wrong not to listen to what you couldn't tell."

Then, Max started to cry as well.  Trish looked to Robbie for insight.

"Why don't we let you two have some time alone," Robbie said to her parents.

They nodded and after murmured good-byes, Trish and Robbie were back on the road.

"They're going to be okay, eventually," Trish talked soothingly.  "It might take some therapy or counseling, but it's better to have everything out in the open."

"I'm sorry I doubted you."

"Don't think another thing about it.  If you rented out the Honeymoon Suite with another woman, I'd wonder about it."

"I should've stayed.  And asked."

"Oh, I think that's a lot to expect, especially in front of Fish Face."

"You mean that clerk?  He was vile," Robbie shuddered.

"I guess he just can't stand the thought of lesbians occupying the hotel."

"I have an idea," Robbie ventured.

"Let's hear it."

"Let's go back."

"To the Brownstone?"

"You've paid for the room, right?"

"I guaranteed it with a credit card."

"Let's see if we can check in this time."

"Okay."

Trish headed back downtown and found a parking place two spots away from their first time.  It must have been break time for Fishy.  He wasn't looming at the desk.  They filled out the registration card and collected their key.  The room was every bit as decadent and gaudy as Trish had remembered.  Even more so now that she was occupant as opposed to uninterested visitor.

"Look at that bed," Robbie had to chuckle.

"It is something else, isn't it."

"I wonder where they get the sheets to fit it?"

"Mary wondered the same thing."

"Great minds think alike."

Trish nodded and then went over to Robbie.

"Why don't we sit down and talk about it."

"Okay."

They sat close together on the red velvet sofa.

"I know you're still trying to sort out everything you've heard tonight. I can imagine it's pretty unsettling."

"It's not so much the past that worries me. It's the current threats that have me most concerned."

"I know. I suppose it was wrong of me to violate your mother's trust, but I was afraid to carry this burden alone."

"She should've told my dad sooner."

"Secrets have a way of being self-perpetuating. I kept Rose's for too long."

"You didn't just find out last week?" Robbie didn't sound at all happy.

"I've known for a long time. I would understand if you were very angry about that."

"I really don't want to stay here," she stood up.

"Do you need some time away from me? Again?"

"Not necessarily. I just want to go home."

"To our home?"

"Yes."

Trish breathed a sigh of relief. At least they were on okay terms. As they drove, Robbie continued to talk.

"I don't know anymore when it's okay to keep secrets. And when it's not."

"I guess I don't know either."

"You did the right thing. How can I be angry at you for doing that?"

"It's hard to tell when you're angry," Trish told a whopper.

"You want me to start throwing things?"

"Senator Fairbanks goes through dishes by the set when she gets ticked off."

"Remind me to price check Tupperware just in case they ever visit."

Trish laughed. It was good to have Robbie back.

## Chapter 10

"I can't believe the price of dishware," Mitch mentioned to Reb across the kitchen table.

"You mean, this old melmac?"

"Hey, it's not so old!" she came to its defense. "And no that's not what I meant."

"Oh, you're talking about the restaurant venture!"

"Or, adventure, as the case may be."

"What do you mean?" Reb queried, only too happy to stay off the subject of Senate business tonight. She often felt that much too much of their dinnertime conversation was about her work. Hearing the latest on Mitch's pet project would be a nice change.

When Mitch first met Reb, it was in a bar called The Lucky U. At that time, Reb was the honorable governor and Mitch was an honorable bar patron. She was actually more than that, having won the lottery and taken to a life of waiting tables for an old friend. When the old friend died, Mitch owned the bar outright. It had been sold after a wrangling over some false charges of bribery and other nonsense. Since Mitch had attached more sentimental value to the former owner than the bar itself, the sale didn't seem to faze her. But it did leave her at loose ends after she and Reb moved to Washington D.C. for a six-year stint. So when Mitch and her new best friend Jane had decided to become restaurant co-owners, it just seemed to be a natural course of events.

"There are so many types of dishware," Mitch began her answer. "And none of them are cheap."

"Tell me about the ones you like so far."

"You're serious?"

"Sure. I wouldn't ask otherwise."

"Okay, well, I was looking at a basic white with this raised pattern around the edge that looks like a paisley design and then there was a blue and yellow checkerboard one I liked but Jane was all hot on some plate that had a fish design made out of what looks like a third-grade ceramic tile art project."

Mitch stopped to take a breath and lapsed into silence.

"So, you and Jane are having your first fight?" Reb guessed.

"It's merely a creative difference."

"Plates are important."

"I can hardly wait until we get to silverware. It's worse than getting married and doing a bridal registry."

"Maybe if you let her pick the plates, you could have your way with other things?"

"I like salmon."

"To eat?"

"The color. I think that salmon-colored tablecloths would be elegant, but Jane wants something a little splashier."

"I have an idea."

"Let's hear it."

"Hire a consultant. Follow his or her advice. Then you and Jane won't waste your time quibbling over this stuff."

"What if we both hate the advice?"

"By the time all the dishes are chipped and the tablecloths are torn, you'll be so successful that it will be easier to agree on things."

"You think we're arguing because we're nervous?"

"I imagine that's part of it. It's also just possible that the two of you have radically different tastes and that's not necessarily a bad thing for business partners."

"I guess not. So, I should get better at compromise and hire a consultant?"

"Ask Jane. Maybe she's tired of making decisions as well."

"I'll do that."

"How's the menu planning?"

"Jane's doing a terrific job of that. I've sampled just about everything so far and it's great. You know, she even does all this fancy stuff with chocolate."

"Really?"

"She can take melted chocolate and spread it over a cold marble slab and then cut and form it. It's quite amazing to watch."

"Do you have the kitchen planned out?"

"We've looked at several layouts. Now that we have the property, it should go faster."

Getting the property wasn't as difficult as it had first appeared. Wagner's the restaurant that Mitch had had her eye on, went up for sale right before the trip to Kansas. By the time they arrived home from the funeral and the other various side trips, Mitch's real estate agent had the papers ready to sign. Reb hadn't asked the price and Mitch hadn't disclosed it.

"How soon will you have the grand opening?"

"That's still quite a ways down the road. We have to gut the kitchen and start over. The bathrooms need a total upgrade. When the former owners put in the handicap access toilets, all the others got squeezed together in retrofit. We're doubling the size of the ladies room, expanding the gentleman's room and adding a family bathroom for moms and dads with infants. Don't even get me started with the wiring. I'm not sure Wagner's was *ever* up to code."

Mitch stopped her narrative when she saw the amused smile on Reb's face.

"What?"

"I haven't seen you this happy about anything in a long time."

"I'm happy every day you and I share together. I just try to not discuss your plumbing."

"Which thrills me no end!" Reb laughed easily.

"I'm spending a lot of money," Mitch decided to broach the subject they had been avoiding so far.

"You have a lot to spend," Reb noted calmly.

"I hope to make a profit in a year."

"I wouldn't expect you to make money for three or four years."

"Oh no, this place is really going to cook."

"Convenient, for a restaurant," Reb smiled.

"And what about your day at work?"

"Just the usual."

"Now, now, don't be so modest. What about the forestry issues you've been talking about in your sleep."

"I have not!"

"You've been muttering something about spotted owls since Tuesday."

"I've discovered something about myself as I've grown older."

"Please! You're making yourself sound ancient."

"I'm old enough to realize that I've developed a new sense of awe about nature. Remember how you are when you're in Santa Fe?"

"I'm calm."

"Almost reverent. Or spiritual."

"I guess."

"I'm beginning to feel that way about a lot of things. Spotted owls and hundred year old trees and…"

"Me?"

"Oh, you're a couple of rungs above the spotted owls."

"Good thing. I've seen what birds do to cars and such."

After that visual, Reb pushed her dinner plate away.

"Are you finished?"

"Now I am!"

Mitch collected the dishes and rinsed them before stashing them in the dishwasher. Reb probably had about a dozen things to do, but she hung around the kitchen, watching Mitch.

"You think I'm employable?" Mitch wondered why the study.

"Invite Jane over for dinner soon."

"Okay. Any particular reason?"

"I want to see what she can do with chocolate."

"It isn't any better than what you've been known to do," Mitch intoned knowingly. Reb blushed. One of their first intimate encounters involved chocolate frosting and some ingenious uses for it.

"Those were the days," Reb said, almost wistfully.

Mitch dried her hands and then went over to Reb. She kissed her softly, conveying all the possible longing she could manage in one kiss.

"And these are *these* days."

"These days are okay?"

"These days are the best ever. I know people who would crawl ten miles on their hands and knees for five minutes of what we have."

"Pretty soon, you're going to get really busy with the restaurant. How are we going to manage our time?"

"I'll buy you dinner every night."

"What about dessert?" Reb breathed into Mitch's ear.

"I'd better recheck those floor plans. I could add a bedroom?"

"When Jane comes over, let's all take a look at those plans."

"Good idea," Mitch nodded as she raised up and propelled Reb toward the bedroom. The spotted owls would just have to wait their turn for Reb's attention.

Chapter 11

Jane was such a good sport about dinner that she poached salmon and prepared rice as Mitch and Reb set the table. It had been a scant three days in the planning and showed every sign of being a gourmet feast for three. They chatted about the restaurant business as they ate.

"Mitch tells me that you suggested hiring a decorator for the restaurant," Jane mentioned casually in Reb's direction.

"It seemed to me after listening to Mitch that there were a lot of decisions to make."

"I guess it never hurts to get an expert opinion," Jane agreed amiably. "Do you have anybody in mind?"

"Not really."

"I'll ask around," Jane buttoned up that discussion.

"So, tell me your plans for the kitchen layout."

"Rip everything out and start over," Jane said. "I can't believe Wagner's could deliver any kind of food with the way things were."

"Mitch and I agree. Tell me how the place will look when you get done."

Jane was pleasantly surprised. "You want to hear all the boring details?"

"It won't be boring. I promise."

"Well, we've made the major decision to have part of the kitchen open to public view."

"That was a major decision!" Reb agreed, although she hadn't heard any part of it from Mitch.

"And Jane came up with it," Mitch added.

"You give me too much credit," she gently countered. "Other places have an open kitchen."

"But that doesn't mean that the customers see everything, does it?" Reb prompted Jane.

"No. Not at all. We'll have an exhibition kitchen and a prep kitchen. The front kitchen will have a steamer, fryer, three 6-burner ovens, a charcoal broiler, a convection oven, a mixer, and a raft of under-the-counter refrigeration."

"What will be in the back kitchen?"

"Along with a lot of counter space, a bigger mixer, a dough machine, a pizza oven, another standard oven and a stock pot."
"Don't forget the griddle and the smoker," Mitch tacked on.
"And we're thinking about a wok or two, depending on how my stir-fry creations shape up," Jane was cautiously optimistic.
"All your creations are scrumptious so far," Mitch was ready with reassurances. The truth was easy to tell so fast.
"All three of them? We need at least a dozen plates to start."
"Plates?" Reb remembered that discussion. This couldn't be the dinnerware debate? Could it?
"A dozen entrée selections," Jane explained.
"What do you have so far?"
"The salmon I cooked tonight…"
"It's terrific."
"Thanks. And then, a pepperoni chicken number, and a vegetarian pasta dish."
"You have a lot more than that," Mitch bragged on her behalf. "You do tuna and steak and chicken salad with the greatest of ease."
"But we still need the side dishes to accompany those."
"Which would be a good use for the wok. A nice serving of crisp-tender vegetables is always a nice addition."
"I thought I was going to serve *your* famous potato salad with everything." Jane gave Mitch a smile chock full of tease.
 "Only if we are desperate!"
"What famous potato salad?" Reb wanted to hear this one.
"Am I the only person who puts bacon grease in potato salad?" Mitch asked it like she was begging for salvation.
Reb and Jane looked at each other and nodded in unison.
"What are you going to call the place, The Clogged Artery?" Reb laughed.
"You haven't told her?" Jane checked with Mitch.
"Told me what?" Reb was such a nosy one lately.
"We've settled on a name for the restaurant."
"Really? What did you decide?"
"Fairbanks's," Jane announced.
For a moment, Reb couldn't speak. Then, she said, "You named it after me?" She was truly touched.

"We wouldn't have gotten together if it hadn't been for you. It was the right thing to do," Jane explained.

"I'm honored. I'll try and live up to the reputation."

"You already do," Mitch said as she cleared dishes. It was her automatic response after every meal.

Jane turned her full attention to Reb. "Mitch said you wanted to watch me work with chocolate."

"I've been looking forward to it all day."

Jane worked with smooth efficiency as she melted chocolate and then spread it thin on a chilled slab of marble that Mitch had purchased yesterday. Jane used a sharp knife to cut out simple shapes. At least, that's what she called them. To Mitch and Reb, they looked like oak leaves, snowflakes, and butterflies. Any one of these served with a dish of ice cream or a slice of chocolate cake would add a perfect touch of elegance. She could also slice the chocolate and wrap it around cylindrical portions of homemade ice cream.

"Of course, we still need to hire a pastry chef," Jane reminded Mitch.

"And about a hundred other people," Mitch added with just a touch of pretend panic in her voice.

"Hiring them is the easy part. Keeping them is the tough part."

"Mitch never had trouble keeping help before," Reb expounded. "People love working for her."

"I'm glad you brag about her," Jane tattled. "She never does it herself."

"That's one of the many reasons people like working for her," Reb reasoned.

"Are the two of you done talking about me like I'm not even here?" Mitch was bordering on a blush.

"Are we done talking about her like she's not even here?" Jane asked Reb thoughtfully.

"Let me think about it," Reb struck a meditative pose.

"Enough already!" said Mitch. "I'm eating this oak leak."
She held up the delicate form.

"Better hope it's not poison ivy instead!" Reb giggled.

Jane worked with the chocolate for a while longer before calling it a night. After she left and Mitch had the kitchen scrubbed up, Reb was still curious.

"When were you going to tell me that you were naming the restaurant after me?"

"I left that little announcement to Jane."

"Was it your idea?"

"I suggested it and Jane liked it. It sounds cool."

"Sounds like the two of you agree on more than you disagree."

"We do. If I could just talk her out of those ugly tile fish dinner plates, I'd be satisfied."

"I kinda like the fish plates."

"I'll buy a thousand. First thing tomorrow."


Maybe it was just the fact that it was Kansas that made the court dockets manageable. Before Mitch and Reb had barely gotten over their last trip to Utopia, they were contemplating another trip to witness the first hearing on the competency of Aunt Bunny. The operative word was "contemplating." Mitch was about as enthusiastic about another visit to the homestead as a dip in a hot tub full of piranha.

"You can wipe that look off your face," Reb intoned with just a hint of schoolmarm.

"What look?" Mitch pulled an innocent expression out of her facial repertoire.

"That 'hot tub full of jellyfish' look."

"It's piranha this time."

"Whatever. Besides, counsel tells me that we don't need to be there."

"And you probably shouldn't go anyway. You'd probably want to punch BeBe in the nose for insinuating that Bunny was over the edge."

"The lawyer said that from what he's seen so far, BeBe doesn't have a case."

"Well, let's not count the chickens before they hatch."

"What do you mean?"

"One day, you'll need to decide what you're going to do with a whole farm."

"That time's coming sooner rather than later, I think."

Reb was right. It didn't take the legal system long to decide that Aunt Bunny was of sound mind. Choosing one relative over another was less an oddity and more of a cottage industry in the will-making business. The court appointed Rebecca's lawyer to perform the necessary paperwork as per Reb's instructions. After all, she couldn't run back and forth to Kansas once a month to take care of all the details of settling an estate. BeBe, Henry and Miranda moved out lock, stock and barrel even though as far as Reb was concerned, they could have stayed on the property for as long as they wanted. Reb had no intention of evicting them and soon regretted their hasty decision. There was no one to keep the house in good order. This fact nettled Reb. Mitch, even when mired knee deep in restaurant-building details, couldn't help but notice.

"What's wrong?" Mitch asked after a protracted silence one evening.

"Nothing."

"Is it a big nothing or a little nothing?"

"I can't decide."

"Tell me. I'll decide."

"I'm worried that the farmhouse is sitting vacant."

"That's a big worry."

"You think so?"

"You bet! You don't want the place to fall into disrepair."

"What should I do?"

"Isn't it obvious?"

Reb thought it over, taking way too much time.

"Have Mary and Lisa move in," Mitch provided the logical answer.

"Mary and Lisa?"

"Sure."

"But Mary is working and going to school."

"They have schools in Kansas. Besides, taking care of the property is enough of a job."

"What will they do for money?"

Mitch watched Rebecca for about fifteen seconds without speaking.

"Why are you looking at me that way?" she asked, finally.

"Because I don't understand why you think there's a money problem."

"The estate isn't settled yet. All the assets are frozen, so to speak."

"So? You can pay Mary and Lisa out of your own pocket to keep things in order. Makes more sense than paying complete strangers."

"We don't even know if they would be interested," Reb said matter-of-factly. Too matter-of-factly for Mitch. Mitch picked up the phone.

"Call them and ask."

"Right now?"

Mitch checked her watch. "Somebody's bound to be home." Reb took the phone from Mitch's outstretched hand and dialed the number. After two rings, Lisa picked up.

"Hello?"

"Hello, Lisa."

"Oh, hi, Senator."

"Is Mary there?"

"She should be home in a few minutes. Can I take a message?"

"No, that's okay. I can call back."

"I've been responsible for taking messages since I was six."

"I'm sure you have been, but this is family business."

"Must be about the farm in Kansas," Lisa the omniscient guessed correctly.

"Just have her call me."

Reb disconnected the call. Abruptly. Rather too abruptly to suit Mitch.

"That was a bit short," she stated.

"I probably have to call back later to talk to Mary."

"About the *family business*?"

Mitch's emphasis wasn't lost on Reb.

"What's your point?"

"My point is that Lisa is family, too. Didn't it bother you when BeBe and her family treated me like an outsider?"

"It's just their way."

"Well, is it hardwired in the family DNA?"

"You don't exactly get along so well with Lisa yourself."

"I have an excuse."

They stopped talking. Arriving at impasse usually had that effect on them. Mitch and Lisa were once lovers. It was about once enough for Mitch. And Reb. After all, Lisa was drop-dead gorgeous. Even someone as beautiful as Rebecca could foster a sense of insecurity in the very presence of her. Their wandering separate thoughts were interrupted by the ringing of the phone. It was Mary. Surprise.

"Hi, Mom. How are you? Is everything okay? Is Mitch okay?"

"Everything is fine, dear."

"Lisa thought maybe something was wrong. We were worried."

"I'm sorry. I didn't mean to worry you. I'll talk to her in a minute, but I wanted to ask you something first."

"Sure. What?"

"Well, how is school going?"

"School? You called to ask about school?"

"Can't a mother call to ask about school?"

"Yeah, sure. School's fine."

"And work?"

"Work's fine."

"And Lisa?"

"Lisa's fine. Her work is fine. Everything is fine. What's going on?"

"Mitch and I had an idea."

"An idea?"

Mary's tone of voice belied her true feelings. At least she hoped. Because everybody knew that when Mitch got an idea, it was usually hold-on-to-your-hat time.

"Well, you know that your Aunt BeBe and everybody moved out of the farmhouse."

"No, I hadn't heard that. Was that part of the court order?"

"Not at all, and I didn't ask them to go. They just apparently got huffy and left."

"That's too bad," Mary was still on edge. She knew there was more.

"It really is. Now, the place is abandoned. Open to vandalism and all sorts of stuff."

"Oh…" Mary was finally beginning to see the point.

Reb hurried to the finish, "So Mitch and I thought to offer the place to you and Lisa, if you want to live there."

"Hang on a second," Mary asked as her end of the phone line grew quiet. Then, she was back quickly. "Okay," she answered.

"Okay?" Reb repeated the answer to make sure she heard it right.

"Lisa thinks it's a wonderful idea. Me, too."

"You don't mind uprooting your lives?"

"We're young. Uprooting our lives is something we're good at."

"I guess so," Reb trailed off.

"So, how much more rent are you going to charge us?" Mary asked all business-like.

"Mitch thinks we should pay you to live there."

"Tell Mitch I like her ideas," Mary laughed.

"Why don't you tell her yourself?"

"I have a better idea. Why don't you talk to Lisa first."

"Put her on."

There was a rustling, and then Lisa was there. Reb started to speak, "I wanted to apologize for being abrupt earlier-" was all she managed to get out of her mouth before Lisa interrupted her.

"Don't think another thing about it. I understand how important it was for you to discuss this with Mary first. You should've been here to see her eyes light up. It's such a nice offer and such a nice thing for you to do and-"

"Whoa, hold on, take a breath," Reb said.

Lisa laughed, "I'm sorry. I just got so carried away."

"Now, there's probably a lot to think about, but one of the first things you'll need to do is to pick out some furniture. I'm pretty sure that whatever wasn't nailed down was hauled away by the former occupants."

"Oh, that's okay! Mary and I can get along with very little. We are right now, so that won't change much."

"I'll make sure you have a few things. Can I talk to Mary again?"

"Oh! Sure! And thanks for everything!"

Reb and Mary talked a few more minutes before hanging up. Mitch had been sitting there with a rather mysterious Cheshire-cat expression on her face. She never did get her chance at the line, but that was okay. Reb studied her smugness, and the asked,

109

"So, tell me, what's it like to be so incredibly wise about every damn thing?"

"It's fucking incredible."

"I imagine so," Reb replied drolly.

"You were wonderful, too." Mitch followed up with a compliment.

"Lisa is good for Mary."

"Yup," was all Mitch could come up with as a reply.

Chapter 12

It took a while, but the third letter arrived at the Goldstein household on a bright, sunny Wednesday. For a few days after Rose's revelation, things had been uneventful. Actually, quite quiet. Maybe a little too quiet. Robbie hadn't talked much more to Trish about the subject and Max had closed up tighter than a clam shell to all parties concerned. Trish's guess was that it was anger, but fear was a close runner up. When the truth was on the table, Trish contacted Detective Forrest to see about protection and the next logical steps. He was more than happy to run a patrol car past the house from time to time but anything more than that would require the arrival of another threatening letter. Or, in the case of a bodyguard, more money. For whom, Trish was more than willing to chip in, but Max didn't want some hulking 250 pound bag of muscles shadowing Rose day and night. And it wasn't just because he was the jealous type, he made it clear.

So, in a strange way, the arrival of the letter brought a sense of relief. It gave everyone something to do. Rose called Robbie who told Trish who notified Detective Forrest who showed up at the Goldstein's about the time Robbie and Trish pulled up. He wore gloves as he bagged the unopened letter for a trip downtown.
"Isn't it important to know what it says?" Rose asked the question directly to him.
"It might be the most crucial clue," Detective Forrest agreed. "Would you like to come with me to the lab? He made the offer to all, but held eye contact with Trish while he waited for an answer. It was obvious that he would really like to show Trish around. Maybe two or three times.
"Why don't you go, Rose. You, too, Max," Trish all but pushed them out the door.
"Call us when you know something," Robbie added as an afterthought.
Only four or five rubbernecking neighbors watched as Max and Rose were driven off in a police cruiser. Robbie went back in the house and faced Trish.

111

"Detective Forrest has eyes for you."

"You noticed," Trish remarked.

"Should I have noticed sooner?"

"I think he's been fond of me for quite some time."

"He wears a wedding ring."

"And so do I. I guess mine means more to me."

"I'm sure it does. Especially all we've been through."

"And all we have yet to go through. How can we talk your parents into getting some protection?"

"Maybe this third letter will bring them around."

"Hopefully it will have a fingerprint or another clue."

Robbie nodded and then went to the kitchen to make some coffee. It was going to be a long day. In the meantime, Trish wandered into the family room and turned on the TV. She settled on the couch and then pulled Robbie close when she came in with coffee, cream and sugar.

"You're going to spoil me for anyone else."

"By serving you coffee?"

"By being thoughtful twenty-four hours a day."

"Drink your coffee, you sweet talker!"

After sipping the brew, they sat side by side for so long that Robbie dozed off in Trish's arms. Apparently she had perked decaf. Trish sat quietly, treasuring the time. She was holding a most beautiful, loving woman in her grasp and sniveling hotel clerks who couldn't keep their opinions to themselves could tip over backwards off a cliff. The longer they sat together, the more Trish's arm fell asleep. It went from tingly to prickly to non-responsive in about ten minutes. As she shifted to relieve the thrumming sensations, Robbie stirred awake as well.

"Um, did I fall asleep?"

"You and my arm."

"Here, let me rub it for you."

Maybe it wasn't a medical miracle, but all of a sudden, Trish felt a lot more awake because of Robbie's touch. She had to keep reminding herself that they were in the parent's house and more importantly, the folks were still at the police station perhaps tracking down a nutcase.

"If you were a spy in World War II, what would you be doing now?" Trish asked of Robbie.

112

"Collecting Social Security benefits?"

"Do you think you'd still be talking about the good old days?"

"The veterans of World War II were sure luckier than the men and women who came back from Vietnam, that's for sure."

"In what way?"

"They could talk about their experiences because they were heroes. America didn't embrace the Vietnam Vet."

"So, do you think you'd still be talking about it to anyone who would listen?"

"Did spies talk at all, then or now?"

"That's something I didn't think about," Trish admitted.

"You know what they say about loose lips," Robbie admonished in a way that made Trish's toes tingle.

"What about lips?" she asked quickly, wanting very much to keep the topic going.

"Loose lips sink ships."

"Oh, of course. Can I pretend to be the ship? I've been needing a really good sinking lately."

"No, you haven't!" Robbie was just beginning to pink up around the ears when they heard a car pull up.

"I guess we should leave the nautical stuff until later," Trish said as she stood up to go to the door. Robbie was right behind her. As expected, Detective Forrest had accompanied Rose and Max back home. He was a gentleman, after all. And if all it took was a smile now and then from Trish to continue this kindly attentiveness, well, she could smile with the best of them. Max appeared unruffled by the events of the day, but Rose was a shade wan. Rather than pretend to be the perfect hostess, she allowed Robbie to steer her to a chair and pour her a cup of coffee. Detective Forrest readily accepted a cup as well and sat next to Rose as she talked about the visit and the letter.

"You said there were no fingerprints?" she checked the facts by running them by Sam in pop-quiz form. Who knows how many times they had had this same conversation before now?

"There were no fingerprints," he corroborated her statement. By then, everyone else had settled around the table to hear the rest.

"Except on the outside of the envelope, of course," Max added.

"And all of them probably belong to a raft of postal employees," Sam tried his hopelessly pained look out on Trish. She smiled a sympathetic smile back, as if she shared his pain for keeps. Even though she hadn't become straight during the time he had been gone, it rendered him speechless anyway. A fact not lost on Robbie. She spoke up, perhaps trying to break the spell.

"So, what did the note say?"

"It was awful."

"The note said 'it was awful?'"

"It didn't say that. It said, 'you will pay.'"

"That's the most threatening of the three so far," Trish checked Rose's face. She would either need to lie down or get a blood transfusion.

"That settles that," Robbie made up her mind. "We're getting you a bodyguard and I don't want to hear any arguments. Can you help us out with some advice, Detective?"

He broke off his study of Trish's eyelashes long enough to volunteer for anything that would keep him welcome at the house. Unfortunately, he couldn't be the actual bodyguard. Overall, come to think of it, he was kind of thin and weedy.

"I have a few ideas," he answered.

Robbie, being the lady that she was, refrained from making any pointed comments about what she thought his salient ideas were about and followed up instead with, "Can you give us some names?"

He took out his notepad and jotted down some information as Rose looked on in a strangely detached manner. She needed some rest, and sooner rather than later. Robbie the nurse continued to exert her self-appointed authority.

"Come on, Mom. You need to go lie down for a few minutes."

"What about our guest?" Rose asked in an automatic voice.

Robbie eschewed making a silly remark like, "If our guest needs to lie down, I'll put him on the couch," and instead said, "Let's just worry about you right now."

Rose allowed herself to be guided by Robbie and Max to the other room. In the meantime, Detective Forrest was passing a note to Trish like they were in junior high. It read, "Have dinner with me?" Trish tried to not groan out loud. Lest it be mistaken for something other than just plain, old-fashioned non-sexual frustration.

"Sorry, I can't"

"Don't you eat?"

"I do all my eating with Robbie," Trish admitted before she realized how it might be taken. Too late.

"So, it's really that way?" he said with disappointment. Real or faked, Trish couldn't be sure.

"Why is that so hard to believe?" Trish felt her hackles rise. Straight people didn't have to defend their feelings, did they?

"Well, it's just hard to believe that you would settle for some pudgy, middle-aged woman when you could have me."

"And why would you feel that way?" Trish ignored her irritation and supplanted it with honest curiosity.

"Uh, well, I have so much more to offer."

"Well, like what?" Trish couldn't seem to stop herself now that she had ventured this far into the shallow end of Detective Forrest's pool.

"I thought maybe it was obvious...?"

Trish cast an appraising eye over whatever might be obvious. Alas, it wasn't.

"You're just not woman enough for me," was the kindest thing Trish could come up with on such short notice. They were spared further embarrassment by the reappearance of Robbie.

"Did the two of you come up with anything?" she was still exuding authority and didn't notice the shifting of bodies brought on by a too-ambiguous question.

"There are three people to call that I can recommend for protection," Sam tore off another sheet from his notebook. The action reminded Trish of the incriminating note she held wadded up in her hand and it was all she could do to keep from rolling it into a tiny ball and popping it into her mouth. Ink could taste so foul.

"Thank you, Detective Forrest. I'll start calling them now. Will you please stay for dinner?"

He looked from Robbie to Trish and back again.

"No, thank you. I need to get back downtown to check on the lab reports. Do some calling around," he trailed off. Guess hanging around the Goldstein's, watching Trish light up every time Robbie walked in was losing its appeal. He wasn't, after all, a glutton for punishment.

Robbie was on the phone before the door closed. Bodyguard interviews would commence in two hours, which didn't give them much time to compile a list of questions. Max had, by now, rejoined them.

"What do you ask a bodyguard, anyway?" he wondered.

"I guess you start by asking how much money they charge?" Robbie offered her opinion.

"Let's not worry about that," Trish said gently but firmly. "I don't want to cut financial corners where safety is concerned."

"I agree," Max said, "although we can't afford somebody forever."

"I'm paying for this," Trish made it clear.

"We'll pay for it," Max forwarded his opinion in turn.

"I'm paying!" Trish assured him pointedly.

"Look, before the two of you start wrist wrestling over the bill, let's get somebody hired!" Robbie got them back on track.

"I guess references are okay to ask for," Trish said thoughtfully.

"People who were protected by them?" Max asked.

"Right."

"I wonder if we'll get somebody who's guarded a famous person," Max brightened considerably and then added with sudden gloom, "unless it's a famous person who has just been attacked. You know, successfully?"

"That would certainly be something to research." Robbie nodded, trying to think if any celebrities had been attacked lately.

"Do we need to ask if they carry firearms?" Trish ventured into gun territory.

"Rose will not allow guns in the house," Max said firmly.

"Under normal circumstances, I might agree," Trish said, "but these aren't normal circumstances."

"Maybe if we don't ask, he won't tell."

"Our first interview is with a woman."

"A woman?" Max made sure he heard correctly.

"She was first on the list Forrest gave me," Robbie explained. "I figured we'd start there and if we needed to move down the list, we could do that later."

"Well, if she was first on the list, are you sure it wasn't in alphabetical order?"

"Her name is Silver."

116

Trish almost made a Lone Ranger joke and then stopped herself just in time. Maybe later, when death threats were laid to rest.

"Are you okay?" Robbie asked her.

"I'm fine, really," Trish was still restraining a giggle and it all came out sounding strained. Max patted her hand to help her be brave but Robbie knew the truth. There was a Tonto joke lurking in Trish's eyes. Maybe she thought she was covering it well, but she was wrong.

"What is Ms. Silver's first name?" Max was writing all this down like the secretary at a PTA meeting.

"Silver is her first name," Robbie noted.

If Silver's last name was Bells, Trish was going to have to leave the room. Perhaps the house. Maybe the neighborhood. She could go get some Chinese food and bring it back for the long haul.

"Smith," Robbie read it off the note.

"Silver Smith?" Max repeated it as he continued to make notes.

"Anybody in the mood for some Chicken Lo Mein?" Trish changed subjects instantly.

"Chicken Lo Mein?" Max looked up, wondering if maybe he should be writing this down as well.

"We won't have time to cook amid the preparations for this interview. I'll go pick up something to eat."

"Does it have to be Chicken Lo Mein?" Max asked carefully.

"No, of course not. I'll get anything you want. What sounds good?"

"Turkey empanadas, stuffed tomatoes, soda bread and berry trifle."

"Maybe it was just the perplexed look on Trish's face, but both Max and Robbie said at once, "So So's."

"Sosos?" Trish asked.

"It's a little bitty place three blocks down and four blocks over."

"And they have this stuff?" she couldn't remember it all to repeat it.

"I'll give So So a call. See what's on the menu today," Max got out of the interview questions assignment. He was smooth. In fact, so smooth, that after he got off the phone, he took off to So So's personally. Which was okay since Trish had fended off the giggles and turned serious again.

"I think we need to ask what these people did before they became bodyguards."

"That's a good question. Do you suppose that we'll need to do anything else like install a sophisticated security system?"

"People do that without ever getting threatening letters. It couldn't hurt."

"Do you think I'm going overboard on this?" Robbie needed sudden reassurance.

"No, I don't. I think we're doing the exact right thing."

"You all sound very confident," Rose said as she entered the room. She looked considerably better.

"Daddy went to So So's to get dinner."

"Then, we'll need another pot of coffee."

"A Ms. Smith will be here in a few minutes for an interview."

"A female bodyguard?" Rose said thoughtfully.

"She was first on the list."

"It's okay with me," Rose shrugged. "Maybe she would like some tea?" Rose padded off to the kitchen.

Because life could sometimes fall into place and actually work out, about the time that Rose had coffee and tea ready, Ms. Smith was holding the door open for Max, who had his hands full carrying paper bags bulging with take-out containers.

"There's more in the car," he mentioned to Trish as he went to unload in the kitchen, but Silver was one step ahead and brought the rest in with ease. Trish liked that sort of quality in a person. How many people in the average day ever stop to help? There's a national epidemic of impoliteness surrounding us and if you don't believe it, just go to a mall and drop something on the floor and see who comes to help. Take a dust mop; cobwebs could form.

Rose and Robbie set the table and put the food on platters and in bowls. Max must've bought the pregnancy special, as if all the females were eating for two.

"What would you like to drink, Ms. Smith?"

"Please call me Silver, and I'll have some coffee."

"Cream or sugar?"

"No. I take it strong and black," which quite coincidentally was a rather on-target description of herself. She was every ounce of two-hundred fifty pounds, looked like she could bench press

118

everyone else at the table all at once, and had a deep coloring that was breathtaking. Somewhere, Trish figured, between French Roast and Kona.

"You went to So So's!" Silver smiled broadly as they passed the food.

"You know the place?"

"It's been a favorite spot for years."

"Have you lived here all your life?"

"Since I was three. My family moved here from Alabama."

"Oh, really?" Rose asked amiably. "Was it a work-related transfer?"

"No. They just got tired of having to get off the sidewalk every time a white person went by."

Max nodded. Jews in Germany were made to scrub sidewalks. By hand.

"So, how did you get into the bodyguard business?" Robbie directed the conversation to the issue at hand.

"Because I'm good at it," she answered quickly.

"Then, how were you able to arrange an interview at this short notice?"

"My last client is dead."

The entire Goldstein clan demonstrated great restraint in not exchanging knowing looks.

"He died of *natural* causes," Silver followed up with due emphasis.

"How natural?" Rose thought it wise to check, just for the record.

"He was ninety-two years old."

"Your last client was ninety-two?" Trish asked. She was wondering how much guarding a ninety-two year old person really needed.

"He was an active ninety-two year old man."

"How active?" Max was now on the curiosity bandwagon as well.

"Very active," Silver nodded sagely.

Max became quiet. Very quiet.

"So, have you always been a bodyguard?" Robbie was checking things off her list efficiently.

"I was a teacher for a while."

"What grade?"

"Middle school."

"What age is that?"

"Thirteen, fourteen, fifteen."

"Why did you quit?"

"It was easier being a bodyguard and the pay was better."

"How much do you charge?"

"It depends."

"On what?"

"Who needs the protection?"

"Rose does," Max avoided being the target of concern.

"And what is your typical day like, Rose?"

"Well," she began somewhat uncertainly, "I get up and make coffee. Except, I use the, you know, ladies room, and then I get the paper and work the puzzle which takes me a while. I don't know some of the new-fangled words." She paused to breathe. And think. "Like computer terms?"

"You mean, like byte?" Silver suggested.

"Is that one?"

"Do you go out much?" Silver probed, hoping to get past the puzzle page.

"I shop."

"Can someone else do that for you?"

"Uh, well, I don't know?"

"We can have groceries delivered," Trish offered her best idea. "And I'll check them before they are brought into the house. Do you have a security system installed in the house?"

"No. Should we?" Rose looked directly at Silver for advice.

"Just what kind of problems are you having?" Silver asked as she finished off one turkey empanada just about the time Trish dished her another.

"There are letters from Cleveland," Rose answered quietly.

"Letters from Cleveland?" Silver asked, just mostly to make sure she heard correctly.

"Three letters."

"Cleveland is a long way away."

"Anybody can get on a plane."

"Not with a gun."

"Do you carry a gun?" Rose was calm and decisive.

"I have three."

"That's a lot."

"You don't always get time to reload."

"I guess not. You need that many shots?"

"I'd rather be safe than sorry."

"Us, too. That's why we want to hire you."

"Good choice," Silver smiled. "Do you have a spare bedroom?"

"Yes. Why?" Rose asked in a most perplexed way.

"You do want twenty-four hour protection, right?"

"Oh, of course. You'll just have to forgive me. I've just never hired a bodyguard before."

"That's okay. Most people haven't."

"So, you'll take the job?" Robbie asked, sounding hopeful.

"Do you order from So So's often?"

"Every night, if you want," Max saw a chance to find an ally in the diet-breaking department.

"I'll move in tonight. We'll call a security place tomorrow. Get this place outfitted properly. Tom Cruise won't be able to break in."

"Tom who?" Max asked.

"Think Peter Graves," Trish translated smoothly.

"Peter Graves wants to stop by?" Rose was now very interested. "I just love his gray hair!"

"He can't come unless he brings Barbara Bain along," Max nodded, finally catching on to the context.

"Until all that happens," Silver made it clear, "I'm answering the door."

"What about the phone?"

"Ever hear of anyone getting shot through a phone?"

"No, but I did see a movie once where somebody answers the phone and they hear a secret code word because they've been hypnotized and they go and kill somebody in a trance," Rose was now on a roll.

"Were they in a trance or was the person they killed in a trance?" Silver asked politely.

"I think they were," Rose answered, clearing nothing up.

Silver nodded like she knew it all along.

As Rose and Max cleared the table, Trish took the opportunity to get down to brass tacks with Silver.

121

"How much do you charge?"

"For a job like this, I'm thinking five-thousand," she mused.

"That's pretty reasonable," Robbie said.

"A week." Ms. Smith tacked on.

"Oh." Was all that Robbie could say. She was thinking in terms of months.

"That's very reasonable," Trish nodded, not wanting cost to stand in the way of peace of mind.

"But I also have a senior citizen discount plan, so I'll cut it to two-thousand."

Trish shook her head. "Not a penny under ten-thousand a month."

Silver checked to be sure that Trish was serious. She had never been on this end of the negotiations.

"I like the way you treat Rose," Trish answered the unasked question.

"Then, you got yourself a bodyguard."

"Send me the bill. If Rose and Max fuss, just tell them to spend their money on takeout from So So's."

So the deal was set. Trish and Robbie promised to hold down the fort until Silver could go home and pack. Actually, it would've been more accurate to say, "check out," for at the moment, Ms. Smith had been living out of a motel that was more famous for its monthly than nightly rates. Rose busied herself by changing the sheets on the guest bed, even though they were clean. It was her way of keeping her nerves in check. After freshening up the bed and fluffing the pillows, she dusted out the already empty dresser drawers and vacuumed the floor, including the carpet in the closet. This could very well prove to be a serious upgrade from the motel particularly with the scented candles that Rose lit. You would've thought she was opening a bed and breakfast. Perhaps in this situation, it was more of a bed and breakfast...and lunch...and dinner.

Silver was back in an hour, carting in two bulging suitcases like they were as light as French pastry. Somewhere in all that were three guns, which remained out of sight for now. On Silver's list of things to do next was a thorough check of the residence. For a modest suburban home, it had a lot of rooms, mostly because it was built circa 1900. The stairway to the basement was steep and narrow and once a person arrived at the bottom step, it was a puzzle to know which way to go next. There was a small room which seemed to open labyrinth-like into other rooms. It was like spelunking without the cavern. A small washer and dryer were the only big draws in the main room. To the immediate left was a small room with frayed carpet.

"This was the playroom," Rose explained as she served as tour guide down memory lane. "Robbie would spend hours down here, especially on rainy days."

Silver nodded politely, but was more interested in checking window wells than listening to reminiscences. Every window had a lock. That was good. Of course, windows made of glass were always breakable. They could either have them wired when the security system was installed or board them up for the duration.

"Don't do any laundry for now," Silver instructed Rose.

"But I can't do without it."

"I'll take care of it," Silver assured her.

"You do laundry?" Robbie asked.

At these prices, it seemed like a fair trade to Trish, but she kept her mouth shut.

"For the time being, I'll do everything that requires a trip down here. I don't want anybody in the basement unless I escort them. Understood?"

Everybody nodded slowly. Silver checked each room one more time, as if she was memorizing every nook and cranny. Then, she more or less herded everyone back upstairs for the room-by-room tour of that level. It didn't take long, Silver was really quite efficient. Trish was feeling better already and convinced Robbie that they could go home once Silver had checked everything. They weren't two blocks down the street before Max was dealing three-handed pinochle to a couple of cagey card players. All was right with the Goldstein's world. If they minded the semi-automatic on the table, they didn't let on. After all, it was a friendly card game.

Chapter 13

When a couple went from rich to poor, there wasn't much to
pack. Mary and Lisa gave the fair two week's notice to their
respective employers, and Mary withdrew from her class.
Maybe there would be time for that in Kansas. She would know
more after they settled in to farm life, and found herself softly
whistling the theme song from "Green Acres" as she packed all
but the essential toiletries. One thing that they were never short
of in the house was beauty products. Lisa, being naturally
gorgeous, hardly needed such an inventory. If this was going to
be "Green Acres," Lisa was Eva Gabor and Mary was Eddie
Albert. Casting was still in doubt for Arnold the Pig.
"There's just one part of this I don't quite understand," Lisa
brought up while taking a break from cleaning.
"What's that?"
"How do you make money on a farm?"
"Oh, you are a city girl, aren't you?" Mary smiled kindly.
"Haven't seen you with a sprig of alfalfa lately, either, Miss
Raised in a Mansion."
Mary laughed easily. "You know as well as I do that I didn't
move into the mansion until after my formative years."
"Which still doesn't answer my question," Lisa suspicioned a
tiny bit of evasiveness.
"Ever slopped a hog?"
"Does waiting tables suffice?"
"Close enough."
Lisa sat quietly for some moments. At this rate, she could've
entered a contemplative order, at least as far as the silence was
concerned.
"You okay?" Mary asked tentatively.
"Oh, sure. I'm fine. Really," Lisa nodded honestly.
"We can still change our minds," Mary went right to the heart of
the matter, in more ways than one. She loved this woman so
much that she could hear the unsaid.
"Is slopping hogs very hard?"
"Actually, there aren't any hogs. I was teasing about that."
Lisa tried unsuccessfully to hide her abundant relief. Wouldn't
matter. Mary was tuned in as usual.

124

"But maybe there are chickens?"

"Do they bite?"

"They peck."

"Hard?"

"You wear boots and heavy duty overalls and you don't feel a thing."

"And all you do is toss seeds at them, right?"

"You're getting the hang of it already," Mary patted Lisa's shoulder.

"So, it's a chicken farm? Do we sell eggs or chickens?"

"Probably neither right now. From what my mom said, there's not much left of anything."

"Well, what do we sell, then?" Lisa was back to her original question.

"My Aunt Bunny leased land to other farmers."

"You can do that?"

"Sure. You lease land to other people and they do the farming. Aunt Bunny was getting too old to do anything herself."

"What about the others?"

"I don't quite know what they were doing," Mary admitted. Lisa took the hand that Mary had been using to pat her shoulder and kissed it. Somehow, the fact that land was leased and no pigs needed slopping made this impending trip all the more palpable.


A couple hundred miles of flat, never-changing landscape only put a bit of a damper on the spirit. Mary, who had been at the homestead only too recently after the demise of Aunt Bunny, disembarked first. Lisa was mysteriously rooted in the seat of the car. At least she rolled down the window. Finally. After the swirling dust had subsided a little.

"You going to get out of the car, Sweetums?" Mary was leaning down to make eye contact.

"I'm Sweetums now?" Lisa leaned an elbow on the door frame.

"Just since we crossed the state line."

"Oh, so it's a Kansas term of endearment?"

"I'll look it up in the dictionary just as soon as we unpack. The operative word being, 'we.'"

"Do you know how rich you really are?" Lisa looked directly at Mary.

"Uh, well, no. Not really. Not exactly. The book value of a farm can be hard to pinpoint, wouldn't you think?"

"Oh, gee. I haven't owned a whole fucking huge farm lately so what would I know about book values on a couple gazillion acres of prime farm land in Kansas."

"If you don't get out of the car, I'm coming in after you."

"I haven't heard *that* line since my first date. With a guy."

Lisa stepped out on to the gravel driveway and stretched. Meanwhile, Mary grabbed a suitcase and led the way to the front door. She unlocked it with a key mailed to her by her mother, compliments of the court system, and stepped across the threshold. Her first gut instinct was to call the sheriff and report a robbery. A really big one. Then, common sense prevailed and she pondered calling animal control instead to get an update on any recent vulture activity. This place was picked cleaner than fish bones at a feline reunion. Lisa, who had no point of reference, was scanning the remains with a set jaw and philosophical eyes.

"Were they Amish?"

Mary shook her head and then laughed. Just a little. Anything to relieve the anger. Otherwise, she'd probably be hurling suitcases at the wall. Every stick of furniture was gone. The drapes had been removed along with the rods. Cupboard doors were taken off and all other kitchen fixtures were missing entirely. You've heard the saying, everything but the kitchen sink? Well, the kitchen sink was gone as well.

"Why would anyone take cupboard doors?" Mary asked out loud like it was a mystery weekend and this was the mystery.

"Firewood?" Lisa mused.

"Firewood?" Mary looked at Lisa.

"It sounded better than revenge."

"I think this goes way beyond revenge. You want a picture of a serious dysfunctional family, this is it," Mary had it all pretty well figured out.

"Well, there had better be a toilet in this place, or I'm going back to the car and checking into the nearest motel."

Lisa took a short, self-guided tour and returned in five minutes.

126

"Well?" Mary asked.

"We can stay. But we need to make a shopping list. Quickly."

"How quickly?"

"Let's just say that it was damn good luck that I had some Kleenex in my pocket."

"Quickly works for me. Let's go to the store right now."

"Shouldn't we lock up?" Lisa asked as she followed Mary out the door.

"You're afraid somebody's going to steal the toilet?"

"It would be our luck."

"Come on."

Mary was deeply silent during the first ten miles back into town. This gave Lisa time to scribble notes on the back of the last scrap of paper she had in her wallet. She would've saved it had they not been going directly to the grocery store.

"How's the list coming along?" Mary finally spoke.

"I put toilet paper right at the top."

"Good thinking. What else?"

"Uh, soap, coffee, coffee pot, towels, bread, something to put between bread…"

"Shit!" Mary muttered.

"Oh, I'm not sure that would be something we need to buy?"

Lisa got a case of the giggles. Maybe it was the dust infiltrating her brain.

"You think this is funny?"

"I don't feel the loss that you do, so it's all on the ridiculous side as far as I'm concerned."

"That's an interesting way of looking at it. Tell me more about this loss that I'm supposedly experiencing."

"The material loss is obvious, even to the casual observer. That's me."

"But I never owned that stuff to begin with."

"Then," Lisa the amateur psychologist continued, "there's the loss of all those golden childhood images where family was like Robin Hood. All for one and one for all."

"I think that was The Three Musketeers?"

"Whatever. They pretend in front of the children that everything is peachy rosy and then when you grow up, you realize that they hate each other and they've always hated each other."

"Is that why you never talk about your family?" Mary asked, suddenly aware that after all their time together, she hadn't probed much into Lisa's life history.

"What? Why?" Lisa's defense mechanism clicked into place. The sound was almost audible.

"Because they were like mine?" Mary opined, hoping to illicit a co-conspirator type response.

"When people can pretend so well to like other people, doesn't it make you wonder if they were, you know, pretending with you as well?"

"Don't you talk to your parents anymore?"

"They don't talk to me anymore."

"After you came out?"

Lisa only nodded, a gesture Mary caught out of the corner of her eye as she drove. Why was it that important information came out at fifty-five miles an hour?

"What else do we need at the store?" Lisa changed the subject back.

"Every damn thing. I'm calling my mom. Maybe she'll wire some money."

"I saved up some from tips."

"Enough to buy a bed?"

"Maybe a couple of sleeping bags?"

"I'm not sleeping in some damn bag."

"Oh, come on. We could pretend we are on some wonderful extended camping trip."

"How extended?"

"I can maybe get a job tomorrow?" Lisa offered.

"You're not getting a job. I'm calling my mother. Now, let's plan dinner."

"I love it when you get all authoritative."

"Doesn't count. You love everything I do," Mary winked.

"Darn, you found me out!"

"Mom said the diner in town is pretty good. Well, actually she said that Mitch said it was good. She went in one day while they were here for the funeral and ordered one of everything."

"Just one?" Lisa asked dryly.

"You want to eat first or shop first?"

"Let's eat!"

Mary should've known the answer all along. The way to Lisa's heart had always been through her stomach. They pulled into the parking lot of the diner, walked in, and seated themselves at the behest of the waitress. She took their drink orders of coffee and tea and recommended the chicken salad before buzzing off to another customer.

"I can see why Mitch ordered one of each. This all sounds delectable," Lisa commented readily.

"You're not going to do that, are you?"

The waitress came in at the last few words and asked, "Do what?"

"A friend of ours once ordered one of everything-"

"Oh yeah! We still talk about that! We used up almost all of our take-out containers that day. That means you know Aunt Bunny's relatives, doesn't it?"

"She's a real relative," Lisa ratted out Mary.

"Oh, so, you've seen the farmhouse, already?" the waitress was shaking her head sadly. Mary only nodded and then asked, "What have you heard about it?"

"I heard it was stripped clean. The whole town's been talkin about it."

She didn't say it out loud, but inside, Mary was saying words people learned in church. Like, "hell and damn," for instance.

"So, what are you going to do?" the waitress followed up.

"I'm having the chicken salad," Mary answered, slightly off subject.

"Me, too," Lisa handed over the menus. Having no further pending business, Jessie left.

"You're mad at me, aren't you?" Lisa asked when Mary was quiet for two entire minutes.

"I'm not mad at you! Why would I be mad at you?"

"Well, you don't seem so thrilled about being identified as a relative of your Aunt Bunny."

"I just need to get used to small-town mores. There are no more secrets from anybody. You live in Denver and your house is stripped clean and nobody hears about it but the cops. You live here and everybody hears about it."

"Particularly when you don't have curtains on the windows."

"Put those closer to the top of the list, will you?"

129

"Drapes are pretty expensive. And then we need the hardware. And probably some tools?"

"Thanks for the reminder. I'm calling Washington."

Mary pulled out her cell phone and dialed the Georgetown house. Mitch picked up.

"Hello?"

"Hi, Mitch. It's Mary."

"Well, hi! How are you? Did you get to the farm already?"

"Actually, we're in the diner in town. Is my mom there?"

"She's still at work. Is everything okay?"

"Well, yes and no," Mary fought hard to keep her emotions in check. Now was no time to let her guard down. If she did, the whole town would be talking about that by dinner.

"Are *you* okay?"

"I'm fine. Lisa's fine. The trip was fine."

"Okay, so what's *not* fine?"

"The farmhouse is kind of not so fine."

"Well, that's what had your mother concerned. Was it dusty?"

"Dust is the least of our problems."

"What else?"

Mary went through the whole list of what elses. Mitch whistled softly.

"My sentiments exactly," Mary exhaled slowly.

"So, what are you going to do?"

"A total redecoration, I guess?"

It didn't take Mitch long to figure out the quandary. "Why don't I send you some money to start with."

"I thought I'd ask my mom."

"Oh, let's not worry her about that right now. I'll wire some money today and then maybe later, your mom can kick in something."

"You're not planning on telling her this anytime soon, are you?"

"She's working really hard right now. This kind of news can wait, don't you think?"

"I'll trust your judgment."

"Do you need a hotel room for the night? I can call and guarantee the suite at that nice place in town? It has room service..."

Mary glanced over at Lisa. "That would be really nice." Mary admitted.

"Consider it done. Enjoy your evening and then your money should be there by tomorrow."

"We really appreciate this."

"Hey, no problem! I look forward to visiting when you get everything back together."

"You two are first on the list."

Lisa, who had only heard Mary's side of the conversation, had still gleaned the part about secrecy right off the bat.

"She's not telling the Senator about this, is she?"

"I'm sure she will in due time."

"Mitch never did like to stir the waters too much."

"She's reserving a hotel room for us tonight."

"Isn't that sweet of her!"

"Yes, it is. She's a sweet woman."

They finished lunch, and then drove to the hardware store in the middle of Main Street. It wouldn't do any good to buy drapes until they bought a tape measurer. Along the way, they picked up a few other essential tools, like a hammer and a really nice set of screwdrivers. Lisa picked them out. She just had such a way with this sort of thing. Mary watched as Lisa covetously eyed a table saw. Maybe Mary could budget the money Mitch was sending to squeeze out the purchase. But, first things first, and that included a trip to the dry goods store. That's what it was called when Mary was a little girl and the name stuck. Here was the place where they could pick up a few things for now and get a catalog for future splurges. Not that they couldn't do that online eventually. After they could afford a computer. So, they worked the way down the list, buying only what they needed to survive. Their trip to the grocery store was put on hold for the sake of the perishables.

The hotel suite was ready when they got there, a marvelous treat after such a tiring day. They checked in, ate dinner and fell asleep to the muted sounds of a small town. Had it not been for the jangling of the telephone, Mary might very well have slept past the checkout time.

"Hello?"

131

"Is this the younger Ms. Fairbanks?"

Mary had to think the question over.

"You could say that, I guess?"

"This is Mr. Philbin."

"Do I know you, Mr. Philbin?" she asked, without further inquiry as to whether he was the "younger" of his last name as well.

"Tom Philbin, president of the bank."

"Oh, of course," Mary acted like this made perfect sense, which it didn't prior to a strong cup of coffee.

"I got a call from a friend of yours, a Ms. Tanner?"

"Mitch."

"Right. Well, she wanted to open an account with us for you and you would need to come down here at your convenience and sign some papers."

"I see."

"So, when would be a good time?"

"What time is it now?" Mary figured that that was as good a question as any.

"It's nine-fifteen!"

"We'll be there about ten."

"Fine, fine, I'll work on the forms so everything will be ready when you get here."

"Okay, well, thanks." Mary hung up in the middle of his effusive, "Have a nice day!"

"Who was that?" Lisa asked with barely-opened mouth and still-shut eyes."

"The bank president," Mary patted Lisa on her thigh. "We need to get up. We're supposed to be there by ten."

"A.M. or P.M.?"

"A.M."

"I'll never make it. Go on, save yourself," Lisa turned over to resume her slumber.

"Oh, now. Where's your home town spirit?" Mary cuddled up to her. They were spooning like a couple of old marrieds.

"Gone with the wind."

"A little too south, me thinks. Come with me and afterwards, I'll buy you some *pliers*."

"The set of three with the needlenose?" Lisa was now thinking, which meant she was more awake.

"The set of three," Mary repeated with reverence.

"With the leather holder?" Lisa figured she'd push her luck.

"You're into leather now?" Mary was kissing her shoulder.

"Only where my tools are concerned."

Mary rolled out of bed and took first turn in the bathroom. Lisa was up and about soon after and they made their appointment with seven minutes to spare. Wonder of wonders, they were shown right in like the prodigal daughters.

"I'm sorry to keep you waiting, Ms. Fairbanks," Mr. Philbin had his hand stretched out for the shaking. Mary took her share of pumping before introducing Lisa. He indicated two chairs for them and waited until they were seated before depositing his ample frame in the standard leather banker's chair.

"I hope this sudden meeting wasn't too much of an inconvenience."

"Not at all," Mary promised.

"Let's have some coffee or tea? And maybe some Danish?"

He pushed some magic button on his desk and a woman dressed like an airline stewardess appeared with a tray of goodies. This could explain Mr. Philbin's girth. Everyone was painfully polite as they ate small bites of pastry and washed it down with a brew that made each cup of coffee taste like two combined.

"So, you said you had a paper for me to sign?" Mary had things on her list and it made her restless.

"Actually, there will be a few papers to sign, due to the amount of money involved."

"What do you mean?"

"Well, our accounts are Federally insured for $100,000 as you know, so in order to exercise caution, we opened several accounts. Of course."

"Of course."

Mary looked over at Lisa, who was on her second piece of cherry-filled Danish. She shrugged her shoulders.

"And how many accounts are we talking about?"

"A dozen."

"A dozen?" Mary repeated, squeezing all surprise out of her voice. It wasn't easy. "Sounds like we're talking about donuts."

"Of course, we can rearrange the funds to your specifications at a later time, but for now, we have the paperwork set up so that each account has approximately $ 83,333.33."

"Approximately," Lisa muttered.

"And then, as the accounts accrue interest, you will want to shift the funds as you see fit, if you haven't already spent the money," he laughed a banker laugh.

Then, with a flourish, he produced a stack of paperwork. Mary hurried through the process and before Lisa could polish off the entire selection of bakery items, they were out the door with a brand new set of savings passbooks and one checking account. Their checks were temporary, but Mr. Philbin's last words were, "If you have any trouble cashing those, just have them call me *personally*!"

"Mitch went way overboard," Mary announced in the car. She had just been sitting in it, not even thinking about starting the engine.

"That's always been her style."

"We can't keep all this money."

"I agree, but we need to be careful and not hurt her feelings."

"So, we'll hold most of it in escrow and spend only what we need to spend."

"Good plan. Let's go get those pliers."

They didn't stop there. After the hardware store, they went to a furniture store and arranged delivery of a bed, two chairs and a table. The grocery store was next and then home to begin the rebuilding process.

"I know what we forgot," Mary said as they stepped through the front door.

"I could make many guesses. Give me a clue."

"A phone. I wanted to get something to plug into the wall."

"Tomorrow will be soon enough to hear a phone ringing."

"My main reason was to be able to call in a catalog order."

"Use your cell phone. You'll probably need it to get phone service turned back on anyway."

"I'll do that right now. Can you start unloading the groceries?"

"It's first on my list of chores."

They wandered into different rooms, needing some time away from each other. Mary arranged for phone service, ordered a table saw for Lisa and then took a stroll around the grounds to see if there was any more painfully apparent damage to the homestead. Things seemed in pretty good shape, although all the livestock was gone. She leaned on the split-rail fence and pondered the next logical steps in her life. She must have pondered for a long time, for soon, Lisa was at her side.

"My God, I wouldn't have believed it if I hadn't seen it for myself," Lisa said.

Mary, fearing that it was more bad news about the house, turned to look at her.

"You're even more beautiful here in Kansas."

Mary's eyes narrowed in a somewhat playful way. "Flattery will get you anywhere!" she promised as she pulled her close.

"That's nice to know, but I'll have to take a rain check. The guys are here with the furniture and they need your signature."

"You want a horse?" Mary asked, totally off the subject, like she hadn't even been paying attention.

"Gee, can I think about it?"

"You need to think about a horse?"

"Just the color. Come on. These guys are going to be shifting from foot to foot if you don't get in there."

Mary wouldn't let go of Lisa's hand but allowed herself to be pulled back into the house. They picked one room for their master bedroom and had the men set up the bed as they scoped out the dining room. The table and two chairs would fill up about one-fourth of the space. What the hell, they weren't going to have any state dinners soon. There were bigger problems to solve, for instance, how were they going to cook without a stove and keep food for more than a day without a refrigerator. Good thing they were getting phone service soon. This was going to take some doing.

Whoever these furniture guys were, they sure were efficient and polite. They were also not one bit surprised that the farmhouse had been stripped. Maybe they supped at the diner between deliveries. Mary signed the paperwork, something she was getting good at, and they headed off.

"It's already beginning to feel like home," Lisa smiled contentedly.

"It's a start."

"A bed is a good start. A bed is a great start in fact!"

Lisa waited for a reaction, any reaction, from Mary. The house still had a solemn effect on her, and for a moment, Lisa wondered how long this was going to last.

"It is a nice bed," Mary finally agreed.

"I'll go put those new sheets on it."

"We need a washer and dryer," Mary began formulating the list anew. "Do you have any idea how much all this is going to cost to restore this place?"

"Hey," Lisa said, "Let's just get the basics and worry about everything else later."

"You're right. Why don't you let me help you with those sheets?"

They exchanged knowing looks. Now, it felt like home.

Chapter 14

Mitch was only about ten minutes late for her meeting with Jane. Transferring a million dollars didn't crimp her schedule nearly as much as one would imagine. Today was a big day for the budding entrepreneurs. They were having the first of several walk-throughs of their newly-acquired restaurant property. Gone was Wagner's. One day, hopefully not too far in the future, Fairbanks's would open in its place. Right now, they were taking a good long look at the plumbing. Jane was just shaking her head as she surveyed the ladies room.

"This has just all got to go," she said to Mitch.

"I agree. Which walls are we tearing out?"

"That one," Jane pointed with authority.

Mitch closed her eyes to envision the change.

"Can we move that wall, too?" Mitch indicated an adjoining wall.

"It's your place. You can do anything you want."

"Have you read the building codes lately?" Mitch chuckled.

"You can do anything within the law," Jane amended her statement.

"I want a bigger bathroom. This is too claustrophobic besides being dirt-fence ugly. You can't get a wheelchair in here without a navigational system and a prayer."

"Okay."

"Same with the men's room."

"Okay," Jane started making notes on a legal pad.

"And this isn't just my place," Mitch said belatedly.

"You bought it."

"Maybe so, but you're the one who's going to put us on the map."

"Let's look at the kitchen."

They walked the expanse of the restaurant, now eerily empty, and stood side by side at the entrance to the kitchen. The full impact of the job ahead was just beginning to sink in.

"Watch out. The floor's still slick from grease."

"How in the hell did this place ever pass inspection?" Mitch asked rhetorically as she surveyed the grimy walls and mold-spotted areas. If this was a rock, it would look like moss.

"Let's just say that certain rogue inspectors won't be making any under-the-table profits from us."

"Or anyone else for that matter. We're running a totally honest establishment. No mob. No drugs. No sex."

"It's going to be no nothing if we don't get this kitchen in shape."

They tried at first to divide the thought process into three segments: things to keep, things to replace, and things to repair. That idea was quickly scuttled as they found so much of the equipment totally unsatisfactory.

"Should we just have a garage sale?"

"There has to be a salvage company in the area."

"Probably where they got some of this stuff in the first place!"

"I'll call around. Let's check the dining area again."

An area that Mitch had seen on several occasions bore little resemblance now to those memories. It's true that an area looks larger when it's vacant, but even in this state, the place seemed small.

"We need to raise the ceiling," Jane explained.

"Can we do that?"

"Sure. It's one of those suspended deals. A lot of restaurants put them in to make the room cozy."

"I see. I'm glad we can change it."

"Which means a lot of other changes as well."

"I don't mind that. Let's do it right the first time."

"And it will cost a little more…"

"It's worth it to me. I won't be able to spend hours here unless I feel comfortable."

"Okay. Let's run the changes past our contractor."

"First thing tomorrow?"

"Whenever he can be at a meeting. I'll call and set up a time."

"Call me at home when you find out."

"Okay."

Mitch headed home to the Georgetown residence. Reb was still at work so she took a shower and started dinner. With luck, the gorgeous Senator would be home at a decent hour. Mitch marinated fresh tuna in a mixture of soy sauce, garlic and minced ginger. She debated between white and brown rice and the healthy side won out. Her compromise was lost on the green beans, to which she added ham for flavoring. This concoction bubbled happily along until Mitch heard the van in the driveway. Before going to the door, Mitch started the heat under the rice. Reb was already wheeling up the walkway and fairly zoomed through the open door.

"Something smells wonderful."

"Maybe it's me?" Mitch grinned.

"Did you put pork fat behind your ears?"

"You found out my secret!" Mitch feigned dismay.

"And what else are you cooking?"

"Tuna and rice."

"Ah, yes. Ginger. My favorite aphrodisiac," Reb sighed.

"You and the Gingerbread Man!"

"Did Mary call?" Reb asked over her shoulder as she wheeled into the kitchen.

"Yes," Mitch answered quickly. Maybe too quickly.

"Everything okay?"

"Fine."

"They got there?" Reb continued the questioning and she poured herself a tonic water.

"They are there."

"I think I'll give them a call."

"Good idea, unless…"

"Unless what?"

"You know how it is in a new home."

"How is it?" Reb was lost.

"They're probably *making the bed.*"

"Oh, *that.* Well, when is a good time to call?"

"After dinner. I'm turning on the broiler."

"You go and broil. I can't imagine calling after dinner would be any better than now. I'm dialing."

Reb punched in the number of Mary's cell phone and let it ring ten whole times before Mary picked up.

"Hello!"

"Hi! You sound out of breath."

"I was in the north forty," Mary laughed easily.

"I see. So, you got to the house?"

"We checked in with Mitch."

139

"Yes, she finally got around to telling me. And how was the house?"

"Oh, it's a little bit on the dusty side, but Lisa and I are working on it."

Mary hoped it all sounded so honest. Well, it *was* the truth.

"Do me a favor?"

"If I can?"

"Check to see if your Aunt Bunny's bed is in good shape."

"In good shape?"

"Well, it has some sentimental value."

"I see. You know, I think it may have had some value to Aunt BeBe. I think she might have taken it with her," Mary said this and then held her breath.

"Oh, okay. Well, it isn't worth fighting over. So, where are you sleeping?"

Mary didn't hesitate with her answer. "With Lisa."

Reb thought it over and then refrained from delving further.

"Well, let me know when it's safe to visit."

"Uh, sure, okay. Give us a little while…"

"We will, dear. Bye."

Reb hung up and then looked in Mitch's general direction. She appeared to be minding her own business.

"I don't think we should barge in on the newlyweds for a while," she stated as she munched on a carrot stick.

"Remember when we were like that?" Mitch smiled.

"I don't remember changing. I still love our private time together."

"Me, too."

"So, what did you and Jane do today?"

"We waved our arms around a lot."

"Conducting a symphony?"

"More like a kazoo band. There is so much work to be done."

"And you're just the woman to do it. When do you expect to have the grand opening again?"

"It's weeks and weeks away."

"You want some advice?"

"Sure."

"Savor every day. This is a project you've been wanting to do for a long time."

"You're right. Deep down, I'm loving this, but it will take me away from you more than I'm used to."

"We'll just have to make the best of the time we have together."

"Don't we always?"

"You haven't done a thorough skin check on me in days."

"I'll do that right after dinner," Mitch served up the gourmet meal. They ate slowly, enjoying the calm evening. Afterwards, the promise of a skin check was delivered on by Mitch, who took her sweet time through the process. She never skimped on this important task.

"I can tell you've been taking good care of yourself," Mitch settled in beside her in the bed.

"I need to spend more time in the gym."

"Let me know when you want to go. I could use a few extra sit-ups myself."

"You are in great shape," Reb stroked Mitch's abdomen. It was getting flatter and tighter, due mostly to all the many ways Mitch found to stay out of the refrigerator. How she was going to manage this feat when the restaurant opened up was anyone's guess. Meanwhile, Rebecca's hand moved lower. It was deliciously distracting and Mitch was quick to respond. Well, not *quick*.

"Every time you touch me, I'm helpless. You know that, don't you?"

"I do. And that's why I enjoy it."

Mitch grew silent. She would've given anything if Reb could feel this way again. It had taken Mitch a while to get over the guilt of being the only one who could still have an orgasm, but once she had, it helped her concentrate on new ways to pleasure Reb as well. They would gladly put their relationship up against anyone else's, and yet, they weren't married. Right now, Mitch didn't want to think about it. Another day, maybe. If they ever decided to have children, she would wish for them more security, but they weren't starting a family right now. Maybe never, with Reb in a wheelchair and Mitch knee deep in helping everyone else get on their feet. And asking Mary to lie about it until further notice.

"Did I do something wrong?" Reb asked. She had been watching Mitch carefully.

141

"Sorry," Mitch stirred from her reverie. "What?"

"You sort of drifted away, both mentally and physically. Is something wrong?"

"No."

"There is something bothering you. Why can't you tell me what it is?"

"Because I never want to trouble you with things that you really can't do much about."

"I'm a United States Senator. The list of things I can't do much about is very short," Reb was caught up in her own private power trip.

"Well, okay then, can you make your sister give back all the stuff she took out of the farmhouse?"

"What on earth are you talking about?"

"Well, when Mary and Lisa got to the place, not only was Aunt Bunny's bed gone, but every other bed. And appliance. And drape. And stick of furniture…"

"She wasn't supposed to do that! All that stuff belongs to the estate. I'm calling the lawyer," Reb was just about to reach the phone when Mitch pulled her back.

"Don't call the lawyer. It's after dinner, for God's sake."

"I'm calling him first thing tomorrow!"

"Don't do that," Mitch said quietly.

"Why not?"

"If Aunt BeBe wants that stuff, I think she should have it. Maybe it has a lot of sentimental value for her."

"You think she's emotionally attached to a refrigerator?"

"It happened to me once."

Reb stopped to think about the problem. "So, what are Mary and Lisa sleeping on?"

"Well, they stayed the first night in a hotel and then I wired them some money to get a few things."

"How much money?"

"Enough to buy the essentials. You know, a bed, a refrigerator, curtain rods."

"She took the curtain rods?"

"I guess."

"The *curtain rods*?"

142

"Mary will pick out new ones. Lisa's really good at that sort of thing, too."

"How much?"

"How good is she at that? Well, when we were setting up housekeeping-"

"I meant how much money?"

"Oh, we're back to that," Mitch had hoped she had forgotten.

"Yes, we are back to that."

"I think of Mary as my own child, you know."

"I know."

"And parents want their children to have every advantage."

"How much advantage?"

Mitch took loving, gentle, yet firm hold of Rebecca. Especially her hands.

"A million dollars' worth."

"A million dollars!" Reb was able to wrestle free and was almost sitting up by now.

"Not enough?" Mitch grimaced.

"Do you have any idea how many curtain rods you can buy for a million dollars?"

"Gee, if I'd known there was going to be a math test, I would've brought my calculator to bed with me."

"Don't take that tone with me."

"I wouldn't be taking this tone if you didn't go off the deep end over curtain rods."

"It isn't the curtain rods that are at issue here. You gave Mary a million dollars."

"I figured she was good for it."

"And you didn't think to run the idea by me first?"

"Why should I?"

"If I was going to give away a million dollars, I'd talk to you about it first."

"Why?"

"Why! Because it would be the right thing to do!"

"So, you think that what I did was wrong?"

"Why did you send so much?" Reb was getting calmer.

"I wanted them to be respected in town. And besides, they need too much stuff to spend time going bargain shopping. From what I understand, the only thing left in the whole house was a toilet."

"A toilet?"

"I think you're mad at your sister and you're taking it out on me."

"I just wish you'd tell me things in a timely manner."

"Why? So you can get all worked up in a timely manner?"

"Am I that hard to deal with?" Reb was now laying back down and cooling off.

"You are doing a job that is so stressful and so important that I don't want to load you up with other problems. Especially not ones that can be fixed with money. I think we should give Mary and Lisa a month and then invite ourselves to dinner. You know, see what they've done with the place."

Reb thought this over.

"I appreciate everything you have done, from the first day we met until right this minute."

"I haven't done anything right this minute."

Reb tousled Mitch's hair.

"The night is still young."

Chapter 15

As quiet as the Goldstein household was, Silver Smith hadn't rested easy until the security system was installed. It was a real system, not one of those fake deals where people just put shiny-looking tape on their windows. No, sir. This was the real deal. Some sort of beeper beeped whenever a door or window was opened. Max had set it off a good half a dozen times before getting the hang of it. Rose was edgy, which made getting the system seem counter productive at first. But since there hadn't been any new letters, they were now in a cautious holding pattern. Every morning, Silver would inspect the premises, eat breakfast, shop with Rose, come home, inspect the premises, monitor Rose's activities, eat dinner, play cards with Max, get the mail, do any other necessary chores and then rest after battening down the hatches for the night. A visit by Trish and Robbie was a welcome event.

"Hello, you two!" Rose fairly ran to the door to greet them. Silver refrained from frisking them. After all, they were paying the bill. Rose, Max, Trish and Robbie all settled down to a meal while Silver took a well-deserved nap. It always took her a while to get used to new surroundings, but she still slept with her gun close by.

Meanwhile, Rose chatted on and on to Robbie mostly, and Trish somewhat, until she had run clear out of things to say. It took a while. It was more than obvious that most of the conversation was borne out of nervousness.

"Don't get me wrong," Rose started to explain clear out of the blue, "I like Ms. Smith. She's really very nice. Really."

"But?" Robbie prompted.

"And I know you only have my best interests at heart," Rose's voice dropped to a whisper.

"What's on your mind, Rose?" Trish asked genuinely.

"I don't know how much more bodyguarding I can take."

"But, you said you like her, right?"

"Oh, yes! She's wonderful. A lovely young woman. And a wonderful house guest."

"But you still feel uncomfortable with the protection?"

"She practically walks ahead of me to check for land mines."

"Well, maybe it won't last much longer. Haven't they got any leads?"

"Cleveland is a big place. This could take weeks."

The conversation sort of ground to a halt, so Max started another thread about sports. When Silver awoke, she joined them for coffee and cake. If nothing else, this gig had great food. Overall, things didn't seem too oppressive, even with a loaded 22 on the table. But then again, Trish and Robbie didn't have to live this way day after day. They stayed longer than they had planned and Trish was pensive on the drive back home.

"What are you thinking?" Robbie asked a couple miles from home.

"I'm thinking that whoever is sending letters to your mother spends about a dollar a month and we're out ten thousand and your mom is still miserable."

"There's not much we can do..." Robbie trailed off.

"There's always something we can do. All I have to do is figure out what."

"Do you even have a starting point?"

"I've been researching people who were spies for our side in World War II. I can call one of them and see what they know."

"Are there any in Colorado?"

"There's one in New Jersey, one in Florida and one in Hawaii."

"Let me guess. The best lead is the one in New Jersey."

"How did you know?"

"Because Florida and Hawaii are so nice this time of year."

"You'll love New Jersey. It is the Garden State."

"Make the call the minute we get home."

Chapter 16

Lisa looked on as the two men unloaded a truck for the third time this week. It wasn't the third time they had unloaded this particular truck, but rather the third truckload of stuff to be delivered this week. Despite the fact that it seemed as though they were out in the middle of nowhere, things moved quickly. The first truck had held the bed, table and chairs. A second truck brought a refrigerator, washer, dryer, bathroom and kitchen sinks and a dishwasher. So, whatever was in this third truck piqued Lisa's interest, for she knew of no other pending deliveries.
Mary came up behind her and asked, innocently enough, "What's this?"
Lisa had watched her facial expression and knew that Mary was totally guilty of whatever was going on.
"Why don't you tell me?"
"What makes you think I would know?" Ms. Angelic asked back.
"It says on the box that it's a table saw."
"Oh that! Well, I thought it would come in handy. We could make new doors for all the cabinets."
"And about a hundred other things we need as well, but where can we set it up so the sawdust doesn't bother us?"
"I hadn't thought about that."
The delivery men were on the same line of thought.
"Where d'ya want this, lady?"
"How about the front porch?" Mary offered her idea.
"If it was my table saw, I wouldn't leave it out on the front porch," the larger of the two men answered thoughtfully.
"Back porch?" Lisa asked.
"Same problem. Anybody with a truck would have hisself a new saw."
"You think someone would steal it? Out here in the wilds of Kansas."
"Kansas has its fair share of thievery," the smaller man remarked readily.
"Well, bring it on in the house and we'll go from there," Mary sighed philosophically. The contraption was heavy enough to require at least two people to shuffle it from place to place, so

they decided to set it up in the empty bedroom at the back of the house.  As Lisa fiddled with the accessories, Mary started another shopping list, beginning with a heavy-duty canister vacuum to keep the sawdust under control.  Other things that came to mind included a couch, a TV set, and a computer.  And, of course, wood for Lisa.  As she took a moment to reflect on other ideas, she glanced out the window.  Not that it was terribly out of the ordinary, but a car was driving slowly down the street, as if the driver was checking for signs of occupancy.  Mary made a point to stand up and be visible and then walked through the house to check on Lisa.  She was attaching a blade to the saw, preparing for a test run.

"How's it going?"

"I'm being overly cautious.  A table saw is nothing to fool around with."

"Good plan."

"But I'll need some wood."

"I put it on the shopping list.  You want to go now?"

"In a while.  Why?"

"We just have a curious passer by."

"Really?"

"Maybe somebody's lost.  I'll go check again."

"I'll go with you.  Maybe it's the welcome wagon."

They walked to the front porch, but no one was out there.

"I guess they found their way," Lisa surmised.  "You still want to go shopping?"

"You need wood, don't you?"

"Let's go."

They locked up the house and headed into town.  After lunch at the diner, they went to the hardware store, where they were instantly recognized by the manager.  Lisa selected enough lumber to get a good start on a bookcase and cabinet doors and then conferred with Mary on a vacuum.  It was all paid for and what didn't fit in the car was set up for delivery later in the day.  With any luck, they would have several hours of daylight to begin the repairs.  It was only with a mild curiosity that they noticed a car close to the house when they arrived home.  As they pulled up in their driveway, several people got out of the car and opened the trunk.  In two minutes, they had formed an

148

orderly picket line, holding signs that said, "Citizens United for Morality," and other such sentiments.

"So much for the welcome wagon," Lisa shrugged her shoulders as she carried in a load of lumber. Mary followed with the vacuum and then watched the group for a few minutes from drapeless windows.

"I'm putting curtain rods and drapes on the top of the list."

"Don't do it on my account," Lisa remarked matter-of-factly.

"What do you mean?"

"I don't care if they can see in and I, for one, want an unrestricted view of them. Besides, they are in the front yard. If we want privacy, we'll sit out on the back porch."

"I wonder if what they're doing is legal?"

"You mean, trespassing?"

"Maybe I could call the sheriff."

"You could, but my guess is that this group knows what is legal and what isn't."

"You're probably right. I never did understand why Aunt Bunny built the farmhouse so close to the property line."

"She probably wanted access to the road. I'm sure they measure snow by the foot around here."

"How long do you suppose they'll be out there?"

Lisa didn't know what answer Mary was asking about. Did she want to know how long today or how long period?

"It wasn't that hard a question, was it?" Mary checked back after the silence.

"Just until dark, I'm sure. They have dinners to eat as well."

Mary helped Lisa carry in the rest of the wood and watched with safety goggles as Lisa made expert cut after expert cut on the boards. Truly, Lisa had a knack for this. She would have a sturdy bookcase put together before they had books. Maybe they could get a library card and fill it with loaners. The rest of the lumber arrived before nightfall and Mary and Lisa worked through midnight before going to bed.

The next morning, bright and early, another car arrived soon after breakfast and the picketing started up all over again. There were a few more participants, but Mary spotted a couple of familiars as well.

"Looks like we have company, again," Lisa observed calmly as she continued working on the bookcase.

"Do you think the wood we got for the cabinet doors matches the cabinets?" Mary asked.

"It's about as close as I could guess. Do you like what's already up there?"

Mary gave it a good, long look. Once she had, she realized just how ratty it had become over the years. Why BeBe had bothered to take the doors was anyone's guess.

"How hard would it be to redo the entire kitchen?"

Maybe it was just her imagination, but she thought she saw a glimmer of pure joy in Lisa's eye.

"I think we could manage that," Lisa nodded slowly, already making mental calculations.

"Now, what kind of wood shall we use?"

"How about knotty pine?"

"How 'knotty?'" Lisa winked.

"Oh, not too 'knotty.'" Mary indicated out the window.

"What? You don't want to offend the Citizens United for Morality patrol?"

"They must be the same group who showed up for Aunt Bunny's funeral."

"I suspect so. How many anti-gay groups could Kansas possibly be famous for, after all?"

"Hopefully only one."

"I can think of one more thing to put on our master shopping list."

"What?"

"One of those really nice patio furniture sets with the round table and umbrella."

"I would love one of those," Mary nodded.

"Well, then, we'd better buy two sets."

"Two?"

"I was thinking of our company first."

"Why buy a set for them?"

"Because the weather can be ominous out here in Kansas. Besides, I wouldn't want any of them to have sun stroke or something worse. We'd be saving ourselves the trouble of calling the paramedics every time something happened."

150

"Mitch had them throw the food she offered them on the ground. What do you suppose they would do to patio furniture?"

"That doesn't concern me. We can only show them how to be hospitable. How they react is their problem."

Mary and Lisa spent a companionable day removing the old kitchen cabinets from the walls. Now, instead of having old, dingy cabinets, they now had kitchen walls that appeared to have broken out with a case of oversized rectangular measles. The contrast between where the cabinets had been and not was striking.

"I'm really glad that we did this!" Mary exclaimed. "I had no idea how faded the walls had become."

"Looks like we have our work cut out for us. We'll need to scrub and repaint everything."

"This is turning into quite a project. I'm glad now that Mitch sent substantial funding."

"She has indeed come to our rescue."

"First thing tomorrow, let's go into town and pick up some paint swatches from the hardware store."

"And a couple gallons of some type of cleaning solution."

"And a mop."

"And some rags."

"And a couple of ladders."

"And a couple of buckets."

"The people who run the hardware store are going to be our new best friends."

"Let's not forget rubber gloves."

"What should we do with the old cabinets?"

"Let's put them out on the back porch. Maybe we'll get lucky and someone will steal them."

"We should be so lucky!"

At dusk, the GHF patrol broke camp and went home, leaving Mary and Lisa alone to enjoy the evening. Their day of hard labor had left them dusty and grimy, so they took turns helping each other wash up using only the supplies they had on hand and several buckets of water. It was a slow process, but anytime these two engaged in physical contact, it was anything but

151

tedious. When they weren't kissing, they were giggling. Now, *this* was Mary's idea of a camping trip.

"I'm still putting a bathtub on the list," Lisa remarked later in bed.

"It would help to soak away sore muscles."

"And we're going to have our share of those."

"Beginning tomorrow morning."

They were quiet for a while, on the verge of sleep, when Mary stated quietly, "Now I know we love each other."

Lisa thought about it. "Why now?"

"Because if we didn't love each other, this would be intolerable."

They held hands until they went to sleep.

Lisa groaned. A night's worth of soreness had crept into her shoulders and she felt its grip as she turned over in bed. Mary was up and the smell of strong coffee wafted from the kitchen. It enticed Lisa out of bed and she wandered out in her jammies. Mary was drinking a cup of coffee at the table.

"Good morning," Lisa said cheerfully, in spite of her physical condition.

"You might want to put your clothes on," Mary answered back.

"Why?"

"We have company again."

Lisa checked out the window. There must have been two carloads out this morning.

"Don't you think I'm decent in my pajamas?"

"I do. But then again, I think you're decent in anything."

"I'm glad you find me so upstanding," Lisa brought her coffee to the table.

"You'd think they would have better things to do," Mary was beginning to sound amazed.

"Gimme a kiss," Lisa leaned forward.

Mary didn't.

"I don't want to give them the satisfaction."

"And so, no more good-morning kisses?"

"Not in front of an audience!"

Lisa leaned back and studied Mary for so long that Mary felt the need to defend herself.

"You think I'm caving in, don't you?"

152

"I don't really know what you're doing unless you talk to me about it."

"If we kiss in front of them, that just gives them more ammunition."

"To do what? Go report on the big, bad lesbians on Aunt Bunny's farm? Who's going to listen to them?"

"The whole town, for starters."

"And so what? Don't you think the whole town already knows?" Lisa made the obvious point.

"I guess so."

"And we still seem pretty popular in town."

"Our patronage is popular."

"There's nothing like commerce to keep the lines open. Let's be sure to thank Mitch out of earshot of your mother."

"Let's pick up a phone today and give the phone service a whirl."

"Then we can get a computer and shop online for what they don't have in town."

"Good thinking. But before we do that, come closer."

"Why?"

"For your good-morning kiss, of course."

Lisa followed orders well and lingered over the moment. If people's eyes had popped out of their heads and were rolling around on the ground, Mary didn't notice. She was too busy getting ready for their daily trip into town. Nobody waved any sort of fond farewells as Mary and Lisa took off down the road, and the knot of people was a mere speck as they drove up and over a small hill. Out of sight, out of mind.

"I'm hungry," Lisa announced before they were halfway there.

"We forgot to eat breakfast."

"I'll buy you a stack of blueberry pancakes at the diner," Lisa offered.

"With a side of bacon?"

"With a side of anything you want," Lisa ran her hand up and down Mary's thigh.

"Save that for later," Mary twinkled good naturedly.

"Apres drapes?"

"Apres dinner!"

It wasn't as if they had their very own table at the diner, but they had sat in the same place before. Jessie put coffee in front of them without asking and stood waiting for their order like she knew they had already decided.

"I'll have the-" Mary started to say.

"Is it true what they're saying?" Jessie shoe-horned in her first question.

"Is what true?" Mary asked.

"That those *people* are out there?"

It would've been snide to comment on just how "out there" the visitors really were, so Mary just nodded.

"Well, what are they *doing*?"

"Walking back and forth," Lisa replied succinctly.

"Well, you *think* they'd have *something* better to do with their time! You made up your mind what you're havin?"

"I'd like the blueberry pancakes."

"I'll bring you a tall stack for the price of a short one."

"Don't forget, you wanted a side of bacon as well," Lisa reminded with just a hint of a smile.

"It's on the house. What else?"

"A cheese omelet for me, thanks," Lisa added.

"Biscuits are fresh. I'll bring you a couple to taste. Tell me if they're any good, ya know," she cracked her gum and winked at the same time. Her synchronicity was superb.

"I think she likes you," Mary smiled sweetly. "I bet she doesn't let just anybody taste her biscuits. Ya know."

"Now, you know I'm not a bakery sort of girl," Lisa blushed just a tad.

"Oh, yeah, right!" Mary teased and then turned serious, "We are the talk of the town."

"Seems so, but it's not all bad. You're getting free pancakes and I'm getting a taste of…small town life."

Breakfast arrived without delay. Their order had been put at the top of the stack. Everything was wonderful. Especially the biscuits. Lisa raved about them to Jessie when she brought extra jam and butter. And more coffee. And more syrup. And more of everything but a check. They ate until their hunger was a distant memory and left enough money on the table to cover the still-absent check and a generous tip. Their next stop, the hardware store, was equally fruitful. The man in charge of plumbing answered all their questions about showers, bathtubs and Jacuzzis and offered to come all the way out to the farm to size up the situation free of charge.

"I'm not sure we're quite ready for inspection," Mary grimaced a bit.

"Oh heck, I've seen stuff you wouldn't believe." he assured her jovially. "Flood damage, tornado damage, renter damage. Hard to say which can be worse. Nuthin shocks me. Been in the business thirty-two years."

"I see."

"So, you want me out there this afternoon?"

All salient information about Mary and Lisa had leaked out by now, apparently including their bank balance.

"I'd hate to have you drive all that way just to look. Why don't we pick out a tub that you think will work and install it?"

"Tell ya what. I'll bring two or three and check your pipes as well. If anything's busted, I'll call Charlie. He's an *honest* plumber." He said the last sentence like it was considered a contradiction in terms.

"But if you bring so many bathtubs, you won't have room for all the other stuff we need!" Lisa was beginning to enjoy this.

"What else is on your list?"

Between Lisa and Mary, they mentioned enough items to cause his brow to furrow.

"I can get Buster to help out."

"He won't mind?" Mary asked.

"His wife'll be thrilled."

"That's all that matters!" Lisa nodded like she understood this all too well. The appointment was set for three o'clock.

Then, Lisa insisted on another trip to the grocery store.

"We're having two gentleman dropping by the house at tea time. Trust me, we're going to need a couple of six packs and a big bag of pretzels."

"I sincerely hope you're thinking about grape soda rather than beer. I don't want two inebriated handymen zigzagging down that dirt road after dark."

"They won't be there after dark, and yes, I will buy soda. And beer for me."

They barely got back to the house in time to ice down the pop and fix some snacks. At two-thirty, two trucks came barreling down the road and stopped rather suddenly right beside the protestors. A plume of dust swirled around. Mary went out to the gate and opened it for them. They pulled onto the property and slowed to a more gentle stop close to the house. Jeb, the man from the hardware store, introduced Buster. He was a round, grizzled man with one gold tooth and another missing entirely. But overall, he was clean and shy. Mrs. Buster could've done a whole lot worse for herself.

Mary showed them the main water shutoff and they began to fiddle with the bathroom fixtures. By five-fifteen, Mary and Lisa were the proud owners of a working bathtub, bathroom sink, dishwasher, washer and kitchen sink. For good measure, Jeb and Buster checked the hot water heater, dryer and furnace. They replaced a couple of parts here and there that needed fixing and were sitting quite contentedly under the umbrella of the new patio table with a cold drink by five-forty-five.
"You must remember to charge us for overtime," Mary placed food in front of them and refilled their drinks.
"Oh, no, ma'am. You're eligible for the new customer discount."
"We are?"
"Sure. Besides, we know a loyal customer when we see them, right, Buster!"
Buster only nodded. His momma had told him early in life to never talk with his mouth full, and right now, it was jammed with crackers and cheese. Lisa pushed the food closer to him. He had worked up an appetite helping with all those mechanical things.
"So, how long do they stay?" Jeb cocked his head toward the front. They were seated out in the back, well out of line of sight, but everyone knew who he was referring to.
"They leave at dusk."
"Well, we can't wait around for that. Let's hit the road, Buster."
Buster eyed the remaining food with regret. Mary put it in a container for his long trip home. He was eternally grateful and they left without further incident. After the rest of the group left,

Mary and Lisa put together the other set of patio furniture and then hauled it out to the area where the group was sure to be bright and early. Then, they took turns in the bathtub, Mary getting the honors of the first baptism, Lisa took the next turn and then they went to bed between clean sheets.

The protestors were there bright and early and so was the sheriff. Mary was awakened by an incessant pounding at the door. She threw on her clothes and hurried to the door so the noise wouldn't wake Lisa.

"Howdy, Ms. Fairbanks," Sheriff Clouber was polite and tipped his hat.

"Good morning, Sheriff. Would you care for some coffee? I'm just about to make some."

"No, thank you, ma'am. Just following up on a complaint."

"There must be some mistake. I haven't complained or called about anything," Mary opened the door wider as Lisa came up behind her.

"Come in, Sheriff," Lisa said.

"Just for a minute, maybe."

"Do you like your coffee strong? I'm afraid that's all I know how to make."

"Strong is fine."

He fiddled with the brim of his hat, which he had removed upon entering the home.

"So, you're here about a complaint?"

"It's a matter of dumping."

"Dumping?"

"Well, littering doesn't really apply."

"But I haven't signed a complaint about anything," Mary was still unsure about the nature of the visit.

"Oh, I know that, ma'am. It's them," he jerked a thumb toward the picket line. They were all marching up and down, not even availing themselves of the shade of the umbrella.

"Them? What are they complaining about?"

"They say you dumped some junk out on the road."

"The patio furniture!" Lisa got it first.

"Right."

"It was intended as a gift."

157

"Well, you know the old saying about one man's junk..." the sheriff trailed off.

"Is another man's patio furniture," Lisa finished the statement with originality.

"This is mighty good coffee."

"Thanks. So, do we have to pay a fine or something?"

"Tell you what. If you get it moved by tomorrow, I'll drop the whole matter."

"Why wait until then?" Lisa asked Mary. "Let's do it while the good sheriff is here to witness."

Lisa led the way outside to the item in question. She grabbed one side while Mary took the other just like the night before. They moved it just to their side of the property line and then Lisa went back in the house, got everyone's coffee and served it right in front of the group. If the delicious aroma wafted their way, so be it. The sheriff took off after a couple more sips. Hopefully, there were more important crimes to investigate. That left Mary and Lisa sipping their brew slowly.

"You want some breakfast?" Lisa asked Mary after draining her cup.

"I'll cook. Tell me what you want."

"Bacon, eggs, toast and jelly."

"You have quite the appetite this morning."

"Dining al fresco has that effect on me."

Mary whipped up a breakfast fit for the most beautiful woman on earth and made sure she knew it as they ate their feast for two. They would've been more than happy to share the food, but they knew better than to try. After picking up the dishes, they went inside to begin their cleaning project. Scrubbing a ceiling was rough on the shoulders and long before noon, they took a well-deserved break. Mary worked on Lisa's shoulder muscles, deeply massaging them until they relaxed a bit. Then, she held her close from behind.

"I'm crazy about you."

"I'm grimy and sweaty."

"Then, I'm crazy about a grimy, sweaty person."

"I'm really glad we got the tub hooked up," Lisa murmured.

"Me, too. You want to go first this morning?"

"I'm not done working yet.  There are still hours and hours of work to do."

"I think we should *pace* ourselves."

"Pace ourselves?"

"As far as work is concerned.  You can go as long as you want to in other endeavors."

"Is that a challenge?" Lisa leaned into Mary's arms.

"More like a dare, I'd say."

"We don't have drapes and it's still light."

"We have sheets."

"To hang over the windows?"

"To snuggle under."

"Well, then, what are we doing here?"

They bathed and then cuddled up in bed.  Here it wasn't even noon yet and already Lisa, who never took a dare lightly, had already teased Mary to the verge of an orgasm twice.  Lisa couldn't really take much of the credit, because it hadn't taken that much teasing.  As Lisa kissed Mary over the edge, she moaned sweetly.  When Mary could talk again, she asked, "How do you have so much energy?"

"You inspire me."

"Come over here and I'll inspire you some more."

Mary took her own sweet time as well, and when she was finished inspiring Lisa, they both fell asleep in each other's arms.  It was dark when they stirred awake and were relieved to have the place to themselves.

"What do you want for dinner?" Mary asked before they even got out of bed.

"You."

"You had me for lunch, remember?" Mary laughed.

"Oh yeah. We had dessert first.  I remember now."

"Come on, you sweet talker you!  You can make a salad."

"Okay."

They wandered out to the kitchen in their robes and admired their partially clean ceiling.

"This is looking better already," Mary observed.

"It is.  We should have the kitchen done by the end of the week."

"Can I ask you a favor?"

"Sure, anything."

"I want to go to church on Sunday."

"You do?" Lisa sounded moderately surprised.

"Yes."

"That's okay, I guess."

"And I would like you to go with me."

"You want *me* to go with you?"

"Well, I don't see anybody else in the room," Mary looked around.

"You know what I mean," Lisa was suddenly prickly.

"I'm not exactly sure," Mary admitted. "Tell me."

"You've already seen the kind of welcome we're getting from the religious community around here," Lisa commented as she started frying potatoes. So much for the salad idea.

"That doesn't mean you wouldn't be welcome at the church I went to when I was young."

"Even if we didn't have the posse out here every morning, what makes you think that we'd be seen in any favorable light in church under any circumstances?"

"If it makes you feel any better, I think the Kansas State Legislature outlawed stoning people to death in the last general session."

"And they say Kansas is against evolution! One small step for man, one giant leap for Cro-Magnon," Lisa came back as she added more oil to the already drowning potatoes.

"Hey, hey! Take it easy on the cholesterol over there."

"I'll drain them before we eat. What else do you want?"

"Salt and pepper."

"I meant, what other dish? How about some corn?"

"That would be okay."

"Do you want any meat?"

"No, not tonight."

Dinner was served in ten minutes. Simple food on a simple table with simple chairs. It was deathly quiet for about two minutes. You could've sworn they were saying grace. Silently.

"You don't have to go," Mary said.

"I didn't say I wouldn't go."

"But you really don't like the idea."

"I don't like to go where I'm not wanted."

"You came to Kansas."

"I'd follow you anywhere."

"You would?"

"Even to church."

"You mean it?"

"Of course. I wouldn't want to miss *all* the fun."

"What do you mean," Mary asked warily.

"Well, what church do your relatives go to? You know, the ones who stripped the place clean, Aunt and Uncle Tornado."

"Oh, no problem. They go early."

"And you don't?"

"I go to the drunkard's services."

"The drunkard's services?"

"The ten o'clock service."

This got a laugh out of Lisa. Mary's heart tingled at the sound.

"You only get until ten o'clock to get over a hangover around here, huh?"

"Well, sitting in a pew isn't exactly like running a marathon. Take a couple of aspirin, wash it down with a Bloody Mary and you're ready for anything."

"I'll take your word for it. I don't plan on getting falling-down drunk on Saturday."

We can go to church and then have brunch afterwards at the hotel. I'll call and make reservations tomorrow."

"Is it a champagne brunch?"

"You think you'll need one by then?"

"I might need two or three by then."

By the end of the week, they had established a routine. Lisa was up first and made coffee. She took a cup out to the front yard and savored the morning sun as she awaited the arrival of the "Kansas 25." Off and on throughout the day, picketers would come and go, so that by day's end, somewhere between twenty and thirty adults and children would walk up and down the property line. Lisa wasn't interested in striking up a conversation, she was merely keeping an eye on the proceedings. She did feel especially sorry for the little boys and girls who endured the hours without shade. In forty years, their dermatologists would be able to retire early. What a shame. So, after Lisa drank down her coffee, she went in the house and started working. Her muscles fairly glistened with the sweet sweat of hard work.

"You look absolutely fetching," was Mary's form of "Good morning" these days. By the shameless way Mary buttered up Lisa, you would've thought they owned a cow. Speaking of livestock, they added a little more meat to their diet, mostly to be supportive of the local economy. The best eggs on earth were sold three farms down, which, as those in this part of the country knew, was miles away. Still, Mary was a customer and she had nearly perfected her omelet-making skills by Friday. Saturday, they drove past the picket line to go into town to buy some new clothes for church. Lisa, who normally selected silk, went to a subtle shade of linen instead. Other than feeling like she was wearing a tablecloth, it was perfect. Mary, ever the pragmatist, went cotton straight down the line. They would both be wrinkled, but presentable. Saturday night's dinner was modest and they went to bed early.

In the morning, Lisa was surprised if not shocked, to find a few picketers. She guessed that nobody gets a day off in this day and age.

"How many do we have this morning?" Mary asked sleepily as she meandered into the kitchen.

"Only a handful."

"Guess everybody's still at church."

"What time should we leave the house?"

"About nine-fifteen. Then, we won't have to rush around."

"Gives me a good hour to work," Mary yawned out the conviction.

"I have a better idea!" Lisa bragged.

"You always do!"

Even though the plan was to leave early, it just didn't work out that way. Oh, that Lisa and her better ideas! Still, they arrived at the church in plenty of time to find a parking place and enter the building. It was surprisingly cool. Apparently, the congregation had sprung for air conditioning between Mary's childhood and adulthood. What a difference a dozen years and a few hundred thousand dollars can do.

Lisa followed Mary as she picked out a row to sit in, not too close to the front to appear proud but not so far away to appear penitent. No one else was in the row, so they situated themselves in the middle so people could share their pew. The drunkard's services were more crowded than Mary remembered from childhood and by five minutes until ten, the church was almost full. Several fellow worshippers had approached Mary and Lisa's row and then passed on to other places, leaving them in some sort of solitary confinement. When services commenced, people chose to stand in the back or crowd in to other pews rather than sit next to the newcomers. It wasn't cramped, but it was obvious as hell. Lisa managed to stand and sit at all the right times and marveled at Mary's singing voice. Her pitch was as clear as her eyes and Lisa forced herself to look away for fear of showing her undying love through unguarded facial expression. Just when Lisa was settling into proceedings, it was over and people filed out to chat in little circles. Little, tight, non-inclusive circles. Mary led the way to their car and they headed over to the hotel for brunch.

"That was nice," Lisa chatted amiably. She had actually enjoyed herself.

"I'm so embarrassed by how we were shunned! God, I didn't think I was Amish!" Mary, by contrast, hadn't enjoyed herself.

"Oh, I wouldn't let it get to you. Maybe everyone is just shy?"

"They aren't too shy to take our money when we go shopping! Did you see that sales clerk from the store practically sit on that man's lap to avoid sharing our pew!"

"Never confuse shopping with religion. Then, we'd be calling you Trish."

Mary nodded and even smiled a teensy bit. But she wasn't placated. However, she was determined to be in good humor for their meal. They were seated the minute they arrived in the hotel's main restaurant and two glasses of champagne were brought by a gregarious waiter. A special menu was left for study. It would sit unstudied for a while.

"Why didn't you tell me you have such a lovely singing voice?" Lisa asked as she sipped her champagne. She was thirsty, but was careful to not overindulge. In the meantime, Mary was looking over one shoulder and then the other.

163

"Yes, I'm talking about *your* singing voice!" Lisa tapped Mary's hand.

"I can creak out a tune and that's about it."

"You could give Madonna a run for her money."

"I'm not blonde."

"Neither is Madonna."

"But you are."

"I can't sing."

"What are you having for brunch?"

"I don't know. Let me look."

It took about two seconds for her to decide. "The crepes sound good."

"Me, too."

They placed their order and then sipped more champagne as they planned next week's work schedule.

"We should be able to get the entire kitchen painted by Tuesday, unless you continue to distract me," Lisa said all business-like.

"It's going to be wonderful," Mary said mysteriously. Lisa didn't know if she meant the painting or the distracting.

"Then, we can start on the dining room," Lisa made it sound so inviting.

"The dining room?" Mary wasn't so sure.

"Everything is going to need scrubbing and repainting," Lisa explained. "Is there another room you'd rather do next?"

"The bedroom."

"The bedroom?"

"We spend one-third of our time there. Sometimes more, if we're lucky. I want to redo it as soon as possible."

"What color do you want?"

"Something that will stir your passion."

"Then, we'll need to find the blue that matches your eyes."

"You say the most romantic things," Mary stroked Lisa's fingers. It was a subtle sign of their affection, one that was meant to be unobserved by all but the most nosy. After brunch, they took the rest of the day off to observe the Sabbath. Too bad the protestors didn't. After noon, a huge contingent showed up to wave signs and read out loud quotes from the Old Testament. Mary began to despair ever doing serious gardening in the front yard. The small patch of lawn was getting absolutely ratty.

"What are you wishing for?" Lisa broke into Mary's reverie.

"A riding lawnmower."

Lisa giggled. "For that tiny bunch of sod?"

"I was thinking that the roar of the engine would drown out the reading of the Gospel."

"Did they switch to the New Testament and I missed it?"

"You know more about religion than you let on."

"All I know is that Jesus never said a bad word about gay people."

"Oh, but that argument never holds water with this group. They just turn around and say that Jesus never said a bad word about molesters, either, so you can't go by what Jesus didn't say."

"You have a point there, which is why I don't put much stock in Christianity. It's all up for interpretation."

"Not according to Bible literalists."

"Too bad they don't realize that they take something literally that has been passed down orally and translated. And we all know how bent out of shape that makes messages."

"So, I guess you won't be wanting to go to church anymore?"

"Honey, I wouldn't miss it for the world. Having a pew all to ourselves in an air-conditioned church once a week is too good to pass up!"

"I wonder when someone will get brave enough to sit next to us?"

"It can only be a matter of time."

Chapter 17

The plane ride to New Jersey was cramped. First class had been
filled by a group of morticians going to a convention, so Trish
and Robbie endured economy class. It was only to the east coast,
for goodness sake. They had cheap wine, peanuts and each
other. By the time they landed, Trish had a case of heartburn
second to none. She wanted to blame it on the legume luncheon,
but knew in her gut that it was the impending meeting with her
contact that was causing the distress. They claimed their luggage
and then took a limousine to their hotel. This, Trish insisted be
first class and they were in a suite by tea time.
"I'm ordering a scotch and water from room service." Trish
announced. "You want anything?"
"I'm more hungry than thirsty."
"Let's go out to dinner then."
"Isn't it a little early for dinner?"
"I'm sure we can find something."
They found what they were looking for on the second floor of the
hotel. It was an upscale 24-hour restaurant where you could
order any type of meal at any hour of the day. Rack of ribs at
one in the morning if you were in the mood. Robbie was more in
the mood for meatloaf, which they served gourmet style, one half
covered with standard Italian red sauce and the other half
drenched in Alfredo white. A glass of Chianti made it all go
down smoothly. Trish, who was secretly seeking a cure for her
indigestion, ate a hearty meal of teriyaki chicken, rice, and stir-
fry vegetables. After dinner, they walked around the hotel for a
few minutes until fatigue got the better of them. They dragged
themselves back up to the room and fell sound asleep.

Trish was up first and called the woman she had first contacted
two weeks ago. If the entire truth were known, Trish had made
this journey on faith. The woman, one Helen Montague, hadn't
been at all forthcoming with certain information during their
preliminary conversations. There was no reason to believe this

would radically change now. It might have been that the trip via economy was all for naught.

"Hello?" the voice answered.

"Helen?" Trish wanted to be sure she had dialed correctly.

"Who's asking?"

"It's Trish."

"Where are you?"

"At the Darcy Hotel."

There was a long pause. Then, "We can't meet there."

Trish resisted the urge to comment sarcastically that this much was evident with all the dozens of spies lurking in the lobby and simply asked, "Where do you want to meet?"

"Not at my house!"

"Okay."

"There's a park where all these young hoodlums go to skate and smoke dope."

"Sounds perfect to me."

"You wouldn't say that if it was in your neighborhood!"

"I guess not. What's the name of the park?"

"Sanders Park. Corner of Sanders and Fifth. Go to the gazebo on the south-east corner. Ten o'clock. If I'm not there by five after, the meeting's off. If I don't see you there, I won't stop."

She hung up without further comment. Trish woke Robbie up.

"The meeting is at ten."

"What time is it now?"

"Eight. You want breakfast first?"

"Sure. Something light, though."

"Sounds like we might just as well go to the second floor again?"

"That would be fine."

In thirty minutes, they were once again seated across from each other in a booth, this time studying the breakfast page of the menu. After ordering fruit and cereal, Robbie started in with questions.

"So, what's the plan?"

"We're meeting a sweet little old lady in a skater park to exchange espionage information."

"How will you recognize her? Will she be wearing a red carnation in her lapel?"

"She said she would find us. We're to wait in a gazebo."

"And what exactly is she going to tell us?"

"She's hopefully going to tell us about the good old days and if there are any Nazi nutcases living in Cleveland."

"Why would she know?"

"Because Helen Montague was a spy for our side."

Breakfast was late, but edible. They were out of the hotel by nine-fifteen. That gave them a good half hour to walk the mile to Sanders Park. It was a nice park, if not very established. Most of the trees were barely more than saplings, but dotted here and there along the walkway were a towering tree or two. Several nicely-pruned bushes enhanced the path and birds took advantage of the cover. A small lake was home base for a family of ducks and placed strategically along the route were sturdy benches. Even at this early hour, there were many people making good use of the park. Folks of every age and shape walked dogs of every age and shape. Trish wanted to own a kennel in her next life, and stopped once or twice to comment on a particular dog breed. Everyone who walked obeyed the rules of the road, walk on the right, pass on the left. Those who rode bikes or skates gave fair warning of their approach before zooming around at five times the speed of walking.

Robbie spotted the gazebo first and they sauntered over to await Ms. Montague. It was four minutes past ten and no one was in sight except a bicyclist who had passed Robbie and Trish earlier in their walk. She recognized the lime green jersey. It was practically fluorescent. The cyclist passed by the gazebo and then doubled back. Trish was getting nervous. This might rattle Ms. Montague and botch up the meeting. As the cyclist approached, Trish was unsettled until she took a good look at the face.

"You Trish?" the woman asked.

"I'm Trish."

"I'm Helen."

"You cycle?"

"Since the war."

"And you're not afraid of hurting yourself?"

"I fought the Nazis! You think I'm scared of a bicycle?"

"Guess not. Anyway, this is my friend, Robbie."

"Yeah, I know. You're the two that got married."

"You know that?"

"Saw it on TV. Good for you! Those right-wingers are the second coming of Hitler as far as I'm concerned."

"Can you tell me about groups in Cleveland?"

"A woman after my own heart. Right down to business. There's only one person who I know of in Cleveland. I keep track of things on the Internet sometimes. But I still keep in touch with the old network. Lucy has kept her eye on Ohio all these many years."

"Lucy?"

"Never mind her last name and forget you ever heard her first. She was a decoder during the war. Smart as a whip. She kept track of Nazi sympathizers in the Ohio valley area."

"There were a lot of them?"

"More than you could believe. You think it was just happenstance that America dragged its feet getting into the war?"

"I thought it was political."

"That's right."

"So, Lucy, who doesn't have a last name, gave you a lead?"

"Over the years, the Nazis active during the war have died away, as have my circle of friends," Helen explained the attrition with a wistful voice.

"I understand," Trish prompted.

"And so, there aren't too many left in Cleveland," she nodded sagely. "Lucy had it easy."

"I see," Trish nodded.

With that explanation, Helen pulled a small piece of paper out of her fanny pack and pressed it in Trish's hand.

"Good luck," she said and then rode away.

Trish unfolded the paper. It had a name and address clearly printed. Hans Cooper, 2301 North Pipe Street.

"You want to go now or after lunch?" Robbie asked.

"Let's go back to the hotel and see about airline reservations. We may be stuck here for another night."

Nothing was available until the morning, so Trish and Robbie spent their lag time resting and planning.

"What are you going to say to Mr. Cooper?" Robbie asked.

"I haven't figured that out, yet."

"We could pretend to be in cahoots with him."

"We probably can't pretend to be anything other than who we are. Even Helen Montague recognized us."

"I hope that when I'm seventy, I'll still be bicycling."

"You're not bicycling now!"

"I might start any day."

"There's only one thing I hope I'm still doing when I'm seventy," Trish nuzzled close to Robbie's ear.

"Me, too."

The only difference between the flight to New Jersey and the flight to Cleveland was that it was shorter. Oh, and it wasn't full of morticians.

"You aren't just going to waltz into Mr. Cooper's house and demand he stop sending letters to my mother, are you?"

"No, I think I could get into trouble doing that."

"So, what can we do? Without getting into trouble."

"Well, we can watch the house for a few days to see if he makes a lot of trips to the post office."

"But if he posts his letters at his own mailbox, it would be a clue as well."

"Except if we meddle with the mail, we could be facing a federal offense."

"So, there's not much that we can do."

"There is one thing we can do."

"What's that?"

"We can gather evidence."

"What kind of evidence?"

"Useful evidence, hopefully."

Trish didn't elaborate further and instead closed her eyes and slept through the rest of the flight.

They rented a car at the airport after once again rescuing their luggage from the baggage carousel. As Robbie deciphered the map included in the car rental, Trish negotiated the streets of Cleveland. It didn't take long to find Mr. Cooper's residence, a painfully modest frame house in a neighborhood that had seen better days.

"I guess being a crackpot Nazi isn't as lucrative as people think."

"I guess not," Trish agreed thoughtfully as she headed around the block. There was no clear vantage point from the back, so Trish drove down the street one more time before scouting for a shopping center.

"We didn't come all the way to Cleveland by way of New Jersey to go shopping, did we?" Robbie asked pointedly.

"I need a few things. Come on."

Trish led the way through the discount store, picking up a clipboard, a tote bag, several expensive pen and pencil sets, a box of drawstring style trash bags, a package of manila envelopes, a box of file folders, a briefcase, a set of kitchen towels, a white cotton lab coat, latex gloves, a computer disk, a ream of white paper, and a jar of dry roasted nuts.

Robbie was amazed what you could pick up at these chain stores. "I just have one question," Robbie asked as they loaded the stuff into the trunk of the rental car.

"What?"

"Why the jar of nuts?"

"I'm hungry."

"Okay. What now?"

"I need to go to a copy center and rent some computer time."

"You can do that?"

"I hope so. I'd hate to have to buy a whole computer tonight."

"Speaking of tonight, where are we going to stay?"

"Let's get a room now and I'll do this work later."

Just for a change of pace, they rented a hotel room across town from Pipe Street. The place boasted an Olympic-size swimming pool and Trish and Robbie splurged on new swim suits in the hotel shop. Afterwards, they went to an all-night copy center and created some very official-looking survey forms.

"You're going to do a survey?" Robbie was beginning to catch on.

"Right."

"About plants?" she needed more details.

"I noticed that although the neighborhood was older, many residents, including Mr. Cooper, kept rather nice gardens."

"And so, you're going to ask him about his garden? How is that going to help us figure out if he's the one sending the letters?"

"It isn't going to help directly. But it might help indirectly. Now, we need to go to the bank so I can cash some travelers checks."

"You need cash?"

"People who take surveys expect some form of remuneration. I can't very well write a check."

"Guess not, but why did you buy so much of everything?"

"Because we're going to survey the entire block."

"Good thing I packed my comfortable shoes."

Midmorning of the following day, the "ladies" from Green Fingers Inc. started at the corner on the opposite side of the street from Mr. Cooper's house. It took them three doors before someone was home, or brave enough to answer the door.

"Good morning!" Trish chirped when an elderly lady about the same age as Helen Montague opened the door.

"Are you sellin something?" she asked point blank with obvious disdain.

Trish held up a crisp new hundred dollar bill.

"We want to give you this brand new hundred dollar bill," Trish started to explain but was cut short.

"How do I know it isn't counterfeit?"

"I just got it from the bank. You can call them and ask."

"Maybe I will. Meantime, what do I have to do to get it?"

"I have a two-page survey about gardens. You qualified for the survey because of the beautiful plants in your yard."

Okay, so it was an out-and-out lie. About the only plant of merit in the front yard was a rose bush that looked like it hadn't been pruned since Ronald Reagan was president.

"Let me see the two pages."

Trish held up the copies they had made the night before. Each sheet only had four questions on it. Eight questions were all Trish and Robbie could come up with between the two of them.

"How long will it take?"

"Maybe two minutes per question?"

"And that's all for a hundred dollars?"

"Did I mention that you also get a lovely pen and pencil set?"

"How lovely?" she was still skeptical.

Trish held up one of the many sets she had bought. They were a beautiful shade of mahogany.

"I don't like red much."

"I have blue as well."

"Let me see them."

Trish rummaged around in the tote bag until she found a blue set. This gained them entrance into the hallowed halls of the Rose Bush Lady.

"I won't put my name on the survey," she said as she led them into the tiny kitchen. After looking around, they both passed on the offer of coffee.

"We insist you don't use your name. In fact, we would have to tear it off or scratch it out if you put it on the paper, because we want this survey to be totally anonymous."

"Do you have another pen I could borrow?"

"You don't want to use the one I just gave you?"

"I'm saving that for good."

Trish nodded. It made sense. The woman began page one. It was mostly benign demographic queries. Did you rent or own? How many years had you lived in the house? How many people lived there? Level of household income?

These four questions gave the woman pause.

"Are you from the census and you're lying to me?"

"We're not from the census. If you don't want to answer the questions, we'll just be on our way."

"I didn't say I wouldn't answer! I was just wondering."

"If you want to think about those questions for a moment, you can just go on to the next page."

She went on to page two after making a few marks on the first sheet. The next four questions were specific to gardening with emphasis on bulbs, seeds, perennials and succulents. This part took considerable thought and the woman furrowed her brow intently.

"All I got is a rose bush and some grape hyacinths."

"Then, just write that under 'bulbs.'"

"A rose bush ain't a bulb!"

"My supervisor will sort it all out," Trish stated, hoping to come across as bored rather than worried.

"Is she your supervisor?" the woman indicated Robbie.

"I'm just the trainee," Robbie piped up.

"I'm done. Do I get my money now?"

173

"Of course," Trish handed over the hundred. The woman held it up to a light and nodded like she would know a real bill from a fake any old day. And she probably did.

"By the way, what are you selling really?"

"We are working on a marketing venture."

"What are you venturing to market?"

"Fertilizer."

"Oh well, good luck."

Trish followed Robbie as they took their leave. When they were out of earshot. Robbie repeated, *"fertilizer?"*

"It was the closest word I could think of."

Two more houses were non-responsive and then they found another lady at home. If Mr. Cooper ever went without a date, it wasn't for lack of opportunity. Things went about the same all down the block. Folks were skeptical at first and then, when Trish and Robbie readily handed out money, they got all sorts of information about gardening. If anyone was suspicious that they knew more about the subject than the ladies from Green Thumb Inc., no one opined about it.

By the time they crossed the street and approached Cooper's house, their nerves were settled. When the man opened the door, it was more or less routine. He was skeptical at first and then grudgingly cooperative at the promise of money. He scratched in the answers to the questionnaire and then accepted the money and pens without any glimmer of recognition or hint of being wise to Trish's plot. If Robbie had studied him more intently than any previous neighbors, she hid it well. They finished out the block and then went back to the hotel for a much-deserved rest.

"What do you think?" Robbie asked as she stretched out in bed next to Trish.

"I think this has been a colossal waste of time."

"Why would you say that?"

"Well, because Mr. Cooper didn't recognize us."

"Did you expect him to?"

"Whoever we are seeking out recognized your mother after forty years. Since we were in the wedding footage, he would've known us as well."

174

"Maybe he did and he's just hiding it well. Or maybe he had been concentrating so much on my mom that he blanked the rest of us out?"

"I guess either one of those could be true."

"So, that's it? All that survey and money just to see if he knew us?"

"Oh, heck no. We now have much more than that!"

"We do?"

"We now have his fingerprints, a sample of his handwriting, and the knowledge that if he uses our free pen to address envelopes, a match of the ink. That is, if he's our man."

"My God! But didn't you handle the paper, too?"

"Minimally. I stuck it in a plastic bag to preserve it."

"I had no idea what you were up to."

"I know. I didn't want you watching me too closely. That could've tipped off Mr. Cooper."

"So, I was an able, if ignorant, assistant."

"Do you feel left out?"

"Not really. I understand your reasons. Can we go home tomorrow?"

"Absolutely."

Robbie was quiet for so long that Trish was sure she had dropped off to sleep. She was surprised to hear her ask, "What are we going to do if it's him?"

"We're going to thank Silver very much and send her packing."

"Why?"

"Because Mr. Cooper isn't good for anything but mailing cryptic letters."

"Are you sure?"

"He uses a walker, for God's sake."

Robbie nodded and then said, "I'm hungry."

"I'll buy you a pizza."

"You're on."

One pepperoni, onion and black olive pizza sated their appetite and they slept soundly after making flight reservations for noon of the following day. Rising early, they packed, checked out and arrived at the airport in time to walk leisurely amidst the general stampede that occurs when people are running late. Nothing like needing to be at gate 99 with five minutes before takeoff. Only a couple of bumps disturbed an otherwise glorious flight.

"When I grow up, I want to be a pilot," Trish revealed another deep secret to Robbie.

"When all this is over, you could get a pilot's license."

"I suppose I could try."

"Then, we wouldn't need to make airline reservations all the time."

Trish smiled broadly, prompting Robbie to ask, "What?"

"That's what I love about you. You're always supportive of everything I do."

"That's because you do the coolest things."

"I do, don't I."

After landing in Denver and getting the car out of parking-garage hock, they checked in with Rose and Max. Things were fine. Silver was making the rounds, checking the perimeters of the Goldstein property.

"So, where did you go?" Rose asked as she served blueberry pie and coffee.

"We went east," Trish replied.

"To Cleveland?"

"Eventually."

"What did you do?"

"We followed a lead from a contact."

"Was it dangerous?"

"No."

"How do you know?"

"We're back safe and sound, aren't we?"

"I guess so. You're staying for dinner?"

"Of course," Robbie replied.

Trish slowed down on the pie consumption. "How are things with Silver?" she asked.

"We're doing okay."

"Does it still bother you to have the protection?"

"Maybe she's relaxing a little or maybe I'm just getting used to it. We're doing okay lately."

"Well, if our evidence shows that this guy in Cleveland is our man, then I think you could probably dismiss Silver at the end of the month."

176

"You mean, fire her?"

"No, not fire her. Just let her know that you don't need her anymore."

"Oh, I'm not sure about that," Rose backpedaled somewhat.

"So, she makes you feel safer?" Trish picked up on the tone.

"Is she too expensive?" Rose answered with a question of her own.

"Don't worry about the expense," Robbie said quickly.

"I'm just, well, getting used to her. We're doing fine."

Trish had kept mental count. They had gone from two "okays" to a "fine."

"You want to keep status quo?"

"For a while. Maybe?"

Trish thought it over. The auction was fast approaching. She had tried to keep that event out of her conscious thoughts. All things considered, it wouldn't be a half-bad idea to have some security during that event. Postponed twice, mostly to stir potential buyer frenzy, the sale of Trish's gift from Albert, "Paradise on Earth," was scheduled for a scant few weeks from today in New York. The painting was valuable. Some of whatever they really pocketed would need to go toward the care of Connors Rosenthal. That would take a huge chunk of the proceeds, but Albert had counted on Trish to do the right thing.

"What are you thinking?" Robbie asked Trish. Even Rose was waiting for this answer.

"We should have stopped by Glens Falls when we were in New Jersey."

"You were in New Jersey, too?" Rose asked as Max joined them at the table.

"That's where the contact was," Robbie explained.

"You can go see him when you go to the auction," Max knew who and what they were talking about now.

Silver didn't. "What auction?" she asked as she pulled up a cup of coffee and sat down. She looked fit, rested and ready.

"I, we, own a painting and we're going to sell it to pay for some special medical care for a man."

"That's very generous of you."

"Well, I don't think it's going to take the whole 65 million," Robbie noted calmly.

Silver only broke the cup when she dropped it. The sauce survived the crash. Rose started to clean it up as Silver blurted out, "Say again?"

"Oh, I guess it's just sort of usual for us, but I can see how that would surprise somebody new," Trish did her best to downplay the news.

"Y'all own a painting worth 65 million dollars?"

"Well, we're not sure about its true value. It's a painting that disappeared during the Holocaust. It took us a while to find it."

"Did you go to Europe?"

"No, actually, we found it in Washington D.C. in the home of a Senator."

"Name wouldn't happen to be Schnell, would it?"

"Actually, yes."

"Holy good grief! I read all about that in the newspapers. He got shot dead!"

"And right in front of us."

"My God in heaven. And somebody else got wounded?"

"One of our friends."

"And another senator was there as well?"

"Another friend of ours."

"Let me see if I got this all down. You have a senator for a friend?"

"Right."

"And a painting worth 65 million dollars?"

"Right."

"And a crank letter writer threatening your mother?"

"Right."

"It's worse than I thought. I'd better go buy a couple more guns!"

Chapter 18

Mary and Lisa started right in on the bedroom next. It wasn't as complex as the kitchen. There weren't cupboards to tear down and grease to scrape off the walls. Just a simple room with four walls, a ceiling and a floor. The flooring throughout the farmhouse was hardwood. Forget about oohing and ahhing, it was old and worn and ugly. It would either need to be sanded or ripped out. The decision had been staring Mary and Lisa in the face, which had so far prompted their top down approach. But it would need to be faced eventually. The bedroom ceiling was a cinch, but the walls were nicked, gouged and holed from years of hanging pictures and banging about with furniture. Lisa managed to do a lot of patchwork as Mary painted. They had indeed chosen blue for the color. No surprise there.

The only surprise at the beginning of the week was the appearance of a local TV news crew. Mary had feared for a moment that they had caught her in a not-so-photogenic mode but soon realized that it was neither Mary nor Lisa whom they wanted to film. The protestors were the main attraction and the crew got them in all their glory. The only surprise at the end of the week was Mary and Lisa's ability to take a drive to town. Roads for a quarter mile in every direction were clogged with network satellite trucks. To offset this phenomenon, several hundred more protestors had gathered at the site and further blocked access. Lisa drove the car down the driveway to shouts of, "Here they come now!" by reporters. She drove slowly to avoid hurting anyone as Mary sat stiffly in the passenger seat. They were past the worst of it in a few minutes.
"What prompted all of this?" Mary asked after she had stopped gripping her seat belt like it was the harness of a parachute and she was making her first jump.
"Must be a slow news day."
"Slow, hell! Things would have to be going backwards to warrant this kind of coverage."
"I think backwards is an apt description," Lisa chuckled.
"Will they be there when we get home?" Mary's voice wavered just a bit.

"We could stay out after dark. They're usually gone by then."

"Will we need to stay out after dark all the time?" Mary asked with a bite tougher than sarcasm.

"It's going to blow over sooner or later. TV stations won't stay if there's no real story and then, after the protestors make their point, they'll go away."

"What if it somehow becomes a story?"

"If we don't react, there won't be a story. We just need to keep our cool and go about our business."

Business which started at their favorite hardware store, talking with Jeb about flooring. He was a tad on the reticent side about it all.

"You feeling okay, Jeb?" Mary asked.

"Sure, just been watching the news this week."

"We don't have a TV," Lisa explained.

"You probably don't need one. You are the news."

"We are?"

"Every night for three days on every channel."

"Not that much has happened," Mary stated.

"Not much needs to happen to make the news around here."

"In the meantime, we still need some supplies."

"Could you wait on that for a while?"

"Why?"

"I don't want to get on the news myself."

"It could be bad for business?" Lisa got to the point.

"None of the protestors buy from me anyway, but there's talk of a boycott."

"A boycott?"

"Yeah. Talk is that anyone who does business with you is on some list already."

"Well, that's a lot of businesses. You, the bank, the grocery store, the hotel, the diner..." Mary went down the list.

"And don't forget the church." Lisa added. "And the nice lady who sells us the eggs!"

"Don't get me wrong. It's not that I don't want to stop doing business with you. I just can't see me and Buster trying to get the truck down the road what with all the crowd there."

"That makes perfect sense," Lisa nodded. She knew how tough it could be in a car, let alone a delivery truck. "Besides, we don't really need anything delivered for a while. But I do need a gallon of deep blue paint for trim."

"Got about three shades to choose from, but you think you need a whole gallon?" Jeb and Lisa went off to confer about the finer points of latex. He helped her pick out a shade that matched Mary's eyes, although he had no idea that that's what they were doing.

The next stop was the grocery store, where they smiled at the gawkers who recognized them from TV as they filled up a grocery cart with all the essentials and a variety of frills including gourmet coffee, chocolate and strawberries. It wasn't until the checker asked for three IDs that Lisa noticed a change in the demeanor of the woman waiting on them.

"Three IDs?"

"It *is* a temporary check."

"Why don't I just wait here while you call Tom Philbin at the bank?"

The woman looked like she was arguing with herself. And losing. So much for the bright idea of the multiple IDs. She ran the check through the machine and handed over a receipt.

Nobody offered to help them out, but they were two able-bodied young women. They stashed the groceries in the car and then debated whether or not to go to the diner for a late lunch.

"I could use a break from cooking," Mary said.

"Okay."

As they stepped into the restaurant, their favorite waitress, Jessie, practically shoehorned them into their usual booth and brought water and menus immediately.

"It's nice to be openly welcomed somewhere," Mary observed as they studied the menu they had already practically memorized.

"Oh, it hasn't been that bad. Just a little bumpy here and there."

"You're always willing to give people the benefit of the doubt."

"It can't be easy, having the town newcomers on the nightly news."

Further private conversation was put on hold when Jessie returned to take their order. "Is it as bad as it looks on the news?" she asked.

"That depends. How bad does it look on the news?"

"It looks like lots and lots of really angry intense people in your front yard."

"It's not that bad."

"It isn't?"

"They only look that way when the camera is on them. Otherwise, they look hot and hungry and bored."

"Lots like most of our customers. You heard about the boycott yet?"

"Just this morning."

"Well, don't you worry none about that. You're welcome here any day. Special today is Salisbury steak. Take it from me, stick to the burgers. Better yet, the hot turkey sandwich is fresh. You know I'd tell you otherwise."

"Sounds good to me," Lisa said.

"Me, too."

"Good. Turkey all around."

In five minutes, they had steaming hot plates full of turkey, potatoes, dressing and gravy. A small dish of canned cranberry came with it as did coffee and pumpkin pie. You would've thought it was Thanksgiving. In a way, it was. They were extremely thankful that those enlightened folks at the diner paid no nevermind to boycotts and such. After lunch, they headed home. The road rose and fell in now-familiar ways as they had become more used to the trip back and forth.

"Did you know that they sometimes intentionally put hills and valleys and curves in roads?" Mary asked as she navigated the drive.

"They do?"

"Keeps you from going to sleep," Mary explained.

As they drove over the final rise and headed downhill to the farm, an interesting sight met their eyes. The group of people who usually milled about was now laying or sitting in front of the driveway, thereby preventing Mary and Lisa access to the farm. Mary had done a lot of things in her life, but running over a bunch of people in her car wasn't one of them. She wasn't about to begin now.

"What are we going to do?" Lisa asked.

"We could go back to town?" Mary considered options.

"But we have these groceries that will need refrigeration soon."

"Maybe we could get out and walk around them?"

As they were talking this over, the group of protestors began to stir and chant ugly slogans. It was intimidating enough to warn Mary off the walking-in plan. She pointed the car to the right and drove due east on the road, passing by all the confrontation.

"Where are you going?" Lisa asked.

"To the Bixby place."

Lisa nodded. That would be the farm next door. Next door in Kansas was measures in acres, which gave them time to digest both lunch and the new developments.

"Isn't what they're doing against the law?" Lisa groused after a few moments.

"I suppose so. But if we make a fuss, that's all the news cameras will show and then we'll look like the bad guys."

"Speaking of news coverage, you should check in with your mom to see if we're on the news as far away as D.C."

"I'll give them a call as soon as we get home, whenever that may be."

Mary pulled up to the road that led into the Bixby farm. That house was quite a way from the main road, but Mary thought it better to walk in. Lisa followed after she locked the car. No use adding car theft to their growing list of problems. It only took about five minutes to cover the distance, but in the hot sun, it seemed longer. Mary stepped up to the front door and knocked. And waited. And waited. She heard shuffling long before the door opened, and steeled herself for the appearance of old man Bixby. He had seemed ancient way back when Mary had visited as a child. Lord knows what the ravages of time would have been visited upon him after all these years. As the door creaked open, he stood as tall as possible with the aid of a walker.

"Hello, Mr. Bixby."

"Do I know you?"

"I'm Mary Fairbanks."

"Oh, yeah. You've been on the TV box every blessed night. You and her," he motioned toward Lisa.

"Unfortunately, yes. Can I ask you a favor?"

"No."

"Expecting a 'yes,' Mary was taken aback.

"You won't do me a favor?"

183

"Your family stole twenty-five acres from me and now you come wanting favors?  Got a lot of nerve for a girl."

Mary ignored the "girl" part and concentrated on the "stole twenty-five acres" part.

"Which twenty-five acres are we talking about?"

"The twenty-five acres where that idiot Henry replaced the fence last year."

"Henry put up a new fence in the wrong place?"

"He got some som-a-bi-," Bixby started to get warmed up and then his manners caught up with his vocabulary.  "Sorry, but that no good Henry found hisself a lyin, cheatin surveyor to lie about the property line."

"Isn't it kind of hard to lie about twenty-five acres?"

"Well, it isn't a block of five acres square that we're talking about."

"Oh," Mary nodded as she shifted from one foot to the other. There were groceries deteriorating in the car.

"Hell, uh, heck no.  Tisn't one big chunk of land.  Just one real long stretch of land.  Goes for miles."

"Henry put up miles of new fence?"

"Had to do something to get out of the house, if ya know what I mean."

"Wouldn't a divorce have been easier?" Lisa spoke up.

"Not in these parts, young lady.  Doing a whole new fence is loads easier than getting deevorced from BeBe Knight Buckmaster!"

"Guess so," Lisa nodded and then, ever curious, turned to Mary and asked, "Does that mean your mother's maiden name was Knight or Buckmaster?"

"Knight.  My dad was Fairbanks.  What does it matter?"

"It really doesn't.  It's just that the name of the homestead is getting longer.  Knight, Buckmaster and Fairbanks.  Sounds like a group of lawyers."

"So, you young ladies as fond of each other as they been yakkin about on TV?"

Mary couldn't figure a graceful way out of the question, so she just said, "Yes."

"Well, don't just stand there sunning yourselves on the porch. Might as well come on in," he backed up real slow.

184

"We'd love to stay and catch up on old times," Mary stepped in tentatively, with Lisa the Shadow at her elbow, "but we have a car full of groceries that we need to get in the ice box."

"You do?" he sounded a twinge disappointed. Company didn't stop by all that much anymore.

"Yes, and we can't get into our house."

"Lock yourselves out?"

"No, but the people who've been picketing our place all decided to sit in the driveway so we can't get through."

"And so you come here to borrow my Frigidaire?"

"Actually, we're looking for a back way into our property."

"Oh, yes, you're lookin for the church organist's gate."

"We are?"

"It's not too far. Come on and git your groceries and I'll take you over in my vehicle."

"Your vehicle?"

"Yours'll never make it. Get stuck or high centered. C'mon. Ain't got all day. Got to be home for Jeopardy. It's College Week!"

Mary and Lisa looked at each other with one of those "What have we got to lose" expressions and fetched the groceries from their car after moving it closer to the house. Then they all climbed into some sort of behemoth truck that by all rights belonged in the Smithsonian and bumped off down the road. About a mile into the drive, they came across a gate in the fence. As Bixby revved the engine, Lisa did gate duty. What Bixby lacked in walking skills, he more than made up for in driving. They soon approached the farm from the back and would've probably remained unnoticed except for all the telephoto technology. Not much could be done by the blockade except to begin the parade all over again.

"Looks a lot smaller in person," Bixby noted from his vantage point behind the steering wheel. "TV makes it look like a mob riot."

This reminded Mary to be sure and call her mom just as soon as the perishables were put away.

"Come in for some lemonade and cookies," Lisa cajoled as only Lisa could. Bixby was quickly becoming her new best friend. She really liked his truck.

"What kind?"

"What kind of cookies?"

"No, what kind of lemonade?"

"The kind made from lemons, I guess?" Lisa felt like she was auditioning for Jeopardy College Week.

"My doc has me on a restricted diet. Can't have sugar."

"How about tea?"

"Got any beer?"

Lisa thought this over. Wasn't beer just about as bad as lemonade? She didn't feel like getting into a nutritional discussion with a guy who looked about five years older than a Model T.

"We've got that diet beer," Mary put the clincher on the topic.

"Sounds wet," Bixby eased himself out of the truck and onto the back porch.

"Come inside and sit. It's cooler now," Mary said.

He hesitated. "I haven't been welcomed in this house for over twenty-five years."

Mary caught a glimpse of misty eyes before she spoke. "Well, you're welcome here now. Follow me and watch your step. We're under construction."

Mary helped Bixby get settled in one of their two good chairs while Lisa took a beer out of the fridge and put the milk in. She popped it open and handed it to their guest. He took a long, refreshing draw with a steady hand.

"Now, that's a dust cutter," he nodded his appreciation.

Lisa agreed and started one of her very own. Mary stuck to lemonade. One of this wild bunch had better stay sober. At least long enough to call Washington. Mary, having put the task off as long as she dare, settled into the other good chair and placed the call.

"Hello?" the voice answered. It sounded strained.

"It's me, Mary."

"What in *the hell* is going on out there?"

So much for salutations.

"Well, Lisa, and Bixby and I are having a cold beer," Mary stretched the truth. Besides, at this rate, she might start in on the brew any minute herself.

"You're on the news and you don't have your phone hooked up yet?"

"We're on a waiting list."

"And what about your cell phone? Why do you have it turned off."

"I've been saving the batteries."

"And you couldn't call?"

"We've been real busy being the Goddam moral lightning rod of Utopia, Kansas!" Mary was finally showing the strain. Lisa, feeling more and more like a member of the family every day, took the phone from Mary before things escalated into a real fight.

"Hi, Rebecca. This is Lisa."

"Put Mary back on the phone!"

"I will in a minute. She's getting another beer. In the meantime, I just wanted to reassure you that things are more peaceful here than the news lets on."

"Is that really the truth?"

"Absolutely. We've been having breakfast on the front porch every day. Swear to God. Things are okay."

"So, that explains why you can't get up the driveway?"

"That's just a temporary inconvenience."

"It sounds like the troublemakers are getting more organized rather than less."

"They all decided to sit down at once. That's not much in the way of organizational skills. Is Mitch there?"

Lisa could tell by the rapt silence the consideration Rebecca was giving to the question. A thousand one. A thousand two.

"Yes, she is."

"Could I talk to her for a second?"

"About what?"

"About mixing paint, unless you happen to be the expert on painting?"

"Mixing paint?"

"Well, she did go all the way to Santa Fe just to learn about it."

"I'll put her on."

Lisa took another swig before Mitch got total custody of the phone.

"Hi. What about paint?"

187

"You have to answer questions like I'm asking you about painting."

"A picture or a house?"

"That's good. You've got the idea. Now, in numbers that sound like proportions, tell me how bad it looks on TV."

Mitch thought for a moment and then replied, "About 5 to 1."

"Now, keeping that number in mind, how worried is Rebecca?"

"About 20 to 1," Mitch was catching on quickly, "if you use a good primer."

"And how many times have you had to talk her out of getting on an airplane and flying out here?"

"Seven to one."

"Okay. You know, maybe a trip out here isn't such a bad idea. Once you see how calm things really are, it will put your minds at rest."

"I see."

"This won't go on forever. Some of these people must have a life. I hope."

"We'll see, but Rebecca wants to talk to Mary again."

Phones were switched back and the interlude helped to calm everyone's nerves.

"Lisa is telling Mitch to bring you out for a visit."

"I see. We'll make arrangements to stay in town."

"Oh, no, you can stay out here."

"I didn't think you had a spare bed?"

"We'll work on that."

"How are you going to get it delivered over the sea of bodies?"

"I don't know yet. How soon are you coming?"

Rebecca thought it over. "Are you really sure things aren't as bad as they look?"

"I'm sure. Besides, Mr. Bixby is helping us out and we have good friends in town."

"Old Man Bixby?"

"Right."

"Okay. So, you think you can get a bed?"

"We'll find you a bed!" Mary was sounding much happier.

"She can have mine!" Bixby spoke up. "Not every day you can claim a senator slept in your bed!"

Two things were clear. Bixby was a funny drunk and he hadn't been to Washington D.C. lately.

After a few more words of encouragement, including Bixby's offer of a couch as well, Mary signed off. Bixby was starting in on another beer and making quite good conversation about the farmhouse. "If BeBe had had time, she'da steamed the wallpaper right offa the walls!"

"Things were a bit on the empty side when we got here," Mary chatted.

"So, tell me what you've done so far?"

Mary indicated that Lisa could tell this story far better, and then listened with half attention. The other half was tuned into the protestors. They seemed to be quieting down somewhat. It would be okay for the "folks" to visit. Really it would. Maybe the furniture store would deliver in the evening, like, say two a.m.?

"Maaaaarrrrryyyyy…"

She popped back into the realization that everyone was watching her.

"Sorry. What?"

"I offered to go over with Mr. Bixby to get the car. Do you want to hang out here or go with?"

Mary thought it over.

"Jeopardy's on soon," Bixby wanted to hurry along the decision-making process.

"Tell you what. I'll stay here and work on dinner."

"You sure?" Lisa sneaked a glimpse out front.

"I'm sure," Mary nodded. She'd be double damned if she was going to let a few noisemakers make her afraid. Even if she was outnumbered.

"Okay," Lisa agreed. "I'll be home before you know I'm gone."

Lisa and Bixby managed to tiptoe out the back door, sans tulips, and head across the now very plain access road to what had he called it? The church gate? Mary would ask later. Right now, she set forth baking a couple of pieces of chicken, peeled two huge potatoes for boiling and cleaned some farm-fresh cauliflower. This last item she would steam. Lisa liked her vegetables tender crisp. So intent on her cooking, she didn't notice until she heard the noise that Lisa was on the back porch.

She had driven Bixby's truck back. Something wasn't right. Mary met Lisa halfway through the house.

"What happened? Where's our car? Where's Bixby?"

"Which one do you want me to answer first?" Lisa was calm. Too calm.

"Where's the car?"

"What's left of it is in smaller, chunked-up pieces."

"It's what?"

"You know, ready for the scrap heap. Apparently, that's where some of our detractors drifted off to while we were having beer and cookies."

"They demolished our car?"

"It's totaled. I wonder if our insurance covers this?"

"They totaled our car?" Mary asked again and then looked like she was in need of either a chair or a good stiff drink. Or both. Which Lisa arranged quickly.

"It's only a car," Lisa patted Mary's hand reassuringly.

"It was *our* car."

"Well, we'll just get a new one. And then we'll lock it up in the barn or something."

"Where's Bixby?"

"You wouldn't believe me if I told you."

"Try me."

"He's sitting guard over the remains with a double-barrel shotgun. He insisted on loaning me the truck until further notice. His words."

"Was anybody still there?"

"No. It didn't take too long to turn the car into a good imitation of a bumper car reject."

"Should we call the police?"

"I think it would be a good idea to start documenting the actions."

"Exactly. We already have them for trespassing onto Bixby's property."

"It's going to be our word against theirs."

"What do you mean?"

"It seems that before they wrecked it, they picked it up and took it off the premises."

"They picked it *up*?"

"Either that or they matched the tire tracks exactly while rolling it. But it was locked and the brake was on. So, I figured they just picked it up."

"I think the sheriff should investigate it."

"Okay, let's give him a call."

"I'll do it. Would you check on dinner for me?"

"Sure."

"I think I steamed the cauliflower way past crisp."

"It's okay. I can eat not-crisp cauliflower once in a while. You going to be okay?" Lisa smiled bravely.

"I'm going to be okay." Mary smiled back.

Lisa took over the cooking chores as Mary placed the call. It would take him about forty-five minutes to get to the Bixby place. It was, after all, the dinner hour. This meant that Mary had plenty of time to put the finishing touches on thoroughly mushy cauliflower.

"This is great!" Lisa lied between bites.

"Don't lie with your mouth full," Mary had regained some of her sense of humor.

"So, what kind of car should we buy?"

"Can civilians buy tanks?"

"You want a tank? Isn't that a bit of an overstatement?"

"Maybe a tractor? That would have a nice farmy sort of feel to it. Like to see them try to carry a tractor around."

"Maybe just a nice, solid, four-wheel drive vehicle."

"With an electric warning device that delivers a shock!"

"Oh hell, just leave the sticker price tag on it. That alone shocks most ordinary mortals."

They were in a giddy mood by the time they got in the truck to meet the sheriff at Bixby's. They called ahead to warn him and to avoid getting shot. It worked. By the time they arrived, the sheriff was taking Bixby's statement, nodding along as the old man told his story, but not writing much of anything down.

Mary and Lisa disembarked from the ancient but reliable truck and joined the investigation.

"So, which one of you came back over with Bixby here."

"I did," Lisa answered.

"And did you see anybody around here?"

"No."

"Neither did Bixby."

"So, you think the car beat itself up?" Mary could feel her temper starting to rev up.

"No, ma'am. I just figure that whoever did this worked real fast."

"And they're keeping pretty close tabs on us as well. We wouldn't have been down here at all had it not been for the fact that our driveway was blocked."

"Blocked?"

"Right. The protestors were sitting in our driveway."

"Why didn't you give me a call then? We would've come out and cleared a path."

"I understand that. Let me try to tell you why. My mother-"

"The Senator," the sheriff was already nodding.

"Right. My mother, the Senator, is already very agitated about the activities to date. She's ready to charter a flight and come out here and fix the problem."

"She might have a problem or two doing that," the sheriff interjected.

"You may be right, but try telling that to a United States Senator."

"I see your point."

"And if she sees the sheriff trying to remove protestors and smashed-up cars, she's going to be very difficult to deal with."

"Well, what do you suggest, Ms. Fairbanks?"

"I suggest that we put the smashed-up car under wraps before the media gets footage to up-link and then try to figure out several ways to get access to the property so that pretty soon, the protestors will lose interest."

"The first part sounds easy enough. The second might be tricky."

"They can use my place," Bixby offered. "It worked once."

"My fear is that they'll catch on and then block your place as well."

"And how would that look on the news?" Lisa asked.

"I'll tell ya what it'd look like," Bixby was getting the hang of this. "It'd look like a buncha mean people was pickin on an old man is what it'd look like!"

"And that's an image that they would want to avoid," Sheriff Clouber agreed.

"So, when they come to my driveway, I'll just teeter out to the truck and try to drive through but only if the TV folks are here which I could probably call and get em out here pretty quick."

"Let's not go out of our way just yet to gather a crowd," Mary steered everyone back to the original problem. "What we need more right now is another car. What do you suggest, Sheriff?"

"Maybe we can rent you something for now? Might have something in the garage that only needs a coupla parts?"

"A coupla parts?" Lisa, who had driven the best in her short life time, tried to hide her angst.

"Oh, nuthin major. A fan belt. Plugs and points. New muffler wouldn't hurt. And the thing that sprays the cleaning stuff on the windshield gets kinda clogged up. But if it isn't snow season, it should carry you through."

The sheriff was finishing up his soliloquy to car parts when Mary threw in another complication. "How easy would it be to land a helicopter?"

He didn't have to think long. "Lots of open space. Just kick up a fair amount of dust about all. Why? You thinking about getting a chopper?"

"Not for myself, but my mother might need one. With her medical condition and all, any delay in arriving at the farmhouse could be problematic."

"So, she's coming for sure?"

"If your daughter found herself in similar circumstances, what would you do?"

"My daughter isn't a homosexual in the middle of Kansas."

"Lucky her," Lisa answered, just a bit on the drippy side of sarcasm.

"I don't mean no harm by it, it's just that you two are, well…"

"Out?" Mary offered.

"I was thinking of 'obvious' but if 'out' is the right word, then 'out' it is."

"We're not trying to make a statement, we're just trying to get on with our lives. It isn't us who go milling around in front of other people's homes."

"Let me find you another car," Sheriff Clouber rose to leave. "Then, we'll work on clearing access to your driveway."

He lumbered out to his official vehicle and drove off down the road in a cloud of dust. After he was gone, Mary and Lisa used Bixby's truck to tow the remains of their car into his barn. As an afterthought, they covered it with a paint-splattered tarp, just in case of two things. Number one, the TV crew poked a camera through the window and number two, anybody ever thought to dust it for prints. Then, Bixby insisted that they take his truck and go home.

"How are you going to get around?" Lisa asked.

"I don't have a hot date tonight. You two gals go on."

"What about tomorrow night?" Mary asked with just a hint of a smile.

"If I get a date tomorrow night, you'll be the first to know," he guffawed as only an old geezer can. On that note, Mary and Lisa headed across the field. It was well past dark by the time they got home, secured the truck in the barn and went to bed. Things were quiet. There wasn't much left to say, it seemed. Lisa finally thought of something.

"We can't possibly be the only lesbians in Kansas."

"Then, why does it feel that way?" Mary asked.

"Because," Lisa explained succinctly, "that's how they *want* it to feel."

Chapter 19

Trish, Robbie and Rose passed on the gun-buying trip. Max
went along with Silver, if only to ride shotgun, pun intended.
She picked out two for good measure, as she had planned. Max
was no expert, but they looked deadly enough. This activity had
happened soon after Trish and Robbie had returned from
Cleveland with their possible evidence packet. When Trish had
called Detective Forrest to report, he was more than happy to
stop by and check the evidence. He was impressed with their
technique, but scolded them on the risk involved.
"You should leave this kind of thing to the professionals," he
chided, a lot too snippy for Robbie's taste.
"And what would you have done?" she asked back.
"Well, I would've taken a couple of detectives out there and
done some…detecting."
"Wow, why didn't we think of that," Robbie gee-whizzed in his
general direction.
"You don't think I can handle this?" he asked back, bristling a
bit himself.
"To date, I'm not dazzled," Robbie said quietly and then excused
herself to check on coffee and cookies.
"She doesn't like me much, does she?" he asked of Trish after
Robbie was out of earshot. Barely.
"It's been hard on her to have her mother threatened. I'm sure
you understand."
"Sure, sure. Now, let's talk about what you have."
Trish and Sam discussed the various details of the packets of
surveys and pens.
"What you did wasn't legal, but I guess you're used to that sort
of thing."
Trish didn't dignify the crack with a reply and held the door open
for the detective. He took the evidence and left. Trish went to
the kitchen to find Robbie. She was just studying the last of the
coffee dripping from the pot.
"What does Detective Forrest take in his coffee?"
"Doesn't matter. He's gone now."

"Is that a reproach I detect?" Robbie was well tuned into Trish's moods by now. And subsequent tones of voice.

"You were effective."

"It's not against the law to refrain from fawning over the police."

"Are you always going to be this jealous?"

Robbie thought about the question for an awfully long time. Her answer, by comparison, was short. "I don't know."

"I never thought of you as the jealous type, whatever that is," Trish wandered around the subject.

"I don't think I ever was before."

"What makes people jealous?" Trish asked.

"People in general or me in specific?"

"Whoever you feel like talking about."

"I can talk about me. Talking about me is okay."

"Okay."

They sat down at the kitchen table with coffee and a plate of cookies between them. Trish ate while Robbie nibbled.

"Everyone thinks you're attractive," Robbie said quietly, somehow veering off the subject of herself long enough to concentrate on Trish.

"They do?"

"Detective Forrest, that woman at Glens Falls residential care center…"

"Okay," Trish had more or less forgotten all about the woman in New York. "That's two people."

"There are lots and lots of others. You just don't notice them."

"But, you do?"

"It's a little hard not to. You really have no idea how attractive you are."

"I'm not that attractive. If they're looking at anyone, it's you."

"It is not. Stop it!"

"Why do you have a hard time believing that?"

"Because I'm not at all the cover-girl type. I'm big and not blond."

"Honey, there are billions of women on the planet. Less than one-thousand of one percent are cover-girl types. I didn't marry you for your hair color or body type. I married you for the special way you make me feel inside every time I hear your voice or see your face or touch your hand. I love you for the tender way you remind me what my name is after you kiss me. Detective Forrest can drool until he creates high tide and I wouldn't care."

"And I shouldn't either," Robbie had a sheepish look.

"You know what you really need to be worrying about instead of Detective Forrest?" Trish challenged.

"What?"

"You need to worry about how to spend all that money after the auction is over!"

"I'm trying not to think about it."

"Why?"

"Because I've never thought of the money as mine."

"It'll be ours. I wouldn't have met Albert had it not been for you."

"But we still have Connors to think about."

"Yes, we do. But I'm still spending some of the money on you so either you have a list ready or be content with my selections."

"I always have been before, content, that is," Robbie finally smiled.

"Well then," Trish followed up with a dare, "Let's try for something way beyond content!"

Chapter 20

"Are you sure two suitcases are going to be enough?" Rebecca
called out from the other room.
Mitch closed her eyes and pretended not to hear. Word had
leaked out on the fate of Mary's car and as they say in the good
book, that was the straw that broke the camel's back. Or maybe
that wasn't in the good book? Mitch pondered. Mitch was still
pondering this as Rebecca wheeled back into their bedroom. She
had a lightweight suitcase balanced on her lap and tossed it
unceremoniously on the bed. Mitch tried to ignore this as well,
but Reb started peppering her with questions.
"Did you hear me? Are two suitcases going to be enough?
Where's the makeup bag? Did you remember to pick up my dry
cleaning?"
Mitch only shut her eyes tighter and feigned snoring. Not loud,
but noticeable nevertheless. Things got very quiet. Too quiet.
Mitch opened one eye. The Senator was looming over her, at
least as much as anyone could loom in a wheelchair. It was, for
the most part, psychological.
"Yes. I hope so. In the top dresser drawer. Don't I always."
Mitch provided all the right answers and in the right order.
"You think I'm making a big deal out of this, don't you?" Reb
asked in the tone of voice she usually reserved for fights.
"No."
Mitch's unwillingness to be drawn into an argument made
Rebecca even testier.
"They march around, block the driveway, smash up her car and
you want me to just sit here and twiddle my thumbs!"
"I've never seen you twiddle your thumbs yet. Why would you
start now?"
"You're just upset because you can't come," Reb noted for the
record.
Mitch thought of a least one interesting reply, but bit her tongue.
Lately, she was the only one interested in that particular pursuit
anyway, but now just didn't seem like a good time to bring *that*
up.

"I'm not upset," Mitch raised up on one elbow, mostly just to make eye contact.

"That's the nicest word I could come up with."

"Well then, let's hear the not-so-nice words."

"Okay, how about…insufferable!"

"Insufferable? Oh gee, that's pretty not-so-nice!" Mitch almost laughed, which made Rebecca's eyes narrow even further.

"Why don't you just call me an asshole. Maybe that would make you feel better?"

"Well, it might make me feel better, but imagine how denigrating that would be to assholes all across the nation to be compared to you!"

Mitch didn't say anything but held eye contact with Reb until she looked down.

"I'm sorry. That was really uncalled for."

"It's okay," Mitch sat up and reached out to lightly touch the side of Reb's face. "I think you're right, or at least close."

"I don't think I'm right nor close. I don't know what I'm thinking."

"Then, forget for a minute about thinking," Mitch took Reb's hands into her own. "Tell me what you're feeling."

"I'm angry."

"At me?"

"No! At all those people who are bothering Mary."

"And Lisa?"

"And Lisa."

"And what are you going to do when you get there with your two suitcases full of all that dry cleaning I picked up?"

"Change my clothes a lot, I guess," Reb said with a smidgen of humor. At least it was returning.

"Now, that's a sight I'm sorry I won't be there to see," Mitch teased back.

"Well, I could change my clothes in front of you a couple of times before I go. Maybe that would hold you until I get back?"

"It's what I live for."

"I know the real reason you're being such an…insufferable jerk."

"You do?" Mitch raised both eyebrows. This she had to hear.

"It's my first trip away from you."

"No, it isn't. You went all the way to Japan once without me."

199

"I meant, you know, apres accident."

Mitch thought it over. She was right. "That's French, isn't it?"

"Don't pretend to hide behind a language barrier. You're going to miss me while I'm gone and worry every minute and you don't need to."

"I don't need to miss you?" Mitch pretended to be so dense as to lose track.

"Oh, you need to miss me like nobody's business," Rebecca pulled Mitch closer. "You need to miss me before I even finish packing."

"Hell, I miss you before you've even started."

"But you don't need to worry."

"Why not?" Mitch wanted details.

"Because it's just Kansas. It's not like I'm going to Mars."

"A trip to Mars wouldn't worry me."

"So, you admit I'm right to be concerned."

Mitch made a note for her memoirs. Don't ever expect to win in a debate with a Senator.

"I never said you weren't right to be concerned. I just don't know what you can do that the local law enforcement hasn't already done."

"I'm a mother. There's very little I *can't* do!"

For once in her life, Mitch refrained from stating the obvious. It kept her out of trouble. For the time being. Although it was awkward, Reb pulled Mitch into a kiss. One of those slow, long-drawn out ones that brought out all of the compliant genes that Mitch had. There were an awful lot of them, and Reb knew them all by heart.

"Now, are you going to help me pack?" Reb asked.

Mitch couldn't trust her voice, so she just nodded. If it wasn't for the fact that Mitch and Jane were expecting several major deliveries to their opening-soon restaurant, she would be packing for two. Maybe in a way, this was best. They hadn't been apart for any length of time in months. Mitch didn't need a break from all the extra things she did for Reb, but Reb probably needed a vacation from Mitch's constant nurse-maiding.

"Does Mary have everything you need?"

"I doubt it. Last I heard, she was still trying to get a bed delivered."

"Single or double?"

"Does it matter?"

"If we ever visit together, it does," Mitch unzipped the first suitcase. "It would be terrible if you had to sleep on the floor over Thanksgiving!"

"You don't think I can, do you?"

"Hell, I haven't slept on the floor since high school."

"Maybe you could practice while I'm gone?" Reb was in a full teasing mood by now.

"Anything would be better than sleeping in our bed without you," Mitch sighed.

Now it was Reb's turn to hide the tremor in her voice. It took her a while to remark, "Then I sincerely hope it's a double."

"I can fly out later in the week, if you want?"

"Why don't we play it by ear?"

"Did you say something about playing with my ears?" Mitch was eager to know.

"You wish!" Reb giggled. It was good to be over the worst of their discussion. It was only concern and tension that caused them to squabble and deep down, they both knew it.

"You did say 'ears,' right?"

"What if I said 'rear' instead?"

"I'm gonna call Jane and tell her I won't be there!"

"No, you can't do that!" Reb was adamant. "You need to be here for Jane and that marvelous restaurant you've named after me."

"And you need some time alone with Mary," Mitch surrendered gracefully.

"And Lisa." Reb added this time.

"And Lisa."

"Besides, your ears will still be here when I get back."

"So will my rear."


Mary only paced about half the finish off the already worn down floor waiting for the bed to be delivered. Lisa feared for the floor itself by the time the week was over.

"Honey, why don't you sit down and I'll get you a cup of coffee," Lisa offered.

"I don't want a cup of coffee."

"Maybe a cup of hot tea instead?"

"It's already eighty degrees and it's only eight in the morning. Does that sound like hot tea weather to you?"

There were times when Lisa wished that she had a better communication with Mitch, just to be able to crib notes on how to deal with the Fairbanks women. This was one of those times.

"Guess not," Lisa replied calmly. Perhaps too calmly?

"I don't fucking believe this!" Mary suddenly and vehemently stated.

"What don't you believe, fucking and otherwise?" Lisa was calm.

"I don't believe that I need to get a police escort just to have a bed delivered for my mother!"

"Well, I think it's nice that the sheriff-"

"That's not the point!" Mary interrupted tersely.

"It isn't?"

"No!"

"Well, what is the point?" Lisa fished cautiously. These waters could be tricky.

"No one should need a police escort to have some stupid furniture delivered."

"You're right, of course, but it is nice to get cooperation from both the sheriff and the furniture store."

"That's why we pay taxes and delivery charges, and at time-and-a-half, I'm sure!"

Lisa had to agree, Mary did have the time-and-a-half part right. In fact, this might be closer to triple rate pay or perhaps combat? After notifying Sheriff Clouber that the honorable Senator from Colorado was visiting her daughter and lesbian lover deep in the heart of Kansas, as they say in church, all holy hell broke loose. The sheriff had been considering calling in more help before now, and the consideration had gone straight to serious after Mary's phone call. Of course, things like this never remain a secret very long, and before the sheriff could beef up his reserves, the protestors had gone and done likewise. The press followed suit and before you knew it, an entire two-mile stretch of road was filled with the curious and the curiouser. How anyone was going to manage to get a delivery truck down it was anyone's guess.  Lisa, who had been silently weighing all this in her mind must have had a troubled look on her face, for Mary touched her hand and said, "I'm sorry."

"What?" Lisa came back to the moment.

"I don't mean to snap at you."

"Don't think another thing about it.  I didn't take it personally."

"I'll take that cup of coffee if you're still offering it."

"Coming right up."

Truth be told, the stress was beginning to get to Lisa as well. When they had first moved in, although the place was bare, it was quiet.  It was a lover's paradise where they could make love and know that there was no one within shouting distance to hear them.  Now, all that had changed.  After pinning up rather thin sheets on most of the windows, they were still finding it harder and harder to maintain any sort of intimacy.  Just the thought of being in the vortex of all this activity messed up their powers of sexual concentration.  Not that that was all that kept them together.  They were, after all, several months into their relationship.  There were so many other things that were important.  Maybe not as much fun…

"Hey, you gonna get me that coffee today or next week?" Mary prodded Lisa into action.

"I'm workin on it!" Lisa hurried along to cover up her dawdling.

"You're distracted.  Are you okay?"

"My mother-in-law is coming for a visit.  I have a God-given right to be distracted."

"Does she still make you nervous?"

"She's one of the hundred most powerful people on the planet. Gosh, why would *that* make an ordinary daughter-in-law nervous?"

"You're not an *ordinary* daughter-in-law," Mary assured her in positive terms.

"If you say so."

"I say so.  And I'm the daughter of that most powerful person on the planet."

"Ooohhh," Lisa tried to sound really, really impressed.  Mary pulled her close despite the ever-present gawkers to see how much more she could impress her.  It only took a couple of kisses to make a really good impression.  Lisa melted into Mary's arms and held on tightly. It felt good. Better than anything they had had lately.

"I miss you," Lisa breathed quietly.

"What are you talking about? I've been here all the time."

"I miss having you all to myself. Away from the maddening crowd."

"We could always soundproof the bedroom."

"We'd need to soundproof the whole house to suit me."

"The whole house, huh?" Mary had a excruciatingly tender tease in her voice. "You're planning to make love to me in every room of the house?"

"Once at least," Lisa smiled.

"A day?" Mary wanted to clarify the situation.

"You don't think I can, do you!"

"I look forward to it!"

"Me, too. Just as soon as we reassure our pending houseguest that everything is okay out here in the wilds of Utopia."

"Which would be a whole lot easier if we had a bed for her."

"Which is coming down the road as we speak" Lisa remarked with a mixture of hope and dread.

Mary turned to see the spectacle for herself. A truck with a bed in it surrounded by four motorcycle police was inching its way through the crowd of protestors. Two police cars were in front and a contingent of officers on foot were decked out in riot gear. By contrast, the protestors were all moderately well-behaved, demonstrating, no pun intended, none of their more assertive tactics to date and instead giving the impression that they were poor helpless citizens being picked on by the big, bad government. All in all, it made Mary want to throw up.

"Well, at least there's hope for getting your mother in here safe and sound," Lisa said with gusto.

"We're not bringing my mother in here in a truck."

"Oh yeah," Lisa nodded. The ETA of the helicopter was still a state secret, but it was due very soon.

"Come on. Let's go get the bed set up."

"I'm right behind you."

By noon, things were eerily quiet. The bed had been set up along with some heavy-duty drapes in the guest bathroom. The most privacy that could be afforded was the best gift Mary could offer. Meanwhile, part of the police escort withdrew alongside the delivery truck, still leaving a substantial contingent at the house. Mary had used the remaining time wisely, cooking a modest dinner of pork roast, green beans and scalloped potatoes. A puffy lump of bread dough was doing its best to rise to the occasion.

"Sweetie, why don't we go to bed for a while," Lisa thought that sounded like a good idea while they waited.

"I *can't*. I'm too nervous. Besides, my mother is due any minute!"

"I didn't mean *that*," Lisa explained.

"*That?*"

"I just meant that every little bit of rest would help. Why don't you go put your feet up for a few minutes. I promise I'll guard the bread dough."

Mary thought it over. "Okay, you talked me into it. But wake me up the minute anything exciting happens."

Lisa monitored the progress of the dinner for a good thirty minutes before she heard the unmistakable beating of helicopter blades on unsuspecting air. As the noise got louder, Lisa peeked in on Mary. She was sound asleep, not even stirring once. Lisa let her be and went to the back door. She stayed inside until the chopper was down. It scattered bucketfuls of dust before it was over. There had to be at least five guards around the general area and it took three of them to lift Rebecca out in her wheelchair. She maneuvered her way to the back porch and was greeted by Lisa at the door.

"Mary's asleep."

"Asleep?"

"So, could you direct everyone to keep the noise down."

"I'll do what I can."

Rebecca chatted briefly with someone who appeared to be in charge, at least where decibel levels were concerned and in moments, Rebecca's luggage was placed noiselessly in the spare bedroom. Soon afterward, the helicopter was buttoned up and on its way. This left Lisa and Rebecca facing each other in awkward silence.

"Come on in," Lisa spoke quietly, leading the way to the kitchen. Not that Rebecca needed leading. She was just trailing behind a bit, scanning the rooms as she followed.

"You want coffee, or tea, or maybe a good stiff drink?" Lisa offered.

Reb thought it over carefully.

"I'll take that drink," she answered as she wheeled closer to the front window. The protestors were watching intently with zombie-like stares. It gave Reb a chill.

"You're shivering," Lisa remarked.

"I'm cold."

"It's over ninety degrees."

"It's still cooler than Washington, what with the difference in humidity."

"I suppose," Lisa put a double bourbon in front of Rebecca. She took a couple of sips before asking, "So, how long has Mary been asleep?"

"Not very long. She was exhausted.'

"The worry is getting to her, isn't it?"

Lisa didn't know exactly which worry Reb was referring to, so she kept quiet. A stunningly wise choice, she thought.

"Your silence is deafening," Reb noted after another sip.

"Well, it's not every day that a helicopter drops a senator off on your doorstep. Not much to say after that."

"You don't approve of my coming, do you?"

Lisa wondered if it was too late to call Mitch and ask for that advice.

"I'm glad you're here. Nobody else wants to visit much, what with the picket line."

"It's worse than I thought."

"A lot of that crowd today is due to your arrival. I expect traffic to die down. Maybe by Thanksgiving."

Reb found herself smiling.

"What?" Lisa asked.

"Mitch was just talking about Thanksgiving before my flight."

"And how is old Mitch?" Lisa asked as if they were talking about a distant acquaintance. Or maybe more like a faithful horse or trusty dog.

"Old Mitch," Reb paused for emphasis, "is just fine."

They looked at each other in that unique way people do when they have shared the bed of the topic of conversation.

"And how are you?" Lisa followed up politely.

"I'm still dead from the waist down."

"Puts you ahead of a number of your colleagues who appear to be dead from the neck up."

"Oooh, ouch!" Reb would've giggled if it were Mitch saying this, but she wanted to keep some reserve with Lisa. So, she simply took a good long drink from her glass and then excused herself to freshen up and unpack. Somewhere in this process, she took a moment to check the new bed for comfort and dozed off. She awoke to the sound of voices taking turns in a muted conversation. It was Mary and Lisa. Words drifted by…

"I told you to wake me up if something exciting happened!"

"Nothing exciting has happened as far as I can tell."

"My mother got here."

"That's nice, but not exciting."

"Well, what would fall under the category of exciting?"

"If all the protestors went away. Now that would be exciting."

The voices died away and a clattering of pans and dishes took their place. This pleased Reb. She was starving after her long day. After wrestling herself out of bed and running a brush through her hair, she wheeled into the kitchen. Mary looked up from her cooking.

"Hello! Did you have a nice nap?"

"I could ask you the same thing," Reb smiled as Mary swooped down for a hug.

"I cannot believe I slept through the helicopter!"

"They are making them quieter all the time."

"I probably snored right through it."

Lisa only nodded quiet agreement. That would explain it. She finished up the cooking chores as Mary and her mother chatted. After all the years, they had become quite good at this, not succumbing to the dysfunction that so many mothers and daughters fall into over time. That quiet, "I could tell you but I won't" sort of family warfare that makes for uncomfortable silences around many people's dinner tables. No, they talked all through dinner and halfway through dessert before noticing that two things had happened. The protestors had gone home for the day and Lisa hadn't said much of anything.

"You're pretty quiet tonight, Sweetie," Mary touched her hand as they picked up the dishes.

"Couldn't get a word in edgewise with the family reunion," Lisa smiled.

"Does my mom look okay to you?"

"Sure. She looks fine. You don't think so?"

"She just looks a little thin to me."

Lisa thought it over and was going to remark that it was probably due to the wasting that can happen to paraplegics, but kept her mouth shut. At least, about that prognosis.

"Once she starts eating your cooking, she'll plump right up."

"Oh really? Like how you *haven't*?" Mary played with words.

"I've gotten a little on the chunky side myself lately," Lisa made it sound like bragging.

So much so that Mary stood back to get a full survey for her own determination.

"Hey, you better knock off ogling me like that in front of houseguests."

"Oh yeah," Mary edged closer. "And what are you going to do if I don't?"

"I'm going to start by making you do the rest of the dishes," Lisa warned playfully.

"Why don't I do that anyway and you go put your feet up. You're the only one who hasn't had a nap today."

"I'm fine. I'll finish up here. You go in and talk to your mom. You're better at that than I am."

"For obvious reasons, I guess."

"Yeah, I guess."

Lisa finished up her chores and went to bed early. She felt Mary slip in between the sheets about midnight.

"Long talk?"

"Lots to do before bed. It isn't easy when someone has a lot of health issues."

"Umm," was Lisa's last reply before dozing back to sleep.

Chapter 21

Saturday dawned bright and clear. It was a week before the auction. Trish had spent the morning on the phone making reservations. Since the art auction was going to be held in New York, she thought it best to make plans ahead of time. She had almost waited too long, but managed to reserve a nice suite at the Marriott. Not the honeymoon suite, mind you. Trish had had enough of that for one lifetime. Not honeymoon, just honeymoon suites.

"You certainly have a curious look on your face," Robbie sat beside Trish on their couch. It was a lumpy, snugly worn out old thing that folded out to a single bed. Hence the lumps.

"I do?"

"Yeah. It was an interesting mixture of pleasure and dread. Is it the trip to New York that makes you look so?"

"I'm sure you're right," Trish fibbed. No use dredging up past misunderstandings.

"So, you got us a room?"

"Two, actually," Trish showed her the notes she had made."

"Goodness! You put us on the concierge level?"

"Whatever that is?" Trish shrugged her shoulders.

"Those are going to be very nice! And you say you booked two rooms?"

"One for us and one for your parents."

"That only leaves one question."

"What's that?"

"Who gets Silver?"

"Should I have gotten another room?"

"No, she's there to be a bodyguard, after all."

"So, that means you and I get a room all to ourselves," Trish tossed her notes aside to concentrate on *those* plans.

"Now, don't get ahead of yourself," Robbie said with a hint of playfulness in her voice. "We still need to *talk* about a couple of things."

"Okay," Trish put her arm around Robbie, just so she wouldn't get away. "What do you want to talk about?"

"I was wondering if you've heard from Detective Forrest?"

"I have," Trish nodded.

"And?"

"And nothing. None of the fingerprints matched up with anything."

"So, he could have still used gloves."

"Oh, sure."

"And what about the handwriting?"

"Nothing that would be admissible in court."

"And since there's been no recent letter, no use checking the ink."

"We are definitely in a holding pattern," Trish was hoping the words would mean more than one thing.

"Speaking of which, did you make airline reservations?" Robbie was touching all the bases, except one.

"Exactly how much more talking do I have to do before I get a kiss?"

"Exactly?"

"Yeah?"

"Coach or first class?"

"Kiss?"

"No, flight!"

"You're just going to have to wait and be surprised."

"Can I take a carry-on bag or will we need to check all the luggage?"

"How much luggage are we talking about?" Trish asked like there was going to be a surcharge.

"It's New York! That's a lot to pack for."

"Have you taken your mom shopping yet?"

"She's hesitant."

"About spending a lot of money?"

"I told her I'd buy her things, but she doesn't want to leave the house."

"Well, then, why don't we bring the store to her?"

"Can you do that?"

"It's worth a shot, don't you think?"

"How would we go about it?"

"Where does your mom like to shop?"

"She likes Marleys."

"Let's give them a call. Maybe they'll bring a few things over to the house."

"That's a terrific idea. I can give them her size and preferences to help them narrow down the selection. Who do I call?"

"Maybe they have one of those personal shoppers. I'd start there."

"Will do. Now, what else do I need to do?"

"You need to quit stalling and kiss me before you drive me clear up the wall."

"You wanted a kiss?" Robbie batted her eyelids, which only served to melt Trish even more. "Why didn't you just say so!"

"I didn't?" Trish played along as she put her other arm around Robbie.

"Maybe you did?" Robbie turned her full attention to Trish. It was almost too overwhelming and Trish struggled to keep her kisses soft and teasing. It was what Robbie liked best so early in the process and soon, she was glad she had. Robbie was setting the pace, and Trish was happily being carried along.

Their fun was rudely interrupted by the phone. Trish checked the caller ID. It was Mitch.

"You'd better take the call," Robbie breathed patiently. "She doesn't call unless it's important."

"Okay, but don't you go away. I'm just getting warmed up."

"I'm staying right here," Robbie vowed.

Trish answered the phone, "Hello, Mitch!"

"How'd you know it was me?"

"We have one of those ID things."

"Oh, yeah. Well, how are you?"

"I'm sitting next to the most beautiful woman on the planet. How's that for an answer?"

"Oh dear, is this a bad time to be calling? If it is, I can call back."

"This is a fine time to call. What's on your mind?"

"Well, I remembered that you're coming to my end of the continent one of these days, and wondered if we could get together?"

If Trish didn't know better, she might have thought that Mitch sounded lonely.

"We'd love to get together, are you okay?"

"I'm fine," Mitch heard the rush of words and knew to address them all. "It's just been a little quiet around here, what with Rebecca in Kansas."

"That's right!" Trish emphasized, "We've been hearing snippets of that on the news. Is everything okay there?"

"What have you heard?"

"We heard about the small protests."

"Is that all?"

"Is there more?"

"There's been a bit of vandalism to Mary's car."

"A bit?"

"It sort of got smashed to smithereens."

"Geez, we didn't hear about that!"

"Well, Rebecca did and now she's there and I'm here and you're coming when? Or is that a delicate question?" Mitch asked diplomatically.

Trish laughed. We'll be there in about a week. In New York, that is!"

"Just up the road."

"And we're taking a swing through Glens Falls to visit Connors and set up some more permanent funding for his care."

"So, do we get together before or after all this activity?"

Trish had been watching Robbie as she talked and as if somehow Robbie had been privy to both sides of the conversation, answered, "How about after? We can extend our visit by a day or so."

"Make it a week. You can stay here."

"Oh, that would be too much. Remember, we're a party of five lately, what with our bodyguard."

"You still don't have any good leads on those threatening letters?" Mitch swept away the cobwebs on that particular subject. After the topic of the letters had become general knowledge, Mary had told her mother, who in turn had told Mitch.

"Not yet, but we're keeping an eye out for an old man who uses a walker."

"And you need a bodyguard for that?"

"Well, that and the check from the auction that we're supposedly going to be carrying around."

"That makes sense, I guess. But back to the old guy. He uses a walker?"

"Yes and he's our prime suspect and we're just waiting for another letter to nail him."

"What if you don't get another letter?"

Trish hadn't thought about it that way. "I don't know. I guess we'll have a bodyguard for life. She's not that bad, once you get used to her."

"A bodyguard for life? Maybe it's okay for you, but I think that would drive me batty. Probably the only reason I'm not running for president!"

"Well, maybe you're not, but what about Rebecca?"

"Rebecca? Last I heard she wasn't planning on getting reelected to the Senate, let alone launching a presidential bid."

"Really? Well, what is she going to do with herself in six years?"

"You're just going to have to ask her for yourself when you get here."

"Okay, but in the meantime, you get the spare bedroom cleaned up."

"I'll change the sheets on the bed personally!"

"We're looking forward to seeing you again."

"Me, too."

On that note, they hung up. Trish sat quietly, most if not all of her playfulness fading away.

"What's wrong?" Robbie asked, puzzled at Trish's sudden change. Half of the conversation hadn't sounded that bad.

"I don't know. It's just that I get these funny feelings once in a while that things aren't going to turn out the way we plan them."

"Good funny or bad funny?'

"I can't tell yet. Just *funny*."

"How about I go make that phone call to Marleys. Maybe now is a good time?"

"I'm sorry I'm being such a wet blanket."

"Don't worry about it. We'll catch up on that later."

"Okay."

Trish checked her notes again after Robbie went to use the extension phone. She had hotel suites on the concierge level, a charter jet, and a rental limousine lined up. Everything they would need for their appointment with fate. Maybe that's what was giving her all these strange feelings. They were destined to gain or lose a fortune in practically the same length of time that most people have for vacation. What their life afterwards would be like was anyone's guess. Whatever it was, she would have Robbie by her side. And as this comforting thought crossed her mind, Robbie returned.

"I made the call."

"Come over here," Trish indicated the still-warm spot on the couch.

"And they said that they could be most accommodating."

"So can I," Trish said as she pulled Robbie into another kiss, this one a bit more direct than the previous ones. Which suited Robbie just fine. She was ready for more than teasing by now anyway.

"Let's go to the bedroom," Robbie breathed in Trish's ear.

"You got something against the couch?" Trish wasn't budging.

"It's lumpy," Robbie reminded her.

"So am I and it hasn't bothered you yet."

"Oh, but you're lumpy in all the right places. That's the difference!"

"I see. You lead and I'll follow."

They spent a magnificent forty-five minutes in bed. Thirty of those minutes were pure physical joy. The remaining fifteen were spent in quiet conversation. As a couple, their relationship had evolved to the point where they were entirely comfortable with each other. Robbie, once shy over her plump body, had moved beyond that. As for Trish, she was just getting used to the fact that she had the most wonderful partner in the universe. They were a perfect match.

"Did you ever get your funny feelings figured out?" Robbie wanted to know for sure.

"I think I'm just apprehensive about our upcoming trip."

"Why?"

"You know me. I don't like to be the center of attention."

"Funny, you didn't give me that impression about twenty minutes ago," Robbie traced with a lazy finger places that hadn't been touched lately. Like about twenty minutes ago lately. She was an equal opportunity teaser.

"Well, that was twenty minutes ago," Trish smiled and caught Robbie's wandering finger and held on gently, lest she forget what she was saying.

"You're worried about the auction?"

"I assume there's going to be a lot of press coverage. Like at our wedding."

"Personally, I don't mind that so much."

"You don't?"

"I figure that you and I have been given a chance to be a somewhat high-profile gay couple for a reason. It means having a lot of responsibility, but imagine the positive impact we could be having for other gay couples everywhere?"

"It doesn't seem to be working out so well for Mary and Lisa."

"Well, that's different," Robbie philosophized.

"Really. Why?"

"Because they are in Kansas."

Somehow, it made perfect sense when Robbie said it.

Chapter 22

"You want to do what?" Rebecca sounded incredulous.
"Which part didn't you understand?" Mary countered. It wasn't that difficult a concept.
"You want to go to church tomorrow?"
"She's been going lately," Lisa popped in with her two cents.
"I didn't ask you," Reb snapped without even looking over at her.
"In that case," Lisa knew when to bow out," I think I'll go take a bath."
Lisa hadn't even cleared out of the room yet before the debate resumed.
"I went last week and the world continued to spin on its axis."
"Last week was different."
"Not really. In fact, the protestors sort of take a break on Sunday morning."
"And so you think you'll be able to drive down the road?"
"I won't know until I try."
"Will Lisa go with you?"
"I'll ask her later. Why?"
"I just worry about you, that's all."
"Nothing has happened to me yet at church."
"Well, wake me up before you go, okay?"
"Okay. I'll even cook you breakfast."
"Don't go to any trouble. I'm your mother, not a guest."
"So, you don't eat breakfast anymore?"
"Mitch makes me a cup of coffee."
"Doesn't sound like much."
"You haven't tasted Mitch's coffee lately. I have no idea how she's going to run a restaurant."
"She'll probably do that like she does everything else."
"How's that?"
"One day at a time."

Chapter 23

Mitch and Jane nodded their approval. It looked damn good, this new kitchen of theirs. Of course, it wasn't done. But it looked damn good.

"This looks good!" Jane ran her hand along a shiny new counter top.

"Plenty of space to work," Mitch nodded her approval.

"You like it?" Jane knew the answer but wanted to hear it.

"I love it."

"We'd better. We're going to spend a lot of time here."

"But, we are going to be able to hire some help," Mitch reminded.

"Some. But if we don't start right off the bat working toward a breakeven point, we're going to be sunk."

"With you as chief chef, we'll do terrific."

"You have a lot of faith in me."

"You deserve it."

They fell silent, all out of compliments.

"You want to go get a drink?" Jane asked tentatively.

Mitch thought it over for about one-fourth of one second. "Sure. That's a great idea. My treat. Where do you want to go?"

"How about Skeeters?"

"Fine. Let's go."

Skeeters was far enough away that they took separate cars. Jane had finally gotten a driver's license and a car. She knew that she could no longer rely on the bus, subway or taxi to meet her hectic schedule demands. They found two parking places relatively close and entered the bar together. Nobody sat up and took notice, like they usually did when Mitch and Rebecca went anywhere together. It was nice for a change. They sat in a corner booth and ordered an expensive bottle of wine. Jane, in her pervious life as a hooker, had gotten used to being served the best. Mitch tried to not disappoint. They sipped for a few minutes in silence before Jane spoke up.

"You sure miss her, don't you?"

Mitch looked up. "I guess I'm not being very good company."

"I didn't say that. It just seems like about half of you is missing."

"My better half," Mitch smiled. It made her sound so…married. The effect was not lost on Jane. "What is life like with her?" Mitch could've answered the question from several standpoints, which was probably by design on the part of Jane.

"What part do you want to know about?"

"What part do you want to talk about?"

Mitch didn't recall mentioning wanting to talk about any part of it, but thought it better to talk than to appear recalcitrant.

"Have you ever had the sensation that you're about two feet taller than you are?"

"No, not really."

"Well, that's how it feels."

"How what feels?"

"Life with Senator Fairbanks."

Jane thought it over. "That's an odd description."

"It's an odd life."

"Are you very worried about her being in Kansas with all those protestors?"

"Not really. Rebecca, Mary and Lisa are three very resourceful women. Even I try to not tangle with them on any given day."

Jane raised her glass. "Here's to three resourceful women."

"Five, counting us," Mitch added.

Chapter 24

Sunday started out hot. Mary couldn't believe it. She hadn't
even gotten out of bed yet and she was warm and sticky. Lisa
wasn't to blame, either. *She* was still asleep.
"I'm getting up to cook breakfast," Mary gave fair warning.
"Hum?" Lisa muttered awake.
"I said I'm cooking breakfast."
"None for me. I think I have a cold. I'm going back to sleep."
"How bad do you feel?"
"It's just the sniffles. I'll be fine tomorrow. You go on to
church."
"Are you sure?"
"I'm positive. I just need some rest."
"Okay."
Mary got out of bed and hurried to make early services. She
could be out and gone before the protestors arrived and then
sneak back in through Bixby's place. Her mother and Lisa could
certainly fend for themselves.

The first thing Rebecca smelled was smoke. At first, it irritated
her. If Lisa had started smoking, she was going to raise the roof.
Didn't she know that was bad for her? Irritation soon turned to
concern when the smokiness got thicker. Maybe Mary was
burning breakfast? She called out Mary's name and then true
terror sank into her gut when she realized that it was more than
breakfast that was burning. Much more. She discerned the
unmistakable crackle of flames making quick work of hundred-
year-old wood. Instinctively, she started to scream names.
Mary's first and then Lisa's as she struggled to get out of bed
and into her wheelchair. Halfway into the task, Lisa stumbled
her way into the room. Without delay, Lisa helped to hurry the
process, unceremoniously cramming the half-dressed Reb into
the chair and aiming her in the direction of the front door. She
stopped long enough to locate the cell phone that Mary left
behind and tossed it into Reb's lap as they went toward the front
of the house. It was too late for safe exit so Lisa wheeled Reb
around and propelled her toward the back door. It would be
tough to negotiate the back steps, but it would be doable. Thick

smoke blinded them as they made their way and in the confusion of the noise, panic and limited visibility, Reb felt as if she was moving half speed through the house. She reached the door, felt it for temperature, opened it and looked over her shoulder to yell instructions to Lisa on how to take her down steps. When she focused through her terror, she realized why she had moved so slowly the last few yards. Lisa had collapsed on the floor, a prisoner of the smoke and fire. Reb turned to wheel back in and was pushed back by the hell-hot air.

Frantically, she sped to the porch steps, and using every trick they taught her in rehab, bounced her way down the steps and onto the dirt path. From there, she dialed 911 on the cell phone and alerted the emergency operator as to the seriousness of the situation. All professional and volunteer firefighters would be notified. Next, she patched a call through to the helicopter service who had delivered her in the first place. They would deploy in minutes, they promised.

Rebecca could feel the heat begin to radiate from the house, mostly the front however, and tried her best to stay close to the door anyway. Her vision was blocked as much by tears of frustration and she chided herself to snap out of it. She then placed her third call to Mitch. Thank the lord, she answered on the second ring.
"Mitch!" Rebecca yelled into the phone.
"Hello. How are you?"
"Listen carefully. I need you to do something for me!"
"Okay."
"Find out the name of the best burn center in that area."
"I already know that."
"You do?"
"Sure. When you're in the restaurant business, that's one of the first things on the list. It's Maryland General."
"Maryland General?" Reb hollered into the phone. Noise from the oncoming rescue crew was drowning out the connection.
"Right," was the last thing Reb heard before the connection was lost.

Church had been very quiet. Mary enjoyed the silence and solitude, until bells started to go off. Without concern to being sacrilegious, several beefy guys stood up and left the building. "What's going on?" she whispered to a woman whose husband left.

"Fire alarm."

Mary got up and followed her instincts out the door. An informal convoy was wasting no time heading down the street and she tailgated. As the trail became all too familiar, a sickening feeling crept into her gut and only primal strength kept her going. The scene was activity incarnate. Long before the Senator's helicopter touched down, a truck with two volunteer firefighters had careened into the driveway. Reb had waved them down and told them with what was left of her voice that there was still someone inside. With the type of stunning bravery that is reserved for fire and police personnel, they charged into the roaring fire and brought Lisa out. Once a safe distance from the house, they placed her on a stretcher for transport. Reb looked at her. This wasn't going to be good.

"Is she still alive?" Reb asked just to be sure.

"She's still breathing and pretty good for what she's been through."

They placed an oxygen mask on Lisa's face, both the burned and unburned areas. The burns started there and went down her neck to her left arm. Her hair had been partially burned, some clear to the scalp. The unmistakable stench of burned hair and flesh made Rebecca woozy. Paramedics now on the scene fixed her up with an oxygen mask of her very own and then loaded Lisa into the helicopter for her first destination, Topeka Medical Center.

As firefighters worked to drench what little was now left of the farmhouse, the cell phone started to ring. By now, Rebecca had a splitting headache and an extremely sore throat. An attending paramedic answered the phone and then asked Rebecca if she knew someone named "Mitch?" She nodded and croaked, "Tell her to stay put and please answer her questions."

"Sure thing, ma'am," he nodded.

221

From what Rebecca could discern, Mitch was asking short but profound questions. Nothing was omitted from the paramedic's explanation.

"She says she loves you," he conveyed the message.

"Tell her I love her back," Reb whispered. He did so and then disconnected the call. He had things to do, not the least of which was get a United States Senator to the hospital. As they loaded up and prepared to depart, Mary came into view.

"You want to ride along or drive yourself?"

"I'll drive myself."

"Okay. We're heading to Topeka."

"Where's Lisa?" Mary hid her panic well.

"She's being transported by airlift."

Mary looked at her mother. A thousand silent words passed between them and then Reb said quietly, "She's got to be okay. She saved my life."

"Let's go."

Once off the dirt road, they traveled quickly. And as fast as they arrived at the medical center, steps had already been taken to pull Lisa from the brink of death. So much for breathing good at the scene. By the time the admitting physician consulted with Mary and Rebecca, Lisa had been placed on a ventilator and been given medications to subdue her. For all intents and purposes, she was paralyzed by the drugs to keep her from fighting the ventilator.

"Can we see her?" Mary asked.

"In a while. I want to prepare you for what you're going to encounter."

"That doesn't sound good."

"Senator Fairbanks, Ms. Fairbanks, we're preparing to transport Ms. Beaumont to a burn center. Did you have a preference?"

"Maryland General, if possible," Rebecca answered in her best Senator voice. It was slowly returning, but still awfully scratchy.

"I'll begin the process. Do you have a second choice?"

"What about here?" Mary looked confused.

"We can't handle the case. You want Boston General for an alternative?"

"Sounds good," Reb nodded.

"What can't you handle about Lisa's case?" Mary started to tremble.

"Ms. Beaumont has third-degree burns that will require extensive treatment. Right now, we're treating her with 100% oxygen to counteract carbon monoxide poisoning and working to replenish her fluids."

"Why would she be poisoned?" Mary asked about one thing at a time.

"When someone is in an enclosed area, we suspect carbon monoxide poisoning."

"And the fluids?"

"Burn patients lose a lot of fluids through the burn wound. Those need to be replaced. We call it resuscitation. The amount of fluids we replace depends in part on how much of the body is burned."

"How much are we talking about?" Mary asked. She hadn't seen Lisa carried out of the house.

"We use what we call the rule of nines. The body is divided into areas and then we figure from there."

"I don't understand?"

"One arm is roughly nine percent of the total body area. One leg is eighteen percent. Numbers like that."

"I see. So, what percent of Lisa is burned?"

"We're still trying to calculate an exact number."

"Give me a guess. I won't hold you to it."

"Somewhere between ten and twenty percent. The burn extends from the left side of her face down her neck and left arm."

"Oh, dear God," Mary put her head in her hands.

The doctor looked at Rebecca and said, "I'm going to begin the necessary steps to transfer Ms. Beaumont to one of those burn centers you've requested. I'll let you know when I hear something. In the meantime, I'll arrange for you to see Ms. Beaumont. Please make your visits brief and assume she can hear everything you say."

"Thank you, doctor."

He was long gone by the time Mary was able to compose herself.

"I'm so scared," she admitted with a shaky voice.

"I know, but we need to put on our best brave faces."

"Did you call Mitch?"

"Yes. I told her to stay put."

"How did the fire start?"

Rebecca had intentionally put that particular thought out of her conscious mind. There had been more important things to worry about at the time.

"I don't know."

"You mean, it wasn't you or Lisa?"

"It wasn't me. I was asleep."

"And Lisa was going to sleep in as well. She wasn't feeling well."

Mary looked directly at her mother. Reb looked back.

"It was one of them," Mary said.

"Them?"

"The protestors."

"We can't be sure. Whatever you do, don't say that in front of anybody else."

Mary was about to say something when a nurse came up to them.

"Are you waiting to see Ms. Beaumont?"

"Yes," Rebecca answered.

"Please follow me."

It took a moment to get started. Rebecca was still on oxygen, but had been switched to a nose plug set up with a portable tank which hung conveniently on the back of her wheelchair. Still, they went slowly. By the time they got to ICU, Mary had steeled herself for the sight. It wasn't as traumatic as she had visualized. Lisa's wounds had been covered in some sort of special gel packs and covered with gauze, the attending nurse explained. Still the sight of her head and arm heavily bandaged was sickening. The ventilator was doing its job methodically. Lisa's chest went up and down. Up and down. A heat shield was keeping her warm.

Mary asked, "Why does she need that?" It seemed so out of place.

"When a burn patient loses so much skin, the body loses some of its ability to maintain constant body temperature."

"What about infection?"

"That's a concern, but there are other things to do now."

"Like what?"

224

Rebecca wheeled over and squeezed Mary's hand, more as a warning than for comfort.

"We can ask the doctor later," she said in her best authoritative way. Mary caught on. She leaned in as close as she could and tenderly kissed the side of Lisa's face that wasn't bandaged quite so heavily. Lisa shivered.

"You're blocking the heat," the nurse admonished.

"Sorry."

Mary left the room reluctantly, followed closely by Rebecca. They took up vigil just outside her room.

"Are you going to be okay?" Rebecca asked point blank.

"No."

"No?"

"No. I'm not going to be okay until we get Lisa well and whoever started this fire behind bars."

"Honey, listen to me. You just concentrate on Lisa and let everyone worry about everything else."

Mary went back to holding her head in her hands and didn't notice the visitor shuffling toward them. He took his time, having no other choice. Rebecca was the one who recognized him first.

"Bixby?"

"Well, I got here. Didn't think I would," he puffed.

Mary stood up and took hold of him in an awkward embrace. His walker wasn't helping matters. Then, she motioned for him to sit in her chair as she pulled up another less comfortable one for herself.

"How did you get here?"

"Ona them nice church ladies brought me. I'm a widower, you know."

Mary nodded like she understood the connection between the first and second sentences

"Thank you for coming, Mr. Bixby," Rebecca smiled at him.

"They told me Lisa got the worst of it."

"She's in intensive care."

"She gonna be okay?" his bottom lip began to quiver.

"She's steady so far, but the next few hours are crucial."

"I see," he said and then muttered as an afterthought, "Damn bastard protestors."

"You think they're responsible?" Mary held on to his arm like he was slipping down a cliff.

"I know damn well they're responsible. This is the third burnin down, by my count."

"You mean, they've done this before?"

"It didn't dawn on me until the drive up here. All the while the Widow Fremont was droppin hints about what good marriage material she'd be, I was thinkin bout two other suspicious fires. Course, nobody would admit they were. But it all makes sense now," he nodded all along to show his confidence in his theorem.

"What other fires have there been?"

"Well there was the problem with the library."

"The library burned down?"

"No, but people were setting books that they didn't approve of on fire and then dropping them down the book return chute. That was causing a big mess. Smoke damage and all."

"What else?"

"Well, a fire gutted a book store downtown last year. Guess it had a book about sex or somethin? The news said it was faulty wiring but I talked to Joe Stewart and he said he did all the work way above standard. He didn't get no business for months and he has a family to support."

"So, why didn't he say something?"

"Too scared, I guess. Hell, if I'da put this all together sooner, maybe I coulda warned you girls."

"Don't blame yourself, Bixby. You didn't light the match."

"I just hope this don't get swept under the rug."

"I guarantee it won't," Rebecca assured him. Assurances from Senators still meant something to folks of his generation. His eyes welled up.

"Thank you."

Further discussion was interrupted by the attending physician, who came to inform them that Lisa would be transported by air to Maryland General Hospital within the hour and they should prepare to depart.

"You have to go all the way to Maryland?" Bixby sounded panicked. It must be way worse than they were telling him.

"We requested a burn center close to Washington D.C."

Bixby only nodded. Or maybe he was just shaking real hard.

"Go with us, Bixby," Mary said suddenly.

"I'd only be in the way."

"No, you wouldn't! When Lisa wakes up, she's going to need all the friendly faces we can find."

"But what about my house?"

"Maybe the Widow Fremont will house sit for you?"

"If she does, I'll never get her out of the place!"

"Well then, fly out with us and then you can head home after a few days. You'd be a big help," Mary cajoled. It convinced him.

"What the heck, I ain't never been to Maryland."

And so the travelling party was established. They were a reserved group once they were seated on the plane. Lisa had been wheeled on earlier and secured with all of her medical machines. No less than four trained specialists traveled with her, monitoring her vital signs and continuing with the fluid resuscitation. They were taking no chances with the friend of the daughter of a United States Senator. Power did have its rewards. This was one Reb wished she would never have to reap.

Much to her surprise, Mary slept through most of the flight. She would need the rest. When they touched down, Lisa was tended to before anyone else. She was loaded into an ambulance and taken the five miles to the hospital at a moderate rate of speed. Mary, Rebecca and Bixby were provided separate transportation and arrived just moments after Lisa. Waiting in the admitting area was Mitch. She looked solid and reassuring, ready to absorb all the anger, fear, and uncertainty that Rebecca and Mary could dish out. Reb was first, holding her in one of those grasping embraces that conveys thankfulness that she hadn't been there as well. Mitch returned a softer embrace. No use bruising both of them. Next came Mary, who felt quite simply like a damp dish rag and Mitch guided her to a chair. She would need to begin filling out paperwork, but for now needed to get something to eat and gather her wits. It would be a few minutes before they could see Lisa again. She was being settled into the burn center room that would be her home for a while.

"Mitch, this is Bixby. He's our neighbor,"

"Hello, Bixby," Mitch shook his hand. "Thank you for coming along. I'm going to get some food for everyone. What does everyone want to eat?"

"I'm not hungry," Mary said first.

"Okay, I'll find something anyway. Anybody want to go along?" Mitch looked directly at Rebecca. Rebecca looked back. She got the message. "I'll go with you. We won't be long. Will we?"

"Shouldn't take too long," Mitch reassured.

"We'll be here when you get back," Bixby patted Rebecca's hand. Already he was a good choice to bring along.

"Okay."

Rebecca wheeled alongside as Mitch walked down the hall.

"I suppose you already know the way to the cafeteria," she observed.

"Oh, you know me," Mitch replied in a reassuring way, "Stomach first."

"Thank you."

"Huh?"

"For being here when we got here."

"Where else would I be? Mary is going to need all the support she can get. In the meantime, what's with the oxygen?"

"I inhaled some smoke. Lisa saved my life."

"She did?"

"One minute she was wheeling me full speed toward the door. The next thing I knew, she was on the floor. I got out." Rebecca stopped talking. Mitch surveyed the situation and wheeled her into an empty family conference room and started handing her tissues. Rebecca knew it was safe to fall apart out of sight of Mary and anyone else watching. Mitch held her firmly and waited out the tears.

"Why don't you take out your oxygen tube for a few minutes. It makes it easier to blow your nose."

"Okay."

Rebecca snuffled for about five more minutes before settling down.

"I guess I've been holding that in for a while."

"I'm glad you let go. I've been really worried about you."

228

"I'm not the one you need to worry about. Lisa's in really bad shape."

"Well, she's not so bad that they couldn't bring her all the way out here. I think that's a good sign."

"You always were an incurable optimist."

"So, all optimism aside, how bad is Lisa?"

"Part of her face is burned. Part of her scalp. Her left shoulder and arm. I saw her when they brought her out of the house. Mary didn't. She doesn't know."

Mitch took all that in and worked it over in her mind. Slowly, to avoid saying the wrong thing.

"How much of her total head area is burned?"

Rebecca looked thoughtful. "I'd guess maybe one-fourth. Why?"

"Well, with the couple of spare minutes I've had waiting for you to show up, I've been reading some of the literature around here."

"You couldn't have had much time."

"I'm a quick study. From what you've told me, Lisa is burned on about fifteen percent of her body."

"The doctors in Kansas said between ten and twenty. What does that mean?"

"It means that her prognosis is good if she can get through the next few days."

"Maybe she'll live, but how will she ever learn to cope with the scars on her face. You know how important her looks are to her."

Mitch nodded and then sort of smiled at a time when most people would think a smile was out of place.

"What are you thinking?" Reb asked.

"I'm thinking that Lisa will get through this the same way that most people get through any crisis. She has a strong, loving partner."

Rebecca studied Mitch. "You're talking about you and me as much as you are Mary and Lisa, aren't you?"

Mitch just shrugged and then changed the subject. "I only got two hotel rooms. Who's going to sleep with Bixby?"

"He's only staying a couple of nights. Just long enough to see Lisa when they take her off the ventilator."

"She's going to be here a while. Maybe I should try to rent an apartment?"

"That sounds like a good idea. Right now, Mary will want to stay at the hospital for a night or two anyway to begin with."

"But we need to keep from wearing herself out. She's going to need her strength for later."

"I'll help you find something later. We'd better deliver on that promise of food."

"What does Mary really like to eat? Something she can't resist?"

"Fried chicken."

"Then let's see what we can scare up in the cafeteria."

The cafeteria didn't have fried chicken, but it had the next best thing, a chicken-fried steak special with potatoes and gravy and corn. Mitch ordered four of these to go and then picked out some salads and desserts while Reb got the bright idea to check on the availability of the family conference room for an impromptu dining room. Apparently no one in the hospital was any good at saying "No" to a United States Senator. Maybe they just lacked practice? Soon, the four of them were seated around a beautiful mahogany table, far enough away from all things hospital and yet close enough for emergencies. Conversation was strained, but Mitch managed to keep things going by chatting with Bixby. All the while they talked, Mitch was wondering where in the world they were going to buy a spare set of clothes for his two-day stay. Maybe there was an overalls store in the suburbs of Maryland?

About halfway through dessert, no less than four people arrived either with news or well-wishes. Hilary, of all people was first on the scene.

"I heard about the fires on the news. You picked a great burn center."

Mary didn't know what to say except, "Thanks."

"If you need anything, you know where to find me."

"I do."

"Keep in touch."

"I will."

Maybe it only sounded like wedding vows to Mitch. She wisely kept her opinions to herself. After Hilary came the director of communications for the hospital. She had a security guard with her.

"Senator Fairbanks, I'm Wanda Peterson."

"Hello, Ms. Peterson."

"The press corps is beginning to assemble at the hospital. Do you wish to give a statement?"

Reb thought it over. Here she was, in the news again. Most Senators would give their right arm for this kind of coverage. The irony was not lost on her that Lisa nearly did give her left arm. "I'll have a statement in about an hour."

"The security officer is here to talk to a Mr. Bixby. That might be you, sir?" Ms. Peterson looked at the old man. He was, after all, the only guy in the room.

"That's me."

"I'm afraid I have some bad news, Mr. Bixby," Officer Blake started out. "There's been another fire at your place."

"How bad?" he asked.

"I'm afraid it's a total loss."

Bixby ruminated for a minute and then stated philosophically, "Well, at least that'll discourage the Widow Fremont from movin in anytime soon."

Mitch only nodded. She suspected two things. One, that he was insured up to his eyeballs. Two, that they'd need to go clothes shopping a helluva lot sooner than expected.

"Better make it a three-bedroom apartment," she said to Reb in an aside.

"So, that's why Hilary talked about fires in the plural," Mary said to Bixby mostly.

"Guess so," he agreed. His lower lip seemed to be getting a whole lot steadier lately. The fourth person to descend on the group was Lisa's new doctor. He introduced himself as Roy and sat down like it was his standard practice to make himself at home with the family of the victim. Mitch liked him already.

"I'm prepared to consult with you, Ms. Fairbanks, and anyone else you wish to include in the discussion. Would you like a few minutes to prepare questions?"

"Maybe five minutes?"

"Sounds fine. Do you want to talk here?"

"Can we use this room?"

"Certainly. I'll check back in ten or fifteen minutes. That will give you a few more minutes to finish your meal. That's the chicken-fried steak, isn't it?"

"Yes."

"Don't tell anyone but it's my favorite. Adds two, three miles to my daily jog, but it's worth it!"

He smiled and was gone.

"And I have one more message for Miss Tanner?" Ms. Peterson announced.

"That's me," Mitch almost raised her hand like she was in school.

"A Ms. Trish Sullivan or Trish Weingarten has been calling for you."

"Oh, right. I'll call her right now. Thanks."

Mitch knew Trish's number by heart and dialed it into the nearest phone. It barely rang.

"Hello?" Trish answered quickly.

"Hi, it's Mitch. Sorry I didn't call sooner."

"Oh, thank goodness. You're all over the news. What is going on and is Lisa okay?"

Mitch more or less tried to tick off the answers in reverse order.

"We're going to consult with the doctors in about five minutes, but Lisa is still alive. We just heard about the other fire. What does the news say?"

"Apparently, there's a rash of fires in Utopia."

"I know why they burned down Mary's house. Any clue as to why they burned down Bixby's?"

"Rumor has it that they burned down the Bixby place because he helped them out once or twice."

"Gee, I hope that doesn't become a habit. Who knows who's next in line?"

"You want me to come there? I can get on a flight and be there today?"

"Aren't you coming out this way later in the week?"

"Right."

"Well, I suggest you stick to that schedule. By the time things calm down for you and the art auction, they should be a little more settled around here as well."

"Okay. But you'll call if you need me. Or us?"

"I'll call you with updates. How's that?"

"Perfect."

About the time Mitch hung up, the doctor was back. He sat down and surveyed the group. Bixby had excused himself from the conference to go make some phone calls of his own. That left Mitch, Rebecca, and Mary to hear the news.

"Ms. Beaumont's blood gases are improving," he started right in.

"What does that mean?" Mary asked, not knowing exactly what the terms meant.

"It means that there is sufficient oxygen in her blood, which in turn means that we will be able to take her off the ventilator soon. She didn't sustain permanent lung damage from the smoke. It's my guess that there weren't a lot of toxins in the smoke."

"Toxins?"

"Burning plastics. Paint. Things like that."

"We had some paint in the house?"

"Well, apparently not enough to do a lot of damage. Ms. Beaumont still must have only inhaled mostly wood smoke."

"Which isn't as bad?"

"It could have been worse. Now, I know it will seem like we're moving quickly, but barring a set-back, we will begin working on her burn wounds in a couple of days."

"That soon?" Mary sounded stunned.

"In the last ten years, we're learned a lot about burns. We used to leave wounds too long and they tended to contract as part of the natural healing process. That led to disfigurement in many cases. So, beginning very soon, we'll begin the process of debridement."

"Debridement?"

"That's when we take a dermatome and cut the dead part of the wound away. Usually, it's done after the wound has been soaked. We call it tubbing."

"Does it hurt?"

"I'll be honest. It's not unusual for the nurses to wear earplugs."

"Oh, God," Mary was beginning to go pale.

"Don't you use pain medication?" Reb asked.

"Yes, we do. Pain management is important to the overall procedure. But we also use other techniques as well. You'll hear more about that later from the real experts on that, the nursing staff. But burn treatment is painful. I won't pull any punches."

"I appreciate that. How can I help?" Mary was once again involved, having regained a bit of color.

"Most burn centers recommend that your presence not be associated with the worst of the process. My advice is for you and others to be there for support after the debridement and dressing processes are over."

"How many will she have?"

"Of the debridements? That will depend."

"On what?"

"On how soon we can cover the wound. There are several options and the team is trying to decide the best option."

"What are the choices?"

"I'm leaning toward skin grafts. Ms. Beaumont has a good source of donor sites and she's young."

"Donor sites? Does that mean you're going to use her own skin?"

"Right. We take a patch and mesh it so it stretches and then we use it for the graft."

"So, she could be wearing skin from her leg on her arm?"

"That's the general idea."

Mary grew silent.

"Did you have another question about that process?" Roy was very tuned in.

"How well will her face heal?"

"That's going to be a challenge. It's going to be a lengthy process. Why don't we worry about getting her off the ventilator and getting her voice into the discussion for the next few days?"

Rebecca nodded. "Good idea."

They followed the doctor to Lisa's room.

"My suggestion is that you sit out here until we remove the vent and allow her to wake up. It could be a while."

They all followed the suggestion except for Mary, who paced the floor and Mitch, who went in search of Bixby. Which left Reb, who didn't have much choice but to sit anyway.

Bixby had wandered down to the main lobby of the hospital to watch TV footage of his house burning down. They watched together what could very easily have been the hundredth or so airing.

"You'd think with all those TV cameras around, they'da gotten a shot of the guy who did it," he said in a detached sort of Sherlock Holmes kind of way.

"What makes you think it was a man?"

"You think a woman would go around torching places?"

"I've seen a few women in my lifetime whom I wouldn't put it past. Men don't exactly have the market cornered on lunacy."

"That's refreshing to know, in an oddball sort of way."

"Has anyone taken your statement yet?"

"There's not much to tell. I was on the way here when it happened."

"When will you hear from your insurance agent?"

"Already have."

"You have? That was fast!"

"I called him. He called right back."

"Pretty good service."

"I'm a pretty good customer."

"So, you had coverage?"

"I have coverage on everything you can get coverage on. Fire, theft, tornado, flood and crop failure."

"Everything but marriage?" Mitch was teasing.

"I got ona them too. My lawyer has a prenuptial agreement all ready just in case."

It made sense to Mitch, particularly when she realized the net worth of a place like Bixby's. Or Rebecca's, for that matter.

"I hope Mary and Lisa are covered," Bixby said.

"Me, too. I'll ask Rebecca next time I see her."

"Well, not next time," Bixby said.

"Why not?"

"Because she's on TV."

Mitch turned the sound up on the set. Somewhere close, there was a press conference.

"I'm going to read a prepared statement and then answer as many questions as my health will permit."

Mitch noted that Reb had put her oxygen tube back into her nose. And she was still photogenic.

"Today, my family's homestead in Kansas was burned to the ground, along with the neighboring house. I owe my life to my daughter's significant other, Lisa Beaumont. She's in a struggle for her life as we speak. I call on all appropriate branches of law enforcement to fully investigate this incident and bring the perpetrators to justice."

Reb folded the paper and looked into the camera.

"Are there questions?"

"Senator, do you suspect arson?"

"I'm waiting for the official report. I'll have a comment then."

"What about your injuries?"

Rebecca talked about her health, downplaying the seriousness of her smoke inhalation but resisted giving details about Lisa.

Some people should get to retain a certain amount of privacy.

"Are you going back to work?"

"As soon as humanly possible."

When she tired of the questions, she coughed, pointed to her oxygen tank and wheeled away.

"I wish she'd move to Kansas," Bixby said.

"Why?" Mitch asked.

"So, I could vote for her someday. Better than any of the bozos we send to the Senate."

Mitch raised her eyebrows. Perhaps she was in the presence of a closet liberal.

"Maybe you could move to Colorado and vote for her there?"

"Give me a coupla years to think about it. In the meantime, I need to get some clean socks. And other…things."

"Let me check in with Rebecca and then we'll go shopping. We need socks, an apartment, and other…things."

Chapter 25

At first there was nothing.  Just like in the Bible.  Then, things were fuzzy.  Then, things hurt like bloody hell.  It would be fair to say that Lisa came out of a coma ready for a fight.  Maybe in her mind, she was still fighting the fire.  She was gently restrained until the world made some sense.

"Hello, sweetheart," Mary leaned in close.  Half of Lisa's face was still heavily bandaged, but she managed to open one eye.  It was, frankly, filled with terror.

"What?" she was barely able to croak out through her sore throat.

"Hi, Sweetie.  How are you feeling?"

"Hurts," she replied succinctly.

"I'll tell the doctor."

"You won't need to," the nurse at Mary's elbow explained.

"He's already ordered something."

"What has he ordered?"

"A morphine drip."

"A what?"

"A morphine drip.  It's a device where the patient can press a button to administer morphine in the I V."

"What will keep her from overdosing, *accidentally*?" Mary hoped the emphasis on accidental was clear.

"The machine is set so that it will only administer the correct dose.  She won't get morphine every time she presses the button.

"Oh, good.  That's good.  Is it set up?"

"I'm going to do that just as soon as Lisa wakes up a little more."

"Oh, okay."

"So, you go ahead and talk for a few minutes and then I'll be back."

As the nurse vanished, Reb came into view.

"Hello, Lisa," Reb said.  For once, she was taciturn.

"Hi.  You came all this way to see me?" Lisa asked.

"I was in Kansas with you."

"Oh, yeah.  Really?"

"Right."

"And when can I go home?"

"You're in a hospital in Maryland."

"Maryland?"

"They had an opening in the burn center here."

"Maryland? I'm really in bad shape, aren't I?"

Mary and Reb knew that they had to strike a balance between optimism and realism.

"We brought you here so both my mom and Mitch could visit a lot."

"Where is Mitch?"

"She and Bixby are out buying socks."

"Bixby came to Maryland?" Lisa asked with a voice that was quickly filling up with fatigue.

"He offered to come with us. He'll be in to see you later."

Further explanations were interrupted by the nurse.

"I have that morphine drip ready. You can stay while I get it all hooked up."

"That's okay," Reb answered. "I'll wait outside."

Mary elected to stay. Reb wheeled down the hall and found a quiet waiting area. When she looked up, Hilary was waiting there as well.

"Hello, Senator."

"Hello, Hilary."

"I was between classes and thought I'd stop in to check on Lisa."

"And Mary?"

"And Mitch."

"That's a lot of checking."

"I had an hour. How is Lisa doing?"

"I'm really not at liberty to say."

"Well, I can wait around and ask Mary."

"She may be a while."

"I study here. I'll be able to check in a lot, Senator."

"Don't you think Mary has enough to worry about already?"

"I prefer to think of myself as a resource, not a source of worry. You won't believe how difficult the next few months will be. What Lisa is going to go through is a whole lot worse than your rehab ever was."

"What makes you say that?" Reb got a tad huffy.

"Because you didn't have the kind of pain Lisa is going to experience."

238

Their debate was cut short by the arrival of Mary.

"Oh, hi," Mary said in Hilary's direction.

"How are you doing?"

"I thought it was Lisa you were concerned about."

"I am. How is Lisa?"

"She's asleep."

"Good. She's going to need her rest. Are they running a morphine drip?"

"Don't you think that's confidential patient information," Reb was beginning to snap.

"Actually, it's routine procedure."

"Then, why do you ask!"

"Because I care," Hilary answered quietly.

"If you really cared-"

"Mom!" Mary interrupted decisively. "Let's not fight. If Hilary wants to stop by and check in from time to time, so be it."

"Whatever you say," Reb pulled herself up as tall as she could manage and then wheeled off down the hall.

"I don't mean to cause trouble between you and your mother."

"It's okay. We're all a little on edge around here."

"So, she's on morphine?"

"They started the drip."

"That's going to make her woozy and forgetful. She might not remember visitors, so don't get impatient with her."

"I wouldn't anyway."

"You two have everything patched up, then?"

"Yes we do."

"Then I'm happy for you. You know that I'll help in any way I can. You picked a great facility."

"My mother selected it."

"Tell her for me that she made a great selection."

"I will."

Hilary patted Mary's hand and stood to leave.

"Thanks," Mary remembered to say.

"You're welcome."

Mary got five minutes all to herself. She managed to make good use of the time by closing her eyes and falling asleep sitting up. When she woke up, an hour later, someone had covered her and put a small pillow under her head where it had slumped over.

239

The someone was nowhere to be found, so she dragged her stiff body out of the chair and wandered down the hall. Lisa was awake and staring into space.

"Hi, Sweetie."

"Do me a favor."

"Sure, what?"

"When they take off the bandages, I want a mirror."

"A mirror?"

"There's not one mirror around here."

"Oh, I'm sure there is somewhere," Mary hedged. She hadn't given the matter much thought and hesitated being definitive.

"I'm going to look horrible, aren't I?'

Mary didn't know how to answer.

"You've seen me already, haven't you!"

"No, I haven't."

"Well then, I don't want you here when they unwrap me."

"Why not?"

"Because I don't!"

"I'll do whatever you want. Just don't be afraid to change your mind."

"I want a mirror."

"If the doctor says it's okay, I'll bring you one."

On cue, the doctor appeared. He was making evening rounds.

"How are you feeling, Ms. Beaumont?"

"Druggy and you can call me Lisa."

"Does the morphine take the edge off the pain?"

"Barely."

He turned to Mary. "I'm glad you're here. I wanted to talk about tomorrow's procedure. We're going to begin working on the burn wounds."

"So soon?" Lisa asked. She hadn't been inclined lately to make eye contact with Mary, let alone touch her, but now her hand sought out Mary's.

"We know that the sooner we begin, the better."

"Why?"

If Roy hated the fact that he found himself explaining things twice, he hid it well.

"We don't want the skin to begin contracting around the wound."

"No, I guess we don't."

240

"Right. Now, I know this is tough to believe, but in a way, you are one of our luckier burn patients."

"I don't feel very lucky."

"I realize that but the reason you are fortunate is that you're young and healthy and, very important point, you have a lot of healthy skin that we can begin the grafting process with."

"I do?"

"We use the skin on your lower torso and thighs for the process."

"How is that going to work?"

"We take a full-thickness layer of healthy skin from the donor site and mesh or poke holes in it, and then attach it to the clean edge of the burn wound."

"The clean edge?"

"We start with a procedure called debridement. We excise the burned skin and replace it with the graft."

All the time he talked, Lisa kept squeezing Mary's hand until Mary had to use her other hand to allay the pressure. Roy noticed this as well.

"It's okay to be worried about the process. It's no fun to go through."

"How would you know?" Lisa was in a snappish mood all of a sudden.

"I happen to have been a burn victim myself once," he answered with quiet confidence, and then added with a twinkle, "I'd show you my scars, but I hardly know you!"

Lisa laughed for the first time since the fire. It hurt, but it felt good.

"So, any questions about tomorrow?"

"It will hurt?" Lisa was just checking again, to be sure.

"It hurts like hell, to be honest."

"How long will I be here?"

"In the burn center?"

"Yes."

"A lot depends on how extensive the wound is and how good a healer you are. But be forewarned that the total healing process takes months."

"But not here, right?"

The doctor looked at Mary. "Is she always this inquisitive?"

"Yes."

241

"Good!  Never underestimate the power of the 'When am I getting outa here' attitude!"

"I did have one more question," Mary spoke up.

"Sure?"

"Lisa wondered why there are no mirrors here."

"You want a mirror?" he asked.

"Can I have one?" Lisa asked back.

"If you want a mirror, you can have one.  I can't guarantee that we'll ever make you look the way you used to, but we will make you look better than when you got here.  How's that?"

"Okay.  I just wanted to know."

"If you think of anything else, we can talk tomorrow morning, okay?"

"Thank you, doctor."

"Call me Roy."

"Thank you, Roy."

About ten seconds after Roy left, the visitor contingent arrived. All things considered, they were quite the sight.  Reb in her wheelchair, Bixby with his walker, and Mitch with her crooked arm.  They looked like poster children for rehab.  Bixby took the initiative, tottering over to the bed and patting Lisa's good arm.

"You're lookin real good, darlin."

"I'm feeling good, Bixby," Lisa was braving it out for his sake. "It was sweet of you to come all this way."

He nodded silently.  Mitch, Reb and Bixby had all decided against bringing up the torching of Bixby's house.  One mysterious arson per week, please!

"We've come to pick up Mary and take her to the hotel for the night," Mitch explained.

"I'm staying here," Mary explained back.

"I want you to go to the hotel," Lisa added her explaining to the glut of explaining.

"You do?  You sure?" Mary studied her for possible lying.

"I'm going to be in morphine-induced sleep all night.  You go and take a hot shower and relax.  I'm fine."

Either Lisa was getting perfect at lying or she meant every word. Whichever was the case, Reb commended the decision.

"Lisa's right.  Come on, Mary."

Mary leaned over and kissed Lisa goodbye.

"I'll see you in the morning."

If Mary said another word, she knew she would cry. The party of four headed out of the room and down the hall. It was a short elevator ride to the parking garage where Mitch had snagged the last handicapped parking space. Five minutes later, they were on the highway heading north to the hotel. It was everything Mary had hoped for and more. They were escorted by hotel security through a back entrance and ushered into their beautiful three-room suite. It was equipped with two bedrooms and a main room with a huge TV and bar. The chairs were recliners and practically begged you to sit in them. May did so at the behest of Mitch and reclined until her feet were level with her heart. Slowly, the ache drained out of them and threatened to relocate in her head. Mitch gave her a double scotch and then untied her shoes and pulled them off. Next, she peeled off her socks and then sat beside her in the other chair.

"You must be exhausted as well with all the errands you've been running."

"I'm fine. Did I tell you we found an apartment?"

"No, you didn't."

"It's nice. Three bedrooms, two baths, enough closet space for Imelda Marcos..."

"Who?"

"Never mind. And a kitchen that makes me jealous."

"How is the restaurant coming along?" Mary asked with the kind of concern that comes when you're tired of talking about yourself.

"It's shaping up real nice, but we still have a long way to go."

"I don't want you to neglect it because of the accident."

"Oh, I won't. Besides, Jane is quite the businesswoman."

"That's what I understand from Mother."

"Why don't you go to bed?"

"I'm going to sleep here."

"No, you're not. You're sleeping in that room," Mitch pointed to where Reb had disappeared.

"That's your bed."

"It's yours until further notice. No arguments."

"There's only one problem."

"What's that?"

"I can't get out of this chair."

"Oh, that's no problem. I'll carry you over my shoulder. Come on before I get any more tired myself."

Mary allowed herself to be pulled up on her feet and walked on her own to the bedroom. She was asleep before Rebecca emerged from the master bathroom. She, too, got forthwith into bed, which left Mitch and Bixby to their own devices.

"I'm glad Mary got out of that chair," Bixby said.

"Why?"

"I'm sleeping there."

"You don't have to," Mitch protested.

"I've been sleeping in a chair for eight years. This isn't time to start sleeping in a bed again."

With that revelation, he settled into the chair and closed his eyes. Within two minutes, Mitch was being serenaded by the beautiful three-part harmony of snoring. She went to the empty bedroom and crawled between the cool, clean sheets. Tomorrow, she would buy some pajamas for everyone. On that note, she joined the chorus.


Lisa tried so hard not to scream. From the minute she had entered the hospital, they had been cleaning and dressing her wounds. For those occasions, she had been under the influence of the drug Pavulon. It was, in effect, a paralyzing agent and had been administered every few hours to keep her sedated. Otherwise, she would have hurt herself fighting against the ventilator. And even in a coma, they had given her pain medications. Things were different now. She was fully awake for the debridement of the wound on her arm and even though she had been given something for the pain, it was excruciating.

Her company, comprised of Mary, Reb and Mitch, had arrived early and wished her well. Then, in a manner orchestrated by the staff, made themselves scarce for the actual treatment. Or at least, that's what Mary wanted Lisa to believe. In truth, she sat just down the hall while Reb and Mitch went to the cafeteria. So it was Mary alone, by choice, to hear the horrible screams of Lisa emanate through the doors of the treatment room. And now, as much as Lisa tried to hold back the screaming, so did Mary try to hold back the tears. They were both unsuccessful. Mary wanted to cover her ears and run down the hall, but sat frozen in her chair. And cried.

Hilary could only observe from afar so long before she went over to her.

"Are you going to get through it?"

"I don't know."

"What are you thinking?"

"Tell me why it's her and not me in there?"

"I can't."

Another piercing scream permeated the air.

"I'm not supposed to be in there, you know. I guess that if I'm there, then Lisa will associate me with pain."

"And then, she'll resent you," Hilary finished the thought.

It created another awkward silence between them mostly because it summed up their previous relationship.

"So, I sit out here and then pretend later on that I never heard a thing."

"When are they going to begin the skin grafts to her face?"

"Well, I thought it was today, but I misunderstood. Things are so jumbled up. I guess they do two different things, because the burns are in two different places. They will do something different with the burn on her face. Something about a natural separation of..." Mary couldn't remember the term.

"Eschar?" Hilary offered her guess.

"That sounds right."

"So, they are going to excise her arm wounds now and wait a few weeks for her face wound to lift off by itself."

"Yeah, I guess so?"

"They do wonderful things these days, Mary. Everything from growing skin in a laboratory to matching the pigmentation of skin grafts with tattoos. You want my advice?"

"You're dispensing advice now?"

"Let the doctors and nurses do the medical stuff. You just concentrate on the emotional stuff. Lisa is so very lucky to have you by her side."

Mary nodded. It couldn't have been easy for Hilary to be saying all this, but Mary didn't want to be distracted right now. In about five minutes, Lisa would be wheeled out, and Mary didn't want to be seen. She said goodbye to Hilary and headed for the cafeteria.

"I can resign my Senate seat," Reb told Mitch for the third time. And for the third time, Mitch shook her head.

"I don't think you should."

"This isn't like a case of the measles," she argued back. "Things aren't going to be back to normal in a week. Even if it was just Lisa's condition, it would be time consuming enough. But with everything else added in…" her voice trailed off.

Mitch didn't answer at once, and instead thought over all the other issues. There was, of course, the case of the burned-to-the-ground family homestead and Bixby's place as well.

Bixby had opted to stay at the hotel today. He needed his fix of The Price is Right and some rest. Mitch told him to order all the room service he wanted and enjoy the day. Even though he had an insurance settlement forthcoming, it would still take a long time to rebuild his place. Of course, there was still the official investigation and hopefully an arrest and conviction. But it wasn't like Rebecca needed to tend to all that personally.

"What would you do if you quit?"

"Resign."

"Okay, resign. What then?"

"I could be supportive of Mary."

"That's a noble gesture. Have you run that idea past her?"

"No. Why would I?"

"Well, maybe she isn't going to need wall-to-wall people around here all the time."

"I'm hardly wall-to-wall, whatever that means," Reb answered tartly.

Mitch chalked it up to stress.

"It seems to me that the hospital staff has things well in hand. If anybody's got a messed up future, it's Bixby. What are we going to do with him?"

"There's got to be a place in Utopia where he can stay until his place is rebuilt."

"I'm sure there would be, but I don't know if he'll want to go back. He might not be so lucky next time."

"Well, what do you suggest?"

"Maybe he'd stay with us in Georgetown? The place is already handicap accessible."

"And where, pray tell, would he sleep?" Reb asked with that twinge of steel in her voice that meant she was mentally biting her tongue.

"In a chair. Guess he has for years."

"I don't think you've really thought this thing through."

"I guess we're in the same boat. Both of us have some thinking to do."

And so, painted in their proverbial separate corners, they fell silent. However, any deep thinking was quickly pre-empted by Mary's arrival. She looked like hell as she pulled up a chair and sat down.

"What is it, honey?" Reb asked in that mom tone of voice.

"Oh," Mary's voice was already shaky and she wasn't past word one. "I was just, you know."

She stopped to breathe and started to cry instead. Rebecca gave Mitch one of those patented, "I told you so" looks and reached out to Mary.

"Is Lisa okay?"

"I just…didn't know…you know?"

"What didn't you know, honey?"

"I've just never heard screams like that."

Mitch and Reb could only nod.

"I mean, like *ever*."

What could you say to that? It wasn't like Mary spent her life around screamers. However, that didn't seem to be the thing to say, so Mitch kept her mouth shut.

"She probably didn't know you were listening, sweetie," Reb reminded. "It probably gave her a good release to yell."

"I know she didn't know and I want to keep it that way."

"Whatever you say, honey, but are you sure you want to keep doing that?"

"I have to know what she goes through so I can be the best possible help to her."

"I'm not sure that's the best approach," Mitch just couldn't keep her mouth shut any longer. Neither one looked like they wanted to hear more, but Mitch ventured on anyway.

"I didn't need to sit around and hear your mother scream to be useful to her."

"That's because I never screamed," Reb defended her honor.

"But if you had, it still wouldn't have made any difference."

"Well, what's your suggestion?"

"When Lisa talks to you, listen with ears that love."

"What do you mean?"

"You have to hear everything that goes unsaid."

"That doesn't sound so easy?"

"I know. But if I were you, I'd start by talking about that mirror she insists on having."

"I just assumed she wanted to know what she looked like?"

"No doubt about that, but why?"

"I don't understand?"

"When your mom got hurt, and couldn't feel anything below her waist, we talked about it. Eventually. Because it's tough to talk about loss. The sooner you know what Lisa's concept of loss is, the better things will be."

With that, Mitch left mother and daughter to talk things over. She wandered back upstairs to Lisa's room. Whatever they had given her for the pain was just kicking in.

"How you doing?"

Lisa checked the room for other visitors, and when satisfied that no one else was present, answered bluntly, "Oh, fuckin peachy keen, and you?"

"I've been eating hospital cafeteria food. Whaddya think?"

"Do me a favor?"

"If I can."

"You're a millionaire. You can do anything, remember?"

"Okay, what?"

"Please make Mary take a break."

Mitch had to think about how being a millionaire would help her with this one.

"A break?" she stalled.

"I don't need her here all the time."

"That may not be as easy as it sounds," Mitch mused out loud.

248

"Come over here and sit down by me," Lisa patted a spot on the bed that was pretty narrow. It would be a tight fit. Mitch managed it, barely. Lisa placed her hand on Mitch's thigh, a familiar-enough action between former lovers to not be too terribly distracting.

"Are you outnumbered?" Lisa asked succinctly.

"You could say that."

"I know what you mean. You give those Fairbanks women an inch and they take an acre!"

"I guess so. So, what do you suggest I do with Mary?"

"Isn't that art auction coming up this week?"

"You've been keeping track of that?"

"Just because I've been holed up in Nowhere, Kansas doesn't mean I've lost touch with the real world."

"You always did try to keep in touch," Mitch stroked Lisa's arm as she talked.

"So, you take Mary to New York and have a girl's day out with Trish and Robbie."

"Well, that only takes care of a day," Mitch was keeping track.

"And you're opening that restaurant pretty soon, right?"

"It'll be a while."

"Mary's got a flair for decorating. You need another interior decorator?"

Mitch thought about it. She and Jane had already butted heads on a number of issues. Bringing Mary into the process didn't seem to be a level-headed idea.

"Jane's already done most of that," Mitch admitted, "But I can try to distract Mary with other things."

"Name one."

"Bixby."

"Name another."

"If I'd known there was going to be a test, I would have cribbed notes!"

Lisa patted Mitch's thigh. "When haven't I been just one big test for you?"

"All things considered, it was mostly good, especially the pop quizzes," Mitch said and then leaned down to kiss her on the cheek.

"Everything good in my life is a result of knowing you," Lisa said quietly. The pain medication was beginning to set in and she had a dreamy look in her eyes.

"You go to sleep and let me worry about Mary."

"Okay," Lisa closed her eyes and drifted off to sleep. Even in bandages she was beautiful. Mitch crept out the door and ran smack dab into Mary and Rebecca.

"She's just dropped off to sleep," Mitch whispered.

"So, I guess we could wait out here?" Mary said.

"I have an idea. Let's go back to the hotel and check on Bixby."

"Oh, he already called me," Mary reported.

"He did?"

"Yeah. He made airline reservations to fly home. He's leaving this afternoon."

"Really?"

"Yes, really. He's going to pack and call a cab."

"How's he going to get home, or where ever, once he gets to Kansas?"

"He mentioned something about a widow."

Mitch appeared troubled, not at the thought of Bixby's fate as much as the precipitous exit of her number one distraction.

"He might need help packing," Mitch pondered. Her next idea was to try and get Mary to volunteer to go with her to see. "You want to go and check with me?"

"No, I'm staying here so I can see Lisa the minute she wakes up."

"I figured I should start moving all our stuff into the apartment. You want to come, Reb, and supervise?"

"I'm going to stay here as well."

"So, you want me to do all the moving myself?" she tried to scrub all the irritation out of her voice. It was tough.

"We trust you to take care of things," Rebecca answered with maddening calm.

Mitch gave up and took off down the hall to use the stairway. Waiting around for elevators right now would only make her cranky. Okay, who was she kidding. She was already cranky. One simple favor Lisa asked of her and she couldn't deliver. By the time she got to the hotel Bixby was gone. That left her all alone with very little to pack and too much time to contemplate

250

why she couldn't get the sensation of Lisa's hand on her thigh out of her mind. Lisa was, after all, one of the favorite people in her past. Mitch often tried to come across as the fourth billy goat gruff around Lisa, but watching her as she maintained her composure during this frightening experience made Mitch feel like a lump of silly putty. Had Lisa grown up that much? Mary had such a good influence on everyone, but this transformation might fall under the category of miracle.

Mitch loaded up the van, checked out of the hotel and drove to the apartment. Thank goodness it was on the first floor. Mitch wasn't in the mood for marathon training. Since the apartment was furnished, it took scant time to unpack. Mary in one room, Mitch and Reb in the other. It was soon time to go back to the hospital. Mitch wanted to drag her feet, knowing that Lisa wouldn't be happy with her lack of success.

Things were quiet in the burn center. Lisa was still drowsing in and out of sleep. Mary was sitting in a chair scooted right up next to the bed and Reb was posted on the other side.
"Hi, everybody," Mitch thought she had been relatively quiet, but no.
"Ssshhhhh! The news is on."
"Are we in it?" Mitch stage whispered.
"No, but the art auction is."
Mitch turned just in time to see file footage of Trish and Robbie's wedding day. The dulcet tones of the news anchor informed them that, "with two days left before the biggest art auction since Van Gogh, the art world is aquiver with anticipation…"
Mitch didn't pay much attention to the signoff and instead turned her attention toward Lisa. She had one of those, "You couldn't do one simple thing" looks on her face and Mitch felt the flush of embarrassment creep up from her neck.
"I got everything moved," Mitch announced, mostly to break the spell, but also to fish for compliments.
"You weren't gone very long."
"There wasn't much to move."
"See there, we knew you could handle it all by yourself."

"You were right as usual," Mitch ended up doing the complimenting. Lisa looked like she could use some real rest. "Why don't we leave and let Lisa get some deep sleep?" Mitch suggested.

"You two go," Mary said. "I'm going to just sit here and be as quiet as a mouse. Lisa, honey, you can just go to sleep and I'll be right here if you need anything."

Lisa only smiled weakly. She was too exhausted to argue.

Mitch and Reb went down to the cramped lounge that faced due west. The sun filtered through specially treated windows so that not one ounce of harmful rays were left. It was, for Mitch, quite depressing. She preferred the sun in all its destructive glory and would've liked to be soaking up some right now in places far away, like Santa Fe, for instance.

"You're awfully pensive," Reb nosed in.

"It's been a long day."

"What's troubling you?"

Mitch, who was transparent to Reb and, why fight it, said, "Lisa doesn't want Mary hovering all the time."

"And that's what the two of you were discussing while she was patting your thigh and you were kissing her cheek?"

"Yes," Mitch admitted. "Guilty on all counts."

"We're not in court," Reb said with that Senator inflection in her voice.

"Oh, good," Mitch answered back quietly, realizing that she had taken a small part in ratcheting up the rhetoric and should take part in toning it down.

"So, don't treat it like the Inquisition."

"Then, don't frame your questions like it is."

Reb sat for a moment, having no other real choice. Then, she spoke in a calm, level voice, "I'll go and get Mary and find some sort of distraction for her. Give me the key to the van."

Mitch handed over the key ring which now had the apartment key attached as well.

"And you watch over things here. Is that suitable?"

"That's fine."

Reb turned and wheeled down the hall. Mitch stayed behind. She wasn't finished being depressed yet and no good would come of her infecting Lisa with this added malady. That would come all too soon.  The doctors and nurses had promised as much.

Soon, from her vantage point, Mitch saw Lisa being wheeled down the hall for more treatments.  In order to try to alleviate some of the trauma, the people at the burn center tried to keep one place "safe" for the patient.  By that, they meant that the most painful procedures would not be performed in the "sleeping quarters" of the patient.  It was their safe harbor, if you will.  Mitch had no intention of being within earshot of whatever they were doing to Lisa now and went for a stroll outside.  By the time she ventured back in, Lisa had been once again medicated.  Mitch checked in on her.

"How are you feeling?"

"Like hell."

"Can I get you anything?"

"No.  I'm going to try and get some sleep.  Is Mary here?"

"No.  She and Reb are out keeping busy."

"Oh, good.  You go somewhere, too."

"Okay."

Mitch did as she was told, dropping off to sleep in the artificially darkened lounge.  She was awakened by the sound of Mary's voice.

"How long have you been asleep?"

The first answer, "Not long enough" never got to the voicing stage.

"I don't know.  What time is it?"

"It's five."

"A.M. or P.M.?"

"P.M."

"Then I dozed for about two hours.  How's Lisa?"

"I peeked in on her.  She's sleeping."

"Oh, good."

"Were we gone long enough?"

Mitch studied Mary's face, no easy feat after just waking up.

"What do you mean?"

"My mother rarely pulls punches.  She told me that Lisa needs time to herself."

"Sometimes people rest better when no one's around."

"Okay. I'll remember that."

"But she still asked about you."

"I'll go and see about dinner. You're supposed to go back to the apartment." Mary handed over the keys to the van.

"I can stay a little longer."

"No, you can't. Go. Now!"

Mitch acquiesced. Mary was back and in charge. Definitely in charge. Traffic was heavy at this time of the day, so Mitch didn't get back until six. She walked in the door and was greeted by an unusual sight. A table for two was set up in the dining room, complete with candlelight and flowers. Reb appeared from the kitchen area and greeted her.

"Hello."

"Hi."

For two people who had shared all things intimate, the moment was awkward.

"Are you hungry?" Reb asked.

Mitch turned her full attention toward Rebecca. She had on a new outfit, and appeared rested and refreshed.

"You look wonderful. Did you get a chance to rest?"

"A little. Are you ready for dinner?"

Mitch went over to Reb and bent down to eye level.

"I'm ready for a kiss."

"Aren't you always ready for a kiss?" Reb had that twinkle in her eye. You know, the one that never failed to drive Mitch clear off the edge. She held steady for now, holding onto Reb wheelchair. Barely.

"So, if you had a chance to rest, who did all this?" Mitch indicated the table and all its accoutrements.

"Mary helped."

"That Mary, she's a real gem."

"Yes, she is. Now, do you want dinner or not?"

Reb threw out the question like she knew the real answer.

"I'm starving. What did you make?"

"I didn't make anything, but it seems there's this really good restaurant just up the street that delivers."

"That's nice."

"But you have to let go of my wheelchair so I can serve it."

"Not quite so fast. I haven't gotten my kiss, yet."

"No you haven't," Reb's voice was causing a meltdown in Mitch's knees. "Well, come closer."
Mitch obeyed. Mitch always obeyed. Always always.

How it was that one kiss from Reb could convey the message that there was lots more where that came from eluded Mitch. As did Reb, who slowly wheeled backwards and away from Mitch's grip. She had kitchen things to attend to. Whatever restaurant that was down the street specialized in chicken cordon bleu with rice pilaf and French green beans. Mitch could only guess what was for dessert. As she sat at the table, Reb served. It was hard for Mitch to eat slowly, but she forced herself to do so.
"How was Lisa when you left?"
"I don't know."
"You don't know?" Reb sounded like a head nurse.
"I didn't check up on her when I left. Mary was there so I figured she was in good hands."
Reb only nodded.
"This dinner is great," Mitch chatted on.
"I know that what has happened to Lisa deeply affects you."
Ah, now we were getting down to it, Mitch said to herself. Out loud, she stated, "This entire event has been a shock. I realize that you could have been killed in the fire."
"Had it not been for Lisa," Reb nodded.
"Do you feel guilty about that?" Mitch probed.
"That must be what it is. I've been a bearcat, haven't I?"
"No, you haven't been a bearcat. All things considered, you've been a pillar of strength."
The pillar of strength now took this opportunity to dissolve into tears. A natural reaction for which Mitch posed a natural solution.
"Let's go to bed."
Over protests about dirty dishes needing washed, Mitch carefully guided Reb's wheelchair to their new apartment's master bedroom. Without even undressing, they arranged themselves in a comfortable embrace. The Pillar continued to cry, although monsoons soon dwindled to periodic sniffles. The warmth of her body permeated through Mitch's clothing and skin, and she soaked it up and craved more.

"Am I always going to be this jealous of Lisa?" Reb asked.

Fools are credited with a lot of interesting characteristics. For instance, they go in where angels fear to tread. For another, they are soon parted from their money. So far, Mitch had met the criteria hands down. Fools also try to answer rhetorical questions.
"I guess so," was her response to Reb. It sounded safe. Reb raised up on one elbow.
"You think so?"
"Well, it's always been an issue between us, but, don't you think it's strange that you're jealous of a woman whose face is about one-fourth burned off? Not to mention her neck and arm?"
"It hasn't got anything to do with looks. It never has."
"Oh, sure it has," Mitch, AKA the Fool, forged ahead. Wasn't that Fool's Hill up ahead?
"In the beginning, it was all about looks."
For a moment it looked like Reb was gearing up for either another bout of crying or a good fight. Then, she suddenly relaxed.
"You're right, you know."
"I know. You always felt like the ugly duckling and you needn't have."
"I never felt like an ugly duckling!'
"Well, how would you characterize it?"
"I felt like I was just a smidgen less gorgeous. That's all."
"A smidgen?" Mitch figured it was safe to ask for a clarification.
"A tiny smidgen."
"Tiny?" Mitch pressed her luck.
"Miniscule."
"That's pretty small."
"I suppose you want some Noble Prize winning scientist to do an accurate measurement?"
"Nah. I'll take your word for it," Mitch was agreeable.
"But then I realized something important about you."
"You did?"
"I realized that it's never been about looks as far as you were concerned."
"I guess."

256

"In fact, it's never been about a whole lot of obvious things where you were concerned. So, it's been an interesting journey with you, wondering just what it was that did matter to you."

"And did you come to any conclusions?" Mitch was now very curious.

"Oh, sure."

"You did?"

"Yup."

"Are you going to tell me?"

"Nope."

"Why not?"

"Why should I be the one to tell you things about yourself that you must already know?"

Mitch squinted her eyes. The logic was inescapable.

"I bet you win your share of debates in the Senate with logic like that."

"Speaking of the Senate, I'm resigning this week."

Mitch didn't jump right into this next conversation. Maybe that was one of those things Reb admired most about her. Her thoughtful demeanor.

"Did you hear me? I said I'm resigning. You don't have anything to say about that?"

Well, maybe that wasn't one of those qualities Reb admired most.

"You already know how I feel about that."

"But you don't know how I feel about it!" Reb made her point.

"I assumed you wanted to resign in order to help Mary."

"That's only part of it. I've been thinking."

"What's the other part?"

"Well, notwithstanding the fact that the entire election was rigged from the beginning-"

"That's water under the bridge," Mitch interrupted.

"Let me finish."

"Okay," Mitch held her a little tighter.

"The Senate is taking me too much away from you."

Mitch tried to remember if she had mentioned this in any of their conversations. She didn't recall any specifics. On the other hand, she couldn't think up a plausible retort. They did spent a lot of time apart. She finally hit on a good idea.

"Starting up the restaurant shares part of that blame."

"Not even close. If I'm not in session, I'm meeting with constituents or in subcommittee meetings or fending off would be lobbyists. I'm the one who's never home."

When Mitch didn't say anything, Reb continued, "And when I get home, I'm buried in paperwork and phone calls."

Mitch still didn't reply.

"Say something!" Reb commanded.

"If you quit, then I'm quitting, too."

"But Jane depends on you."

"The citizens of Colorado depend on you."

"I can easily be replaced. People were lining up the minute I got elected. But Jane deserves this second chance, and you're the only person who's stepped up to the plate for her."

"So, I can be a passive business partner. I can help her with financing and an occasional bit of consulting. Otherwise, she can do it all herself. I've watched her. She's good."

They were both quiet for a moment. Reb spoke first.

"You realize that we're lying here making major life-altering decisions."

"It's kind of exciting, isn't it?" Mitch caught the sudden uplifting spirit of the mood.

"And I haven't even given you dessert yet," Reb said, and then added, "And I'm not referring to the confection in the refrigerator!"

"I had hoped you weren't," Mitch admitted.

As Reb's hands traveled over Mitch's body, it erased all other thoughts from her mind. It was just Mitch and Rebecca and a hundred-thousand tingly feelings. For starting out in argument mode, they both ended up in a perfectly fulfilling state of being. Even Reb was glowing.

"I should go and get you your real dessert now," Reb said after what seemed like an endless amount of restfulness.

"I'm not letting you out of this bed," Mitch was emphatic.

"You're not, huh!"

"And what do you mean by 'real dessert' anyway?" Mitch nuzzled Reb's ear again.

"I meant to say, 'your other dessert.'"

"What is my other dessert?"

"Cheesecake."

"Well, why didn't you say so in the first place," Mitch feigned astonishment but continued to nuzzle. In the land of no orgasms, nuzzles were king. Reb enjoyed the royal treatment.

"With strawberry goo," she whispered.

"Too bad I didn't know about the strawberry goo about ten minutes ago."

"There's always next time," Reb intoned wisely.

"And the time after that."

"Oohhh, getting a little ambitious, are we?"

"You know, now that we've made some monumental decisions about what we're *not* going to be doing, what exactly *are* we going to do?"

"Whatever it is, it will be fun doing it together."

Mitch thought this over. They had never had this opportunity before. They had always been so...busy.

"You're awfully quiet all of a sudden."

"I guess I'm tired all of a sudden."

"You want to save the cheesecake for breakfast?"

"Sure."

Mitch closed her eyes and almost instantly fell asleep, the exhaustion of the day finally catching up with her.

# Chapter 26

Trish stirred awake. Robbie was nowhere to be found in their bed. Damn. She got up, stretched, and wandered into the bathroom for morning chores. When she emerged, Robbie had covered the bed with open suitcases and clothes. So much for going back to bed.

"Good morning!" Robbie was perky and almost sang the greeting.

"Mornin," Trish answered.

"You want me to get you a cup of coffee? Or maybe some toast or are you really hungry? Bacon and eggs hungry?"

"Whoa, hold on a minute," Trish signaled for a timeout. Robbie slowed down, sort of. "Maybe just a bagel?"

"Maybe a kiss, for starters."

"Oh sure," Robbie came over and pecked her quickly. "Now, you want breakfast?"

"Could I have another kiss? Maybe this time in slow motion."

"Oh, you wanted a *kiss*. Why didn't you just say so?"

"I thought I did?"

Robbie came close to Trish, wrapped her arms around her neck and gave her a nice, long, warm kiss. Too bad the bed was covered with stuff.

"We have a lot to do," Robbie said as if she had read Trish's thoughts.

"Are you nervous?" Trish asked suddenly, finally catching on.

"We're leaving for New York today to prepare to auction off your 65 million dollar painting. Gee, who would be nervous about *that*?"

"I guess," Trish sounded way less enthused.

Robbie held her close. "I'm sorry. I keep forgetting about your friend, Lisa. You must be worried sick about her."

"I don't know how much help I'm going to be. I've never seen someone who has been burned."

"I know you're scared. I'll be right there with you all the way."

Trish nodded. "Okay. Let's grab a bite to eat, and then I'll help with the packing."

They ate a leisurely breakfast in spite of Robbie's excitement level and then chatted about what to pack.

"I think we need something really nice for the day of the auction," Robbie ventured an opinion.

"I suppose so. Anybody who has millions to spend on a painting probably has some nice duds in the closet."

"I helped my mom pick out some new clothes, but I have no idea about my dad. Or Silver?"

Trish smiled. Just the thought of having Silver make the trip was heartening. Of course she had been required to go to the airport yesterday in order to have her weapons transported under separate cover. Apparently, bodyguards knew all about these rules. Much like big game hunters. Unknown to everyone but Robbie and Silver, Trish had chartered a jet for the trip. Her rational was that it would be easier to secure a charter against possible attack. Her fantasy was that it would be like flying around in Goldfinger's jet. A few shaken martinis and before you knew it, you were touching down in style, just like James Bond. After the flight, there was little else that Trish could do to control security. She was depending on Silver. Silver didn't seem worried, so why was Trish?

"You are miles away, Trish." Robbie noted.

"Can I wear my jeans on the plane?"

"I guess so. I'm wearing my rayon blouse and black slacks."

"You'll be lovely as ever."

"Oh, stop!"

"Of course, you're even lovelier without your blouse and slacks…"

"Now you're making me blush."

"All over?"

"I'm not telling!"

"Can I see for myself?"

"No! If we start that, we'll never make our flight."

"They'll wait for us."

"When was the last time a commercial airline waited for late passengers?"

Trish had slipped up. Oh well.

"I guess you're right. Let's get going!"

Trish helped with the rest of the packing and then they drove over to the Goldstein's. To Robbie's delight, there was a stretch limousine parked in front and two uniformed personnel were loading luggage into the trunk. They pulled up behind so that it would be easy to transfer their bags. After that chore, Trish stowed their vehicle in the garage for safekeeping. By that time, the Goldstein women had been around each other long enough to get each other all stirred up again.

"I hope I packed all the right things," Rose was asking Robbie.

"I hope so, too. Did you pack your comfortable shoes?"

"I put them in at the last minute."

"She's taking more for this one-week trip than either of us brought with us to America!" Max expounded.

"We didn't have anything when we came to America."

"So, we do now and you're packing enough for three weeks. Maybe a month!"

"How about you, Max?" Trish interjected.

"I packed my new suit."

"You got yourself a new suit?"

"I was outnumbered."

"Aren't you always?"

"You get to wear your jeans," he pointed out. He was decked out in new slacks, a white shirt and a sports jacket. Rose better keep an eye on him. He was a dandy.

"I'll get dressed up when I have to. Is everybody ready to go?" Everyone deferred to Rose, who led the parade to the limousine. With expected flourish, the attendant held the door open for her. Soon, everyone was settled in a comfy seat and served their choice of champagne, cocktail, or ginger ale. After a nudge, Trish talked Robbie into champagne. They toasted each other and then sat close in companionable silence as they traveled to the airfield. When they arrived, they bypassed the usual terminal crowds and instead were delivered to their own private jet. Robbie's jaw was slack for about a second.

"You didn't?" she finally had a statement in the form of a question. Just like Jeopardy.

"It was a purely common sense decision."

"A plane all to ourselves?"

"It made the security precautions easier."

"I suppose there's champagne on board as well?"

"You catch on quickly!"

Of course, Silver insisted on checking out the jet before everyone got on board. She looked for the usual stuff, packages that ticked, whirred or otherwise leaded fluids. But she was also on the lookout for things that could be disguised, such as errant pagers and other electronic devices. Oh the daily challenges of a bodyguard. When Silver had deemed the aircraft safe, she escorted Rose up the steps and placed her in the front row of seats. Next to her was Max and then across the aisle sat Silver. Everybody else was on their own. Trish and Robbie sat together farther back in the cabin, after promising to trip any suspects if they walked up the aisle from the back of the plane. Rose didn't find this terrible amusing, but she had over time warmed up to the idea of being the only lady on the block with her very own bodyguard and was feeling rather worldly for such sophomoric humor.

Once Trish realized that she and Robbie were pretty much out of the line of sight of everyone, she began to behave like she and Robbie were back home on the couch. She began to gently stroke the inner part of Robbie's thigh as they prepared for takeoff.
"What are you doing?" Robbie asked.
"Just making sure you're not nervous."
"I'm not nervous."
"Not at all?"
"I'm excited."
"Oh good!"
"About the flight!"
Trish laughed. Robbie was so good for her.
"And here I thought you were excited about me?"
"I'm that, too. But we're in an *airplane*!"
She said the word "airplane" in a way that was meant to convey her hesitation.
"Yes, we are," Trish agreed.
"With my parents and a bodyguard who's going to be checking the plane every ten minutes!"
"Well, you know what I can do in ten minutes." Trish arched her eyebrows.

"I've seen you do a lot of things in ten minutes. Eat dinner, shave your legs, check your e-mail-"

"None of which I had in mind right this minute," Trish continued to touch Robbie until she gently took hold of Trish's hand.

"I want you to save your energy for New York."

"Why?" Trish asked, but didn't fight the restraint.

"Because, you're going to need it," Robbie promised.

That was good enough for Trish. Robbie always kept her word. Trish had just one more thing to say. "One of these days, I'm going to charter a jet just for you and me and then we'll see about those ten minutes."

Robbie only blushed at the prospect.

After the jet had achieved cruising altitude, Trish got restless. No surprise there. She wandered up to the front of the plane and chatted with Rose, who also seemed a tad jumpy.

"Are you excited about the auction tomorrow?" Trish figured she might just as well ask stupid questions as smart ones.

"I'd be a lot more excited if we had found the person who wrote those letters."

Trish nodded. So far, the investigation had gone down one long blind alley. Their only suspect was either very clever or very innocent. Trish had pinned her hopes on him, mostly because she didn't think they had much to fear from a tottery old man. In fact, Trish had relaxed about the case in general. Even if one old man was off the list, it was still logical to assume that the body of suspects only included people Rose and Max's age. And although that entailed a substantial part of the population, it still was hard to get all worked up over a few wacko letters from an octogenarian.

About that time, a flight attendant approached the front of the plane.

"Would anyone care for a cocktail?"

Max was about to name his pleasure when Rose gave him a look that conveyed, "If you get drunk on this airplane, you'd better have a parachute strapped on good and tight!"

He ordered a beer, a fair compromise by his standards. Rose requested coffee. Silver wanted tonic water.

"And you, ma'am?"

264

"I'll stay with champagne. No use mixing up my brain any more than it already is!"

The super model floated back down the aisle and Trish followed behind, though not too closely. Robbie was still sitting in the same spot. Still strapped in. Still behaving herself.

"You doing okay?"

"Yes, thank you."

"I ordered more champagne. You want some too?"

"I don't think I need any more champagne."

Trish settled in beside her.

"Honey?" Trish wanted to talk.

"Yes?"

"After tomorrow, you won't ever have to talk about things in terms of needs. The only thing I want you to think about from now on are strictly wants. You tell me you want something, and I'll get it for you. Anything you desire. Anything at all."

"That's really nice, but I already have what I desire."

On a scale from one to ten, Trish's heart was about nine and a half on the mush meter. Her brain was still at four. Where was that champagne?

"Of course, we still need to take care of Connors," Trish spoke solemnly.

"Of course."

"And I don't know how Mary and Lisa are doing, money wise."

"Whatever they need. However much." Robbie said.

"Let's just get through tomorrow." Trish was suddenly serious. Maybe her nerves were starting to show as well. Robbie didn't say anything more. She just held Trish's hand. It was all she needed right now.

Chapter 27

Mitch woke up late. Really late. There was a note on Reb's pillow. It read:

"I haven't left you a note in a long time. You look so sweet when you're asleep. I couldn't bring myself to wake you up, even for cheesecake.

My plans are to go to the hospital and bring Mary home for some real rest. Aren't you expecting to hear from Trish soon? Let me know if you find out anything.

Sincerely,
Ex-Senator Fairbanks"

Mitch chuckled at the ending. What a sit-down comedian Reb was becoming. Mitch pulled herself out of bed and showered for the day. Trish was due in and staying at that extremely fancy hotel. She called the place and left a message and a number where she could be reached. If things worked out, Mitch and Mary would hop on a commuter flight for the auction. If not, Trish could swing by the next day and visit. Either way, it would be a good distraction for Mary. Speaking of whom, she was in the kitchen eating cheesecake when Mitch wandered in looking for coffee. There was none made, so she set forth to perk some.
"Did you spend the night at the hospital?"
"They set me up with a cot."
"I bet you're ready for some good sleep."
"Actually, I rested quite well."
"Good. Say, you want to go to the art auction tomorrow?"
"I think I'll stick around here. Thanks anyway."
"Trish really wants us to be there." Mitch was stretching the truth, something she was good at.
"I'm sure she'll understand."
"You could use the time away."
"You're beginning to sound like my mother."
"Worse things could happen," Mitch defended herself.

"If it was Rebecca in there, we'd need a couple dozen sticks of dynamite to blast you loose."

Mitch couldn't argue that point. Mary was a hundred percent correct.

"I guess so."

"Why don't you go?"

"I'm beginning to get the feeling that Trish and Robbie don't need any more security problems. I think I'll stay out of the way as well."

"I think that's a wise choice."

"Yeah, besides, it's just an art auction."

"Right. A 65 million dollar art auction."

"I wonder how much my 'Study of Nude Woodpecker' would bring?"

"Probably not enough to buy birdseed!" Mary laughed.

Chapter 28

The charter jet touched down after another bottle of champagne
had bit the dust. During the flight, the Goldsteins and guests had
been treated to a first-run movie and a four-course gourmet meal.
It helped to soak up the bubbly. They were transferred to
another limousine and whisked to the hotel. Security brought
them in a separate entrance and the uniformed guards escorted
them up to their suites. Not rooms. Suites. Silver did a walk-
through with the head of security and was satisfied with the
preparations. Then, they were left on their own, except of
course, for the contingent of guards posted at each outer door. If
they had been dressed in red, you could have easily mistaken the
place for Buckingham Palace. Meanwhile, his royal highness,
Max was busy trying out the bed, bouncing on it like a groom.
The brochure had it listed as a California King and Max was
dwarfed by it. He might need a map to find Rose later in the
evening. Trish had hoped to not have similar problems with
Robbie, but put that thought out of her mind. There was, after
all, still the unpacking left to do. The hotel staff had offered to
help with the arduous task, but the group collectively passed on
the opportunity. Rose didn't want strangers handling her
garments, particularly her "under" kind. Only a couple of items
required pressing and the valet was at the door before you could
say, "You want starch with that?"

Then, undaunted by anything as trivial as death threats, they all
headed downstairs into still another limousine and toured around
town. Seeing the Statue of Liberty through eyes that had looked
upon seventy summers didn't diminish the effect for Rose and
Max. They had seen it many years ago and for them, it had not
lost its symbolic beauty. Freedom by way of Ellis Island had not
been a snap, but had truly saved their lives. Next, they drove
around Central Park and then stopped for bagels and coffee at a
small eatery.

At five-thirty, they were scheduled to meet with the director of
the auction house for a final briefing on the process. The
building was quiet and everyone sat in the room where the

auction would actually take place as Silver was taken on a special tour of the facilities.

"This is awesome," Robbie said.

"Just like in the movies," Rose nodded.

"Just don't pull on your ear tomorrow like you do at the breakfast table," Max admonished Rose, "or you'll be the proud, broke owner of Trish's painting!"

"I don't pull on my ear at the breakfast table."

"You do when you're reading the paper!"

Silver rescued them from further discussions about ear pulling. "Everything looks secure."

"Good," Trish jumped up. "Let's have dinner!"

They dined fashionably late and then arrived back at the hotel in time to relax before bedtime. The hotel staff had finally managed to locate the message left by Mitch, and Trish sat holding the paper as she and Robbie talked.

"Does it feel to you like our entire lives will be changed tomorrow?" Robbie asked.

"It feels like I'm going to fulfill a promise."

"And that's important."

"Promises are always important to fulfill."

"Call Mitch. It's important to keep in touch with friends, too."

Call it a hunch or a lark, or maybe just an early midlife crisis, but Mitch got it in her head to show up at the auction. This decision happened soon after she and Trish talked by phone after dinner. They had chatted happily into the late hours, and then Mitch went out and got a rental car and drove the two-hundred some miles from Baltimore to New York. That was the easy part. Getting to the hotel was another story and she arrived with scant minutes to spare. They had time for quick hugs all around, after Mitch was checked over by security and then the group was ushered into a waiting limousine. In the car, Trish asked more questions.

"How is Lisa, really? What couldn't you say over the phone?"

"It could have been a whole lot worse," Mitch cushioned the real news.

"I guess she was lucky?"

"As you heard, probably, Rebecca managed to call for help very quickly. It didn't hurt to have a helicopter handy."

"It's nice to have a Senator in the family."

Mitch only nodded. It wasn't her place to blab Reb's news.

"So, they haven't found yet who set the fire?"

"Not that I've heard. But from what I understand, there's no shortage of suspects. The authorities are combing through a lot of TV film footage to see if they can pinpoint a suspect."

"Didn't they burn down two places?"

"Right. A nice, old guy named Bixby is going to have to rebuild his place from the ground up."

"That's horrible," Rose got into the conversation.

"I guess it depends on who you talk to. Apparently, his house was a bit rundown and he's insured to the hilt. This could be quite an upgrade for him."

"I know you're excited about the auction," Mitch had repeated what everyone else had been saying for about three days.

"I guess it is quite the event of the year!" Rose trilled like it was the first time anyone had said anything. She was very much into the spirit of things now and had even practiced not pulling on her ear all through breakfast.

"Is it true that a lot of bidding is done over the phone?" Mitch asked.

"That's right. Some of the bidders prefer to remain anonymous. It's all fascinating to me," Robbie was getting antsy now. Mitch and Trish exchanged glances. Mitch knew about the real reason behind all the security measures. She hoped to be more help than hindrance, but Trish wasn't able to give her any more clues about possible suspects. So at this point, Mitch could only hope to be a spare pair of eyes. Everyone else was no doubt going to get all caught up in the moment.

They pulled up to the front and disembarked under the watchful eye of Silver. She would've hoped that everyone would just go in and sit down but, no. It was mingle time and, boy, could these art types mingle. Much to her chagrin, Mitch was recognized by several people as "that Senator's significant other" and although it was flattering, it kept her from riding shotgun. People whom she had never met greeted her with a mixture of awe and curiosity. So much so that she wondered for a time if they had mistakenly gone to the zoo. Mitch was congenial to a point and then searched for a quieter place where she could simply observe. As she scouted for dangerous retirees, she thought about all the decisions she and Reb had made. Would Mitch miss all the attention she got by being associated with a Senator even if the same Senator was often notorious for her absences during these types of functions. Or would Mitch truly prefer hanging out full-time with an ex-Senator? Full time. That's what was catching in Mitch's mind. Between Rebecca being a governor, a Senator and a rehab patient, they had never really had much in the way of full time togetherness. When old people did this, they called it retirement, got on each other's nerves and took up hobbies. What would this bring for Mitch, who wasn't really very good at hobbies? Except, maybe, getting into trouble?

Trish materialized at her elbow and said, "It's time to go and sit down. I managed to get a seat for you in the second row."
"I could just as easily stand," Mitch answered, "I don't want to be a bother."
"You're no bother. Come on."
Trish led the way to the second row and indicated a chair next to Silver, who was seated directly behind Rose. This meant that Mitch was behind Max. So far, so good. Robbie sat next to Rose and Trish flanked Max. If some old geezer in a walker even looked their way, things would happen. Big things.

As previously arranged, the minimum bid started at forty-million dollars, quite the chunk of change in and of itself. Trish found herself holding her breath, as if no one would make that first bid. She needn't have worried. The opening bid was made and immediately eclipsed by another and then another. Those who dared, looked around the room to see who was bidding, but many of the signals were tougher to decipher than the Enigma. Max was taking no chances, he held firmly onto Rose's hands. There would be no errant ear pulling on his watch.

The civilized tension was rising like helium in the rarified air of cubic wealth, and it was just as heady. These buyers, so many of them mystery, were spending millions of dollars faster than a drunk could play the field on a crap table. As Mitch looked around, the bidding hit the magic 65 million dollar mark. On cue, the bidders held firm for just a brief interlude as if it were a sacred moment. Then, some heathen blundered forward and sent the bid even higher. The crowd didn't gasp, that would have been too bourgeois. But the murmur was appreciable. Each bid now had a life of its own, living for a brief moment in the blinding light of extreme fortune, and then dying upon the arrival of the next bid. Mitch watched what little she could see of Trish's expression. She remained unfazed. It just didn't seem to matter to her and Mitch reminded herself to never play poker with her. Never ever.

Mitch scanned the crowd again. Although she had never been trained in any sort of surveillance or security work, something caught her eye. Someone had moved. Mitch thought it over. Probably a lot of people had moved and she just hadn't noticed. It could very well be that people were coming closer to the front of the room to be able to congratulate Trish and Robbie once the bidding was over. That would be natural. Still, just to be on the safe side, Mitch gently touched Silver's leg. When they made eye contact, Mitch mouthed the words, "Red Dress." Silver nodded as if to say, "I had my eye on her all along. But, thanks anyway." Silver could say a lot with a nod.

What happened next sort of all ran together like some slickly scripted action movie. As the gavel came down on the final bid of seventy-two million dollars, Red Dress came motoring up to the front row and over all the applause, started menacingly toward Rose. What she had in her hand would have flashed in the light had it been made of steel, but then she wouldn't have been able to get past the metal detectors. Still, it was sharp, honed to a fine point and potentially lethal. Silver was between the woman in the red dress and Rose before anyone else could react. For a large woman, she was fast on her feet. The next sound that was heard was the sickening crack of breaking bones.

Silver, perhaps not being too current on the subject of osteoporosis, had used enough force to restrain the likes of a much stronger, younger assailant. It was a bit much for an old lady and she crumpled up in excruciating pain. Rose, always the Good Samaritan, wanted to help.

"Someone call 911. And give the woman some air!"

Everyone did as they were told except Trish, who bent down to see what she could do to help.

"Who is she?" Robbie asked.

"Don't you recognize her?" Trish answered with a question.

"No, I don't think so."

"Maybe if she had on a fluorescent top. And was riding a bicycle?"

Robbie looked closely at the woman's face and then back at Trish. Being a true lady, all she said was, "Well, I'll be. It's Mrs. Montague!"

Paramedics soon arrived and began their processes. Having nothing better to do, Trish and Robbie now met with the auction director to transact the paperwork of the sale. By the time that was finished, they were millions and millions richer and Helen Montague was in an ambulance heading to the nearest hospital. Rose insisted on following in the limousine and soon, they were all disembarking in the emergency room, where they were told to stay until further notice.

"This still doesn't make sense," Robbie said to Trish as they sat close. "She didn't live in the state where the letters were coming from."

"That is interesting, isn't it? Maybe we'll find out more soon."

Soon became later. It took an awfully long time to set the arm. Silver was painfully quiet, like a child who didn't know her own strength and had been banished from the playground.

"You did what you had to do, Silver," Max consoled her.

"I'm worried about a lawsuit," she admitted. "And other things, too."

"You just leave everything up to us," he reassured kindly.

When visitors were finally allowed in, Rose insisted on going in alone.

"This is between her and me. I'll be fine."

As she walked into the room, the woman stirred.

"Get out."

"Not until you tell me why you tried to frighten me," Rose said in a steady yet commanding voice.

"You are nothing but a Jew pig. You are *nothing*."

"If I am nothing, then why bother?"

"Because you killed my brother. You deserve to die as he did."

"How did I kill your brother?"

"You made him defile himself and for that, he was killed."

It was all beginning to make sense now. Rose chided herself for not seeing the family resemblance, even after all these years. This was the sister of the guard who had raped her.

"I did not know your brother was killed."

"That's what they did to fine young men who were seduced by Jew filth like you."

Rose could only shake her head. A hatred so consuming was punishment enough.

"I'm sorry about your arm. If you don't have enough insurance, I'll pay your medical bills."

"I don't need your rotten Jewish money."

"Fine. It sounds like you have everything you need. I hope you can afford a lawyer as well. I'm pressing charges."

"Get out."

With a shrug of her shoulders, Rose left. Outside, the police were waiting to take her statement. It didn't take too long, they went kind of easy on little old ladies. At least, this one. They took notes and then promised to contact Detective Forrest to follow up on the threatening letters. The press, meanwhile, had gathered at the hospital lobby having heard the news.

"I'd better call Rebecca before she hears this on TV. She'll have kittens until she hears we're all okay."

Hospital personnel guided Mitch to a private area where she could make her call. Rebecca could either be at the hospital or at the apartment. Mitch called the hospital first. Bingo. Reb was available to talk.

"Hi, honey," Reb chirped. Gee, she sounded perky. "How's the auction going?"

"Uh, well, I suppose we'll be all over the news in an hour or two."

"It went that well?"

"Actually, there was an incident."

"An incident?  What kind of incident?"

Normally, one would ask if the person was sitting down.  Mitch forged ahead.

"There was an attempt on Rose's life.  It was unsuccessful."

"Was she hurt at all?"

"No, but the woman who attacked her sustained a broken arm."

"A *woman* attacked her?"

"Right."

"Why?"

"I don't exactly know."

"Give it your inexact best guess."

"I think it was all tied up with goings on during World War II."

"I see.  Talk about a long-standing grudge.  Okay, we'll check the news.  How are things otherwise?"

"Fine."

"You coming back soon?"

"You just turn down my side of the bed."

"Consider it done."

On that note, they hung up.  Mitch went back out to the group and from here, they went down the hall to one of the service doors and exited the hospital.  They went back to the hotel, where the press was camped out as well.  Through it all, Rose and Max were uncharacteristically quiet.  The ghosts of war had that effect on people.  Silver followed the usual routine, despite the fact that the prime suspect was now weighted down by a plaster cast miles away.  Old habits were hard to break.

Rose and Max sat down on the luxurious divan and held on to each other like they were refugees all over again.  Trish ordered enough room service for a dozen people.  Mitch had a tough choice.  Stay and eat like a pig or get in her rental car and drive her way into Rebecca's arms.

"What did you order?" she asked Trish.

"Steak and lobster."

Mitch almost groaned out loud.  What to do?  Great food or Rebecca?

"I need to be heading back to Baltimore."

275

"You can't stay for a quick meal?" Robbie sounded truly disappointed.

"I'd better not. If I eat, I'll get sleepy. But you are still planning to come to Baltimore, right?"

"You bet," Trish nodded. "We want to see all of you and then we're going to visit Connors."

"So, you're going to become jet setters!" Mitch beamed at Robbie.

"Well, I don't know about that," she smiled back shyly.

"We've got the jet," Trish teased.

"That's a great start," Mitch laughed. "Now give me a hug and I'll see you in a day or two."

By the time Mitch got on the road, she was already hungry. It was worth it. Reb was two-hundred miles away. Too far away to suit Mitch. She drove safe and steady and pulled into the hospital parking lot in time for a late dinner. Reb had waited, God love her. Despite the fact that they were in a public place, they kissed like they had been apart for weeks.

"I forgot to ask if you were okay," Reb admitted right off.

"Oh, heck, I'm fine!"

"Imagine you coming away from a skirmish unscathed," Reb touched Mitch's elbow and then her shoulder.

"That's only because nobody had a gun," Mitch explained.

"Still you could have been hurt."

What went unsaid between them was how difficult Reb's life would be without Mitch. Mitch was friend, lover and support system all rolled into one.

"Both of us have had a scrape with destiny this week. We must be meant to be together. Fate would have intervened otherwise."

"Fate has been awfully busy. It's made Mary and Lisa practically inseparable."

"How is Lisa handling things?"

"I've never heard a person scream so loudly in my life. I don't know how the nurses stand it."

"Let's take Mary out to dinner."

"She's already eaten."

"Maybe she could use some dessert."

"I think you need some dinner and quiet time. Come on. You've worried about everyone else. Take a break."

Mitch fell into agreement. She even let Reb do the driving as they scouted the area for a peaceful dining experience. They settled on a quiet little Italian place with checkered tablecloths and Chianti in a basket. Rebecca ordered pasta carbonara, a sinful dish by any standards. Mitch splurged on oven-baked lasagna. As they waited for their entrees, they munched on soft garlic breadsticks slathered with garlic butter. The sumptuous flavor made their eyes roll back in their heads.

"Is it true that garlic is an aphrodisiac," Mitch asked.

"With you, just about anything is an aphrodisiac," Reb replied.

"Oh, really!" Mitch raised her eyebrows. "Are you saying that I'm horny all the time?"

"I wouldn't put it that way," Reb countered with a smile. "I'd just remark that you have a wonderfully healthy sex drive. And as the beneficiary of said sex drive, I'll feed you all the garlic you can stand."

"You've adjusted so well to your status after the accident," Mitch said out of the blue. "Much better than I ever would have done."

"You would've done just fine," Reb took hold of Mitch's hand and kissed those sensitive spots where the palm met the fingers. It was driving her wild.

"See, there are a lot of places on the human body that feel wonderful when stimulated in just the right way."

Good thing the food showed up. Mitch was beginning to squirm in her chair. Partly from the attention Reb paid to her and partly because people were beginning to stare at them. It didn't matter where you were, people gaped at two women holding hands. The kiss sent the two at table five clear off their nut, causing them to depart mid-meal in what could only be described as a huff. Apparently, they were regular customers, because the owner of the establishment soon thereafter approached Mitch and Reb and asked them to leave.

"Why?" Reb asked pointedly.

"You're upsetting my other customers."

"We are?"

"Yes."

"Do you know that I'm a United States Senator?" Reb asked.

"I can't control the kind of people that get elected."

"I think you meant "who" instead of "that," Mitch interjected, ever the grammarian.

"But I can control the kind of people that come here to eat," he rambled on, displaying his ignorance like a medal.

"Finish up and go."

Mitch looked at Reb. They were only about two forkfuls into their meal, but had simultaneously lost their appetites. As Rebecca put her blazer up around her shoulders, Mitch fished a hundred-dollar bill out of her pocket and left it on the table. It was a classy exit by all standards. Once in the van, Reb asked, "How about we pick up a pizza somewhere and eat at home?"

"That sounds okay."

"Or we could have one delivered?"

"Whatever," Mitch was agreeable.

"I can't believe that something like this could happen in the United States of America."

"Bigotry and prejudice flourish everywhere. Here, there, Kansas…"

"So, when are Trish and Robbie going to stop by?"

"In a day or two."

"Well, at least we know where *not* to take them to dinner."

"Imagine how embarrassing that would have been. Trish could buy and sell that place a dozen times over."

"And she could be tossed out mid-appetizer on a whim," Reb sounded bitter.

"Let it go, my dear Rebecca."

"Gee, you don't use my full name very often."

"Does it turn you on?" Mitch was smiling.

"Of course."

"Well, then, Rebecca, let's go back to the apartment, Rebecca, and have something delivered, Rebecca."

"I knew you'd make up your mind sooner rather than later!"


The next skin graft was scheduled in two days. Good thing company was coming. Lisa was as nervous as a mouse trapped in a maze and could use some distraction.

"I don't want them anywhere near the treatment room when I'm in there," Lisa was making her demands known.

"Okay," Mary noted, "No company anywhere near the treatment area."

"And that includes you."

"I don't hang out there." Mary lied outright.

"Oh, of course you do. Don't you think I can tell? Just by looking at you?"

Mary didn't answer.

"And I want something nice to wear."

"I'll need to ask the staff."

"I'm not talking about all day, every day. Just when people are here. That shouldn't need a ruling from a parliamentarian."

"I'll see what I can do."

"Do your best!" Lisa was getting testy, a natural reaction to everything about being a burn victim.

"I always do my best where you're concerned," Mary got a little testy herself. It ran in the family. Their eyes locked and then Mary sat as close to her as all the hospital equipment would allow.

"I don't mean to be this way," Lisa tried to keep her voice steady. It wasn't working. The day had drained her of her last ounce of reserve and tears stung her eyes. Mary bent close and kissed her forehead, and then eyebrow and then gently worked her way down to her lips. It was their first such contact since the fire, but the burning desire felt by Mary was unrequited.

"I'm tired."

"Of course. I think I'll head home."

"That's a good idea. See you tomorrow."

"Right."

Mary gathered her things and left. They both needed some rest. By the time she got to the apartment, there was enough hot pizza to feel the Mormon Tabernacle Choir.

"Mitch went a little overboard," Reb explained as she noshed on a piece covered with barbecue chicken and green peppers.

"What are you eating?" Mary asked Mitch.

"This is a taco pizza."

"I see," Mary answered with zero enthusiasm.

"Taco pizza isn't your thing, I gather."

"Got any pepperoni?"

"Sure. I got two."

"Two?"

"She got ten total," Reb tattled.

"Why?" Mary was now curious.

"I just felt like it."

"We got thrown out of an Italian restaurant so Mitch is making a point to support the competition. It was all I could do to keep her order to ten-"

"You got thrown out of a restaurant?"

"Yes."

"How did that happen?"

"Your mother kissed my hand," Mitch explained and then added, "She's such a hopeless romantic."

"Let me see if I understand this. My mother kissed your hand and that alone got you thrown out?"

"You know how some people can be about public displays of affection, particularly between gay people."

"I think you should do something about it," Mary remarked.

"I am. I'm taking economic measures."

"Ten pizzas are hardly going to make a difference," Mary said as she checked out the other combinations.

"Who said I'm going to stop at ten?"

Mitch had that millionaire-with-a-cause look in her eye.

"Why do I get the feeling that we're going to be eating pizza for a month?" Mary was almost afraid to ask.

"You, me, us, and the entire staff of the burn center, for starters."

"That's a lot of people. Must be a hundred or more."

"So, that's still only fifty pizzas at about twenty dollars apiece which is a thousand dollars a day," Mitch did the math.

"Which is about thirty-thousand dollars a month. Money well spent, in my opinion. A good lawyer would cost easily that much, couldn't guarantee results and not taste as good."

"Hopefully, Lisa will be out of the hospital by then," Mary mused.

"That might be a bit on the optimistic side," Mitch warned.

"I know Lisa better than anybody. She's going to be back to normal in no time!"

"Are you trying to convince us or yourself?"

"Do you doubt me?" Mary challenged quickly.

"Uh, no." Mitch said carefully and then added, ""You want to talk to your mom alone?"

"Why?"

"I figured you might want to tell her what's bothering you," Mitch gave her arm a squeeze. "I'm going to take a shower and plop into bed. See you in the morning."

When they were alone, Reb asked, "Is there something bothering you?"

"Not really bothering me. Just, well, things are so jumbled and complicated."

"She's pushing you away, right?"

"How did you now that?"

"I did the same thing with Mitch. Big time."

"Really? So, what did Mitch do about it?"

"She got me in a swimming pool. I came to my senses soon after."

"A swimming pool. I don't think that's going to work with Lisa. By the time she's discharged, she might never go in a tub or pool ever again."

"I can understand that."

"So, what do I do?"

"Just do what you've always done before. Make her feel special in every way you can conjure up. Is there something you can do starting tomorrow?"

"She want's something nice to wear for company."

"Then, I suggest you go shopping and pick out something nice. Maybe in silk?"

"I can do that."

"Oh and one more thing…"

"What?"

"She's pushing you away to exert her power. Let her do some of that. It's healthy for her."

"Okay. Anything else?"

"Be patient with her. And don't skimp on the physical affection, even if she's not responding like usual. Start slow."

"Okay. I can do this. I know I can do this. Would you go with me tomorrow?"

"Of course."

"I don't know how I'm going to cope with all this when you and Mitch have to go."

"We're not going anywhere."

"What do you mean?"

"I'm resigning from the Senate."

"Does Mitch know?"

"She's the first one I told."

"And it's okay with her?"

"Why wouldn't it be?"

Mary looked like she was all ready to say something and then she stopped herself. Reb, the master at reading her daughter's nuances, asked again, "Why wouldn't it be?"

"I'm sure it's fine," Mary became monosyllabic.

"But?" Reb kept on.

"Mitch once told me that she loved you so much, she'd follow you to Orion. I checked it out. That's a long way."

"Yes, it is."

"I guess I just figure that when Mitch said that, she meant that she'd follow you there, and, well, stay."

"Meaning?"

"I think that Mitch needs to put down roots somewhere. If you keep going back and forth from here to there, it will be to the detriment of Mitch."

"I'll keep that in mind. Meanwhile, let's go shopping first thing tomorrow."

"Okay. Goodnight."

Mitch was still awake when Reb came to bed. In fact, she was reading the late edition of the paper.

"What are you reading?" Reb asked in a voice that conveyed she'd rather be doing something different. Like, talking, for instance.

"The paper."

"I can see that," Reb got closer. "Which part?"

"The part about the art auction and subsequent fiasco."

"That must have been scary."

"It was terrifying. Look at this picture. They didn't even get my best side!'

"How could they," Reb was warming up her comedic skills, "Don't you usually keep that covered?"

282

Mitch gave Reb one of those, "I'd be laughing hysterically if you were on stage" sort of looks and then tossed aside the newspaper. "You're in a mood," she pulled her close.

"I want to ask you something."

"Okay."

"Is it really okay with you that I resign from the Senate?"

"Sure."

"You'd really say so if it wasn't?"

"Yes, I'd say so if it wasn't."

Reb considered the answer carefully.

"Was it okay that I ran in the first place?"

"I thought we already talked about all this?"

"Have you enjoyed being in Washington?"

Now it was Mitch who had to do the thinking. "Just what exactly did you and Mary talk about tonight?"

"Stuff," Reb answered with obvious mystery.

"Stuff like what?"

"Oh, stuff like Lisa wants something besides a hospital gown to wear when she is expecting company."

"That sounds like a good sign. What else?" Mitch continued to fish.

"Stuff like how she thinks you need roots."

"I need roots?"

"Mary thinks that if I continue to drag you halfway across the continent on one whim after another, that that will be bad for you."

"Gee, you'd think that Mary had enough to worry about to concern herself with my roots."

"Is she right?"

"In a way, yes, but probably not how most people see it."

"At the risk of sounding dense, could you run that by me in English?"

"Oh sure," Mitch snuggled up closer to Reb so she could begin to fiddle with her best side. "Most people think of roots as a place or a house or a plot of land. And although this may sound unflattering, I think of you as my roots. Not that I'm likening you to a couple of acres of dirt, mind you. I just mean that wherever you are, that's my home. So, Mary's right in that if I didn't have you, I'd be lost. Was that in enough English?"

283

"Not only was it in enough English, it was perhaps the most romantic thing you're ever said to me."

"It was! Really?"

"If it wasn't, it was a close second to telling me that you'd rather sleep on the floor than in our bed without me."

"So, in a nutshell, you think that the truth is about the most romantic thing on earth?"

"Only when you say it."

"Now, that's romantic," Mitch leaned in and kissed Reb.

"I'm learning at the foot of the master."

"Oh, now, don't go all kinky on me," Mitch giggled.

"You'd like that, wouldn't you!" Reb got the giggles herself.

"If we don't hush up, we're going to keep Mary awake."

"Okay, ssshhhh!"

They kissed quietly. Well, almost quietly. Mitch couldn't kiss Rebecca without emitting soft moans of pleasure. Nothing that would awaken Mary, but enough to stir Rebecca to further action. Mitch took hold of her hand before she had made much progress.

"What?" Reb whispered.

"Would you believe me if I told you I'm absolutely exhausted," Mitch closed her eyes and they stayed shut.

"I believe it. You go to sleep. I'll catch you first thing in the morning."

"You got yourself a deal."

Chapter 29

Trish woke up first. Everyone else was sleeping in after the long day yesterday at the auction. She wiggled her fingers and toes. Funny, she didn't feel any richer? Robbie was dozing quietly and Trish gazed at her for a few moments. *Now*, she felt richer. She got up and headed for the bathroom. Afterwards, she went down the hall to see if Silver was willing to let her go unescorted to the hotel gym. No such luck. Silver called hotel security and they practically had to flip a coin to see who got the really really bland chore of watching Trish work out. Weren't there any straight guys on the payroll? After fifteen minutes, not one, but two heavily-muscled crisply-uniformed guards appeared in the hallway. How embarrassing was this going to be Trish wondered as they went, not to the gym that all the other hotel guests used. No! They ended up in some private gym that only certain hotel guests got to go to. Great. Each of the guards could probably bench press double their weight. What the hell. Trish started slowly, doing some stretching and treadmill work before hitting the weight machine. It only took about ten reps of six different exercises before Trish needed a break. A really long break. She gathered up her towel and headed back to the room. She was handed back, so to speak, to Silver's jurisdiction by Big and Bigger, who then went back to ostensibly more important business, like patrolling for terrorists. They almost saluted.

Robbie was just waking up. "You're looking absolutely buff," she said sleepily.
"I didn't even break a sweat," she was almost muttering.
"What's wrong?" Robbie sat up.
"Nothing."
"I can tell when something's bothering you," Robbie said and then waited.
"It just gets awfully crowded in the gym with two bodyguards the size of Mt. Rushmore."
"That must have made quite an impression on the other guests."
"There were no other guests. Apparently, when you're a seventy-two millionaire, you get a gym all to yourself."
"That's convenient."

"It's spooky. I mean, what if they weren't real guards? What if they were kidnappers? It would have been easy as pie to spirit me away and particularly after a hard driving workout."

"You said you hardly broke a sweat?"

"Exactly. I wanted to save my strength, just in case."

"Normally, I'd consider that an opening to initiate intimacy, but you seem really upset about all this."

"You know me better than anyone. Tell me what has me so upset. Please?" Trish asked honestly.

"It's probably a combination of things. The bodyguards, the attack yesterday, the fire in Kansas…"

"No wonder I'm a nervous wreck."

"Oh, I wouldn't classify you as a nervous wreck. You're just a woman with a lot on her mind. That's all."

"What's the cure for that?"

"Breakfast!"

"Big or little?"

"Big. Definitely big. No problem is too overwhelming that cannot be tackled by a big breakfast."

"Should we order up or do you suppose the fresh air would be good?"

"I can't guarantee its freshness, but let's opt for the air. I'll tell mom and dad that we're going for a stroll."

"Maybe they'll want to come along?"

"I doubt it. They're still getting over yesterday, I think."

Contrary to Robbie's assumption, Max, Rose and Silver were more than happy to tag along, and their cheerful demeanor had a positive effect on Trish. They walked confidently for several blocks, not at all looking like tourists. Eateries beckoned to them like so many temptations and they eventually surrendered into a cozy place that featured a dozen varieties of Danish along with lox and bagels and bacon and eggs and an aroma of espresso that turned your toes up. The party of five nestled around an undersized table and rather than tax their brains trying to make final decisions, ordered two selections apiece. Trish was bent on satisfying her sweet tooth by ordering several flavors of Danish as well. She narrowed her selection to cherry, lemon and blueberry to start with and at the same time offset the strong black coffee. Max had eggs. He was an eggy type of guy. The bacon he ordered was crisp and crunchy. Trish wondered if you could make a Danish and bacon sandwich for such a length of time that she saw Robbie's hand waving slowly up and down. "Oh, hi!"

"Welcome back. Where were you?"

"In Danish heaven. How's your bagel and lox?"

"Just what you would expect from New York."

"I propose a toast, no pun intended, to Silver," Trish raised her coffee cup. "For going above and beyond the call of duty and for keeping all of us safe and sound?"

"Here, here," they clinked cups and glasses together.

Silver looked pained at all the attention, but Trish wasn't done.

"And as far as I'm concerned, you have a job for life."

"I do?"

"Anyone who has as much money as we now do needs protection. Are you willing to take on the job?"

"I haven't got a better offer."

Trish took that as a yes.

"What do we do now?" Rose asked.

"Something I've always wanted to do in New York. Go shopping!"

Chapter 30

Mitch had awakened stubbornly. Not by design, but rather due to the hectic schedule she had been keeping lately. She knew that Reb and Mary wanted to go shopping early, and they were patient beyond measure while waiting for Mitch to get her feet under her when she expressed interest in going along.

"It's not like they're going to run out of blue silk pajamas," Mitch expounded as she tied her shoes.

"I know. I just want to get to the hospital as soon as we can." Mitch knew in her heart that Mary would wear herself clear out and beyond taking good care of Lisa. And who was Mitch to interfere in the most profound example of family values she had come across lately.

"We better buy a variety." Mitch stated what she thought was obvious.

"You think?" Reb questioned.

"I think it would be a real boost to her to bring a nice selection."

"Okay, well, let's go." Reb's leadership mode went to full blast.

Shopping in the mall was a great American tradition. It was made even greater by the expertise of these three women. When Mitch first met Rebecca, it was not long after that Mary took Mitch shopping for some clothes that looked a little more Republican. As expected, Mitch looked great but felt stifled. Over time, though, her clothes sense improved. It wouldn't take the taste of Anna Sui to improve on a hospital gown, and within two hours, they had filled six shopping bags full of treasures. Money had never been an object where these three were concerned and that fact permeated psychically through all the stores they visited. Once the spending started, like a puncture wound, it was hard to stop. Mary had lost practically everything in the fire, and now that she had a chance to think about it, her buying habits evolved from Lisa's desires to her own basic needs. Like, underwear, for instance. Buying bras in bulk wasn't too challenging, unless you were shopping with your lover's ex.

"You're buying all white?" Mitch was surprised.

"What's wrong with that?" Mary wanted to know, and sooner rather than later.

"Well, nothing, except that that's a whole lot of white."

"You have a suggestion! Make it now!"

"There's that really daring shade of magenta over there."

"Magenta?"

"And there's a really nice tiger print a couple of racks that way."

"I'm really not into animal prints."

"There's always basic black?"

"Do me a favor and see if you can locate a coffee bar in this mall."

"Oh, sure thing," Mitch went off on her errand.

Finding a coffee place in the mall was as easy as finding hay in a haystack, but even with her luck, by the time Mitch returned from her scouting mission, all the underwear buying was over and done with. Meanwhile, Reb had been browsing sweaters. What she and a sweater did for each other had always been pretty incredible, so all Mitch had to do was sit back and oohh and ahh.

"Hush up. People are staring."

"And well they should!" Mitch smiled a goofy smile.

"Did you find a coffee spot?"

"It's about half a mall that-a-way."

"Good. We'll pay for this and then take a break."

"Okay."

Mary attempted to bolt her coffee and ended up burning that terribly sensitive spot just behind her upper front teeth.

"Ouch!" she groused and then became quiet.

"You going to be okay?" Reb and Mitch asked in unison.

"I'm fine. I shouldn't be complaining about a little burn for goodness sake!"

"Pain is still pain." Mitch said philosophically.

"When are Trish and Robbie coming?"

"I guess when they get done with their New York adventure."

"That could be anytime..."


After breakfast, Trish had a shopping spree in mind. A big shopping spree. Travelers know that there are several distinct shopping areas in New York. Trish decided to start at the top.

She arranged for a limo from the hotel to meet them at the restaurant, due mostly to the fact that, number one, two of their party were senior citizens and, number two, cabs in New York could only take four passengers by law. From there, they rode in style to Madison Avenue. After all, wouldn't Max look stunning in something from Giorgio Armani? And if that didn't work out, there were at least a dozen other high class stores to choose from. Add to that the numerous shops for the ladies and you had a place that would keep them busy clear 'til lunch.

Rose and Max, being of the generation that they were, were loath to spend money. Trish wasn't buying it, no pun intended, and insisted they try on anything that even remotely caught their eye. Interestingly enough, they both looked good in bold colors. Maybe it was because they were both warm people? In any event, Rose was busying herself trying to choose from three elegant dresses when Trish informed their salesclerk that, "We'll take all three."
Rose hid her surprise well. Meanwhile, Max, over only slight protest, was being measured for a suit.
"But I don't live here. I live in Colorado."
"Don't worry," Robbie soothed him. "We'll just fly back out for the fittings when the time comes."
Max's mention of chartering another jet got the full attention of the tailor, who snapped to like a sailor on deck. This was going to be some suit. After all this, a compromise was forged. Max wasn't going to spend all his time in a suit, so they scouted around for a more leisurely selection. What he found were polo shirts in lots of colors and stripes.
"If you're not careful, Trish will buy you a pony to go with those," Robbie teased.
"I'd settle for a hot tip on a race horse," he teased back. And this from a man who had never stepped foot in a racetrack.

With further encouragement from Rose, Max bought a week's worth of clothing that would make him the envy of any golf pro. He was downright spiffy. Spiffy enough to accompany four lovely ladies to lunch. There are restaurants in New York that are so popular that reservations are required weeks in advance.

Needless to say, they avoided those trendy places in lieu of a more traditional spot. What was it about Italian food in New York? Other that the fact that is was delectable. Who would have thought to deep fry ravioli and serve it as an appetizer with pungent marinara sauce for dipping. Whoever it was deserved some sort of culinary honor. Was there a hall of fame for cooks? Trish thought about it as they ate this while studying the menu.

"I can't decide," Robbie shook her head.

"What have you narrowed it down to?"

"Well, you know how I am about spaghetti and meatballs," she said with a tone now so familiar to Trish that they blushed.

"I know," Trish nodded.

"But the manicotti sounds good, too."

"That's what I'm having," Silver chimed in.

Trish felt a twinge of guilt. In all the activity, no one had thought to encourage Silver to pick out any new clothes.

"After lunch, let's hit Fifth Avenue," she formulated a plan.

"You youngsters might be up to it, but I'm ready to put my feet up and rest," Rose stated firmly.

"Me, too," Max added.

Trish sensed a mutiny and figured it was manageable. She could surrender Max and Rose to hotel security after lunch and steal Silver away for more shopping. Lunch was a veritable smorgasbord of treats. Everyone ended up ordering something different after all. Silver stuck to her guns and got the manicotti. Robbie went for the spaghetti. Max, the perpetual dieter, ordered pasta with vegetables, and the siren song of pizza was too strong for Trish to resist. Rose surprised everyone by getting chicken sautéed with wine, garlic and oil. Baskets of garlic bread and salads appeared almost instantly and kept everyone busy until the main course arrived. They ate at a slow pace and then sent Max and Rose back to the hotel in the limo. That way, the three of them could hail a taxi and head toward Fifth Avenue. Once Silver realized that this foray was designed for her benefit, she was gracious. Although much of the haute couture was for people of the petite sizes, there was adequate selection for her. She looked good in basic black, somber and proper and just a tad menacing. Everything a bodyguard wanted.

"Do you suppose Gucci makes a gun holster?" Trish whispered to Robbie.

Robbie whispered back, "There's a whole lot better things than gun holsters at Gucci."

She sounded like she knew what she was talking about, too! After another couple of hours of walking and shopping, they were also ready to head back to the hotel and make plans for, as Max put it, the cocktail hour. It sure seemed like they kept their word. Both Max and Rose were rested and refreshed and more than happy to tend bar for the three tired shoppers. Even Silver had a bit of the nip as she checked in with hotel security over the phone.

Trish and Robbie each took a strong concoction to their adjoining room after being hospitable for a decent amount of time. As Trish stretched out on the bed, she watched Robbie begin to go through her parcels. She was beaming.

"Everything is so nice!"

"You have very good taste," Trish agreed.

"Especially in women," Robbie added slyly.

"You think so?"

"I know so," Robbie confirmed.

"Do you think your parents are having a good time?"

"I think they are having the time of their lives. You are so generous to them. I'm sure my mother has never had three new dresses all at the same time. And my dad! I never knew he could be such a clotheshorse. I caught him looking at himself in a mirror when he thought I wasn't watching. He could be a model the way he poses."

As Robbie demonstrated, Trish chuckled.

"I think you're the one who should be a model."

"Oh, hush!'

"Why don't you come over here and make me," Trish made the dare sound irresistible,

Robbie sat beside Trish and almost kissed her, pulling up just a little short at the last second. Trish pulled her close so there would be no more near misses. Robbie cooperated in a manner that conveyed total compliance. Of course there was a knock at the door. Wasn't that just their luck. It was Silver asking about dinner plans. My God, they weren't even over lunch yet.

"What do you want for dinner?" Trish asked of Robbie, whom she hadn't let out of her grasp despite the interruption.

"Whatever you want," she answered.

"Silver, where do you want to go?"

"I haven't had a good steak since the last presidential election."

"Got a place in mind?"

"I'll go start working on it."

"Good, oh and Silver?"

"Yes?"

"Don't get in a rush, okay?"

"Sure, okay. Maybe an hour?"

Trish was watching Robbie, who had blushed clear to magenta. "An hour is fine."

At last they were alone. For a whole hour. Robbie didn't seem to be in quite the hurry that Trish was, which ended up suiting her anyway. There was nothing like a little longing to make things better. And things couldn't get much better.

"You were awfully quiet," Robbie cuddled up close.

"I was keeping in mind that your parents are in the next room."

"For a moment, I thought you had stopped breathing."

"For a moment, I did."

Trish checked the time. They had a few minutes to relax. Trish relaxed alright. Right into a delicious nap. When she awoke, Robbie was elsewhere, probably getting dressed. She appeared as if on cue, and was absolutely stunning.

"My God, you're beautiful!"

"You better get up. We've only got a few minutes."

"I could spend the rest of my life in the bathroom and not look half as gorgeous as you."

"Well, now is not the time to test your theory. Folks are hungry."

"Yes, ma'am." Trish followed orders. She really didn't need another big meal this day, but if it made Silver happy, then that's all that mattered. Over dinner they planned their upcoming schedule.

"Are we going to go all the way to Maryland to see Lisa and then backtrack up to Glens Falls to visit Connors?" Robbie asked

"I think that would be best. I am assuming that we'll have a lot of paperwork to take care of at the nursing home. Besides," Trish went on, "it isn't all that far to the burn center. Mitch drove it in one day."

"Are we driving there?" Max wanted in on the plans.

"Do you want to?" Trish answered with a question.

"We could rent a van," he sounded enthused.

"One of those with a TV set?" Robbie was jumping on the bandwagon.

"And individual bucket seats with cup holders?" Rose put in her request.

Trish and Silver exchanged glances.

"I guess we're getting a van," Trish acquiesced graciously.

Chapter 31

Lisa did her best to eat a few bites of dinner. Thankfully, her mouth hadn't been damaged in the fire but the skin and muscles surrounding the area were still gawd-awful painful. There had been quite the discussion early on in the treatment as to the need for a feeding tube. Lisa had all but signed a blood oath that she would do her best to eat, knowing that the specter of a liquid diet loomed. The truth of the matter was that liquid intake was crucial and administered mostly via IV, but every bit of nutrition helped immensely. Mashed potatoes went down well, as did oatmeal and pancakes. Mary would have brought in anything and Lisa knew it. But for now, she was content with the vast array of sleepwear that the three shoppers had procured. It had been a delicate process to have Lisa try on one of the new silk tops, but she was determined and gritted her teeth through the fitting. The tears in her eyes were partly due to pain and partly due to pleasure. Nobody wanted especially to talk much about the philosophical implications of that and instead talked about something safe: food.

"You want me to go find you some ice cream?" Mitch asked, wanting to be useful.

"All they have around here is raspberry sherbet and I can't stand it," Lisa answered quietly.

"I can go anywhere you want. Let's not limit ourselves to the nurse's station refrigerator."

"I heard you already have gone a little overboard in the food department."

"Who snitched?"

"I did," Mary fessed up.

"You're going to be Mitch, the Pizza Lady," Lisa was fading with each sentence. She would need a nap before dessert.

"That's right. And you get to choose. All your favorites. I know how well you like pizza."

There was just a hint of a smile in those familiar eyes. After Lisa had taken off with a million or so dollars that belonged to Mitch, she had eventually returned with most of the money, a minor infection requiring antibiotics, and a hunger for pizza. Mitch had caved in then. Why should now be any different? Reb tugged at her sleeve.

"Why don't you take me home and bring ice cream later?"

"You don't need to bother." Lisa said as she yawned. "Why don't the three of you go. Tomorrow will be a busy day for everyone."

Mitch agreed. She had gotten word that Trish and her entourage were arriving before noon. They all needed some sleep.

Reb was quiet on the drive home. Mary, by contrast, was quite chatty.

"Did you see how well Lisa ate?"

"Yes, I did," Mitch answered. Lisa always did have healthy appetites. In so many respects.

"That's a good sign, right?" Mary was asking for some hope.

"It's a great sign. Let's be sure to stock up on ice cream. What's her favorite flavor?" Mitch feigned ignorance for Mary's sake. But she knew damn well what Lisa's favorite flavor was. It was butter pecan. She used to buy it by the pint, probably because she was aware of the fat content. And then, on some nights, when she was in one of *those* moods, she would bring it to bed. Just Lisa and a pint of butter pecan ice cream and a spoon...

"You just missed the highway exit to the apartment," Reb jolted Mitch back to reality.

"I did?" Mitch looked around.

"You okay?"

"I'm just tired."

"Is that all?"

"And I'm worried about tomorrow. It's not every day the newest multi-millionaire drops in for a visit."

"Well, at least you don't have to worry about the menu," Mary stated. "We will have pizza and chocolate ice cream."

"Chocolate?" Mitch said as she took the next exit for the scenic route home.

"Yeah. Chocolate. It's Lisa's favorite."

Mitch didn't argue. There was really no point. What was there to say? Gee, I'm sorry but Lisa's favorite ice cream is butter pecan because she used to bring it to bed and feed it to me? Spoonful by spoonful. And what she could do with a spoon..."

"You just passed the street where the apartment is," Rebecca the newly-appointed navigator noted. "Are you *sure* you're okay?"

"I'm going down a block because there's a pothole on the other street," Mitch lied. "Besides, what's one block between friends." Reb didn't say anything. Mitch had the prickly feeling that wasn't going to last much longer. She was right. Once the bedroom door was closed, Reb corralled her as much as she could in her wheelchair.

"What's on your mind?" her question was direct yet kind.

Mitch thought it over. She could continue to lie or just come out with it. Reb would know if she attempted the former, which narrowed the choice to the latter.

"Lisa has been on my mind."

"Current Lisa or taking-a-trip-down-memory-lane Lisa?"

Another former-latter choice to contend with.

"A little of both actually."

Reb waited. She had that "I'm not going to grill you about this, but the sooner you come clean, the better" look on her face.

What could Mitch possibly say?

"Chocolate isn't Lisa's favorite flavor of ice cream."

"Really," Reb tried her Senatorial best not to look too confounded.

"Yeah."

"And this is important because…?"

"It's really not at all important."

"Missing a highway exit and a street with *no* potholes doesn't constitute important?"

"Don't you ever have fond memories about Jeff come floating back to you, just out of the damn blue?"

"Not really. Besides, this isn't about me and Jeff."

"I know that," Mitch replied with an edge in her voice. "This is about what it's always been about between you and me."

"Not really," Reb countered. "It's really about ice cream and former lovers and distracted driving, all three of which I can deal with in moderation. So, tell me, what is Lisa's real favorite ice cream?"

"Butter pecan."

"And what's my favorite?"

"Rocky Road," Mitch knew immediately.

"You have quite a memory where ice cream is concerned," Reb smiled.

"I guess ice cream is to me what perfume is to other people. You know, a…memory trigger?"

"And what memories do you have about Rocky Road?"

"Making love to you after a fight about me being a know-it-all. Butterscotch syrup was involved as well, if memory serves me right."

"You are right! You and your syrup!"

"You want me to go out and get you some Rocky Road right now?"

"Heaven's no! After the way you were driving tonight, I'd worry you wouldn't find your way home."

"Honey, as long as I have you to come home to, I'll always find the way."

"Forget about ice cream. Let's go to bed."


Mitch woke up first. That was a switch. Usually, Reb was up and around but this morning, she was sleeping in. Everyone needed their turn. That gave Mitch a chance to start coffee and breakfast. They would need the energy. Trish and company were on the way. Mary wandered out about the time Mitch had a half a pot brewed and a pan of corned beef hash cooking on the stove.

"Mornin," she yawned and shuffled over to the table. Mitch brought her a cup of strong coffee and a promise of food. While she waited, she asked, "How do you do it?"

"Make coffee?"

"No," Mary clarified after another yawn. "How do you make my mother so happy?"

Mitch had to think about this. When they last parted company with Mary, Reb didn't seem all that happy.

"Happy?" Mitch stalled for time.

"I heard the two of you giggling way into the night."

"I was telling your mother silly stories," Mitch bent the truth. Way over backwards.

"Silly stories?"

"Well, not all that silly."

"Would you answer a very blunt question?"

Mitch nodded.

"My mom doesn't have much sexual response, does she?"

"Not from the waist down. But from the waist up, she's a veritable gold mine of sensuality."

"And that's what keeps you two giggling into the night?"

"That…and my limericks. You want to hear one?"

"No! Thanks anyway. I haven't had my coffee yet."

"Suit yourself. You want toast or toast with your corned beef hash?"

"I'll…have…um…toast."

"Good choice."

"Can I ask you something else?"

"Sure."

"What am I going to do if Lisa resists reestablishing intimacy."

The question couldn't have been any more loaded than if it were sponsored by the NRA.

"Well," Mitch pondered, "How did you establish intimacy in the first place?"

Mary thought it over.

"I stopped running."

"Running?"

"Lisa chased me and I let her catch me."

Mitch knew how that went. In terms of figurative blocks, Mitch hadn't made it past half of one.

"That might just work again," Mitch offered.

"What if she doesn't, you know, want to?"

Mitch had to be really careful here. How could she convince Mary that the chase was in Lisa's blood like a reincarnated pedigree greyhound without sounding like she was a, well, a know-it-all?

"Just don't get too much of a head start."

Mary quietly meditated on this dubious wisdom as Reb wheeled into the kitchen.

"Good morning!" she was perky.

It had to be the limericks.

Having a concierge to do all the dirty work was beginning to have an effect on Trish. This was nice. You want to rent a van in New York and you happen to be rich? No problem! A van with all the amenities was in front of the hotel at ten in the morning sharp. Trish took care of the hotel bill and added a nice gratuity on top of all the tens and twenties she had scattered in her wake.

Everyone was buckled in and drinking Bloody Marys, except for Trish and Silver, who had opted for driving duties. The seats had to have been very comfortable, for the Goldsteins were asleep by eleven. Maybe they were those kind of folks who slept well while traveling? Silver kept a dutiful eye out for highway pirates as Trish navigated the road.

"I never really thanked you properly for saving Rose's life," Trish felt like talking and thought that was a good place to begin.

"It was nothing. Not much needed to subdue a little old lady with a take-out knife."

"Still, you were very brave under the circumstances."

"Thank you."

"Do you enjoy working with us?"

"Yes, ma'am."

"You don't need to call me ma'am. 'Trish' will be just fine."

"Okay."

"So, in your professional opinion, are we past the worst of the danger?"

"Millionaires are never really out of danger."

"I was afraid of that," Trish sighed.

"But you've taken every precaution you can short of barricading yourselves in your house."

"I'm not planning on doing that."

"I noticed."

"Tell me something, Silver."

"If I can."

"Does it bother you that I'm gay?"

"No, ma'am. Everyone is entitled to happiness."

"I wish more people thought like you do."

"We'd have a world full of smart people."

Trish laughed. She was beginning to enjoy this bodyguard stuff.

They lapsed back into silence and never did trade driving duties for fear of waking everyone up. Folks began to stir about ten miles from the burn center.

"My goodness, what was in those drinks? Sleeping powder?" Robbie asked from the back seat.

"Oh gosh, you found me out," Trish made eye contact and twinkled. Robbie twinkled back. Wasn't love grand? She couldn't love this woman any more if she tried.

Whoever thought to have valet parking at hospitals was a genius in Trish's book. The less Max and Rose had to walk, the more energy they would sustain for the visit. Truth be told, they were all a little stiff and sore, except for Silver. Lisa was in treatment right now, which gave them time for a huggy reunion with Mitch. For a minute, Mitch didn't think Trish was going to let go. It hadn't been *that* long. Silver was doing just fine until she met a real live Senator.

"I'm honored, your honorable," she used as many 'honors' as she could think to use.

"Oh, don't worry about all that honorable stuff," Reb put her at ease. "We try to use that only when necessary. Just call me Reb."

"Reb, ma'am?"

"No, just Reb."

If Mitch thought she got a nice hug from Trish, Mary got the royal treatment. By the time Trish got done holding and talking to Mary, she had to brush away a tear or two. They adjourned to the private family conference room, where Mary briefed everyone on the latest developments. Lisa was undergoing another skin graft tomorrow, so this was a good time to visit. Trish nodded like she had a premonition.

"Once they have the skin grafts done," Mary began in the middle of the story, "then they will need to make a special pressure mask for Lisa's face and then she will be fitted for this type of garment," Mary held up a Jobst shirt. It was damn ugly.

"Why will she need to do that?" Rose asked.

"If you don't keep the proper amount of pressure on the wounds as they heal, then the scar becomes lumpy."

"Oh, I know what you mean now," Rose nodded. No doubt she had seen some lumpy scars in her lifetime.

"But, for now, Lisa is bandaged after her daily treatments, so seeing her isn't terribly traumatic."

Their meeting was interrupted by a knock on the door. It was the authorities, not of the hospital, but of the law.

"Oh," he looked surprised. "I was told I could find the Fairbanks family here."

"That's us." Rebecca answered.

"All of you?" he asked, trying his best not to focus on Silver.

"Well, not all of us."

"If I could, I'd like to speak to just those of you involved in the fire that's being investigated."

"Why? Is there some secret involved?" Reb was just checking.

"It's an ongoing investigation, Senator Fairbanks."

He figured that that explained it all.

"Okay, well, it might be easier if Mary and Mitch and I went somewhere else with you."

"That won't be necessary," Trish was already on her feet and the others in her party followed suit. "We'll go out and wait in the lobby."

"Actually, there's a spot close to Lisa's room," Mary said.

"And I can show you where it is," Mitch volunteered. "I can always catch up on the news later."

Mitch led them down a couple of halls and past the tubbing rooms. Screams were audible. Screams were always audible and Mitch didn't pay much attention. Everyone else went a bit pallid.

"Is that Lisa?" Robbie asked in church tones. Or maybe, in her case, synagogue tones?

Mitch paused to listen and then shook her head, "No."

They arrived at the waiting room and were relieved to find it empty. Checking her watch, Mitch confirmed, "Lisa should be back in her room by now and medicated. She'll be ready for visitors soon."

Before Trish could urge Mitch to rejoin the official meeting, Mary and Reb appeared.

"Gee, that was fast," Mitch commented.

"Not much to talk about." Reb replied.

"So, then, there's no news?" Mitch was confused. It seemed to be a lot of fuss for no news.

"I'll tell you later," Reb said in a stage-type aside.

"Sure."

In the meantime, Mary had checked in on Lisa and then happily informed everyone that she was up for company. Quietly to Mitch, she confirmed, "She looks great!"

Mitch nodded. Hell, Lisa made the bandaged look seem dazzling.

Trish and Robbie sort of got pushed to the head of the line and they walked in reverently. Lisa, indeed, was ready. She was sitting up, resplendent in a deep purple silk pajama top. Royalty would've cowered. Trish didn't. Instead, she went over and gave Lisa a big hug and kiss right on the mouth.

"Well, if it isn't my favorite lawyer," Lisa said with a coy smile. This comment elicited a hearty chuckle from Trish, Mary and Mitch. Reb was quiet and Robbie appeared puzzled. "Lawyer?" she asked.

"I'll tell you later," Trish promised.

"Come give me a hug, Robbie," Lisa invited her closer. She complied, but skipped the kiss. Robbie wanted to chat instead.

"So, how do you feel?"

"Not too bad," Lisa was getting better at masking the effects of the pain killers. Either that, or she was building up a natural resistance.

"How many skin grafts will you have?"

"I hope not too many."

"It hurts really bad?"

"They just cut off good skin from places where you'd rather they didn't have to."

"That sounds horrible!"

"Aw, it all grows back eventually. I'm dying to hear about Rose's New York adventure?"

Maybe "dying" wasn't the exact best choice of syntax, but the Goldsteins didn't seem to mind. Rose and Max came closer and before long, Rose was patting Lisa's hand in a classic maternal fashion.

"Our little problem is nothing compared to what you've had to go through."

"But I wasn't chased around by a knife-wielding wacko."

"She wasn't all that scary. Besides, Silver took care of things. Tell her, Silver…"

As Silver and the Goldsteins chatted about the art auction with Mary and Lisa, Reb gave Mitch one of those "let's go talk in the hall" looks. They eased out of the room and went down to the waiting room.

"I forgot to ask. Where is everyone going to sleep tonight?" Reb wanted details.

"I'm sleeping with you. Everyone else has to fend for themselves."

"Yes, but where?"

"I don't know. I assume they are going to some security-laden hotel."

"When is the pizza-for-one-hundred showing up?"

"About four-thirty. You sure have a lot of questions. When is it my turn?"

"Now."

"What did the police have to say?"

"An arrest is imminent. We're going to need to get to Kansas, and soon."

"Why? Can't the police handle a simple arrest?"

"Nothing about this arrest is going to be simple."

Mitch waited for more, but Reb slipped into a contemplative mood. Mitch could wait it out, but there was life to be lived.

"Who's getting arrested?"

"Miranda. And yes, they will read her her rights!"

Back in Lisa's room, a skit was evolving. They were attempting to recreate the knife scene at the auction, sans a player for the part of the wacko.

"And then Silver broke her arm in two places!" Max put the finishing touches on the narrative.

"So, who was she?" Lisa wanted to know.

"She was a woman who was still fighting World War II and I was the enemy."

"I can't imagine anyone thinking of you that way," Lisa remarked. It was obvious that she was tiring quickly. Mary looked at Trish as if they had a prearranged signal and everyone began to wind down the visit. There were kisses and hugs all around.

"You'll be back?" Lisa asked, particularly of Trish.

"We'll be here for dinner."

"Oh, good."

Lisa was asleep five minutes after company left. Mary appeared to need some rest as well.

"Have you all booked rooms, yet?" Mitch asked Trish, but Rose answered. "Silver was kind enough to do that for us. She's been just terrific. A real security specialist. Did you know that all those big hotels have secret entrances?"

"No kidding!" Mitch tried to appear surprised.

"Oh, but you already know all about that, with the Senator in the family."

Mitch was trying to recall if they had ever gone through any secret doors recently, let alone at all. Thankfully, her silence wasn't noticed and she didn't need to elaborate further on the topic.

"Mary, why don't you come to the hotel with us," Trish offered. "You can check out the Jacuzzi and get a massage. My treat!"

Mitch could've kissed Trish for making the offer.

"I usually stay close," Mary hedged.

"Go on, honey," Reb encouraged.

"Yeah, we'll take care of things here," Mitch chimed in.

"Okay, I surrender. I'll go," Mary caved.

"See you for dinner."

Once they were gone, Mitch finally had the chance to quiz Reb on the arrest.

"How do they know it was Miranda?"

"There is a lot of evidence."

"You weren't in the meeting long enough to see a lot of anything."

"They told us there was a lot of evidence."

"So, you're just taking their word for it?"

305

"Gee, you certainly got up on the lawyerly side of the bed his morning."

"And you didn't?"

"They showed us a photo and a couple of receipts."

"A photo?"

"Of Miranda in the crowd at the house."

"I think the operative word there is 'crowd' don't you?"

"They can place her at the scene."

"What about the receipts?"

"She bought a gas can a few weeks ago."

"Well, I own a gas can. I probably own two or three. Anybody who owns a car or lawn mower or snow blower owns a gas can."

"Okay, Matlock, you win," Reb was tiring quickly of the prosecutorial role.

"All I'm saying is that it's nothing but circumstantial evidence."

"Except for the alleged confession."

"She confessed to the crime."

"Yes."

"To the police?"

"To a friend. And *don't* go down character assassination avenue here. I'm not in the mood."

Mitch shrugged her shoulders and remained silent. For all of two minutes.

"I just don't want the wrong person to go down the river for this."

"What are you saying?"

Mitch just shook her head. For a woman who wouldn't hush up a few minutes ago, she could not now be goaded into further speech. They all but waited in separate corners for further developments. The next development was pizza dinner.

When the hospital staff had first heard about the "pizza for a month plan" they were skeptical. Perhaps dubious was a better description. But after all the logistics were worked out, it was less frantic than at first thought. Staff came and went quietly getting their fill of gourmet and not so gourmet pizza. There just was no substitute for pepperoni in Mitch's book. Amidst this process, Trish, Robbie and Mary reappeared. Mary looked about a hundred times better. It's amazing what a massage and nap can do for the body and soul.

"I slept like a dead tuna," she confirmed. It wasn't poetic, but at least it was terribly descriptive.

"Let's get some pizza."

"I'm going to check on Lisa and then I'll be down."

Over dinner in the cramped staff lounge, Robbie remembered to ask about Lisa's comment to Trish.

"Why did she think you were a lawyer?"

Trish looked at Mitch, who started the story by saying, "Oh, hell, that's nothing. She thought Mary was a maid." From the look on Trish's face, Mitch wasn't sure she had been particularly helpful.

"A maid? When did she say that?"

"A year or so ago," Reb clarified. Mitch and Trish seemed to need help with the story, so she went on, "You see, before you married into the family, so to speak, Mitch and Trish and Mary were all involved in a bit of shenanigans."

"You were involved, too," Mitch added.

"I was not," Reb replied.

"You drove the getaway car."

"Only because your arm was still in a cast!"

"As I recall, you were the one who flew up in the governor's jet?"

"It wasn't the governor's jet. Governors don't have jets."

"Do Senators have jets at their disposal?" Trish was wandering off topic, perhaps on purpose.

"Only if they line their coffers with PAC money, which Reb doesn't."

"I see," Trish nodded.

"Except you really haven't answered my question," Robbie persisted.

"I'll clear things up," Mitch assured her. "It's all pretty simple. Lisa, my ex-girlfriend, was trying to swindle some money."

"Lisa was a common criminal?"

"There was never anything too common about Lisa," Mitch answered, "but she did have a habit of taking money that wasn't nailed down. So, we decided to dangle a substantial amount of money in front of her to get her to leave town."

Mitch paused for effect. Should she mention *why* they wanted
Lisa out of the way? She looked at Trish and decided that the
less said, the better.
"But, why did Lisa think Trish was a lawyer?" Robbie kept her
on task.
"Because we told her that Trish was a lawyer."
"Well, why?"
"Why?" Mitch stalled for time.
"How did that convince Lisa that there was money?"
"We told her that there was an inheritance and that I was some
sort of estate lawyer," Trish took over the storytelling duties.
"So, you told her she had an inheritance and she took money that
she thought was hers? That doesn't sound criminal?"
"That's not exactly how it happened," Trish couldn't bring
herself to lie, no matter how convenient. "We told her that a
friend of hers had inherited the money and then we just sat there
and watched as she took the money and ran."
"Oh, I see. So you sort of set her up?"
"Right. Except later, we found out that she was on to us from the
beginning."
"But she took the money anyway?"
"She knew Mitch was a soft touch," Reb explained her theory.
"She just knew she could out drive you," Mitch countered with
her take.
"Well, at least I could drive!"
"You had a broken arm?" Robbie picked up on that thread.
"I had a shot-up arm. Compliments of some of Reb's former
political supporters."
"It was one nut with a gun," Reb said.
"Isn't that all it takes?"
"So, one more question," Robbie the curious one said, "How did
you get this friend of Lisa's to go along with the scheme?"
The staff lounge got very quiet for a moment. Or two.
"She had a lot at stake," Mitch chose her words carefully,
"because she was Lisa's lover."
"Oh," Robbie nodded as everything fell into place. "Now, it all
makes perfect sense."
Mitch breathed a sigh of relief. Now, that wasn't so tough.
Mitch looked over at Reb. She seemed unconvinced that this

settled the whole deal.  It was sure annoying how much information Reb could convey with one glance.

"You haven't told us your news," Trish asked Rebecca, breaking the spell.

"What news is that?" Reb wanted to narrow down the topic, if possible.

"What did the police have to say?"

"Oh, that!  Well, there's an arrest imminent in the fire."

"There is?  Who's going to be arrested?"

Together. Mitch and Reb came out with different answers.  As Reb said, "I can't say," Mitch answered, "The wrong person." There was nothing quite like a camp divided to make things awkward and confusing.

"What did you say?" Trish directed the question to both and got both answers again.

Reb took over the discussion, "I can't say who is being arrested until it's carried out."

"But it's still the wrong person," Mitch wouldn't let go.

"What on earth are you talking about?" Reb finally challenged her in front of everyone.  But before Mitch could forward a theory, Mary came into the room.

"Sorry I'm late, I was watching the news.  They've arrested Miranda!"

After a couple of seconds, Rose asked, "Who's Miranda?"

"The Patricia Krenwinkle of Kansas," Mitch replied mysteriously.

"Who?"

"Never mind, Rose," Reb said kindly.  "It's been a long day for *everyone*."

Everyone meaning Mitch.

"Of course it has," Rose agreed, somewhat perplexed.

As they filtered out of the room to find a TV set, Mitch sat quietly in the lounge.  After a few minutes, Reb came looking for her.

"I didn't know you stayed behind."

"No use watching the news."

"If we started over from scratch, would you tell me what's on your mind?"

"Can we go home first?"

"Sure," Reb agreed.

"Maybe Mary can catch a ride with Trish later."

"I'll make the arrangements myself while you go and get our van."

"You got yourself a deal."

The ride back to the apartment was tomb-like. Reb drove and didn't miss an exit or street all the way home. What a showoff. They even fixed a glass of brandy and sat together on the couch for an extended period of time before resuming their conversation.

"How far back at the beginning do you want to start?" Reb finally broke the ice.

"Wasn't it 1969?"

"1969? What about 1969?"

"I wasn't very old in 1969."

"You must've been in diapers, I'd guess."

"I wasn't that young. But I don't remember much."

"About what?" Reb pressed.

"About the Tate-Labianca murders."

"You mean the Manson Family?" Reb was now thoroughly puzzled.

"Right."

"What on earth does that have to do with Miranda's arrest?"

"Everything," Mitch sounded confident in her reasoning.

"Tell me your idea."

"Did Charles Manson actually kill anyone at the Tate or Labianca households?"

"No."

"But he was convicted, right?"

"Right…"

"Don't you see the parallels?"

"Miranda didn't do it?" Reb was totally lost.

"Oh, I'm pretty sure she lit the match. And she probably burned Bixby's place as well. But there are evil forces at work here, just as there were in the Manson Family case. Evil may have many manifestations, but it's still unmistakable."

"So, you believe that there's some modern-day Charles Manson behind Miranda's actions?"

"I don't think that Miranda came up with this idea all by herself."

"There's one thing you're overlooking."

"What?"

"Miranda had a personal stake in all this. The Manson Family had no personal attachment to the people they murdered. But, Miranda is a different story."

"So, you're willing to believe that this was nothing more than a simple case of familial revenge?"

"Sometimes the simplest explanation is the best."

"Even if it isn't, jail might be the safest place for her."

"We'll need to go to Kansas soon. For a variety of reasons."

"Have you talked to BeBe yet?"

"No. What do you mean jail might be the safest place," Reb finally thought to ask. And change the subject at the same time.

"Think of it as a state-funded bodyguard."

"You think she's in danger?"

"I think she's a liability, particularly for whoever talked her into it."

"You look tired," Reb was in a subject-changing mood tonight.

"*Somebody* kept me awake half the night last night."

"Oh, right."

"And in case I forgot, thank you."

"You're welcome. Let's go to bed and sleep this time."

"I'm right behind you."

Chapter 32

When Trish and Robbie got all snuggled up in bed back at their hotel suite, Robbie asked the question that she really wanted an answer to.

"Did you happen to leave out anything *important* in that story today?"

"Important?"

"I watched Mitch as she told the story. She looked cautious. You guys didn't do anything illegal, did you?"

Trish admitted, "I couldn't say for sure."

"Is there anything else you *could* say for sure?"

"You promise not to leave me alone in this bed tonight?"

Robbie checked Trish to make sure she wasn't teasing.

"Is it that bad?"

"When Mitch and I found out what Lisa was up to, she was living with a woman named Judy."

"And that was the woman who you pretended inherited the money."

"Right."

"And?"

"I fell in love with Judy."

Trish waited for a comment from Robbie. Her body hadn't stiffened in response. That was a good sign.

"I guess I shouldn't be too surprised that you had girlfriends before me. You are devastatingly attractive."

"Yeah, well, Judy didn't think so."

"Really!" Robbie was truly shocked.

"I was too Jewish looking for her tastes."

"I see. And so you began your quest for your heritage and found me."

Trish nodded. "That's right."

"Remind me to send a thank-you note to Judy."

"I never slept with her."

"Maybe I should send her a sympathy card instead?"

"Maybe we should just forget all about Judy."

"Okay. But I did have one other question."

"What's that?"

"Why did Lisa think Mary was a maid?"

"One of these days, when I'm not half asleep, I'll tell you the whole story."


Mary had arranged to get an early ride to the hospital with Trish and Robbie, since they were leaving that same day for Glens Falls. Oh, the hectic life of the ultra-rich. It gave them a few minutes to chat.

"Robbie wants to know how you were mistaken for a maid by Lisa in Texas," Trish figured that Mary was good for the retelling.

"You heard all about that?" Mary checked Robbie's expression.

"I didn't hear about the Texas part," Robbie stated.

"I told her about the Judy part, however."

"Good for you. Honesty is the best policy."

"So, Lisa was in Texas?"

"No."

"Who was in Texas?"

"Nobody. Except for Marge's sister."

"Who is Marge?" Robbie recognized the name only as new to the story.

"Marge was the owner of The Lucky U. Doesn't that take you back about a hundred years, Mary?" Trish said wistfully. "We sure didn't need a bodyguard back then."

"Well, my mom had to have a couple," Mary remembered them well.

"I guess I never paid much attention."

"That's okay. Mitch paid enough attention for the both of you."

"So, Lisa wasn't in Texas?" Robbie tried to get back on track.

"Lisa was in Aspen, with Judy," Trish explained, "And I pretended to be the lawyer of Judy's rich but fictional family in Texas."

"And you picked Texas because Marge had a sister there?"

"I think that was just pure luck. We thought that Lisa would believe without seeing. I guess we should've known better."

313

"So, Marge's sister invited you down to Texas?"

"Actually, we were allowed full run of the ranch for the deception, which included Mary as a maid."

"And we didn't find out until later that Lisa was on to us from the beginning, so she took particular joy in tormenting all of us in our perspective roles. And I guess we had it coming."

"Besides, things turned out okay, until now," Mary became quiet.

"Lisa's going to be fine," Robbie patted her hand. "They are doing wonderful things now-a-days with burn victims."

"I know. But she'll always be scarred. Lisa's looks were always very important to her."

"As long as they weren't important to you, everything will work out."

Robbie sounded like she knew what she was talking about. Mary appreciated the insight.

Trish and Robbie stayed a companionable amount of time at the hospital. Only when it was time for Lisa's surgery did they take their leave. Lisa held onto Trish for a beat longer than she expected.

"You come back and see me when I don't look like a bad screen test for a mummy movie."

"Honey, you don't even look like a bad screen test for a Michelle Pfeiffer look-alike movie."

"Hey," Mary smiled, "You stop makin passes at my girl!"

"Is she always this possessive?" Trish winked at Lisa.

"She's on her best behavior, but you'd better leave before she punches you in the nose," Lisa squeezed Trish's hand.

"Okay. We'll be back. We promise."

They took off to the hotel, where they had managed to convince Silver to stay and guard Max and Rose. Silver was beginning to struggle with divided duties. It wasn't comfortable to have Trish and Robbie gallivanting all around town without protection as well. When they arrived a good hour past when Silver expected them, it was reckoning time.

"If you're running late, it would be best to check in."

314

"I wasn't aware that we were running late," Trish answered calmly yet firmly. Feeling like a chastised teenager grated on her nerves.

"I'm only concerned about your safety," Silver sounded nothing if not maternal.

"I hired you to keep Rose safe. That's the primary job. If we all go out together, I appreciate your presence. But I'm not prepared to have a 24 hour escort for myself."

"Rose and Max are ready to go."

"And safe and sound, thanks to you. If you want to discuss schedules later, I'll be happy to work something out with you."

Mollified, Silver helped with details, including room reservations in Glens Falls. Although it was a small town, it had a couple of nice hotels. Silver secured reservations at the facility that had the most favorable amenities, including a health spa and an exercise room. That would make Trish happy. Robbie and Trish had all their stuff tossed into a suitcase in about twenty minutes. They were becoming expert at the drill. Within the hour, the party of five was on the road again and heading back to New York state. This time, it was Trish who slept, relieved that the visit with Lisa had gone so well. Of course, if they actually had to see her wounds or hear her screams, it would've been different. For now, the medicated, sanitized version was sufficient. She had a dozen questions that she had left unasked. What the doctors planned to do to fix her ear, neck and arm would be revealed in time. No use turning the visit into a quiz show. It had been dicey enough explaining the Texas adventure to Robbie.

Not just anyone can wake themselves up snoring. Trish did so about an hour out of Glens Falls.

"Have a nice nap?" Robbie asked.

"Did I snore constantly?"

"Not constantly."

"I snored all the while, didn't I." Trish shifted to an upright position.

"You were sleeping well. That's what's important."

Trish took a poll, "Anybody else hungry?"

Four hands went up in the air, so Silver pulled into the first restaurant they saw. Its specialty was barbecue but there were less-spicy options as well. Trish was the only one who couldn't decide between two choices, so she ordered ribs and meatloaf. Good thing there was a gym at the end of the line.

By the time they checked in and looked under the beds for kidnapers, Trish was in no mood to spend an hour on a treadmill to work off lunch. She took some heartburn medication and sat in front of a large screen television. News from Kansas was interesting. A seemingly nice young woman was under arrest for the fire that destroyed the Fairbanks's house. As Trish listened, details dribbled out like a Chinese water torture. Footage accompanied the story, including file photos of all the main players. One of those players who Trish hadn't thought about until now was the person in charge of organizing the protests against Mary and Lisa. If the woman was half as mean as her picture appeared, Trish wouldn't want to cross her path unless Silver was close by. This lady, whose name was Lucinda Cornwall, looked like a cross between a vindictive school principal and a whip-yielding dominatrix. Snakes had a warmer look in their eyes than she did. Goosebumps popped up all over Trish's arms, an occurrence which did not go unnoticed by Robbie.

"Are you chilly? Do you want me to get you a blanket?"

"Would you look at her," Trish pointed to the TV, but by then, the image was gone.

"Who?" Robbie asked.

"It was a picture of a scary woman. Apparently the ringleader of the protestors in Kansas."

"Maybe I'll get a look later. Meanwhile, everyone wants to know when we're going to visit Connors."

"Everyone?"

"Well, yes, everyone."

Trish leaned closer to Robbie and put her arm around her shoulders.

"I'm not ready yet."

"Okay," Robbie nodded. "I understand. Just let me know what I can do to help."

"You already are," Trish held her close.

By the following morning, Trish was ready. The five musketeers went to the residential facility, where they were greeted like returning heroes. The director showed them into a beautifully appointed study. It was one of several standard rooms in the facility, but it was still luxurious with leather chairs and pecan wood tables and gleaming light fixtures. It appeared to be rarely used, like a show home in a new housing development. The scent of lemon floated through the air. It made Robbie's nostrils tickle.

Trish assumed that they were brought here to discuss the future financial arrangements for Connors and were not at all ready for the news.
"I have a matter of serious import to discuss with you," Ms. Huber's preamble was directed only toward Trish, as if everyone else in the room had evaporated.
"I'm listening."
"Connors is dying."
Suddenly, the conversation shifted from future financial arrangements to simply future.
"What's he dying of?" Robbie asked as Trish remained speechless.
"Cancer."
"What kind?"
"It's complex. It started out in the esophageal area and spread. There's liver involvement."
"Can he have a liver transplant?"
"That won't do much good."
"Would it buy him some time?" Trish had found her voice again, but it was shaky.
"Doctors are reluctant to perform a transplant for a terminal patient. Too many other people can benefit much more from the limited supply of organs."
"But it might help if the other cancer goes into remission, wouldn't it?"
"I'm afraid that just isn't the case."

"What procedures have you followed so far?"

"Only diagnostic."

"How did the cancer get such a head start?"

"The esophageal area is a place where cancer can grow without detection for an extended period of time. It doesn't cause much discomfort until it's almost unstoppable. If Connors were a typical person, he might still not have caught the symptoms in time."

"Is he in pain?"

"We think we have the pain under control, as well as the nausea. One thing about liver cancer, it really doesn't drag out very long."

"Have you considered chemotherapy?"

"It's an option, but it would increase the nausea."

"But it might shrink the tumor."

Ms. Huber sat quietly for a moment. If Trish's questions were making her feel defensive, she hid it well.

"I'd be happy to arrange a meeting with our physician on staff to answer your questions to your satisfaction."

"I'd appreciate that. I'd like to go and see Connors now."

"Of course."

Max, Rose and Silver opted to stay behind. Trish and Robbie followed Ms. Huber down the hall. It was familiar, even after all the time that had passed.

When they entered the room, Trish went directly to his bedside. He looked so much like Albert that it jolted her. He had aged and was incredibly more frail. His shrunken frame was helpless and childlike in the bed. Eyes closed. Shallow cheeks. Translucent skin. For an eternal second, Trish thought they were already too late. Then, he breathed. Automatically. And then again. And again. But that was about all. He didn't open his eyes when she spoke his name. Nor did he respond when she touched his arm. Before Trish realized, fifteen minutes had passed. Robbie squeezed her shoulder gently.

"The doctor is here."

"Gee, that was fast."

"He's waiting for you in the hall."

"Okay."

Trish tore herself away from her vigil long enough to ask virtually the same questions all over again. The answers were a bit more complex, sprinkled throughout with terms that his parents paid probably about a hundred dollars apiece for him to learn. Bottom line – Connors was dying. There was no point in using invasive procedures. They would keep him comfortable. He promised.

After seeing Connors, all the challenge had gone out of Trish. Even she now saw the wisdom of the merciful decision. Still, it didn't make sitting with Connors any easier. She watched him for a sign. Any sign. Oblivious to the world around her, she was startled when Robbie suggested they have a bite of lunch.
"Why don't you go with your folks?"
"I sent them away over two hours ago."
"You did?"
"Silver took them back to the hotel. They were going sightseeing and wanted to change into comfortable clothes."
"Maybe you should have gone with them?"
"Why would I want to do that?"
"Because I'm not very good company."
"I don't hang out with you because you're good company."
"You don't?"
"Nope."
"Why do you hang out with me?"
"Because you always do the right thing."
"What should we do about lunch?"
"The director said we could get a tray from the dining room."
"Is there a place close that we can walk to?"
"It would be a few blocks."
"I could stand a walk."

Together they walked hand in hand to a fast food place. Thankfully, there had been only one obscene gesture directed their way. Usually, when they walked hand in hand, the gestures were several. Over burgers, fries and milkshakes, Trish commented on the overall friendliness of the town, as if getting flipped off only once was akin to the red carpet treatment.
"This is a nice place."

"Which is good, since I figure we're going to be here awhile."
Trish took a long draw from her chocolate milkshake. "How do
you read my mind?"
"I enjoy novels," Robbie winked.
"I'm more the dime variety," Trish's spirits were lifting quickly.
Robbie had that effect on her.
"At least you're not a hardcover."
"How is all of this going to work out?" Trish floated the
question.
"Let's send my folks and Silver back to Colorado and then see
what's available to rent."
"And then what?"
"Then, we'll do what we always do. Go day by day."

Chapter 33

"Have you called Jane yet?" Reb asked as they killed time in the waiting room.

"Have you called the Senate yet?" Mitch countered.

It wasn't a testy exchange, just one full of trepidation. Reb dug out her cell phone and called the party bosses. It was evident from Reb's facial expression that the person on the other end of the call was having a stroke. Reb listened and nodded and answered by saying "no" and "I *have* given it serious consideration" and "effective immediately." After a few more murmurs and a "thank you" Reb hung up.

"It's your turn," Reb handed the phone to Mitch. Mitch hunted in her pockets for her address book. She finally located it and found Jane's number under "S." She was home and not at all surprised that Mitch was removing herself from the restaurant project.

"I know you'll do fine and I promise to fund you all the way."

"And you will come for the grand opening?"

"You bet."

"Come before then. I'll give you both the grand tour."

"You got yourself a deal."

"How about next week?"

"I'll have to see about my schedule. We need to go to Kansas, too."

"I've been watching that on the news. You be very careful. That whole deal scares me to death."

"Ditto."

After a few more bits of news, Jane said goodbye. She had to go see about a deep freezer. Mitch smiled. The restaurant was definitely in good hands.

Amid flashbulbs popping and cameras rolling, Reb and Mitch made their way to Kansas via first-class airline tickets. News of Reb's resignation had traveled with light speed and the only remark she was prepared to make concerned her strong belief that family values were at the core of her decision. When this remark was run by Lucinda Cornwall, her only retort was to curl her lip and make a remark about "dirty, filthy homos who have no concept of family values."

The press smelled blood. When the plane touched down, Reb and Mitch went directly into a reunion with Bixby. He had adjusted quite well to the circumstances. The hotel room where he had set up temporary housekeeping appeared to be permanent. "How is Lisa?" was his first question. Now, here was a guy who recognized family values when he saw them.
"She is improving, but it is a long, slow process."
"Can she talk on the phone?"
"Yes."
"Would it be okay if I gave her a call?"
"It would be terrific! She can hear perfectly well out of her good ear. But she's just had some surgery, so you may want to talk to Mary first."
"I'll certainly do that. And how is Mary?" he was embarrassed for not asking sooner.
"She's holding up well under all the stress. Thanks for asking."
"The stress hasn't even started around here. You've been watching the news, I hope."
"Bits and pieces. How are you doing rebuilding your place?"
"It's taking a long time. This isn't like the big city here where things happen fast."
"I remember," Reb nodded.
After catching up on old times for another ten minutes, they left. They promised to call. He promised to answer the phone.

Their next stop was the homestead. Despite its devastated appearance, the house still stood like a proud guardian of the land. TV trucks lined the road in anticipation of Reb's arrival. Mitch could have sneaked in the back door, except she would have missed the spectacle. Ms. Cornwall was holding court. "This is what happens when the will of the Almighty God is cast underfoot by the perversions of these sinners."

Gee, Mitch thought, this woman's forte didn't include mincing words. Too bad she was so misinformed.

"Isn't it true that the fire was an act of one of your followers as opposed to an act of God?" one press person asked Ms. Cornwall, the Cruella DeVille of Kansas. Ms, Cornwall gave the poor dear a withering stare. If the press weren't more careful, a tornado might just appear to swirl some sense into the reporter. Alas, the only gust of hot air came from Cornwall. "This fire was an act of God to punish the sodomites."
Reb remained silent, but her jaw was set in that unmistakable Fairbanks' pose. Frankly, it turned Mitch on no end, but now didn't seem the ideal time to discuss that.
"But, Ms. Cornwall, there weren't any gay men living there, so how can that qualify as sodomites?"
Boy, this reporter was really brave for such a small woman.
"These homosexual women are every bit as much a sodomite as are homosexual men."
"Were you peeking in the windows?"
"They bragged about their sin in the eyes of God." Lucinda was getting warmed up to the point where Mitch was keeping an eye peeled for thunderbolts.
"When did that occur?" another reporter took up the questioning. Apparently, they didn't work for any faint-of-heart publication.
"They flaunted their hatefulness of God in his holy house."
"What does that mean in English?" Mitch asked Reb.
"I think it means they went to church together."
"Well, if God didn't mind, why should Lucinda Cornwall?"
This exchange caught the ear of the press, who moved en masse toward Reb. For the record, this galled Lucinda no end.
"Do you have any comment, Senator Fairbanks?"
"Well, first, as you have already heard, I won't be a Senator much longer. I am resigning. The rumors are true."
Things buzzed for a moment and then calmed as Rebecca indicated that she would indeed continue to speak unprompted.
"I'm resigning so that I can spend more time with my family. They come first in my life." As she said this, she squeezed Mitch's hand.
"Can you give us an update on your daughter's companion?"

"She's doing well, considering the trauma she had been put through."

"How long will she be in the hospital?"

"Weeks."

"Are you going to be here for the trial?"

"I haven't decided."

"Will you rebuild?"

"I don't know."

"Are you going to live here?"

"I'll confer with my life partner before making that decision."

"What about it, Ms. Tanner? Do you want to move here?"

There's nothing like having a family conference in front of a few million strangers.

"At the risk of sounding hopelessly in love, I'll go wherever Rebecca goes. She's the answer to my prayers. God gave her to me. I'm not going to question the wisdom."

As the press scribbled, Lucinda burned. She turned such a pretty shade of red.

"So, it sounds like you're moving here," the reporter asked the question in a slightly different form. Mitch replied in a slightly different form, "I'll talk to God and get back to you."

www.ingramcontent.com/pod-product-compliance
Lightning Source LLC
Chambersburg PA
CBHW062036170626
46813CB00001B/352